Of Blood and Stone

A Bill Evers Novel

I0546821

Of Blood and Stone
A Bill Evers Novel

Howard Upton

Copyright © 2017 Still Water Literary, LLC

All rights reserved. No part of this publication may be reproduced or utilized in any form by any means, electronic or mechanical, including photocopying, recording, or by any information storage and retrieval system, without prior written permission from the publisher.

Library of Congress Cataloging-in-Publication Data
Upton, Howard, 1969-
Of Blood and Stone, 2nd Publication

ISBN – 978-1-946811-02-8

1. Action Thriller. 2. Suspense Thriller. 3. Military. 4. Martial Arts.

Still Water Literary, LLC ™

What Readers Are Saying About "Of Blood & Stone"

A Tribute to America's Fighting Men

"Bill Evers is an extraordinary character with real life problems. PTSD is to him what kryptonite is to Superman. This book is a tribute to America's fighting men and women who have returned home afflicted with this terrible disease." Kevin Roper ~ Iraqi War veteran

A Spell-binding Adventure full of Intrigue, Action, and Magic

"Of Blood and Stone is a well-spun story of intrigue and international mystery, intertwined with unexpected twists, nonstop action, double-crosses, martial arts, conspiracy theories, and magic. Howard Upton has an amazing talent for pulling the reader into the story and then keeping him wanting more, right up until the very end. He does an incredible job of integrating military knowledge and martial arts with conspiracy theories, history, and magic, and does so in such a way that makes every part of this adventure exciting and realistic. I even found myself wanting to do further research on some of the mysterious facts that Upton so expertly incorporates throughout the adventure. This is a book that you will not want to put down until you get to the end, and then it will leave you ready for Bill Evers' next adventure." Dr. Bohdi Sanders ~ award-winning author of the #1 bestseller, *Modern Bushido: Living a Life of Excellence*

The Words Rattle and Hum with an Unmistakable Magnetism

"Spies, murder, mystery, martial arts action, testosterone packed intrigue, international suspense, a 2300 year old supernatural curse, globetrotting storyline of characters...no detail is spared as the author weaves his natural southern charm and real-world experience into the fabric of his characters in this story. Like the ancient cartouche at the center of the storyline – the words rattle and hum with an unmistakable magnetism as they fly off the paper and into the reader's mind, simultaneously bolting you to the edge of your seat, and locking your eyes onto page after page, with no chance of escape until the end." Garry Parker ~ martial arts instructor and author of *Chanpuru: Reflections and Lessons Learned on the Dojo Floor*

What Readers Are Saying About "Of Blood & Stone"

Exceptionally Written and Engaging!

"Of Blood and Stone is exceptionally written and engaging. The steady and intensely paced plot captures your attention and keeps you wanting more. The characters are so engaging; some you hate to love and others you love to hate! I'm anxiously awaiting a sequel!" Dr. Bridgette Hester ~ professor and author of *Godwink: On the Wings of Butterflies*

It is Thrilling… An Exciting Page Turner

"If you like shamans, magic, incantations and spells then this captivating fiction is for you! Howard Upton has created resilient, stimulating, macho characters that he strategically places all over the world in a race to find an enchanted cartouche. It is thrilling, as a reader, to follow Evers, the core character, through his winding journey to reveal the connection between ancient civilizations, the cartouche and a spell binding ending you'll just have to read to believe! *Of Blood and Stone* is an exciting page turner that I recommend to anyone craving a spicy new novel to pass around to everyone they know!" Emily Rees ~ administrative professional

An Adventurous Roller Coaster

"Author Howard Upton sets the reader on an adventurous roller coaster that starts in the Talladega National Forest, climbs one peak in Mexico then free falls across different Pacific Islands before stopping in China. Bill Evers, the story's main character, must hunt for an ancient artifact before the spell it contains unleashes the deadliest army the world has ever seen. Magic, mystery and mayhem will captivate the reader immediately!" Rachel Ham ~ academic professional

Dedication

To Mom and Dad – you instilled a passion and drive to always do my best even when I'm at my worst. Mom you continue to be that beautiful, loving spirit that we all adore. Dad, I miss your love, laughter and guidance.

To Courtney and Cassidy – you girls will always be my babies. I never realized how capable of love I would be until you two came along.

To Amanda and Abby, who prove that blood doesn't necessarily make a family.

To Cathy – without your love and support I don't know where I'd be, and have no desire to find out. Your honesty, creativity and life skills have enabled us to live a perfect life. I love you.

Acknowledgments

I must offer a heartfelt thank you to Dr. Bohdi Sanders and Kaizen Quest Publishing for affording me the first opportunity to publish my work. Bohdi, your knowledge and experience are incredible and the copious notes I've taken during our long conversations will serve me well in all of my future writing endeavors.

Tracey Sanders you took so much of your personal time to edit, re-edit, and offer wonderful suggestions to a work that was in dire need of much personal attention. Your ink and insight were wonderful and well placed.

Thanks to the real Kevin Roper who spent numerous hours describing his time in service to our country, his personal struggles with PTSD, and speaking about his own personal experiences in re-acclimating himself in the civilian world.

Thomas O'Brien, thank you for your insights into Afghanistan and covert activities. Our conversations are always educational.

Sensei Dan Dugan your light-hearted sense of humor always makes me smile. Thanks for allowing Bill Evers to search for such a mean bastard. Naturally, anyone who knows you understands that imaginary Dan Dugan has nothing in common with the real Dan Dugan.

A colossal thank you to everyone who took the time to read this manuscript and offer feedback; without you, this work would have remained shelved.

I would be remiss to not thank each and every United States Armed Forces member, both past and present. Your sacrifices have made this country great and this book possible.

Bill Evers Dossier

Name: William Samuel Evers

Aliases: Bill, Will, Buck

D.O.B.: November 2, 1973

Sex: M   Hair: BR   Eyes: BR

Marital status: S

Last known address:	1220 Hidden Cove Rd, Oxford, AL
Military service:	4th Ranger Battalion
Commendations:	Reconnaissance and Surveillance Leaders Course, 1st in class Selected to Ranger sniper school, top 3 percentile
Theater of war:	(Iraq) Mosul, Fallujah, and Najaf (Afghanistan) Kabul, Kandahar
Paramilitary:	Contractual-Liberia, Sudan, Uganda Unconfirmed: Columbia, Peru
Additional training:	High ranks in both judo and karate. Hand-to hand assessment-lethal

Of Blood and Stone
A Bill Evers Novel

Howard Upton

Xi'an, Shaanxi, China
209 B.C., Early Morning

Lu Xiu Chan watched as the fierce soldier beheaded his oldest son as the sword wielding man sat atop his spectacular horse. Blood spurted into the air, his heart still pumping even though his head lay lifeless on the ground. The unarmed Lu Xie Wan had asked the soldier to leave the village in peace, and in response he was slaughtered. Now the elderly Chan stood stone faced, still in shock at the vicious attack Emperor Qin Shi Huang Di's personal envoy levied on a young man simply requesting no blood be spilled on this day.

The helmeted man turned his immaculately adorned mount to face Chan, sword dripping with his son's blood from the razor sharp tip, the sun reflecting brightly off his polished helmet. The powerful steed's head bobbed up and down as an audible snort rolled from his nostrils. A massive front hoof shoveled at the dirt and his tail shifted and swayed.

"Emperor Qin demands your village's taxes be paid, old man, or you will find yourself homeless or dead like this idiot," he said as he pointed at the lifeless body with his chin.

Chan's gaze bore into the horseman, his voice deadly and ominous.

"You killed my son. The Emperor has now been paid. Kill me if you will, as you have taken everything from me. Do your will or be gone!" His eyes were both intent and stolid and his gaze unblinking.

A strong stench wafted through the air. The acrid smell of iron and death hung in the air like stagnant water infested with mosquitoes and moss. Blood oozed over the ground, seeping into the dirt and creating a strange brown-red discoloration that seemed as though it would be impossible to be washed away.

The soldier considered taking the old man's head, but didn't want to explain to the Emperor why he had killed two men and returned with no money. He sheathed his sword and allowed his eyes to wander over the tiny village. Others had stopped to watch the standoff between him and the elder.

He turned his horse in small steps so he could gaze upon those who had gathered. Several similar looking small mud-brick homes sat upon the ground. Their thatched roofs swayed gently in the early morning breeze. Smoke floated from one rooftop as a couple of sheep called to one another from a pen behind one of the homes. The only road leading into the village was wide and well maintained. It appeared that someone took time to occasionally groom the ruts from it, thereby making travel much easier.

"Tomorrow I shall return to claim that which is the Emperor's. You would be wise to have the rice prepared," he proclaimed to everyone within earshot.

"Our taxes are fifty percent of all rice grown and harvested. The village cannot survive the harsh winter on the remaining fifty percent. You and the Emperor know this!" shouted an old lady, watching the scene unfold.

There was no sympathy on the warrior's face as he reflected on Chan and the other villagers.

"If you return here, you will never leave," the old man menacingly growled loudly enough for only the warrior to hear. Feet firmly planted and hands by his sides, Chan's posture was resolute and determined.

The soldier glared at the old man who stood defiant in both voice and stance. Suddenly he laughed and tugged his horse's reins. "Tomorrow, ancient one, I shall return. If your village's taxes are not prepared, I will burn the village to the ground."

The elder's voice became ominous and stronger than usual, "If you return here, you will not leave. This I promise."

The Emperor's soldier laughed once more as his steed turned south and galloped away from the village.

Limping on his aging legs, Chan removed his dusty robe and approached his son's still body. A single tear rolled down his cheek as he bent down and reverently picked up his son's severed head and lovingly placed it on top of the body, covering both with his thread-bared robe. Five of the villagers most respected young men walked with bowed heads toward the body. Gently, they lifted the corpse and began the process of an honorable burial while the old man limped back to his thatch roofed home to consider his options.

Chan served as the local leader of the village, along with his duties as doctor. His medicinal skills were rife with incantations learned and practiced by his ancestors and passed from generation-to-generation to him in his early years. But this night his magic would have to be stronger than anything he had ever attempted before if he hoped to seek revenge for the death of his loving son. His village would suffer either way; they didn't have sufficient resources to pay the tax collector, nor would they be allowed to live should his magic truly work.

He went to work utilizing the small amount of jewelry passed to him by his grandfather. Outside his home the medicine man stoked the fire until the tentacles of flames reached for the heavens. Chan melted the ornate medallion into a shimmering liquid silver that seemed to dance in the moonlight. He then molded the metal into an oblong shape, careful to pour small amounts of water on it so that it would solidify without becoming too hardened to engrave.

For hours, Chan meticulously engraved the object with the required symbols and with the engraving complete, the shaman began the process of crafting the strongest magic of his life. Incense burned and dried roots, flowers and oils were chanted over until an ominous mist appeared and eagerly hovered over both man and jewel. Chan whispered the final incantation only the Gods could hear, and watched as a visible blue aura wrapped itself around the strange adornment.

Outside, a shrill wind howled and screamed. It rolled down the side of the Qin Mountains, entered the village and swirled around Chan's mud-brick home. He shivered as the gust found its way through cracks and crevices of the house and surrounded him like an unseen blanket. Momentarily frozen by the frigid air, Chan could hear his blood pumping through his veins as the spirits of his ancestors gave him courage. Then, as quickly as the wind had begun, it stopped. Exhausted, he released his remaining breath in a long sigh of relief.

He grasped the jewel and staggered to his lumpy bed with his energy all but drained. His frail body sagged, but soon his enchantment would be imposed and his revenge complete. For now he knew he must rest and ready his mind.

The clip-clop of horse's hooves woke Chan. Still in shock and overcome with exhaustion and grief, he looked around to see the early morning sun filtering through his home. From a crack in the wood he could see the sun's rays reflecting off the walls of the massive white pyramid that proudly sat in the distance. Their history did not tell them why it had been built, or by whom, they only knew that it *was*. Emperor Qin was so drawn to the site, he had decided to make it an armory and base for his incredible army.

Fall was always chilly in northern China, but this day was particularly crisp. Although the wind wasn't blowing, there were few clouds in the sky to insulate the Earth. Chan stoked the fire he had built the night before then threw a couple of small logs on top. Flames anxiously chewed at the new wood and small embers floated haphazardly through the air. The cold air gave way to the warm, and slowly but surely Chan's old bones silently thanked him for the reprieve.

As he warmed himself by the fire, he realized he no longer had the jewel in his hand and desperately began searching for it – it had found its way into the folds of his old silk shirt while he slept. A feeling of relief swept over him as he held it tightly in his left hand, his right holding onto a staff he was forced to use when his legs hurt more than usual.

Chan draped his heavy mountain sheep shawl over hunched shoulders. He had exchanged a medicinal prayer and an elixir for the shawl to an ill Mongol a local clansman had brought to his door. The warmth that the blanket provided his old bones was very comforting. He leaned on his staff and limped to his door as the rider and came to a stop outside his shanty. He clung to the oval piece of silver in his hand as the warrior stared directly into his eyes.

"Well, old one," he sneered, "have you gathered the required taxes or do I burn your village? I relish the chance to set flame to this hovel and to burn it to the ground. The smell of dog and pig is so strong here it upsets my stomach. Is it the dogs and pigs I smell or is it you, old man?" He smiled and continued to taunt Chan as he reached across his hip and wrapped his fingers around the well-worn leather wrapped hilt. Smirking, he drew the sword two inches from the scabbard, with the exposed blade glinting in the bright orange sun.

Chan closed his eyes as he began chanting quietly, the jewel held in his outstretched hand. The tax collector furrowed his brow curiously, wondering if the old man had lost his mind. He pondered why was the old man was standing there, eyes closed, extending his hands with his gnarly knuckles tightly squeezed shut. He shook his head in bewilderment, let the sword slide completely from the scabbard and swung it above his head as he bellowed a blood curdling scream.

The old man didn't flinch, his chanting growing more audible. The jewel felt hot as a blue-white glow emanated from his hand while his arm began to shake. His chant grew even louder and the rider's face became confused as he closed the distance on his horse.

Just as he started to cleave the old man's head from his shoulders, the warrior turned to look at his own hand brandishing the sword. Horror crossed his face, his eyes widened, as his arm turned gray and immobile. He watched as the grayness spread across his shoulder, down his chest, to his legs, and finally up his neck. A scream of terror formed in his throat, but lodged itself in his lungs just as they stopped working.

The warrior sat astride his horse frozen in time, never realizing the same fate had befallen his steed.

Chan continued to recite the spell not knowing, or even caring, that the other villagers had gathered to witness the ghastly turn of events. As soon as his chanting stopped he collapsed to his knees in sheer exhaustion. In the distance the wind screamed an unknown language across the Qin Mountains and wound its way toward the village.

He looked upon his countrymen, many of them relatives. "We must leave this place forever, or we will surely perish."

Valladolid, Yucatan, Mexico
July 7, 2013, 12:30 P.M.

The shadow of the large nineteenth century Catholic Church loomed over the restaurant as the older white gentleman entered the eatery. A busload of American tourists turned into a parking lot across the street. Peddlers, well aware of the bus schedule and those utilizing the bus service, appeared along the sidewalks to sell their wares to those more fortunate.

Glancing left and right as he walked into any establishment was a habit the veteran operator could not, and would not, change. His large brimmed hat was pulled low to conceal his features. He took a seat at a table in the back of the large room and waited while a skinny, flat-chested young senorita took his drink order. She handed him the menu as he ordered a beer. His unobstructed view allotted him a visual of the entire restaurant including the entrance. Speaking in Spanish he told her, "Estare esperando por un amigo." The shocked look on her face told him that she was impressed with his flawless Spanish and perfect pronunciation.

"Si, Señor, I will bring another menu." she replied with a warm smile glancing over her bronzed shoulder.

"Senorita," he called, "Por favor, asegúrese de que hace frío,"

"Por supuesto, señor," she replied with a coy glance back at the indignant Americano, assuring him that his beer would be cold.

He nodded his approval and kept an eye toward the door for his "friend" who was habitually late to any and all meetings. As he brushed off the day's dusty car ride in the excessive heat from his pristine white cotton shirt and pants, he reminded himself that this would be the last job this unprofessional asshole would ever do for him. Removing his hat, he ran his fingers through his graying hair, which was in dire need of a trim.

My entire existence relies on this one fucking thing, and the guy I ask to help procure it can't even show up to a meeting on time. This douchebag will never work for me again; in fact, he will not ever take another fucking breath after this thing is done, he thought to himself. He had to remind himself to keep his composure. The damnable Mexican heat was almost too much to bear and he couldn't risk showing any emotion at this time of great importance – a time which potentially could change the balance of power in a perpetually screwed-up world.

Twenty minutes later, he watched a tall, lanky Latino walk into the Restaurante Oasis. He took notice of the man's well-worn cowboy boots and long-sleeved yellow shirt neatly tucked into a pair of pressed Levi Straus jeans. With dark eyes and slicked back black hair, the man's demeanor was one of a well-to-do loner. The same look a lot of the Mexican drug lords brandished. He gave his eyes a few seconds to adjust to the darker environment of the restaurant before walking to the table.

As the lunch crowd ebbed and flowed with tourists heading to and from the ancient Mayan ruins of Chichen Itza and Ek Balam, as well as many locals fortunate enough to have enough money to enjoy a hot meal prepared in a restaurant, the white man stood to greet his associate with a forced smile.

Spoken so others around couldn't hear him, "It's about fucking time you showed up. Be late to one more of my meetings and you'll never have to worry about being late to another one, Rafael. Do I make myself clear?"

They both sat and pulled their chairs up to the table covered with a cheap white cotton cloth. The American adjusted his silverware on his right side then placed his napkin in his lap. The Latino followed suit. By all accounts, the two gentlemen were meeting for a casual business luncheon.

Rafael narrowed his eyes but then quickly softened his facial expression. "My apologies Señor Haden; I had some trouble finding this restaurante. I won't let it happen again."

Haden, his face neutral, replied sharply, "You're fucking-a right you won't let it happen again. And while we're on the subject, I told you this job would require you to be inconspicuous, yet you waltz in here looking like you're on the prowl for some dime store pussy at a two dollar strip club. Are you really that stupid?"

Rafael felt the heat rising to his face and had to fight to keep his composure. But more than that, he could feel something evil or dirty seeping through Haden's aura, and decided that allowing his temper to get the best of him would be stupid and dangerous. Something about the man's heavy gaze told him he would kill without remorse, and had done so many times previously.

Besides, this job would be a major score for him and he didn't want to upset his employer any more than he already had. With some noticeable effort he put his emotions in check, poised himself, and offered a tight smile.

"Señor, dark-skinned people don't like being in the sun. We don't want to get any darker. I think if you look around, you'll see other Latinos dressed just like me," replied Rafael in his thick Mexican accent.

Haden shrugged Rafael's response off as the waitress brought him his cold Sol beer and asked Rafael what he would like to drink. Rafael glanced at her and said he would have the same thing as his friend. The waitress realized nothing would come from flirting with these two, their demeanor said casual but their body language was screaming violence.

"Let's get down to business, amigo. There is an item, native to this area that is of great interest to a special group of my friends. Its intrinsic value is not significant, but its historical value is tremendous within the world of collectors of antiquity. I have been asked to acquire it so that they might enjoy its natural beauty and ponder it privately."

While Rafael listened intently, the skinny waitress brought him his beer. He nodded his appreciation and immediately took a long pull from the bottle, savoring the bitter flavor. His mind wandered to a much simpler time in his small village just outside Cancun, where American and European tourists were happy to throw him money for the easiest of chores. He thought about loading luggage at the airport or working at one of the many all-inclusive resorts found along the strip in Cancun. His skills eventually led him to some visiting "dignitaries" asking where they could score some good Mexican weed. Rafael happily made their purchases and deliveries...for a price. Subsequently, he found himself swimming in the seedy underworld of drugs and corruption, which landed him here with this big mouth American. *Pinche cabron* he thought. *I'd like to pluck out his gringo eyes and eat them.*

"Are you listening to me, boy?" Haden asked as he watched Rafael's mind drift from the conversation.

Curtly, and at his emotional limit, Rafael responded, "Si, señor, I hear you. But I will warn you that I do not take kindly to being called a boy. I can deal with most of your insults, Señor Haden, but if you call me that again, you can go fuck yourself. Comprende?"

Haden pulled deeply from his beer, never breaking eye contact with the Mexican, his face as stoic as ever. He took a deep breath, releasing the unseen tension from his shoulders and lungs. He smiled and said, "You have cajones, amigo, I'll give you that, but if you want to get into a dick measuring contest with me you'll find yourself woefully short. Now pay attention to what I'm telling you."

Rafael didn't respond, but took another drink from his beer and leaned forward to assure Haden that he was invested in the conversation.

"At the National Museum of Anthropology there's an object called a *cartouche*. Have you ever heard of such a thing?"

Rafael's silence confirmed what Haden already knew; he had never heard of the item.

"Specifically, it's a Mayan *cartouche* and, as I've told you, my friends would like it for their private collection. The museum isn't heavily guarded and I don't think you will have much in the way of problems in acquiring it. Do you think you can handle this?"

Rafael had heard of the Museo Nacional de Antropología, but had never been to Mexico City to see it. The poor growing up on the streets of Mexico rarely had the opportunity or luxury to immerse themselves in ancient cultures or travel while trying to find their next meal or score.

"Do I think I can handle this? Si, I can handle most anything. But the question is how much does this job pay, Señor?" Confidence exuded from the Mexican. He reached for his beer and smugly took another swallow.

"Fifty thousand U.S. dollars," Haden responded without hesitation. "But no mistake will be tolerated and absolutely nothing can jeopardize acquiring the cartouche."

"I don't know, Mr. Haden," Rafael began as he switched to the English form of respect, "fifty thousand dollars is a lot of money, but it won't help me if a Federali catches me with a stolen item in my pocket. I can't do this for less than one hundred thousand dollars U.S. I need fifty thousand now and fifty thousand when I deliver this thing to you."

Haden anticipated this amateur's negotiation tactics, but pretended to ponder the counter offer. He took another long drink from his beer, swished the cold liquid around in his mouth and swallowed. He rubbed his chin, making a production of his self-deliberation before responding, "Done. But I will need the cartouche in my hands in short order. July twenty-second. That's when you shall have it to me." Two of his vertebrae popped as he leaned back in his chair. Glorious relief from the pressure the cheap furniture in the restaurant had passed to his aging back allowed a sigh to escape his lips.

Rafael offered a greasy smile, nodded his head and replied, "No problemo, señor. Two weeks I will have this...this cartouche to you. I need to know what it looks like and where it is stored so I can gain access." His weathered hand reached for his beer and brought it to his lips. Lime and hops splashed across his tongue and the cold beverage cascaded down his throat. A thankful nod of appreciation for the chilled beer's refreshing taste was the only acknowledgment he gave Haden.

"Of course," smiled Haden as he slid a picture of a silver pendant with strange raised pictographs engraved on its surface. The pendant was oval shaped, approximately an inch and a half long and a half inch wide. The bottom of the strange looking charm flared to each side and was shaped in dual heads facing away from one another forming single toothed serpents on either side.

Rafael studied the picture for a few moments before sliding it back to Haden who quickly took the photo in his hand, folded it and put it in his shirt pocket. His eyes cut around the room without his head moving to make sure they weren't being observed. Both men understood that a paper trail was not allowable, in the event the mission went awry, so the Mexican would have to commit the photo to memory.

"The cartouche is stored in the conservation lab of the museum. Standard cameras are in place both inside and out. Armed guards man each entry. Every artifact on display is monitored by a heat sensor, including the pendant."

"How am I supposed to get this thing if there are heat sensors around it?" he asked.

"Simple," he replied as he looked around to assure no one could overhear him. "In this bag I'm going to give you, you'll find a small deflection device. It's called a *bi-morph opto-mechanical deflector*. Bi-morph heat sensors have been around for quite some time, but this technology allows you to insert the deflector in close proximity to the desired object, then simply remove whatever item the sensor is protecting. But you must allow the deflector to calibrate to room temperature upon your arrival, as the material is stainless steel specially coated with applied rolled-on nanotechnology. This usually takes no longer than two or three minutes.

"Once you enter the museum, open the bag, or whatever you are carrying it in, and allow the room air to begin working its magic. By the time you arrive in the conservation lab it will be fully calibrated. Simply slide it in place and remove your prize when you see the deflector turn a slight shade of blue on its surface. It's really that easy."

Rafael thought about what he was being told and considered asking if there was more to this relic than someone merely wanting to add it to a personal collection. Stealing a country's precious artifacts was a serious crime and Rafael wanted to know what, if anything, Haden was hiding. Rather than risking the ire of the hot-headed American, he kept his thoughts and questions to himself. *Perhaps this cartouche could be leveraged in some way once I get it*, he pondered.

For a moment it seemed as if Haden was reading his mind. The American eyed him warily then reached for his own beer. He sipped it, enjoying its coolness.

Haden slid the bag containing the deflector to Rafael, nodded at him and got up to leave. After glancing to his left and right, he once more locked eyes with his hired thief. "Remember," he said in low breath, "don't fuck this up. You have my number. Only use it to let me know when you have acquired my artifact."

Haden dropped an envelope on the table with fifty thousand United States dollars. Rafael didn't make any sudden move to grab it, a particular discipline Haden had to respect. He raised a brow at the Mexican and nodded at the envelope and Rafael nodded back ever-so-slightly, noticeable only to Haden.

He turned, put his hat on and walked out the door, careful to check the vicinity for anyone he might consider suspicious. A small, light blue Honda two-door passenger car passed him followed by a local teenager on an old bicycle. The local was wearing a backpack stuffed full of handmade crafts he would attempt to sell to visiting Americans and Europeans for ten times their actual worth.

The rented SUV Haden had parked across the street beeped as he pressed the remote he pulled from his pocket. He took out a pair of aviator sunglasses he had placed in a shirt pocket and put them on. Looking around once more to make sure no one had followed him, he climbed inside the four door Range Rover. As he drove east on Route 180 to Cancun, he replayed the meeting he had had with Rafael in his mind.

That stupid fucking wetback better get this damned charm out of that museum and have it to me in two weeks, or the pain he'll feel for failing me will be like nothing he's experienced. 'Course, after he gives me the cartouche, I'm going to off him anyway, but he'll save himself a hell of a lot of pain if he gets this right.

Haden chuckled to himself when he thought about killing Rafael. The look of surprise on the Mexican's face would be priceless when Rafael finally realized his life was at an end.

His mind shifted to the cartouche and what it would mean to him once he had it in his possession. The secret it would reveal would be worth more money than he could imagine and his "buddies" in the CIA would reward him handsomely for it. Vast amounts of his time had been committed to researching and finding the relic, not to mention the financial investments he had made in doing so. They'd pay alright, and kiss his ass while handing over the money.

Palm, papaya and avocado trees zipped past as he continued driving, his mind not really focused on the road. Little traffic found its way down this stretch of highway, except for the buses carrying tourists from Cancun to the old Mayan ruins.

Fucking Christians in Action. God how I hate those guys, but they do pay well for things they want. And if they won't pay, then some other country's government will pay top dollar for the chance to rule an entire planet. With that thought he broke into another round of chuckles as he made his way to the all-inclusive Royal Sands resort where he had booked his stay. At least he would enjoy some decent food, air conditioning, quality liquor and the thoughts of finally having the cartouche in his hands. Hell, he might even rent a little pussy for the evening, but she would be high-class, not like that trashy waitress from the Restaurante Oasis, and she'd have some big-ass tits.

Mexico City, Mexico
July 9, 2013, 7:45 A.M.

Rafael had taken his time driving south and west from the Yucatan. His desire to avoid unwanted attention from any local police or Federalis on the take forced him to drive off main highways for the majority of the trip and spend the night at a hotel that hadn't changed the sheets on the bed in quite some time. The room smelled like cheap cerveza and even cheaper sex. Still, it provided him with the cover he sought, as few "law enforcement" types frequented the place, unless there was a murder to investigate or they were spending time with a girlfriend or whore they had just arrested. Sometimes a girl turning a trick with a man of the law prevented her from going to jail or having to use her hard earned money as a payment to the cop that had just arrested her.

The extra time had also given him plenty to consider since meeting with Haden. Why was he so interested in this particular pendant? What was its value? He took the time to perform an internet search on his phone and discovered the cartouche was not much more than a charm worn on a necklace. Not far from the beaches of Cancun, rip-off artists made "authentic Mayan cartouches" to sell for American dollars, and naïve tourists lined up by the droves to purchase one after a tour of some ancient Mayan ruin.

Ironically, Rafael had never heard of these ornaments. He supposed street life and scraping to get by trumped learning about some odd piece of jewelry he couldn't afford anyway. But he wasn't a stupid man by any means. As a matter of fact, he knew a man like Haden wouldn't concern himself with some relic unless its value was weighed in more than United States currency.

He sat at the ratty table in his hotel room and drank the disgusting coffee he had brewed. As he raked his long black hair from his eyes, he stared at his coffee cup and thought about his association with Haden.

Rafael's services had been procured by Haden almost exclusively for the past three years. In most cases it was simple thievery of items brought into port areas on either shore of Mexico. Usually, he intercepted small arms for him. Somehow Haden would know when shipments were being made to the rogue nation. Stealing them was pretty easy, as these "imports" weren't controlled by the government, but by other thugs trying to make a quick dollar. He suspected these smuggled guns were from American cities, procured by renegade cops and sold for cash to some dealer.

Haden paid him well enough and he was able to live comfortably in a country where earning pesos meant living in squalor for most of the country's citizens. He owned a small house and horded the extra money he earned; he didn't want to draw the notice of thugs hungry for his small fortune, nor did he want the government snooping around in his business. When he wasn't doing work for Haden, he found employment with other foreigners interested in the drug and arms trade. Most were interested in simply moving the items through the country to drops in the United States. Moving the drugs and guns beyond Mexico's borders was someone else's responsibility, as Rafael didn't want or need the wrath of the United State's federal government coming down on him, so he would arrange for pickup close to the border, yet far enough away to avoid prying eyes.

He had also been a gun for hire when the situation called for it, and the price was right. In his mind he separated the value of human life from what he considered "work." He wanted to hang on to what humanity he could, and while his upbringing had been on the seedy streets of eastern Mexico, he still felt compassion for his people, especially the poor, so revenge killings were something he refused. Justifying murder was a tricky thing, but killing another mercenary made it tolerable. Murdering someone not involved in his usual line of business was something he simply wouldn't do, primarily because most of the jobs he turned down involved an unfaithful husband or wife, or some such nonsense.

He took another sip of his bitter coffee and pushed thoughts of the jewelry's value and his relationship with Haden from his mind. He needed to focus on the task at hand, which included a more elaborate thievery than he'd been part of in the past. Certain that attaining the item wouldn't be overly difficult, otherwise Haden would have hired a professional thief, he figured he would shower, change clothes and do some reconnaissance work around the museum.

After finishing his java and morning preparations, he checked the time – it wasn't quite 8:00. He headed west down the Chapultepec Avenue into an already heady amount of traffic. He navigated the ever-growing presence of eighteen-wheelers and commuters trying to get to their jobs until he found Sevilla Street and turned right. Sevilla merged into one of the hundreds of roundabouts found throughout the metropolitan area. He exited onto the third ramp leading to the museum on the Avenue Paseo de la Reforma. The flow of traffic on Reforma was mercifully lighter than the other major thoroughfares as the morning sun shined brightly in Rafael's eyes. Delicious smells from street markets wafted through his rental car's air conditioning system, which served as a reminder that he had not eaten anything since his supper the night before.

Paseo de la Reforma took him past the museum. He glanced down at the dashboard clock and saw that it was 8:47 a.m., not quite time for the doors to open. He continued driving west for a few more blocks searching for a safe enough neighborhood or parking area for his rental; he didn't want to have to make a speedy escape only to find he had no rims or worse…no car.

Having made a phone call and a couple of inquiries, Rafael knew the museum opened at 9:00 a.m. and tickets were sixty pesos apiece. He decided to wait until 10:00 a.m. before entering the museum as the extra hour would afford him time to walk the area and get a feel for the flow of traffic, both vehicular and pedestrian. After making a hard right on Ruben Dario Blvd, he found a parking lot to leave his car. A quick look around the lot revealed nothing out of the ordinary. Rafael stepped out of his car and pushed his sunglasses up on his nose then brushed his hair back with his hand using his car window as a mirror. The window also served as a mirror that would alert him to anyone standing or watching from his rear. After taking in his surroundings, he turned and bent at the knees in a makeshift attempt to adjust his pant leg and sock. Making these minor wardrobe adjustments gave him time to take in the ebb and flow of traffic, see if anyone looked out of place and note landmarks in the event he had to make a hasty exit. Nothing set off his internal radar.

He crossed the road on foot, careful not to walk in front of the museum where the majority of the tourists and other pedestrians would be. He strolled down the sidewalk on Mahatma Ghandi Drive, which circled a large park behind the museum. Rafael was just another well-dressed tourist enjoying his surroundings and the morning air. The building was enormous and beautiful, a magnificent contradiction in an area devastated with poverty and crime.

He checked his watch after reconnoitering the entire building and saw that it was 10:07, time for him to buy a ticket and check out the inside of the museum. After making his way to the front of the building, he glimpsed the surveillance cameras mounted in strategic locations along the rooftop and atop outdoor light fixtures without so much as lifting his head. His dark sunglasses served many purposes. He sat down on a bench facing the entrance and saw two guards standing just inside the doors next to a metal detector. They passively glanced at the museum patrons as they entered, paying little attention to their coming or goings.

He paid the pretty window teller the sixty pesos, got his ticket and asked her for a museum map. As he walked past the guard he nodded, the guard returning his nod. Careful to keep his head down to avoid looking directly into any cameras, he removed his sunglasses and put them inside a jacket pocket. For the next few minutes he studied the map while standing against a wall in the immense foyer area next to the gift shop. Turning west he saw the small stairway leading downstairs to the first floor which contained the Mayan displays.

Rafael stopped periodically to admire artwork and artifacts on display so as not to draw any undue attention to himself. The truth be known, he was mesmerized with the history of his ancestors. Not wanting to get too distracted by the history housed at the museum, he continued walking toward the elevator marked *conservation lab*. Just to the right of the elevator, he saw a storage closet. He made a mental note of both the elevator and closet, and then turned toward a Mayan statue and pretended to stare at it as he mentally retraced his path back to the front of the building, assuring he had the lay of the museum committed to memory.

Tonight, he thought to himself as he wandered around the museum for another hour before making his way back to his car.

Oxford, Alabama, USA
July 12, 2013, 8:46 P.M.

Silently and resolutely the shirtless man with the karate pants moved forward and backward, then side to side. His focus was primal and intense, and in his mind's eye he visualized an opponent attacking him as he defended. His frayed black belt snapped as he applied an opposite side punch, then immediately dropped his tanden, or spiritual center, into a scissor stance while executing an outside center block. The powerful movement was quickly followed by a sudden snap from the scissor stance into a forward leaning punch. Sweat flew from the man performing the kata and soaked into the ground around him.

As he moved from technique to technique the shrill call of hundreds, or perhaps thousands of cicadas provided a perverse rhythmic symphony, the males' singing rising to fervent pitches and lows. Suddenly, and as fast as he had begun his kata, he finished. A droplet of sweat rolled down his nose as he controlled his breathing and his senses remained acutely aware of their surroundings. Around him he heard each animal and every insect as they moved and called to one another; the Japanese called this altered state of mind *zanshin,* or relaxed awareness.

William Evers, Bill as he was commonly known to the few he associated with, lived at the foot of Mount Cheaha at the edge of the Talladega National Forest. Cheaha stood proudly as the highest point in Alabama, its name taken from the Muskogee Indian tribe meaning "high place." His cabin sat on a fifteen acre spread surrounded by maple and yellow pine trees. The large back yard served as his summertime dojo, or training hall. His achievements of earning high black belt ranks in both Yoshukai Karate-do and Kodokan judo were accomplishments he thought little of; he preferred getting lost in his kata and executing the techniques he'd spent a lifetime learning.

The night air was hot and damp, the sky starlit and the two citronella torches he had lit before training licked the night shadows while keeping the mosquitoes at bay. He reached for a towel that he had earlier draped over his porch banister. As he dried the sweat from his body, he heard gravel crunching in the distance. Bill turned his head to see up his long driveway and saw headlights creeping toward him. Not one to have many visitors, Bill stepped inside his house and grabbed his Glock .45 and tucked it into the back of his gi pants.

He took off his black belt, meticulously hung it on the banister with the towel, and slipped into a t-shirt, careful to pull it over the pistol. Bill walked to the side of his driveway and stood next to a large oak tree and leaned into it with his left shoulder, leaving his right hand free to grab the pistol if needed. The tree provided the perfect cover in case he needed a shield.

The car continued creeping down the tree lined driveway and parked next to the cabin. Its driver turned the ignition off, but left the headlights on for a moment, his eyes casually scanning the area. Suddenly, he flashed his headlights twice – seemingly a signal to anyone watching him.

The driver lowered his window before turning the engine off, the headlights still on. Slowly, two hands emerged from the car followed by a shout, "Billy! It's me, an old friend. I'm going to turn these lights off and get out of the car. I know you're probably packing and I'm just asking you not to shoot me."

Bill recognized the strong, Southern Appalachian accent and a small grin slowly crept across his face.

"Buddy, is that you?" Buddy Smith was an old comrade and presumably retired spook. Evers served with distinction in the United States Army after 9-11 in both Iraq and Afghanistan, but after getting out of the military Buddy recruited Bill to do some overseas work. Fighting other people's wars seemed to be his MO and getting rich on the side had always been Buddy's specialty.

"It sure is, Young Buck," Buddy replied using the nickname he'd given him after his first campaign through Sudan.

It was in Iraq that Bill had taken his first life. That night still haunted his sleep. The recurring nightmares were a lasting reminder that he still maintained a thin grasp on his own soul. Being frightened of the nightmares, but happy they came to him was something only a person who had engaged in mortal combat could understand.

Later, after he had gotten out of the Army, Buddy recruited him to the Sudan where he successfully helped bring about a more U.S. friendly military regime that had created a significant amount of cash being funneled through Buddy's hands as the drug and gun trade amped up in the third world country. Bill had placed a single bullet between a target's eyes at two hundred yards then moved on to the next. The most amazing part of the kill was not the distance, it was the time. At 2:00 a.m. and wearing night vision goggles, Bill had dropped his target without blinking.

"That was a helluva shot there, Young Buck," Buddy had told him in his thick hillbilly drawl. Other mercenaries grew to revere him and his new nickname stuck.

"How're you doing?" asked Buddy when he saw Bill relax. He opened the car door after killing the head lights and stepped into the tepid night air.

"Never better."

Buddy's long gray and brown hair touched the top of his shoulders. It looked as though the old soldier hadn't given his looks much attention for at least a year or two. His face revealed several deeply etched lines across his forehead and beside either nostril that trailed down to the corners of his mouth. Three days of beard stubble displayed more salt than pepper in the once natural black he sported in his younger years. His blue button down short-sleeve shirt hadn't seen the hot side of an iron since its purchase and sweat stains saturated the armpits. The jeans he wore were clean enough with only a few noticeable smudges, and his dusty cowboy boots suggested to the world he had walked the majority of it.

He pulled his stringy hair into a ponytail and tied it up with a rubber band from the morning newspaper. Evers watched him put his hands on his hips and stretch his back. Buddy cranked his chin to his left shoulder, then to his right, the cracking vertebrae audible in the night air. Finally, he rolled his shoulders to loosen them up as well.

"Pretty nice spread you've got here. How much land do you have with this place?" asked Buddy.

"Enough. But did you come all the way out here for real estate advice or is something on your mind?" Bill quipped.

"Damn, Young Buck. I see your pleasant disposition hasn't changed much over the years. You going to ask me inside or are we going to stand here in this sauna all night?"

Bill pointed to the front door with his chin, which served as an invitation. He grabbed his gi top and belt and headed to his cabin. He pulled the Glock from his pants as they walked through the back door into his kitchen. He placed the pistol on the table in front of him within easy reach.

Cool air flowed from the central air conditioning unit's floor registers. The old spook breathed in the gloriously cold air and savored its envelopment over his body that had been mugged by the humid Alabama heat. He wiped his forehead and his cheeks with a dingy white handkerchief he pulled from a hip pocket.

He glanced down at Evers' massive hand cannon. "Is this how you treat all your guests?" Buddy reached for a kitchen chair and sat down, "You've never been much of a trusting sombitch."

Bill leaned against his kitchen counter contemplating what his guest had said, and shook his head. He took a deep breath and calmly asked Buddy, "What do you want? I'm pretty sure you didn't drive your ass out here in the middle of nowhere to talk about the good ole days or the time we spent watching each other's back while the other took a shit."

"I tell ya, Buck, you missed your calling as a poet. You're a cunning linguist if I've ever heard one." Buddy reached into the top pocket of his shirt and pulled out a cigar, a large Cuban Cohiba. Bill intently watched the old man's hand reach into his pants pocket and retrieve a cigar cutter, proceed to snip the end, while being careful not to let it hit the floor.

"Mind if I smoke?"

"Yeah, I mind. Want to do that shit then let's step outside. I don't need the house smelling like a bar," Bill replied matter-of-factly.

Buddy nodded his head and considered stepping outside to smoke his favorite illegal stogie, but placed it back into his shirt pocket instead.

"What happened, Billy? We were always pretty close, but you've become a bit of a mean old bastard since the last time I saw you. For a lot of people solitude is a good thing, but maybe being out here in this," Buddy made a sweeping arc with his left hand, "all by yourself isn't good for someone like you."

"What? Who is 'someone like' me, Buddy? You mean a guy who went to war for his country believing all the bullshit patriotic crap a recruiter told me, only to find out later war and death is really only about money? Is that what you mean? Or maybe you mean the young man who got out of the army who had few skills other than killing people. And that same young man who decided his particular skillset was more useful in fighting other people's wars than it was busting his ass back home for next to nothing. You'll have to excuse me if the realities of the world have made me somewhat bitter. I must admit that I'm not a fan of any country's government, most especially ours."

Some time passed before Buddy spoke again. He weighed his words then said, "Billy, a strong distrust of government is a good thing. Hell, that's what the founders of our country told us to do. You know, don't trust 'em. But walking around being cynical all the time eats at a man's heart. Everyone can't be bad all the time, Billy. You should think about that and let the past die and be buried."

Evers wasn't a man who liked to be preached to and the bitterness he'd described moments earlier still resonated in the front of his mind. He tried to tamp down some of his ire because Buddy, while still his friend, represented everything he'd grown to hate about the puppeteers of the world. These people had a way of manipulating a person for their own end and he'd simply felt like the easiest path was to distrust most everyone.

"I understand how you feel. You know I do. And I know what it's like to walk around wondering if anything you've done really mattered, or if it just benefited some rich asshole sitting behind a desk in D.C. Sometimes a man has to do things for himself, Young Buck.

"But that's enough with the philosophy class, Billy. I came to talk some business. How's life treating you? What do you do for cash these days?"

Bill thought about the directness of Buddy's questions before replying, but he knew Buddy was just being the same old guy he'd known a lifetime ago. He breathed deeply and subconsciously sucked his teeth, a habit he had picked up years earlier.

"Life is fine, Buddy. Since I don't dick around with any of the alphabet soup groups anymore, I sometimes do a little executive protection work. I've tabled enough cash to be comfortable here."

Buddy nodded his head.

"EP work, huh? Bodyguard stuff. I reckon that keeps a man busy. And I see you still practice that kung fu shit, too," Buddy snickered.

"Karate…and judo. Both come in handy in close quarter situations," responded Bill with a slight smirk on his face.

"So does that .45 you're sporting," Buddy snorted.

Bill sighed heavily and walked to the refrigerator and grabbed two beers. He slid one across the table to Buddy then popped the top of the frosty aluminum can he kept for himself.

"Gotta ask one more time, Buddy. Why are you here? I know this isn't a social call, and I don't think you would be asking me what I'm doing for money if you weren't about to propose something."

Buddy laughed before responding. "Boy, you've always known how to cut through the shit and get down to business. That's what I like about you. So here's the deal, an ancient relic was stolen from a museum down Mexico way three nights ago. We'd like for you to find this relic, procure it and bring it to us. There'll be substantial monetary gain for you, including all your expenses, of course."

An array of emotions flitted across Evers' face. Greed, pain, guilt and hate all rolled into one big ball of 'fuck you' is what Buddy saw. It was then he knew this mission was going to be a hard sell.

Bill listened intently to what Buddy had offered before he replied. "I'm not interested. You need to find antiques, go hire Indiana Jones. I've always specialized in other sorts of business and you know that Buddy, not search and recovery of old shit that no one wants other than a museum."

"Yeah, I figured you'd say something like that, Young Buck. But I can't stress to you enough how important the recovery of this artifact is to a lot of people."

"A lot of people? Like who? Who do you associate with now, Buddy…art collectors? What is this relic you want recovered and what's its significance?" Bill stopped and took another pull from his beer, then wiped his mouth with the back of his arm.

"It's a cartouche, Billy; a small piece of jewelry made in ancient China a long time ago. Recently revealed information supplied to us hints that it could be used as one of the most destructive weapons in modern warfare and we need to get it before it falls into the wrong hands." Buddy opened his beer and sipped while keeping his eyes locked on Bill's, allowing him to process the information and form his own questions.

"Wait. I thought you said it was stolen from a museum in Mexico City. Was it on loan from China? And how does a piece of jewelry get confused with some damned weapon of mass destruction? How big is this thing anyway?"

Buddy chuckled and raised the palm of his hand as Bill fired off his line of questions.

"Slow down there, cowboy. Let me answer one question at a time, okay? First, it *was* stolen from Mexico City and no, it wasn't on loan from China or any Chinese holding. It would seem that this particular piece of jewelry has been purposed with some specific thaumaturgy, which has given some folks a reason to be concerned."

"Buddy," Bill began, "you've always been a full time silver-tongued devil and a part-time asshole. What the fuck is thaumaturgy?"

Buddy studied Bill for a moment wondering how much he should reveal to his friend, but said nothing. He pulled the Bud Light to his mouth and took a long, slow drink. A burp resonated somewhere deep in his chest, and he exhaled the bitter vapors through his nose.

"Young Buck, thaumaturgy is a fancy word for magic. But it isn't your run-of-the-mill hocus pocus bullshit you'll see in Vegas on a Wednesday night before all the good strip clubs bring in their pretty gals. This is the real deal…like African juju and island voodoo. You hear me?" Buddy looked seriously into Bill's eyes and continued. "This is the shit you saw when you were traipsing around the jungles of Sudan and Uganda, only worse."

Bill listened to his old war colleague, now slightly intrigued, but not convinced that the American government would have any interest in some piece of jewelry that could supposedly be used as a destructive force against an enemy. Well, maybe that wasn't an accurate thought. The fucked-up American government might be interested in anything that would give them a militaristic or opportunistic advantage in the world, but he doubted with all the technology at their disposal that this particular thing would interest them.

"You said it was Chinese. If it wasn't on loan from China, how'd it get to a Mexican museum?"

"Well, we know it was discovered in the old Mayan temple at Chichen Itza in the Yucatan Peninsula. And maybe my saying it is Chinese isn't one hundred percent accurate. The photos we've seen of the artifact suggest it is of Chinese origin, somehow influenced by Chinese mythology. And some of the hieroglyphs are also very Chinese, at least a very old form of Chinese writing."

Bill chewed on Buddy's words for a couple of minutes before getting up and walking to the fridge for another beer. He opened the door and picked up a can and raised his eyebrows questioningly to Buddy.

"No thanks, Buck. I'm driving. Best if I don't push my luck."

Bill shrugged and popped the top of the beer. "Suit yourself."

"Chichen Itza? You mean the pyramid built by the Mayans? The same people who made the calendar that had everyone going bat shit crazy in 2012? That Chichen Itza?"

"The one and the same, Young Buck. Those jungle monkeys really knew how to fuck with the minds of advanced people didn't they?" Buddy laughed at his own crass joke.

"So, what about the magic? What does this cartouche do? How does it work? And what the hell does it look like?"

Buddy pondered the questions he knew his old friend had asked. "We don't know all the answers to that either, Billy. We just know there's a particular someone who was spotted in the general vicinity of the relic prior to its disappearance. The rumors of the jewel's powers were always considered just that...rumors, but given the special interest from this particular party, we've been asked to recover it, but to do so discreetly."

"Wait. You told me this cartouche could be used as a WMD, but you don't know how, or even if, it works. And the government wants to keep its rediscovery on the QT. Somehow, I don't think you're being completely honest with me, Buddy, and you know I don't like walking into a shit-storm half blind. And before you get the wrong impression, I'm not agreeing to this seek-and-fucking-find mission."

"I'm telling you everything I know, Buck. There are folks who want this thing to see if they can figure out its use. That's what I've been told."

"So, who was in Mexico when the cartouche went missing?" asked Billy.

"Dugan," Buddy spat.

"Dugan? Dan Dugan? I thought that son of a bitch died a long time ago, Buddy." Evers stated as the incredulity rose in his voice.

"Nah. We've been keeping tabs on him for a few years now. He's made a fortune running guns across the Mexican border and the U.S. has sometimes sought out his services when certain things needed to be done clandestinely, if you get my drift."

Bill half chortled. "Yeah, like Fast and Furious, huh? Sneaking U.S. guns across the border to entice cartels into the open so you could take them down. But you didn't know those cartels would wind up killing innocent Americans did you? Are those the kind of things you use this douche bag for, Buddy?"

"We all have a role to play, Buck. It's the end game we all have to keep in mind, especially when we're forced to work with the assholes of the world." Buddy didn't want to remind Evers about their recent conversation on the topic of cynicism, and its ability to eat at a man's heart and soul. He was positive the look on his face let him know he was thinking it though.

"How do you know Dugan was in Mexico?"

"We keep tabs on him just in case he gets out of line. He's a dangerous man and we don't need him going totally rogue. He was traveling with a fake passport and using the name Haden. Seems as though he had a hand in breaking into the National Museum of Anthropology to take the jewel.

"After he got out of the military, he began building a personal network while working as a Blackwater contractor in Iraq about eight years ago. We found out later that he financed small arms sales to AQ on the side through poppy purchases in Afghanistan that found its way to the open market in Turkey. His network was strung out all through the Middle East, and he made a fortune buying and selling drugs and guns.

The military started getting wind of the gun trade inside Iraq and figured there was an insider running it. When the investigation started, Dugan's camp in Baghdad was hit by a mortar, and he suddenly disappeared. The insurgency was in full swing and the military didn't have time to investigate his disappearance further, so they wrote him off as a casualty of war.

We got word a couple of years ago that someone had started up similar activities in Mexico. At first everyone thought the usual suspects were at play – MS13 or the drug cartels. Then we received word that a dirty bomb had been smuggled into Mexico and we knew we were dealing with someone with some serious connections. Fortunately, some of our undercover boys were able to track down the device and retrieve it, but no one knew who ordered it brought to Mexico. I had suspected Dugan for quite some time. Then we caught him on a surveillance video in Puerto Vallarta about eighteen months ago."

Bill nodded, still not fully convinced Buddy was telling him the whole truth.

"I can see on your face you still aren't sure whether you want to do this or not, Buck. You'll make an even million, half when you accept the job, half when we get the cartouche safely to us."

Bill took another sip of his beer, swallowed then narrowed his eyes as he studied his old mentor.

"I have a question for you, Buddy. It doesn't have anything to do with this job, but I want to know what happened to you when we got back to the States. I haven't seen you in a long time and wondered if you had dropped off the face of the Earth."

Buddy smiled, but the smile didn't touch his eyes.

"When I got home I thought about everything I had done and everything we'd seen over there, Buck. I've always believed in a higher power, even after all the shit we'd been through. Something called me to preaching *the word* and that's what I did."

Incredulously, Billy looked at his old friend and remarked, "So you came home and decided to be a preacher. Tell me Buddy, how does a man go from being a spook to a preacher and back again to being a spook?"

Buddy got up from the table and walked toward the door, put his hand on the door knob then stopped. He stared out the window for a moment and, without turning around, said, "I figured out it was a lot easier to take souls than to save them, Buck. Pays a lot more too. You think about this offer. I'll be in touch with you in two days for your answer."

He turned the knob and walked outside, closing the door behind him.

Zacatecas, Mexico
July 12, 2013 8:18 P.M.

Rafael nursed his Modelo Negro, his favorite beer, as he sat quietly at a table in the back of a local restaurant. He had agreed to meet up with Haden in Monterrey on the 22nd of July after calling him to let him know he had the cartouche. Monterrey was a large Mexican city just over 900 kilometers north of Mexico City, straight up Mexico Highway 57, and he decided to begin his journey sooner rather than later.

Rafael had elected to take his time and stay off the main roads as much as possible, as he knew Federalis would be setting up check points in an attempt to retrieve the stolen artifact. He also realized if he were caught with the jewel and a few thousand United States dollars, prison would be the least of his worries. The Federalis were notorious for taking what they wanted and leaving dead people in their wake. There was no way he was giving up his earnings, nor life for that matter, if he could avoid it.

He turned west opting to stay in Zacatecas for a few days. Zacatecas, an old silver mining town, was relatively small, but it wasn't so small that locals would take an interest in him. He took note of the massive number of buildings with gang graffiti on them and made sure he watched for anyone flying gang colors. There was no need to bring attention to himself or invite more trouble into his life.

He checked into the Hotel Posada de la Moneda, a stately and clean hotel for just under forty dollars a night. The stress he had been under after stealing the cartouche, the drive out of the city, and the hot Mexican sun had taken a toll on him. He slept for nearly fourteen hours.

After rousing, he showered, shaved, changed clothes and put on a dinner jacket, not so much for its fashionable statement, but more to hide the Ruger he tucked in his shoulder harness. He took a long look in the mirror to make sure the bulk of the pistol didn't show. Satisfied that it was out of sight, he opened the door to his room, glancing right then left, and walked to the elevator.

Famished and thirsty, he asked the desk clerk where he could find a decent restaurant and was given directions to La Casa Rosa. After making sure he had plenty of pesos in his wallet, he set out for the restaurant. He had hidden his U.S. money in a vent in his hotel room just in case he was harassed by anyone along the way.

As he took another drink of his beer, he allowed his fingers to slide inside his pants pocket where he kept the cartouche. Casually, he looked around to make sure no one was watching him. Most of the people in the restaurant were drinking and talking to friends; none were paying any attention to the newcomer. He pulled the ancient jewel out and felt it *vibrate*, as though it had been awakened. Confused by this sensation, he studied the strange raised markings on the silver pendant, mesmerized by its simplicity and beauty. Rafael wondered how old it was, and why Haden wanted it so badly.

He caressed the cartouche with his thumb and forefinger, feeling a strange life force flowing through it. He broke his gaze for a moment to look around the room and noticed a man glancing his way. *Pinche cabron* he thought to himself. Without looking up, he replaced the relic in his pocket and took another swig of his beer.

The waitress brought him a plate of enchiladas verdes and sliced avocado. He doused the enchiladas with the fiery-hot green pepper sauce she brought with his meal, and then began eating…slowly. Rafael decided he would stretch out the meal and have another beer in hopes the guy eye-balling him would get bored and leave.

While he ate, he watched the man in his peripheral to assure he didn't attempt to get any closer. He also allowed his mind to drift back three nights prior when he stole the cartouche.

He left the museum after scouting it out, knowing he would be seen on the security cameras. After returning to his car, he drove to a local gas station to use the restroom. He bolted the door and changed into a new set of clothes he had packed in a duffle before leaving his hotel. Once he slipped on a navy blue shirt and a pair of neatly pressed black slacks, he stuffed his old clothes into the duffel bag. Finally, he slipped into a comfortable pair of black loafers and pushed a baseball cap onto his head before returning to his car.

He drove around Mexico City for a couple of hours memorizing construction zones and heavy traffic areas. His heart thudded in his chest and sweat rolled down his face despite the car's air conditioning. The realization of what he was about to attempt was making him nervous and jumpy. He knew he would have to get a hold of himself before arriving at the museum.

Around 4:00 p.m., his nerves now under control, he returned to the parking lot he had found earlier, put his car in park, but left it running while he completed his disguise. He checked himself in the mirror to make sure the fake mustache was on straight and looked real. His disguise complete, he reached into the back seat and grabbed a cane and the bimorph opto-mechanical deflector that he had secured in a digital camera bag. It fit snugly in one of the bag's pockets; its size no larger than a lady's compact mirror.

For a brief second he wondered if the device would work as well as Haden had described, or if the American was setting him up. He brushed the thought away before his heart began pounding again. There was little doubt that the man wanted the cartouche, and less still that he would want additional security measures taken by the museum to protect it further, which would make it harder for him to acquire it in the future.

He opened his car door and picked up the cane. A man's ability to disguise himself was relatively easy, but convincingly changing his gait was all but impossible. Between the fake limp he had incorporated as he walked and the cane he used to support himself, the problem was solved.

Once he crossed the street, he dropped his head and pulled his cap over his brow a little further to avoid any surveillance cameras getting a good shot of his face. He crossed the sidewalk and limped into the opening in front of the entrance to the museum. A large set of stairs to the underground parking deck lay just behind him. Several tourists were going in and coming out of the museum while one courteous man held the door for him after watching him approach the entrance. Rafael nodded his appreciation but didn't voice it. He thought it better not to speak, thereby eliminating one more thing for someone to remember him by when speaking with the police.

He had his ticket stub purchased earlier that morning and knew he could use it to re-enter the museum, as the passes were good for a day. His hand reached into his pocket for the ticket and showed it to the guard who directed him to the metal detector. Placing the camera, his cane and car keys on the belt, he struggled through the detector, his limp exaggerated, while another guard opened his camera case to examine it.

The guard carefully removed the camera and studied it for a moment, then looked inside the case itself. Rafael kept a smile on his face as the guard continued to poke around inside the camera case even though his heart was about to jump out of his chest. If the guard found the bi-morph deflector, he would explain it away as being some fancy part of his camera that he had not figured out how to use. Fortunately, when the guard opened the compartment housing the deflector, he gave it no more than a cursory glance before zipping the case closed.

Satisfied that the camera posed no threat, the guard gently placed it back into the bag and handed it and the other items to Rafael. He nodded his appreciation to the guard then began limping into the museum. He made his way toward the area closest to the conservation lab. The museum was scheduled to close at 6:00 p.m., so taking his time and appearing interested in the ancient art and artifacts was crucial.

At 5:45, he spotted the storage closet he had seen earlier. The camera was situated such that the closet was not in its line of sight. He looked around to assure he was alone, then pulled his camera case off his shoulder, opened a small pocket and removed a little screw driver similar to one that would be used to tighten screws on eye glasses. He stuck the flat end into the space between the door and the striker and pushed it against the latch, easily opening the door. As quickly and quietly as he could, he entered the storage closet and settled himself. Rafael knew there would be a final check by security to make sure everyone was out of the museum, and he would probably be in the closet for a while.

At long last he heard footsteps fall outside the small closet. He heard the guard make the circle around the room and the many exhibits of ancient Mexico. The footsteps grew closer to the closet then suddenly stopped. Rafael held his breath and prepared himself to attack should the guard open the door. An eternity passed before he could hear the footsteps echo down the hall to the next chamber. Rafael waited another hour before opening the door.

Once the hour had passed, Rafael opened the door and crept along the wall careful to keep his hat pulled down and continue his limping gait toward the elevator leading to the conservation lab. After pressing the button directing him to the lab, the Otis elevator sprang to life and transported him down one floor. The stainless steel doors opened and as they did, he glanced in either direction looking for cameras. There were none. He saw the door marked Laboratorio de Conservacion and walked straight to it. After another quick glance around the hallway, he looked at the lock on the door. It was nothing fancy, just a simple keyed access on a door handle. Apparently, security was not necessary in an area that never saw a tourist.

Using the same screwdriver he had used earlier, he pried the latch back and opened the door. Quietly, he closed the door behind him then opened the camera case. He removed the bimorph deflector and allowed it to self-calibrate.

He waited three long minutes until he was sure it was acclimated to the ambient room temperature before looking for the cartouche. It didn't take him long to spot the little piece of jewelry, approximately an inch-and-a-half long by one-half inch wide nestled upon a wooden display stand. Such an insignificant thing, but exactly as Haden's picture had detailed it.

Sweat began staining his shirt and his hands shook as he moved to place the deflector in front of the heat sensor that protected the cartouche. He had to be especially cautious that he did not accidentally get ahead of the deflector, causing the alarm to be set off. Rafael made sure the small stand on the deflector was locked in place, its two legs angled correctly to absorb and deflect the sensor itself. The nanotechnology was developed to absorb laser energy and to shed heat. There was no doubt in his mind the United States government had developed the device.

Slowly, he slid the deflector between the sensor and the cartouche until he saw the shield turn a light blue hue. Haden was right! It worked just like he said. Once he was certain the deflector was functioning, he reached into the opening and removed the cartouche from its wooden stand. Just as gently as he reached to grab the jewel, he similarly withdrew his hand. He exhaled loudly in relief when the alarm didn't sound. His hand slipped the prize into his pocket as he retreated to the elevator. Again, the doors to the elevator opened and he slithered into the closet, careful to avoid the mounted surveillance cameras. With the door locked he made himself as comfortable as possible. A storage closet wasn't exactly a Ritz Carlton, but it sufficed.

He dozed in and out of sleep as the night dragged on. A couple of times he heard footsteps outside the door and realized it was just a security guard making his rounds. Rafael checked his watch – 9:08 a.m. He had to slip out of the storage closet and blend with a few tourists before making his way out so as not to arouse any suspicion.

He cracked open the door and looked around for anyone who might see him, saw no one and walked out of the closet. He left behind the cane that he had wiped down before stepping into the exhibit hall. There was no need to haphazardly leave behind fingerprints and make it easier for the police to track him down.

With his cap pulled low, he stayed away from the view of the camera as he stepped into the open. Milling around in different rooms for almost an hour allowed a few tourists and museum goers the chance to start crowding the popular attractions. They would provide him the cover he needed.

He made his way to the exit and left without so much as a glance from the first shift security team. Turning right at the corner of the museum and heading directly toward the parking lot where he'd left his rental, Rafael controlled his desire to run. When he finally reached his car he started the engine and dropped it in drive. Only then did he allow himself a sigh of relief and a wide grin.

Rafael finished his dinner and watched the man at the bar who was still sipping from the same tumbler of liquor he had ordered when he first sat down. He got the attention of his waitress and asked for the check, handing her enough pesos to cover the bill and leave a respectable enough tip, but not so much that she would make an effort to remember him.

He glanced at the man who was spinning the glass holding his drink. It was obvious he was trying very hard to look inconspicuous and bored. Rafael felt the reassuring presence of the pistol under his left arm and walked outside without looking directly at the stranger, but did take note in his peripheral vision that the fellow was Latino, thirtyish and muscular.

Rafael turned on the side street where he left his car and threw himself against the wall of a stucco building. He heard footsteps moving quickly toward him. Not wanting to pull his pistol if he didn't need to, he grabbed the Gerber pocket knife he carried and quietly opened the blade.

Before the man knew what had happened, Rafael grabbed his collar and shoved the three inch blade into his side, below the floating rib. Just as swiftly, Rafael cupped the man's mouth to keep him from screaming, only muffled sounds escaped the wide-eyed Latino. Rafael dragged him behind some boxes and forced him to the ground still holding firm to the knife.

"Quien es, vato?" asked Rafael.

The man winced as Rafael slowly turned the knife making the pain even more excruciating. His eyes widened and he jumped, trying to move away from the knife and the pain burning in his side.

"Who are you? Why are you following me?" he continued to ask.

The Latino grunted then replied, "Some gringo. He paid me to follow you, señor. Please, don't kill me. I didn't mean you any harm."

"I won't kill you if you tell me who this gringo is. Is his name Haden?"

"I don't know, sen...," his words tailing off as his eyes became glassy and he lost consciousness.

"Dammit," Rafael muttered under his breath as he checked around him to make sure no witnesses could see the strange comingling of bodies.

He slapped the unconscious man's face as he attempted to wake him. His victim sputtered and opened his eyes, trying to refocus on Rafael.

"Tell me what this gringo looks like, and I'll get you to a hospital. They can save you. Tell me!"

The man's jaw began moving, but blood dripped where words should have formed. He breathed short raspy breaths that grew more rapid before trailing off. Rafael watched as the man's life force left him. He pulled the knife from the man's side, wiped the blade on his victim's shirt then pocketed the knife. Not taking the time to hide the man's body, he jumped in his car and sped back to his hotel, packed his suitcase, grabbed the money he had hidden in the vent and left without checking out of the hotel.

Oxford, Alabama, USA
July 14, 2013 1:18 P.M.

Evers sat in a rocking chair on his front porch thinking about Buddy's offer. The money would be great, but he feared being sucked back into a lifestyle he detested. He had spent a significant portion of his life in the service of the CIA and fighting other people's wars. The black and white of how the world works was merely a dream shared by most; the gray reality that permeated his mind would scare Joe Citizen to death.

The power struggles, the money, the back door deals with "enemies" were just a few of the reasons he didn't want, or need, to get involved, but the allure of that much cash would afford him his lifestyle without any worries. But more than the possibility of having a significant cash cow at his disposal was the allure of this cartouche. Of all the missions he'd been on, he had never been asked to recover a magical artifact. He would be lying to himself if he thought he wasn't intrigued by the possibility of seeing its magic in person.

Buddy's involvement in this kind of search and find activity was perplexing as well. His old friend had always been one to find a target and take him out, or do things like destroy villages where suspected terrorist holdouts were hiding. To see him involved in this seek and find mission was almost as titillating as the mission itself. He knew he would have to have the discussion about the "whys" sooner or later, but decided to put it on the back burner for now. Buddy had unusually good reasoning skills and a good head on his shoulders and wouldn't be involved in this type of thing without some serious   forethought.

Buddy Smith – he had known the old spook for half of his adult life. Evers' strong distrust of other humans didn't stop with Buddy, but he could honestly say that he had never lead him astray or lied to him, insofar as he was aware. Their shared time on various battlefields also perpetuated a relationship that only forms when certain death is imminent, that is, your death or the death of the targets being hunted.

On more than one occasion, they stood back-to-back fending off guerrilla fighters in jungles and in deserts. Evers recalled a time he took a bullet in his side, and Buddy patched him up until he could receive proper medical care. Still, he was working for the shadow government, and for that very reason alone there was cause for concern. He also knew Buddy was a loner, as were most in their line of work, and that self-preservation trumped any past mission or time spent in the field together.

There was no doubt in his mind that he didn't fully trust Buddy, but for the moment he chose not to focus on him. Instead, he let his eyes and thoughts drift like a thick fog rolling over the mountaintop.

He peered out over his property to the lake that was nestled at the foot of the big mountain. Reflections of the blue Alabama sky and the trees that lined the mountain shone like a postcard. A red-tailed hawk circled overhead before landing on a smaller limb at the top of a large oak tree just to his right. The hawk's superior eyesight was focused on something Evers couldn't see, but he knew whatever was there wasn't long for the world. In a flash the hawk swooped down and snatched a field mouse in its talons. Evers heard the last squeak the little mouse would ever muster as the bird and its prey rose into the air, the hawk flying toward its hidden aerie somewhere in the surrounding woods.

The afternoon air was hot but Evers' garage and house were connected by a covered breezeway which usually allowed for a nice draft. He walked back in his house, opened his kitchen window and turned on his CD player, put on his favorite blues tunes from a band called *Moondog Medicine Show*. The Maryland blues band was a local favorite that he had caught while in D.C. a few years earlier. The female lead singer's raspy voice reminded Evers of a cross between Bonnie Rait and Melissa Etheridge. *She wasn't hard on the eyes either* he thought to himself, then smiled. He poured a glass of water and dropped in some ice cubes before walking back to his porch and rocking chair.

Lana Spence belted out the harsh lyrics in "Bring It On" while he thought about Buddy's offer. His mind drifted to his conversation with him two nights earlier. He wondered what the cartouche was and why Big Brother wanted it. They obviously wanted it pretty badly if they decided a former spook with certain martial skills was the right one to retrieve it.

"And what the hell is an ancient piece of jewelry made in China doing in Mexico," he mused?

He was fascinated by these questions almost as much as he was the money. Evers raised the cold glass of water to his mouth. The water washed over his throat, sating his thirst and cooling his body, but did nothing to quell the uncertainties in his mind.

"Well, Billy," he said to himself, "sounds like you've talked yourself into this gig and you really don't know what all is involved in retrieving this piece of jewelry. You're a dumbass of the highest order." He sighed and stared out at the lake.

Their light armored personnel vehicle stopped one click from the building housing a number of known terrorists deep inside the northern Iraqi city of Mosul. Evers and his small assortment of tactical spec ops spread out and cautiously headed toward their target. The moonless night time operation was orchestrated to be carried out at 2300, long after the streets emptied of hawkers and pedestrians.

The plan called for them to radio in air support once they were in position. Evers and his team would initiate the attack by hitting the first story of the multi-storied building with shouldered RPG's. The ground level attack would force the terrorists upstairs, assuring them of the high ground, a tactical calculation they were willing to take. The Marine's VMA air attack squadron would then begin raining down hell on the cockroaches as they scurried to the top. Their fleet of Harrier II's would level the building while the ground operatives would remain on the deck to assure no terrorists escaped.

"The Desert Pirates" was the name they had given themselves. They even had patches made up of a pirate's face in front of a pair of cross-bones that they sewed on their uniform sleeves. MSgt Weiss acted like he didn't see the patches which were forbidden. Weiss had also convinced their CO that the patch helped build unity in a small band of warriors. Most had gotten the patch tattooed somewhere on their body so their dedication would never be called into question.

Master Sergeant Weiss keyed up his wireless mic that hung on his neck and ordered the unit into position. The team filtered around the building and found whatever cover was available. Evers moved to the front of the building with Sgt Kyle Golik, the sharpest sniper he'd ever met.

Evers looked around for any rag-head bearing gifts of heavy caliber weapons or IED's. He saw only one small boy in the distance, maybe sixty or seventy yards away, a child of no more than eight or nine. The boy stood and stared at him for at least two minutes. Evers could have sworn he saw the boy shaking.

Golik made eye contact with Evers, who in turn put his index and middle fingers to his eyes then pointed to the boy. Golik looked at the kid, turned his head to Evers and shrugged. Both men returned their attention to the task at hand. Evers hauled ass backward, approximately twenty yards, and positioned his RPG launcher on his shoulder. Weiss radioed the rest of the team to do a check down, ensuring all exits were properly covered. The team acknowledged their readiness.

Golik slipped another fifteen feet to his right to avoid any shrapnel from the RPG when it hit the door. He ducked behind a parked car and leveled his M16A4 at the building's entrance. The sniper preferred a Barret XM109, but he was forced to carry the fully automatic rifle when on ground missions.

Evers raised the sights on his rifle and then flipped a switch directing a red laser on the door. He nodded to Golik who called back to Weiss to let him know the door was "hot". Others on the team reported they were hot on their targets as well. Weiss gave the orders to engage on his mark. He counted three...two...one.

Evers squeezed the trigger and a grenade rocketed toward the door. In an instant it exploded. He could hear impacts and explosions from the rear of the building as his team launched grenades from their own RPG's. The concussions of the blasts rattled his teeth. Sulphur seeped through the air and filled his nostrils. He could hear the VMA Harriers moving rapidly toward the building.

He glanced over his left shoulder and saw the young boy walking toward him in a daze. Evers began yelling at him and motioning for him to get away.

His pajamas hung off his small body, obviously too large for the boy, the pant legs dragging the ground.

Two guided missiles hit the top of the building as a Desert Pirate on the back side of the building held the laser in place guiding the ordinance to their target. An insurgent managed to break through a downstairs window in hopes of saving his life. Unfortunately for him, Golik squeezed a burst of firepower from his M16A4 sending his lifeless body against the building.

Still, the young boy ambled toward them. He was closer to Golik than he was Evers when Evers noticed the boy wearing a small backpack. His eyes grew wide as he watched the youngster take four more steps before stopping eight feet behind Golik,

"FUUUUUUUCK! HE'S GOT A BOMB!" Evers screamed as he swung his rifle around and beaded down on the boy. A curious thing about high stress situations is the body's ability to react without much thought and the mind's capacity to slow down time when the adrenaline flows freely. Evers recognized the rush of adrenaline immediately, and vividly saw everything transpire in bits and frames. Seconds seemed like minutes and minutes turned to hours.

There was no thought as he squeezed the trigger, and a burst of bullets pummeled the boy's chest and stomach. Several rounds exited his body and ricocheted off a trash can. A shocked expression crossed his face before he crumpled to the ground. Dark red blood gushed from several openings and seeped onto the pavement all around his little body. He coughed once and more blood spewed from his mouth. Then he was gone.

Evers ran to the little boy's lifeless body while Golik kept an eye on the building. Fire engulfed what was left of the multi-story complex. Wood popped and metal twisted as it fell from the structure. The area looked as though The Apocalypse had begun in one small corner of the world.

With the business end of his rifle, Evers rolled the boy onto his blood-drenched belly. As sweat ran down his chest and arms, he reached for the backpack's zipper and slowly opened it. His heart pounded in his ears and chest as his mind imagined the enormous explosive he would find in the pack. The contents made him gasp. His heart sank and he fell to his butt as tears welled in his eyes.

One stuffed animal and a partially eaten sandwich were in the bag. Much of the area's youth were orphans and begged for U.S. servicemen to give them food or water. Many of these same children were forced to strap bombs on themselves and walk into groups of U.S. military personnel, but this boy wasn't one of those children.

Weiss radioed his team to report. Golik mic'd first to report one DAI – dead ass insurgent. The rest of the team followed suit, reporting positions and number of wounded. Golik walked to Evers and put his hand on his shoulder, looking first to the boy's pack then back to his friend.

"You didn't know, partner. You saw the pack and did the right thing. Get the fuck up, and let's get out of here. No one has to know about this, you

hear? You did the right thing. This little fucker would probably have grown up and tried to kill us anyway, so let's go! Right fucking now!"

Tears trickled from Evers' face as he rocked. Golik had been true to his word and no one ever found out about the boy's death. If they had, he would have been court-martialed and possibly prosecuted for murder. The vision burned vividly in his mind and he could almost smell the little one's death scent. His stomach rolled and lurched as the sense of guilt wracked his heart and mind.

Like a painting, he watched the trees reflecting on the lake as he replayed that event, and several others, in his brain. As clearly as the morning sun shone on the water, the image of the young boy walking toward him etched itself in his brain. Hot, damp Alabama air hugged him like a wool coat, yet he paid it no attention because in his mind he was still in Iraq. After several minutes the memories mercifully floated away to the recesses of his mind, but he knew they were still there waiting to return. They were always with him like a bedtime monster living in a child's closet that only came out late at night.

A couple of hours passed but Evers still sat on his porch having gotten up long enough to pour more water and change CD's. Microwave Dave and the Nukes, an Alabama electric blues band, sang "Beep Beep" while Evers tapped his foot. The music provided an escape from his demons and, for a short time, gave him the chance to still his mind.

He heard the crunch of gravel well before he saw Buddy's car next to his house, but there was no doubt in his mind who it was. The silver Dodge Charger was a nice looking car, but the dust from Evers's driveway had dulled the paint. A car door opened, and the old spook stepped out dressed in a well-worn Hawaiian shirt, faded Levi's and a pair of dusty cowboy boots. A cheap pair of sunglasses were perched on his nose, the wire frames having seen better days. He nodded at Evers as he walked to the porch.

Buddy sat down in one of the extra rocking chairs Evers kept on his breezeway for the company he never had. He popped his neck and straightened his back after the bumpy ride down the long dirt and gravel driveway, removed his sunglasses and looked Evers in the eye.

"How you doing today, Young Buck? You don't look so good."

"Never better, Buddy. Just happy to be above ground one more day, you know? How about you? "

"Finer than a two-dick dog, my man. And that's pretty good right there."

Evers laughed quietly at his colorful euphemism. Buddy pulled a cigar from his shirt pocket and looked at Bill inquisitively. Bill chuckled and nodded as Buddy cut the end of the new Cuban Cohiba. He pulled a box of matches from the same shirt pocket, struck one across the gritty portion of the box then lit his cigar. The pleasant smell of the finely cured Cuban tobacco mixed with the rich odor of sulfur filled the air. Buddy waved his hand to push away the smoke.

"You give any more thought to my little proposal?"

"Yeah, I've given it a lot of thought, Buddy. But before I agree to anything, I need to understand what you want me to do. Is this a recovery or kill mission? What are my objectives?"

"Those are good questions, Young Buck. Here's where we are with this – get the cartouche and bring it back. If we never hear from Brother Dugan again after you retrieve the item, well, that's okay too. It is what it is, Billy. Do you understand what I'm telling you?"

Evers didn't reply to the question, Buddy's meaning was obvious. Not ever hearing from someone again, didn't mean sending them away on an island vacation. "Where am I going? Do you think the cartouche is still in Mexico or has it already left the country?"

"We have every reason to believe it's still in Mexico, but we don't know for how much longer. Naturally, you'll travel under an assumed passport. Anything else you will need will be held for you once you cross the border. Comprende?"

"Yeah," said Evers.

They both watched a blue heron sweep across the lake, pull up suddenly and land on the bank. It stepped into the water, graciously standing on one leg while looking for its next meal.

Buddy took a long, deep pull on his cigar then exhaled a giant plume of smoke. "Billy, I don't need to remind you that Dugan is dangerous. He's in bed with drug cartels and smugglers from all over the world. We both know why he's interested in this cartouche thing, and that makes him even more dangerous."

"Money?"

"Yeah, but it's not just any amount of money. He'll have enough cash to buy a third world country. If our military or government wants this thing that badly, Dugan will try to empty Fort fucking Knox into his personal bank account. But I think it's more than that. He knows something about this damned cartouche and the power it holds. That makes him very dangerous."

Bill nodded his understanding then replied, "I'll fly into Mexico City. Has anyone from our side checked the surveillance tapes yet?"

"No. I wanted to wait until you got there," he said with a slight smile on his face. "I didn't want to scare Dugan this early in the game, plus I figured that would be your first move."

"What made you think I'd take this gig, Buddy?" Evers asked, his eyes cut toward his old friend.

"I know you, Billy. You're a man of conviction. You're a man interested in 'what's out there', and you're a man who can get the job done. You're also a man who will get the shit done right, especially when there's a large sum of money involved."

Evers laughed. "Give me one of those cigars; it looks pretty good."

Buddy handed him one he took from his shirt pocket. "Easy does it with that, big daddy. That there is contraband."

Evers lit the Cohiba with the matches Buddy handed him. He took a long draw on the illegal cigar then exhaled a large puff of white smoke. "I'm going to need a few things when I get there, Buddy. I'll give you a list. But before I go to the airport, I'm going to need that money wired to my account. I'll give you the account number for the direct wire. No dinero, Bill, no leave-o."

"Done," Buddy replied. "What else?"

"Per diem. Two hundred dollars a day wired to my account each day I'm in the field. I'll pay my expenses while I'm out. The per diem will cover anything I spend. Anything required beyond the per diem pay I'll let you know, but I expect to be reimbursed. Also, no questions asked. I control this thing, got it?"

"The per diem is no big deal, Buck, but the no questions thing isn't going to fly. I'm going to need updates periodically."

"I'll give you those updates, Buddy. I'll set up a protected bulletin board account that you can sign into to ask questions. I'll check it periodically; you do the same. But I can assure you, if someone from Christians in Action tries to surprise me, I'll kill him. Then I'll come after everyone else involved!" Evers bluntly replied.

"Fair enough. What else?"

"That's it for now," Evers said as he took another drag off the big cigar. "I'll have the list ready in an hour. Why don't you go down to the lake and fish? You look a little stressed. Uncle Sam must have you working overtime. I'll pull my list together while you're drowning worms. Grab a rod and reel in the garage. The door is unlocked."

He tamped out his cigar after Buddy gathered some of Evers' fishing tackle and walked to the lake. Bill needed time to create his list and get a few things in order before he left. Buddy respected his desire to be alone for a while.

He went to work immediately on the list of things he would need while in Mexico, jotting down basic necessities and items that would allow him to travel lightly. Beyond what he wrote down, he figured he could pick up most anything he would need, without drawing attention to himself, on the streets.

Next, he checked his off-shore account in the Caymans, making sure the untraceable account number he would give Buddy would route and link up with the real account he kept in Belize. The series of dummy account numbers he linked to one another gave him some assurances that his money wouldn't be messed with while he was away. Once the money was safely transferred to his fake Cayman account, it would automatically be forwarded to his secure account in Belize, far from the greedy hand of the United States government.

Finally, he packed a light carry-on bag with a few changes of clothes. He figured Buddy was already working on his pseudo-passport and travel itinerary to Mexico City, assuming in advance that he would take the job.

The thought of taking the cartouche from Dugan, and more than likely having to take Dugan out of the picture enticed him too. Dugan was indeed dangerous, not just because of his alliances with cartels and drug overlords, but because he was a highly trained spook, well versed in the ways of how things worked in the harshest of areas in the world, as well as D.C. That made him a hard target and a very valuable one.

There's no backing out now. I reckon this is what you get for being interested, he thought to himself. He grabbed his list and waited for his old war partner to walk into the house.

Benito Juárez International Airport
Mexico City, Mexico
July 15, 2013 11:20 A.M.

Kevin Roper stepped off the plane and headed toward customs, bag in hand. He stuck his customs declaration he completed during his connection from Dallas inside his passport. Traveling a little over five hours to his arrival destination had left him groggy, both from his early flight and from the decreased amount of oxygen available on all those damnable airplanes.

He approached the customs desk and handed the paperwork to the customs agent.

"Hola, Señor. What is the nature of your visit to Mexico, Señor…er…Roper?" the agent asked while studying his papers.

Roper gave the standard reply, "Business."

"What type of business do you do, Señor Roper?" he asked as he watched the American.

"Textile industry. I work with a distributor here in the city who purchases from a manufacturer in Oaxaca who, in turn, exports to the States.

"I see, Señor. And how long will you be staying in Mexico?"

"One week," replied a hopeful Roper.

The attentive customs agent eyeballed him again then moved his gaze back to the passport. He passed a black light over his identification checking for the watermarked government seal. He frowned then looked back at Roper. Roper's pulse quickened, but his face remained calm.

"Have a nice stay in Mexico, Señor Roper," the agent replied as he stamped the passport.

"Gracias," he responded as he reached for his identification, a forced but relieved smile given to the agent. It was at that moment he appreciated Buddy's connections in the world of identification forgery.

The agent nodded and Roper made his way toward the rental car center. He filled out the required paperwork, purchased renter's insurance, and then headed directly to his hotel.

Roper checked into the Camino Real, a hotel only 750 meters from the Museum of Anthropology in Mexico City. His keycard unlocked his room, and he walked in and opened his suitcase.

His dark hair was a plus, although his complexion was anything but stereotypical Latino. He put on jeans and a blue button down shirt with some embroidered decorations that so many of the Mexican men wore. Next, he put an older cowboy hat on his head and a pair of dark sunglasses to mask his eyes. The sneakers he wore were for practical purposes. Roper needed to blend into his environment, not make a fashion statement.

Out of habit, as he exited the hotel, checked his three and nine, to assure no one was waiting for him. He had gotten an address for a local internet café from the desk clerk when he checked in and decided to walk the short two-and-a-half kilometers to get a feel for the surrounding cityscape.

The downtown area of Mexico City ebbed and flowed with traffic and pedestrians. Roper made several turns and cutbacks to cover his ass. He also ducked into a local trinket and souvenir shop, staying close to the window, to see if anyone's direction had changed or if a person had stopped as though searching for someone. Most would consider his actions borderline neurotic, but his survival skills were in high gear. Besides, most had not been involved in the things he had been a part of in his life.

The internet café stood in the heart of the downtown financial district. The street median was lined with palm trees, the sidewalks clean, and restaurants were packed with business people anxious to taste the glorious Mexican wares fanning over the downtown streets. Bar owners were sweeping entrances to their establishments as they prepared for the nightlife and early revelers. Roper could smell stale beer and human urine from the alleyways as he passed the nightclubs.

Across the street he saw a couple of middle aged men duck into a strip club called the Tahitian. A small smile crept across his face because he knew that men everywhere were similarly hardwired. A tall brunette with dazzling blue eyes and sexy long legs flashed into his mind, but he quickly relinquished her for another more appropriate time.

Roper walked down the sidewalk, an extra block, before reversing course. More often than not this simple act would bring about a sudden motion from anyone tailing him. An amateur would turn around after his target, course corrected, so as not to lose him. He watched on both sides of the street for anyone but didn't see anything out of the ordinary. Confident he was alone, he opened the door to the internet café and walked in.

Inside he found an open terminal and sat down. He opened the internet browser and entered the URL for the secure bulletin and message board he had set up before leaving the States. He sent a message that read:

> *Arrived. Need supplies and pick up site. Advise asap.*
> *Will engage museum after I get supplies.*

He sat at the terminal reading news from various websites for ten minutes before checking the bulletin board again for a response. Remarkably, Roper saw that there was a response.

> *Good to hear. Meet contact at Tamazula, District of Mexico,*
> *6:00 p.m. your time. Tortas are excellent there. Don't eat too many.*
> *Ask for Javier at the desk. Report back findings asap.*

The address for the torta and deli shop was at the bottom of the message. He did a fast search on Mapquest and found that it would take him at least an hour by car to get to the pick-up site. He jotted down the address, took a quick look around the shop, saw nothing out of the ordinary, then closed out the browser and purged the history. Better safe than sorry.

Before leaving, he checked the time on his watch – 3:15 p.m. There was plenty of time to walk a thorough counter-surveillance run before leaving the hotel to meet up with his contact. He checked each direction as he left the café and began walking toward his hotel. Although his destination was to his left, he turned right on the sidewalk heading southeast on Eje Pte Florencia. He crossed over the busy intersection at Florencia and Londres passing in front of a palm tree standing tall and proud in the south Mexico heat. After crossing the street, he made a left, heading in the general direction of his hotel. From his peripheral vision he kept a check to see if anyone made an amateurish movement across the intersection to catch up with him.

He saw a Latino fellow with a white t-shirt and jeans make a sudden turn on the opposite side of the street. *Fuck* he thought to himself. *I'm here a couple of hours and I have a shadow already? What have I gotten myself into?*

Roper focused his mind on the task at hand. He told himself to keep his stride steady and not get in a hurry. He would cross the street at some point and time, but he needed to get a feel for how far away his shadow was. He walked across a construction site where the sidewalk was being dug up and a newer version put back in its place. Quickening his pace, he crossed Hamburg Street before slowing enough to give his shadow some time to catch up. Without warning, he stopped in front of a restaurant and acted like he was just a hungry passerby interested in the menu taped to the window.

His attention focused on the reflection; he waited a moment to see if his follower would pass by the window or stop to wait on him. He saw the man stop and act like he was looking in a window across the street. *Okay, I have a tail. He's an amateur. I need to get him to cross the street,* Roper continued thinking to himself. Forcing his breathing and heart rate to slow down, he calmed his emotions and continued strolling down Florencia, his stride steady.

Roper stopped at the intersection of Florencia and Berna then turned right, taking him on the path back to his hotel, and more importantly, forcing his shadow to cross the street to catch him. He figured his tail was a few steps behind him trying to look inconspicuous.

He stepped into a quiet alley and pushed his back against a dumpster. With this much sunlight, he would have to be as silent as possible to keep from drawing any attention. He could hear the man panting heavily as he ran to catch up to him.

His follower turned the corner to the alley, and Roper's hand shot out executing a shuto, or knife hand strike to the side of his neck. The meaty part of his hand struck the man's brachial plexus, stunning and dropping him to his knees. With little thought, Roper moved behind him cupping one hand around his chin and the other behind his head. In a blur the man's neck was snapped and he fell dead to the ground. Roper looked around the alley for onlookers but saw no one. He dragged his victim behind the dumpster and propped him against the wall, his head lying at a ridiculous angle on his shoulder.

He gave the corpse a fast pat down, checking for any identification but found none. He did find a phone number written on a piece of scrap paper. He didn't recognize the area code or the international dialing code, sixty-three, but assumed it was Mexico's. Roper stuck the paper in his pocket then checked his victim one more time.

The adrenaline rush that came with killing a person was wearing off which meant his body would begin shaking uncontrollably soon. A man with a severe case of the shakes in close proximity to a corpse was certain to garner attention he didn't want. He had to finish and get out of the area before someone saw him in the same vicinity of the now dearly departed *Juan Doe*. A quick look around to make sure no witnesses had seen him gave him some assurance that he could get out of the area before the body was discovered.

Roper proceeded out of the alley back to Berna just as his body began trembling. His breathing quickened and he sucked in raspy breaths. Instead of heading directly to his hotel, he made several more switchbacks and a couple of stops in local shops to see if he was being tailed again. Meeting up with any of the dead guy's friends was not on his wish list.

He didn't see or *feel* anyone else he considered a threat, and now, with the adrenaline rush subsiding, his hands and arms began to tremble. He needed to find a place to sit down and relax for an hour or so before the meet with his contact.

A small, quaint cantina advertising cold Sol beer caught his attention. He stepped into the bar, sat down at a table with his back to the wall, faced the tinted window so he could watch for anyone that looked threatening, and ordered the refreshing Mexican beer complete with a lime.

A cute Mexican waitress brought him his beer and held it out for him to take. He smiled and nodded his head toward the table for her to place it there; he didn't want her to see his hands shaking. She smiled back, put the beer on the table and walked back to the bar.

Mariachi music played quietly as he and one other patron sipped their beers. This gave Roper some time to think about the craziness that had just happened. He let the waves of thought ebb and flow as his shaking hand picked up his beer. The bitter beverage had a hint of sweetness followed by just the right amount of bite at the end.

I'm in the country for four hours, find an Internet Café and get tailed. I had to take a wannabe street thug out because I couldn't risk taking him down and questioning him in the daylight. Who knows I'm here? Dugan? How did he find out? Did Buddy tip him off? Why would he involve me in something like this just to try to have me killed when I was essentially off the grid? That doesn't add up. Something else is going on here. Fuck!

He took another long drink of his beer, the shakes lessening now, his heart rate slowing now that his brain had time to start deciphering this damn cluster-fuck. After finishing his beer, he decided to order another. The pretty waitress smiled as she brought him a second Sol. He nodded his appreciation and took a drink.

The thought of taking another human life began to creep into his mind, but he steadfastly pushed it away. He sometimes thought about his time spent in various war zones when he was younger and the pain he had inflicted; there would be time for self-incrimination later. Right now he had to focus.

His watch told him it was 4:22 p.m. It was time to get back to the hotel, get his car and drive to his meet. Barring no traffic issues, he should make it in time. He paid his bill, left a respectable tip and walked out. A couple more switchbacks and a run around his hotel then he was off to his car and driving to meet his contact. He plugged the address into the rented GPS and listened as a British voice directed him through Mexico City's streets.

Roper drove over an hour through some seedy neighborhoods and on a couple of busy highways. His GPS mapped the "shortest route" but not the preferable one. Mexico City's poor walked the sidewalks. He saw in their eyes the same desperate look he had seen the world over.

Stucco homes and apartments were covered in gang graffiti. Cars that had outlived their engines sat idle, some with broken windows and most with the wheels stripped leaving only shells behind. He heard a gunshot in the distance and knew some other poor person had been robbed or killed, and their meager treasured possessions taken. *It's the same everywhere*, he thought.

At long last he arrived at Tamazula. The smell of fried Mexican food floated in the air. His stomach grumbled reminding him that he hadn't eaten in quite some time and the two beers that had temporarily filled his belly were now only distant memories. Taking a human life had a strange way of bringing on hunger pangs after the adrenaline receded to normal levels.

He stepped inside the tiny restaurant and saw that there were only two tables available for dining, both were empty. A twenty-something young man stood behind the counter eyeing him suspiciously. "Si, Señor?" the young man asked. His question did not escape Roper, for he knew he asked both what he would like to eat and what the hell a white man was doing in this store in this neighborhood.

"Hablas Ingles?"

"Yes," replied Twenty-something, his one word response full of edginess.

"I'd like two tortas and a bottle of water. A friend of mine tells me the tortas are very good."

"Yes sir. Anything else?"

"Yeah. I need to see Javier. He's expecting me. Is he here?"

"Javier? I don't know Javier."

"Look, can we dispense with the pleasantries? He's expecting me. Tell him our friend sent me here to talk to him. Okay?" As he eyed the young man, he reached into his pocket and produced two hundred pesos and handed them to him. The young man considered the money then walked through a door, presumably to find Javier...and hopefully place his order. Famished would have been an understatement of monumental proportions.

The young man soon reappeared with an older Mexican gentleman. "You are Señor Roper?" the man asked.

"Yes, I am. We have a mutual friend who told me to meet Javier. Are you Javier?"

"Si. Follow me to the back."

"Perfect. I appreciate it. I hope my tortas are back there. I could eat the ass end out of a rag doll through a park bench right now."

"Como? What does that mean, señor?"

"It means I'm real damned hungry, sir."

Javier howled with laughter at Roper's explanation of the old southern euphemism before leading him to the back of the restaurant.

"Pablo, bring Mr. Roper's food back here, por favor," he called out to the young waiter.

"Thank you, Javier. I certainly appreciate it," Roper said with all the sincerity he could muster.

They walked through the kitchen area where Javier pushed back a ragged blue and red striped curtain revealing a small office. The office had an ancient computer and an even older monitor with tons of paperwork piled haphazardly around them. Javier sat in one of the two chairs in the compact room. From between the desk and the wall, he pulled out a small black duffle bag and handed it to Roper.

Roper unzipped the bag and checked its contents. He stared at the money, identification and other things he had requested before leaving for Mexico. At the bottom of the bag he saw the pistol, a Colt 1911, and the sound suppressor next to it. A grin crept across his face.

Pablo brought the food and water to him as he zipped the bag. He thought his stomach was going to revolt on him when he smelled the incredibly delicious plate. After thanking both Pablo and Javier, he devoured the meal like it was his first and last.

"You are one hungry gringo, Mr. Roper," said Javier with a thick Mexican accent and a smirk on his face.

"You got that shit right, Javier. This has to be the best food to ever land in my mouth and I have you to thank for it."

"Ha! Thank me all you want, but you still have to pay for it," he laughed.

"I really appreciate you getting these supplies for me, Javier. I'm in your debt," he told the old man as he prepared to leave.

"Our mutual friend made it worth my while. You be careful on these streets, Señor," Javier replied as he patted Roper on the back.

Roper nodded his head and walked back to his car. He needed to make a trip to the museum so he could begin tracking down the cartouche, but that would have to wait until morning. Right now he needed to get to a computer and do some research.

Saltillo, Mexico
July 15, 2013 8:02 P.M.

Rafael's life revolved around cheap hotel rooms and his rental car of late. He pulled back the curtain covering the one window in his room at the Hotel Premier and, in the waning sunlight, looked at his car. All of Mexico's dirt and dust appeared to have covered the blue Toyota Corolla. He scanned the rest of the parking lot to see if any new vehicles had parked since his arrival; there were not. The nice thing about a hundred and fifty peso hotel room was the lack of customers. Apparently, few had the stomach for an occasional roach invader. Only hookers and dregs stayed in those rooms.

He walked back to the little table nestled in the corner of his small room and sat down to a dinner of pasta and salad. His fork swirled around in the baked ziti noodles but his mind wasn't focused on putting any of it in his mouth. He lifted his eyes to the back of the table and saw the cartouche lying there – he thought he could feel it *calling* to him.

His fork fell into the Styrofoam box, and his hand reached for the ancient relic. It talked to him in an unheard and unknown voice…a foreign language that didn't seem foreign at all. None of this appeared strange to Rafael, and as his fingers grasped the cartouche, the jewel began its low vibratory thrum. He closed his eyes and tried to will additional knowledge about its origins into his mind.

He saw a splash of liquid red in his mind's eye and his heart rate accelerated as he heard a scream and a moan. In a trance, he could see a headless body fall to its death, the shocked look on the face of the decapitated was frozen forever. The bodiless head's eyes fluttered and the jaw moved, soundless words forming on its lips. Blood from the lifeless body spilled to the ground, a pool forming as the heart continued to beat, sending its life's liquid to soak through sand.

The cartouche gifted him an array of emotions that ravaged his body and mind. Rage, extreme sadness and pain played an unholy game of tug-of-war with his heart. For a few seconds, he would be seething with anger, the next he would cry, followed by hurt that could only be understood by one who has lost a loved one.

In the distance of his mind, he could see strong, tall mountains covered by lush green trees. Most amazingly were the Asian faces he saw around him. *Who are these strange people* he asked himself? *Why am I seeing this?*

Images flashed through his brain of hands forging the cartouche and strange hieroglyphs etched and formed on the jewel. Fresh vegetation surrounded the ornament and Rafael could almost smell the magnificent earthiness of it all. He could hear strange chanting in the room where the cartouche lay.

These images plodded through his mind for what seemed like hours, but no sooner had the inexplicable story begun to reveal itself when it suddenly stopped. He wiped sweat from his forehead with the back of his hand, struck by what he had just seen.

He pushed the jewel into his pants pocket, the hold it had on him releasing. *Jesus Christ* he thought to himself in English, his legs wobbly as he stood and walked to the bathroom. He turned on the cold water and splashed some on his face not caring that it ran down his chin and chest.

Rafael looked at himself in the mirror and studied the bags under his eyes and the crow's feet, both more pronounced than they were two weeks prior. He grabbed a hand towel and wiped the water from his face, turned toward the toilet and stood there taking care of his business. *This thing...this thing Haden wants...it has power. It has shown me strange things in distant lands. I suspect it has a powerful purpose, but to what end I do not know.*

Even though his instincts told him better, he wanted to go for a walk. Fresh air would do him some good and unless he had been followed from Zacatecas, he figured he should be able to walk in the shadows relatively uninhibited. He got dressed, put on a pair of sneakers and decided a short walk around the streets of Saltillo would make him feel like a new man. He felt the reassuring vibration of the cartouche in his pocket as he stepped through the door.

Saltillo was not the typical Mexican city. While some crime did exist, it was mostly a quiet town forgotten by the drug cartels and crime lords that infected the metropolitan areas of the country. Nestled between mountains in every direction, with only a few mountain passes allowing for car travel, the city provided a perfect escape for someone not wanting to be in the spotlight, especially if that someone happened to have stolen a potentially priceless artifact that had an ability to show the possessor scenes from its past.

Of course, the cartouche might not have any power at all; on the contrary, Rafael may actually have been pushed over the edge, his brain finally falling culprit to all the beer and tequila he'd consumed over the years. He wondered to himself if that was the case.

He stepped into the warm evening air. A Latin form of music known as Bolero boomed from a nearby bar. Bolero was Cuban in origin but had been modified by musicians in Mexico, which meant beautiful ballads with a little salsa. Rafael loved the sound.

He paused outside the bar and stood under an awning with his back to the wall. A cigarette appeared from a pack of smokes along with a refillable lighter whose engraving told him it was made in China. A two inch flame shot from the top of the lighter after he rolled the wheel. Rafael inhaled the unfiltered Camel deeply, another luxury he sometimes enjoyed, especially when he was moderately stressed.

As he drew in another cloud of smoke, his cell phone rang. The quiet ring tone startled him since few people knew his number and fewer still actually called him. His finger hovered over the green button that would connect him to his caller. The number was blocked, but he was certain he knew who it was.

"Bueno," Rafael said.

"Hello, Rafael," replied Haden. "We haven't spoken in a few days and I wanted to make sure you were taking care of our pearl."

Rafael's eyes darted left and right and his head spun quickly to see who might be within earshot of his conversation. He walked down the clean sidewalk and found an area without people loitering about, leaned against a wall so he could see in both directions and began speaking.

"Si, Mr. Haden. I have our little...pearl. It is safe." He allowed his right hand to drift to his pocket and touch the cartouche. Immediately, the thrumming began again, and he had to fight his own mind to remain focused on the conversation.

"And where are you now, Rafael? I've been concerned since you haven't checked in with me. I was praying for your safe arrival to...our meeting destination."

"I am safe, Señor. Now, at least, I am safe," responded Rafael with significant indignation.

"That's good to know. I realize we are planning on meeting on the twenty-second of the month, but I'd like to move that date up to the seventeenth. So, I'll see you then. Same meeting place, same time."

"I'm afraid that won't be possible, Señor Haden. I'm certain I'm being tailed and want to...how do you say...lay low for a few more days. It was odd that shortly after I had acquired our...pearl, that someone followed me. I questioned who had hired him," Rafael responded but didn't elaborate, anxious to see how Haden would follow up.

"What the fuck do you mean that won't be possible?" asked Haden. "And what are you inferring when you say someone is following you? How would anyone know who you are or what you had? What did this guy tell you when you questioned him?"

"What I mean, Haden," he said, as he defaulted to the curt form of address, "is that I'm not meeting you until the designated time, date and place. I'm inferring nothing. I'm simply telling you I was followed the other night and was forced to question the man pursuing me. That's what I *mean*!" he finished.

"What did he tell you, dammit? I want to know what the son of a bitch said!" screamed Haden, no longer able to contain his anger.

"Why are you so anxious to know what he said to me?" Rafael asked. It appeared that Haden had lost some of his composure. Interestingly, it seemed that he no longer held the high hand.

"Don't play fucking games with me, son. I only want to know what he said so we can figure out who he was working for and how he found out about you," he replied gaining some of the composure he had lost a moment before hand.

Rafael considered answering him, but thought better of it. What Haden didn't know was definitely an advantage for Rafael, and he planned on using it. Hardball was a game he was used to playing but not with someone as powerful and well-connected as Haden. Rafael would have to tread carefully. He took a couple of long breaths, both allowing him time to gather himself and think through his response. The wait would also make Haden antsy Rafael figured.

"He told me someone sent him to follow me. I'm hoping you can help me identify who that 'someone' is Mr. Haden. I can think of no other reason for a person to be following me around than the pearl," his voice trailed off as he completed the sentence.

"How would I know who sent him or who he was? Are you implying that I had something to do with this, amigo? Because I certainly hope for your sake that's not what you mean," Haden responded.

"I've implied nothing, only asked a question. As I said, I'm hopeful you can help track down who sent this man. I have a hard time believing he was merely following me because he thought I had money or some such. Either way, it could have resulted in my losing the pearl," he responded.

Rafael heard Haden take a deep breath of his own before he replied.

"I'll see what I can find out, but I would really like to have that thing sooner rather than later. The twenty-second is too long."

"Mr. Haden, I would like to accommodate your request, but I'm afraid it will have to wait until the proscribed time. I don't want to risk another run-in with someone, so I think it's smart if I just take it easy for a while," Rafael quickly responded to Haden.

"I think it's high time you remember who is paying your bills and who has helped your spic ass along the way, amigo," Haden retorted. "If you try to fuck with me, I promise, you won't enjoy it!"

"I understand, Mr. Haden," Rafael replied as a smile touched his eyes. "And I think you should understand that right now I have no desire to be fucked, amigo." He used *amigo* for the first time ever in any conversation he'd had with Haden. He realized the game he was playing was deadly, but it was one he needed to mete out before he dropped the cartouche with his benefactor...*if* he dropped the cartouche with his benefactor.

Haden paused for a couple of minutes, his breathing audible through the phone. Rather than become unnerved and say something he might later regret, Rafael remained silent. He heard Haden gather himself, heard him despite being a country apart.

Haden laughed. Then he laughed a little louder. "You fucking wetback. That's why you're my man. Those balls you wheel around in a dump truck make you a good operator. I'll agree to the twenty-second, but I want to know exactly what that other spic fucker said to you, capiche?"

Rafael shook his head, trying to control his temper after Haden's racial epithets. He took a deep breath, gathered his thoughts then played his card. It was time to take the upper hand in this situation and let Haden know he wasn't merely a pawn in a game of chess played by two mentally challenged children.

"Mr. Haden, here's what I know: I was followed by another Latino who I had never met before. I managed to get to him before he could get to me. Now, I will tell you that he told me he was working for a white man, Mr. Haden. The common denominator appears to be *you*, Mr. Haden. I don't associate with many white people and certainly no white man knew my whereabouts since being in Valladolid, except *you*.

So, Mr. Haden, here's what I'm telling you – if you are responsible for this vato following me and attempting to get your pearl returned to you without paying me the money, or if you're worried that I might know why you want this thing so badly, then you are making a mistake. Should I be followed again, I will disappear with your cartouche," Rafael said with no regard for the unsecured line, "and find someone else who might be interested in acquiring it."

Before Haden had a chance to reply, Rafael hit the end button on his phone, took the back off of it, removed the SIM card and snapped it into quarters. He then threw the phone on the sidewalk and crushed it with his heel. Finally, he kicked the phone into a storm drain and walked away dropping one piece of the SIM card at each corner until he reached his hotel. Having memorized the only four phone numbers he needed, he alleviated any chance that he was being tracked through the device, which he suspected was how it had happened three nights prior.

New York City, New York, USA
July 16, 2013 05:38 A.M.

Dan Dugan ran on his treadmill. He ran as hard as he could, the sweat rolling off his forehead, down his nose and onto the treadmill belt. His mind re-ran his conversation with Rafael, *that fucking Mexican,* over and over. Fortunately, it had been quite easy to keep his true identity from the Latino, and that might come in handy should he be forced to chase him down and retrieve the cartouche.

His mind ran at the same rapid pace as his feet. His options were limited, but as he always did, he planned for the worst. He knew he had an asset on the ground that would retrieve the artifact and return it to him if necessary. Regardless, the loose cannon he'd hired in Mexico wasn't long for this world, of that he was sure.

Dugan finished his five mile stationary jaunt then turned the machine off. He grabbed his towel and began wiping himself down as he walked to a window staring east from his swanky upper west side office. The view of thousands of people walking through Central Park did nothing to better his mood; in fact it worsened it. *Sheep, every damned one of them.* He watched as NYU student groups meditated on a patch of grass near a huge outcropping of rocks. *Smart kids, as clueless as the rocks they sit next to.* He actually allowed himself a chuckle at this thought as he walked into the bathroom and disrobed. He turned on the shower and jumped in when the water was warm enough.

Afterward, he dried himself off, dressed, then moved to his desk and opened his laptop. He checked his encrypted e-mail address known only to two others. His myriad of e-mail addresses and aliases gave him a chance to keep things compartmentalized from some who would love to access his personal information.

He read the note sent to him by one of the two contractors working for him:

Asset is tracking. Half of fee wired to an off-shore account. No questions asked at this time. Awaiting reconnect with asset. No additional information. Advise on other needs if any.

Dugan studied the short e-mail and thought about a response before allowing his hands to touch the keyboard. Outside he could hear the sirens from police cars and fire trucks. At any time of day the prevalent sounds of emergencies were blasting throughout the city. He could smell street vendor food comingled with raw sewage emanating from the city's ancient but complicated sewer system. All of his senses were alert and deciphering the environmental information unconsciously. The sights, sounds and smells of New York City were somehow comforting to him.

He stared at the computer screen and allowed his fingers to rest lightly on the keys. His eyes narrowed as he pecked out his response. His fingers paused momentarily before beginning.

Contact me as soon as you hear from our asset. Once cartouche is acquired, terminate asset and target if still breathing. Confirm receipt.

Dugan clicked the send button on the screen before folding the laptop closed. He could feel how close he was to having the cartouche and all the power and money it would bring. On his desk he kept a photo he had snapped of the pyramid in Chichen Itza, Mexico several years earlier.

He suppressed a laugh as he thought about what he had been fortunate enough to learn about over the last few years. World governments had been involved in strange things throughout mankind's history. In the twentieth century, Nazi Germany had experimented with alien technology in order to develop anti-gravitational aircraft. Many said they had unlocked its secret but couldn't build the ship before the allies attack on Berlin began.

The United States had spent considerable resources engaged in group remote viewing in the seventies and eighties. Amazingly, the results of groups of people focused on distant areas or objects were tremendous. Significant intelligence was gathered on Russian and Chinese military activity at a time when satellite technology was still in its infancy. Later, as always, US military personnel would dismiss the RV experiment as a failure and continue its practice in secrecy, in desolate outposts in Alaska and the fabled Area 51 in the Nevada desert.

Every powerful government had one thing in common: power lust. Control of the skies and oceans for any given country fostered a desire for more. On the global front, development of nuclear arms intimidated smaller, less powerful governments into picking sides and selling their natural resources to the powerful countries all in the name of security. As one powerful government developed a more advanced means of global control, another would discover something even more clever and hideous. The race to control the paranormal was one that conspiracy theorists loved to talk about, and one the world's governments loved to deny.

However, Dugan had a firm grasp on the race to find the next most powerful weapon on Earth. He also knew full well that governments regularly researched means by which to control a burgeoning global population. Billions of dollars were spent annually in America alone on those things most would scoff at: time travel, mind control, alien technology, and other fringe activities.

Dugan's "discovery" would provide the highest bidder with an ability to control the greatest army in world history. He would also become a very rich and powerful man in the process. With Buddy Smith working as his pawn, he knew inroads with the CIA were already paved. His CIA connections would probably land him an opportunity to negotiate with the highest levels of American intelligence and military personnel. He also knew he would have to be very careful or the might of the United States would rain down on him in such a nasty shit-storm; it made him shiver.

Mexico City, Mexico
July 16, 2013 6:31 A.M.

Roper lay in his hotel room thinking about what he had learned the previous night. He laced his fingers behind his head as he stared up at the ceiling, the room's ceiling fan offering a quiet swoop-swoop as it spun, pushing warm air down on him. His eyes followed the blades and his mind drifted.

After picking up his bag of supplies, he drove around the city in search of another internet café, this one a considerable distance from his hotel. He had driven for over two hours, performing switch backs, sudden stopping and parking and two U-turns on quieter roads, all the while keeping an eye out for anyone following him.

Content he wasn't being trailed he plugged a café address into his GPS and found one only eight kilometers from his location. He parked in a well-lit lot just in case someone tried to surprise him. As he opened his car door he took in his surroundings. He walked into the café, found an open terminal and settled in.

He opened an internet browser and searched the word "cartouche." In less than a second, link upon link appeared on the monitor. What he saw confused him even more.

In Egyptian hieroglyphs, a cartouche is an oval with a horizontal line at one end indicating that the text enclosed is a royal name, coming into use during the beginning of the Fourth Dynasty under Pharaoh Sneferu. While the cartouche is usually vertical with a horizontal line, it is sometimes horizontal if it makes the name fit better, with a vertical line on the left. The Ancient Egyptian word for it was shenu, and it was essentially an expanded shen ring. In Demotic, the cartouche was reduced to a pair of brackets and a vertical line.

Roper's hand found his chin and rubbed it. None of this made sense to him. Buddy had told him the cartouche was Chinese, but his research said it was Egyptian. *Worn by royalty,* he thought. *What's the connection?*

He thought for a few more moments, and on a whim he performed a search for "Mexico cartouche." What popped up on his screen this time caused him to furrow his brow. Roper paused long enough to glance around to make sure no one had taken an interest in him. No one he saw made him uneasy, so he went back to his reading.

He began reading about the ancient Mayans and how they made cartouches for their own royalty and spiritual protection. *That's crazy. Half a world away from Egypt and they are making the same damned jewelry? How is that possible? There was no mass transit back then. How could this be?*

Roper was struck by the distinct similarities between both the Mayan and the Egyptian cartouches after seeing pictures of both. Even the hieroglyphs on the different pieces of jewelry were remarkably similar. The shapes were both oval, and the necklace loops were virtually the same.

He read some more about the Mayan cartouche. The entry on the internet page continued, *the Mayan cartouche was believed to keep and protect the individual from those who would do him harm. It was highly regarded as an amulet that would store a person's spirit or could be utilized in incantations and other works of magic.*

While he laid there on his bed, his mind focused on the last thing he read: *incantations and other works of magic.* He could find no other reason that the United States government would be interested in this piece of jewelry than that of potential magic. Roper had been clued into enough clandestine governmental stuff, and had networked with other spooks who knew about things like the government's interest in voodoo and electroshock "therapy" on children, especially those with autistic schizophrenia. Their hopes were to tap into a dormant gene enabling them to perform incredible feats of magic. The government also experimented with mind altering drugs, such as LSD, to aid in magical application.

The U.S. government is always looking for a way to control its enemies AND its citizens. Unbelievable how blind people are to this fact. Well, fuck it. I'm getting paid to retrieve this cartouche not analyze what they'll do with it once they get it. But still, I would really like to know what their plans are for this thing. What does it do that they would pay a hired hand more than a million dollars to retrieve?

Roper got out of the bed and took his body through fifteen minutes of static stretching then found some room to practice kata. The room was large enough to allow practice without having to move furniture. He opened the window and let his eyes adjust to the brilliant sunlight that poured into the room.

His feet moved into the preparation position as he called the kata name out in his mind—*seisan*. His left foot moved into seisan stance, the ball of his left foot touching down lightly on the carpet and his left arm moving into an outside center block. Just as quickly as the block, his right fist shot off his hip in an opposite side reverse punch.

He pushed through the kata, focusing on technique and keeping his head level so his energy moved laterally, rather than bobbing up and down. His hips snapped, and his trailing foot came into the correct position at just the right second each time he moved. The sweat began to form on his body and his kime, focus, became more intent.

The open hand techniques were performed while his mind focused on the targets of his imaginary opponent, both soft targets and nerve strikes. After finishing the kata, he gave himself a few seconds to smile as he thought about his training time with a great American sensei, James Davenport.

Davenport sensei had studied the world over, had been an intelligence officer in the U.S. Army and understood kata application better than anyone he had trained with, including the Okinawans and Japanese.

Roper refocused his mind and prepared for the next kata, Sanshiryu. This advanced kata incorporated spear hand strikes to specific soft targets and several throws that would incapacitate or even kill an opponent. His intent and focus in the kata were incredible, his movement fluid and flawless. He finished the kata then practiced it another five times, each time, changing the cadence of the techniques, letting his mind see his opponent in different combative positions.

He finished his training regimen and walked to the bathroom to shower. With the hot water further opening his pores permitting the impurities to exit his body, he soaped himself and scrubbed with the washcloth. After showering he finished preparing for the day, dressing in a non-descript fashion, the cotton material light against his skin.

With plenty of time before the museum opened, Roper rode the elevator downstairs to eat in the hotel restaurant. He looked around, taking note of everyone, and found a table where he could sit with his back against the wall. From that vantage point he could see both the entrance to the restaurant and the windows to the street outside.

He could smell the food being prepared in the kitchen as he sipped a cup of black coffee. The robust beans offering him a taste of bitter heaven, he savored the blissfully hot nectar of the gods.

He ordered a breakfast of eggs and wheat toast and a glass of orange juice. The sun was bright and the sky cloudless and brilliant. The sidewalks were beginning to bustle with activity, and car horns could be heard in the distance. If he couldn't glean some information at the museum today, he would be at a loss and have to rethink his approach to tracking down the cartouche.

From his pocket he pulled a disposable cell phone, the minutes pre-paid and Buddy's number already programmed. He typed in a simple text, *Going to museum this morning,* and hit send. From his wallet he pulled the pesos needed to pay the chit and walked to his car. A few seconds later he felt the vibration of his phone as he sat down in the driver's seat. He pulled the phone from his pocket and read the text, *Good. Update once you finish.*

Roper navigated the busy Mexico City streets. He arrived at the Museum of Anthropology at just after noon and parked in the underground parking lot. Before he got out of his car, he raised his sunglasses and looked around the lot, acutely aware of the many surveillance cameras placed throughout the garage. He lowered the glasses to the bridge of his nose, stuffed his car key into his pocket and got out of the rental.

He walked up the stairs, which rose to ground level, and was greeted by enormous statues and a Mexican flag flying proudly on a very tall pole, all standing before the entrance to the museum itself. He was able to ascertain two more surveillance cameras at either corner of the roof above the entranceway before walking to the ticket window.

Roper purchased a ticket and pulled his key and phone from his pocket, careful to check himself for anything else metallic before walking through the metal detector. The alarm didn't sound and the guard nodded to him to get his things that had been scanned and inspected by the other security guard on duty. He walked over to the guard after gathering his things and asked to speak with his supervisor. The guard looked at him inquisitively and asked him in English why he needed to see him.

"I was here a few days ago, and one of the guards harassed me. He made me feel very uncomfortable, and I would like to lodge a formal complaint." The guard frowned at the potential of one of his buddies getting in trouble.

"You can leave your complaint with me, sir. I will see to it that my supervisor gets it."

"With all due respect, I prefer to see your supervisor. I'm certain you would make sure he would get my complaint, but I would be more comfortable delivering it in person. Please call your supervisor now."

The guard saw that the American would not relent and radioed his supervisor to come to the lobby. He could hear the supervisor ask, "Por que?" The guard answered that there was someone who needed to lodge a complaint and wouldn't leave until he spoke with him.

An older Mexican gentleman of average height appeared in the rotunda and introduced himself in heavily accented English as Captain Reynoso. "What can I do for you," his voice trailing off as he waited for an introduction from the man who was obviously American.

Roper looked over his shoulder and saw the guard who had called Captain Reynoso eyeing him suspiciously. The guard had moved a respectful distance away, out of earshot of the conversation. Still, he kept his voice low as he reached inside his pants pocket and retrieved an NSA badge, compliments of Buddy and Torta Javier. The badge was a perfect replica.

"Captain Reynoso, my name is Agent Roper with the National Security Agency of the United States. I'd like to have a few words with you about an artifact stolen from your museum a few nights ago."

Reynoso kept his voice low but level. "United States has no jurisdiction here, Agent Roper. I'm afraid I have nothing to say to you. Buenos dias."

Undeterred, Roper stepped closer to the head of security. "Captain Reynoso, I understand your hesitation and admire your position with this wonderful museum. I also understand that having a precious artifact like that cartouche stolen on your watch is very embarrassing. As a liaison of the United States government, I can assure you there is a potential that we will share in far greater embarrassment if you don't afford me a few minutes of your time.

There is a significant risk that the cartouche will find its way into the United States and be sold at auction there, never to be recovered by Mexico or this museum. Do you understand what I'm telling you? Please, also understand that our countries' relations have been somewhat strained over the past few years, and I would hate to see this issue bring about more angst. Together we might be able to prevent this from becoming problematic."

The head of security continued to stare at the large American who stood three inches taller than him. The man's green eyes pierced his own, and something told Reynoso those same eyes had seen many terrible things. His light brown hair was neatly parted on one side and appeared to have been recently cut. Broad shoulders topped an obviously muscular torso, and his arms looked to be those born of hard labor, rather than falsely manufactured in some fitness club. Finally, Reynoso took notice of the man's chiseled jaw that protruded from his face and subconsciously was reminded of a viper poised to strike.

"Let's go to my office, Agent Roper, and speak in private. I do not think the rotunda is the proper place for this conversation.

"Agreed," Roper replied, relieved that the aging Captain Reynoso hadn't questioned his credentials.

Roper nodded to the other security guard who had moved closer in an attempt to overhear the conversation between the American and his boss, but had not picked up on the discussion. A curt nod from the guard back to Roper was the only acknowledgement he gave before turning back to his task of checking tourists entering the museum. He followed Captain Reynoso down a marbled floor to a stained oak door with a "security" sign affixed to it.

Reynoso walked behind a large desk with several security monitors stationed behind him. Roper could see movement in several areas as tourists milled about through the various rooms in the museum. His eyes shifted back to Reynoso who was watching him intently.

"So tell me, Agent Roper, what may I do to help retrieve the artifact stolen from us, and why do you believe it will wind up in the United States?" asked the well-spoken Captain.

"Captain Reynoso, let's be frank here. Your museum is filled with precious and priceless items. It's our opinion that only a collector with substantial means and specific intentions would want the stolen artifact, rather than attempting to steal other more notable items. We also know of a few collectors in the United States and in Europe who would love to have the cartouche in their private collections. What the United States doesn't want is to have this item sold on the open or black market within its own borders. In addition to its return, certain quiet negotiations will be made between our countries. Of that I'm certain," replied Roper as he relayed the story he had rehearsed in his head for the past few hours.

"So, the United States will attempt to blackmail Mexico again, huh? Why should I be a part of that, Mr. Roper? I do not particularly care for you Americans and will not be a part of your country trying to screw mine."

"I understand your hesitation, sir. Needless to say, whatever deal is struck between our countries will be beneficial to both sides. You call it blackmail;

we call it business. But at the end of the day, all that will matter is that I've conducted my job appropriately, and you are still gainfully employed. You don't strike me as a stupid man, Captain Reynoso, so make the right decision here. I offer you your job and the opportunity to right a wrong. Is that really so bad?" Roper finished his logical argument.

The Captain took a deep breath and exhaled. He turned his back to Roper, his hands behind his back, and looked at the bevy of monitors, watching people flow from room-to-room. His mind was temporarily focused on that which he knew so well, and that which made him so respected among his peers and directors. He had a keen eye for anyone appearing not to belong or acting suspiciously, and that was the reason he had beaten himself up mentally for the past few days since the theft.

Reynoso watched an elderly white woman hobble to a display of Aztec pottery, while a group of local elementary school children stood half-listening to their tour guide talk about the changes in landscape around Mexico City as a result of an eruption some 23,000 years earlier from a volcano named Popocatepetl, or "Smoking Mountain." He laughed and shook his head as several of the children fidgeted and twirled around in circles while the female guide spoke to them in Spanish.

"You know, Agent Roper, our museum is one of pride for this great city. We know we do not have the wealth of the United States, nor do we have all the cultural effects of New York City or Washington D.C. But what we do have is an incredible history as a people. Our ancients were the Mayans, Aztecs and Incans. Each of those cultures contributed tremendously to human development in this region of the world."

He continued, "When the Spanish invaded Mexico, the results were not that much different than they were in the United States. Indigenous people here did not have the weapons, similar to our American Indian brothers in your country. But still our people fought with great honor. You realize the long hair so many of our males wear is a tribute to our native lineage, yes?"

Roper listened to a man who obviously had done more at this museum than simply watch people and keep its treasures safe. "No, Captain, I didn't know that. I appreciate you sharing this with me."

"What is it you would like for me to help you with, Mr. Roper? How can I help reacquire that which belongs in this museum, for the world to see, but for Mexico's people to keep and protect?"

"I would like to review the surveillance tapes from the day of the theft, Captain. I'd like to see if I can help spot the person responsible for it." "Agent Roper, I can assure you that we have thoroughly reviewed the tapes, as has our own federal police...you know them as Federales. They were quite thorough in their investigation."

"What was their conclusion, Captain? Do they know who might have stolen the cartouche?"

Captain Reynoso narrowed his eyes and slightly puckered his lips, a look of indignation glossing his features. "They believe it was an inside job,

Agent Roper, but I do not believe this to be true. My guards take much pride in this museum, and I see to it that they are well compensated. Both of these elements reduce the potential of internal thievery. While I do not completely rule out the potential of one of my men doing this, in my heart I do not believe it is so."

"If they're trying to pin this theft on you or one of your men, would it really hurt for me to take a look at the tapes? I might be able to help."

Reynoso considered what Roper was telling him and sighed loudly, "Showing you these tapes could cost me my job, but I suppose my job is still in danger should my superiors deem it necessary to fire someone for this travesty. Yes, you may look at the tapes."

Roper was delighted that Captain Reynoso hadn't seen through his CIA agent ruse. A part of him felt very bad for this man who took his job very seriously and was very proud of his native and Mexican heritage. He also felt badly for having to lie to a good man, despite the need to recover the cartouche and knowing he would not have access to the surveillance tapes any other way.

Captain Reynoso rose from his chair and walked to a large closet with numerous shelves housing compact discs, recordable DVD's, and external hard drives. He thumbed through a few of the DVD's and found what he was looking for, grabbed it and brought it back into his office. He placed it on his desk and Roper took notice of its label: *July 9th, 2013 Zona 4.*

"This is the video surveillance of the sector where the artifact was stolen, Agent Roper. I will place it in this system over here for you to review," he said as he pointed at a computer and a monitor to his left.

"The 'sector' you said, Captain. Which exhibition was the cartouche displayed in, if you don't mind my asking?"

"It was not on display. We kept this precious jewel in the conservation lab because it is so rare."

"But you have surveillance inside the conservation lab, yes? That's what this is that I will be reviewing?"

Reynoso's eyes dropped for a second before he answered. "No, Agent Roper. We saw no need to provide surveillance in areas simply used to store items. We only provide surveillance on our exhibits, I'm sorry to say."

Roper thought about what he'd just been told before nodding his head. "Well, it is what it is, right? I'll review what you have, and we'll go from there. Do you have any inventories of the conservation lab, Captain? Any documented evidence of the last time it was seen in the lab and objective evidence of the discovery when it went missing?"

"Of course, Mr. Roper. Here are the records." He handed him the inventory list, having anticipated its request. "The lab is inventoried each day at noon. This allows our employees to get to work, take care of their required tasks, then assign two individuals to conduct inventories in this sector."

"Who has access to the lab, Captain?" Roper persisted.

"Only five people. The curator, me, one of the senior archeologists and the two guards assigned the responsibility of inventorying each item. Each of us has been interviewed. The curator was off the day of the theft, and our Mr. Rodriquez was in the field. I was in my office doing paperwork the majority of the day. Other surveillance video supports this. My two security officers were interviewed and given lie detector tests that, I'm proud to say, both passed. Would you like to review those tapes as well, Agent Roper?"

"That won't be necessary right now, Captain Reynoso," his gut telling him the head of security was telling him the truth. "I'll review what you have here. Thank you very much for indulging me. Should I find anything, I'll let you know. Is that fair?"

Captain Reynoso nodded his approval, opened his mini-refrigerator and offered Roper a bottle of water which he happily took. He took a seat next to Roper also offering him a pen and paper to take notes.

"I prefer to work alone, Captain. I hope that's okay."

"No, my friend, it is not okay. I will share these videos with you, and should you find something, I prefer to be right here with you...the entire time, sir," Reynoso replied.

"Fair enough, Captain. Thanks for the water and stationery," Roper said as he popped the DVD from its case, opened the door on the computer tower and inserted the disc into the machine. The arduous task of watching people mill around the museum had begun.

Three and a half hours into the surveillance Roper had taken several notes. His stomach rumbled loudly, and Captain Reynoso laughed. He asked Roper if he'd like something to eat from the museum restaurant. He answered in the affirmative. The captain didn't bother asking what he would like and called in an order for both the men in Spanish.

Roper studied his notes: Woman wearing sunglasses at mark 12:08 p.m. Man with baby stroller at mark 4:52 p.m. Man with cane (limping) and baseball cap at mark 5:38 p.m. He finished watching all activity in the area up to the time the museum closed. Next, he turned his attention to focus more closely on zone four, which was closest to the conservation lab, and finally he began fast forwarding through the remainder of the day and into the night. He was careful to watch for anything that looked like human movement in the area. While he fumbled with the computer's mouse, an idea began to gnaw at the fringes of his memory.

"Captain, I'm assuming you have surveillance of the rotunda area from the same day? May I see those as well?"

"Yes, Agent Roper. Why do you want to see those?"

"I think most are going on the hunch that someone entered the building and stole the cartouche during operating hours. That may not be the case. I'm also certain all your external doors and windows are alarmed, correct?"

"That is correct, sir."

A knock came at the door, and Captain Reynoso walked over and opened it. A concierge brought tamales, two large salads and Cokes. He carried the food to his desk and poured them both drinks in the glasses that sat on the trays. Reynoso picked up a plate and offered it to Roper.

Reynoso then fished the DVD from the closet that had the closed captioned surveillance of the rotunda area. It was labeled *July 9, 2013 Zona 1*. He handed it to Roper who promptly ejected the other disk and placed the new one in its place.

Roper fast forwarded to 12:08 p.m. on a whim and began watching. He saw people enter and leave the rotunda, careful to watch for the three people he had taken note of in his previous review. At 1:16 p.m. he stopped the video feed and made a note next to his notation about the woman wearing sunglasses, "Exited. Does not appear suspicious." He wrote down the time she left.

He restarted the video and continued monitoring the activity in the rotunda, Reynoso watching the activity as well. Both reached for food without their eyes moving from the monitor, their movements almost in synch. Roper fast forwarded to the 4:52 p.m. mark and watched intently. At 5:29 p.m. he saw the man and the stroller leaving the museum. As he did with sunglasses woman, he stopped the video feed and made a note of the time he left and his lack of suspicious activity.

Roper then moved the video to 5:38 p.m. and watched for the man with the hat and cane to leave. When he saw no more visitors leave beyond the 6:00 p.m. mark, he backed the DVD back to the 5:38 p.m. timeframe and watched again. He did this a third time, finally satisfied the man with the cane had not left. He grabbed the Zona 4 DVD, plopped it in the computer and watched as the man with the cane did not appear in the feed.

"He's the one, Captain. There's our man. Go ahead and get July 10th's feed for zone one and let's see what time our guy left the museum."

Reynoso sat slack-jawed at what he had just seen, and what he hadn't seen. How had he and the Federales missed that? A million thoughts simultaneously ran through his head. He was elated that a suspect could possibly be identified, and embarrassed that he had missed this crucial evidence. More importantly, he hadn't even thought to look at the zone one surveillance feed.

"Captain," Roper said loudly, "I need you to stop beating yourself up for a minute and help me out here. Anyone could have missed this piece of evidence. I have a lot of experience tracking people down. You weren't the only one who missed this, and now you know it wasn't one of your guys who took it. So, if you don't mind me saying so, get off your ass and help me out. Time is a luxury neither of us has at this point."

Reynoso jumped from his seat, his mind back in the moment. "Yes, Mr. Roper. You are right. I need to focus so we can solve this. Thank you for indulging an aging man feeling sorry for himself."

"There's no apology necessary my friend. Let's just figure out who this guy is."

After he plopped the July 10th surveillance feed into the computer, he watched from the time the museum opened. At precisely 9:14 a.m. he stopped the feed and studied the man walking out. He reset the DVD to 9:00 a.m. and watched again. At 9:14, being a creature of habit, he set the DVD back to 9:00 a.m. one more time, although he was sure of what he *hadn't* seen. The man did not have a cane and his gait was obviously different, but the build and frame of the man was the same. Most importantly was the fact that the man had never entered the museum – he had only exited.

Roper stopped the video feed and did a close up of the man's face, obviously a man with Hispanic features and dressed like a well-to-do gentleman with his jacket and slacks. He looked at the man's face and asked Captain Reynoso if he could get a close up.

"Yes sir, I can do that. Do you need me to crop and paste his face to a jump drive, Agent Roper?"

"That's why you get paid the big money, Captain. You're anticipating my thoughts before I get a chance to articulate them." He clasped Reynoso's shoulder with his hand then patted him on the back before the chief security officer walked back to the closet to retrieve a blank memory stick.

"I'm in your debt, Captain," Roper told the head of security. "I only ask that you keep our visit to yourself while I conduct my investigation. I'll be in touch with you should I find our guy and your cartouche."

Roper reached out to shake the Captain's hand, but when Reynoso withdrew his hand he found five one hundred U.S. dollars.

"I don't need your money, Agent Roper. I simply ask that you return what is ours." He tried to hand the money back, but Roper refused.

"For your time and help, Captain. I'm not buying your friendship. Like I said, I'm in your debt. Buy your wife something nice or take your men out to eat if you'd like."

"Before you go, Agent Roper, there's something else I would like to show you."

Roper raised an eyebrow but held his tongue, waiting for the Captain to show him some other evidence.

Reynoso produced a small metallic piece of equipment with a stainless base. Roper immediately recognized the bi-morph opto-mechanical deflector as one he had used previously in the Middle East when hijacking sensitive material and data from offices with laser and heat sensing electronics. This was a much newer version, but the premise was the same.

Reynoso saw Roper's recognition on his face.

"You recognize this, Mr. Roper. Please take it if it helps in your search."

He simply nodded his appreciation to Captain Reynoso.

With that, Roper exited Reynoso's office to find a thief and to retrieve a priceless jewel that could somehow be used as a weapon.

Langley, Virginia, USA
July 16, 2013 4:33 P.M.

At a bookstore a couple of miles from CIA headquarters, Buddy flipped open his laptop and signed in using the newest generation of encrypted software that made it virtually impossible for anyone to hack into his computer. With his back to a wall providing him a clear view of the store and the front entrance, he glanced around before checking the secret bulletin board. A quiet ping sounded alerting him to a new message. The caricature envelope at the top of the monitor had a cartoonish paper clip wrapped around it indicating an attachment resided within the message.

He read the letter:

> *Suspect identified. Advanced bi-morph deflection used to remove the cartouche. Not something readily available on the open market. Confirm U.S. connection. Suspect's photo is attached. Can you run it and see if he's linked to our friend Dugan? Need information as quickly as possible so I can plan my next move.*

Buddy opened the attachment and studied the face. He didn't recognize the man, but it wouldn't surprise him to find out Dugan had employed a nobody to do his handiwork. He attached the picture of the Latino man to an email and forwarded it to a research analyst at Langley.

> *Please run this photo and see if we have anything in your database. Need information pronto. Everything on the QT until otherwise informed. Thank you.*

He shut down his email, plugged in his ear buds and opened up his iTunes account. He scrolled through his music list and found Gnarls Barkley's *Crazy*.

> *I remember when, I remember,*
> *I remember when I lost my mind*
> *There was something so pleasant about that place*
> *Even your emotions had an echo*
> *In so much space*
>
> *And when you're out there*
> *Without care*
> *Yeah, I was out of touch*
> *But it wasn't because I didn't know enough*
> *I just knew too much*

Does that make me crazy?
Does that make me crazy?
Does that make me craaaaaazy?

Several folks turned to look at Buddy who was sitting at the table singing aloud without realizing it. A few had smiles on their faces as they watched him sing along to the song on his computer. But all of them oblivious to what he was listening to and unable to decipher the song because of his inability to carry a tune, especially with his rough, deep Appalachian accent accompanying it.

Buddy looked up to see all of the folks staring at him and laughing.

"What the hell are y'all looking at? This is good goddam music," he growled loudly. "Y'all should learn to appreciate it, you bunch of young punks."

The onlookers looked away, a couple shaking their heads and still laughing.

"Fuckers," Buddy muttered to himself. "They don't know good music when they hear it."

He shut down his iTunes, glanced around the room and reopened the bulletin board he had looked at earlier. After re-reading the message, he cleared it before closing it down. He snapped the laptop shut and sat at the table for a few minutes before walking over to the snack counter and ordering his favorite Frappuccino. *My buddies think this shit is for pussies, but dammit, it just tastes good.* He smiled at the pimple faced cashier as he handed her a five dollar bill, and soon was sipping what he imagined heaven must taste like. As he walked out the door he gave the music lovers one last nasty look.

Saltillo, Mexico
July 17, 2013 7:06 A.M.

Rafael lay on his bed sipping coffee he'd made fifteen minutes earlier. He stared into the painted fire cast coffee cup that belonged to the hotel. Steam rolled from the top of the cup in small wisps that made their way to his nose. He inhaled deeply, enjoying the aroma of the strong, black rainforest blend. His reflection stared back at him, his eyes as dark as the coffee he gazed into and as blank as the white walls of his room.

He took another sip, savoring the bold flavor, letting it sit on his tongue for a second before swallowing it. Being this close to the United States, the coffee was considerably better than that found in most of the other states of Mexico. He had experienced coffee like this in Acapulco and his home state of Quintano Roo. Ironically, both of these areas had many Americans frequenting them year round, which explained why the best coffee was in those areas. Money buys blissfulness.

After his phone call with Haden, he changed hotels to one on the other side of town. He had not eaten dinner the night before, but his stomach wasn't screaming at him for breakfast. His mind only casually reflected on this fact then drifted to his pants draped across the chair pushed against the desk in his room.

Rafael swore he could *hear* the cartouche's vibration. He had felt it pulsing in his pocket last night like it was trying to convey some message through the old form of Morse code. Although he would not swear to it, something tickled his mind making him think he could almost understand some of the message. The vibration was almost vocal, almost human, and thrummed in an archaic language he couldn't put his finger on, but he felt like he simply...*understood*.

He threw the sheet off his legs and stood staring at himself in the mirror. His arms and legs were noticeably thinner and veiny in appearance. *Probably*, he thought to himself, *due to all the stress he had been under the past few days*. He could see a few of his ribs straining against his skin.

Rafael walked to the desk and fished the cartouche out of his pants pocket. He held it between his left index finger and thumb, examining the strange pictographs that were raised against the silver background. The markings were both foreign and familiar to him. He knew nothing of this type of jewelry, and very little of the Mayan culture that had inhabited his homeland in the Yucatan Peninsula, Southern Mexico and Guatemala.

The cartouche fell into his palm like it had a life of its own, and Rafael's eyes caressed the back of it. Its cold smoothness devoid of interesting markings like the front, but it was all part of everything that made the jewel what it was. His fingers closed around it and he pressed it into his skin.

Without hesitation the thrumming began and Rafael's eyes glazed over like a heroin addict getting his fix.

The thrumming escalated and a series of vibratory sounds etched themselves into words Rafael could hear in his mind: *thrum... thrum... hua... thrum...shi.* The two words made no sense to him, yet he didn't question their veracity or meaning. This feeling of spiritual duplicity passed over him like a soothing, warm bath on a baby's skin. He felt complete, total and without need. And mostly, he felt connected like he had never felt connected to anything before in his miserable life. Something was being revealed to him, but it would be revealed in its own time and not a second before, of this, Rafael was certain and did not question.

The thrumming and vibration stopped and suddenly Rafael was exhausted and confused. *Am I losing my mind? I'm hearing things I don't understand. What is it about this...jewel... that seems to have a hold on me?*

Sweat glistened over the entirety of his body as he stood on trembling legs. He replaced the cartouche in his pants pocket with a shaky hand and staggered back to his bed, falling on top of the dusty bedspread. His eyes closed and he found sleep almost immediately.

Mexico City, Mexico
July 17, 2013 7:13 A.M.

Roper walked to the window overlooking the city. The sky was a magnificent blue and the mountains stood proudly as the morning sun shone on them. The heat had not yet begun waving from the red-brown dirt so prevalent in the region. He sipped some freshly squeezed orange juice he bought earlier at the hotel restaurant and thought about his next steps. Finding out the identity of the thief was one part of the equation, tracking him another, and getting to him before he made the drop with Dugan, if he hadn't already, was the biggest problem he faced.

He hopped on the elevator and rode it to the lobby. The dark marble floors glistened in the morning light, almost to the point of blinding people walking through the area. The business center had four computers, two of which were open. Roper sat in a chair, opened the browser and performed a search for major airports in Mexico. Immediately, a list of over eighteen hundred airports were on his screen, but he quickly eliminated the municipal airports since the international sites were what interested him. He was certain that Dugan would fly to Mexico, rather than risking his asset leaving the country.

Roper quickly ruled out Mexico City, knowing that any good thief worth his weight wouldn't stick around an area while it was still hot. He didn't feel like Acapulco or Cancun were viable transfer points simply because security was much tighter in tourist areas where Americans, Europeans and Asians spent tons of money. The next primary international airport was in Monterrey, some 900 kilometers north of Mexico City.

His gut told him this was the drop site, and that his target was probably in or near the metropolitan area of Monterrey. It just made sense. Dugan would be close enough to the border to bug out in a vehicle if something went wrong, and certainly close enough to the Houston airports to be airborne for a short time. Yes, he was convinced this was the area where the target would pass the cartouche to Dugan, but now the hard part: how to track and find his target before he gave the jewel away. Buddy was going to have to provide some additional help, of that he was sure.

He cleared the internet browser and headed back to his room to call him and find out whether or not he had been able to identify their subject. The door closed behind him, and he folded the security latch over the metal bulb mounted to the door to prevent housekeeping or other unwanted guests from barging in.

Roper put the battery in his phone and turned it on; one could never be too cautious with regard to personal security and tracking. He flipped it open and dialed Buddy's secure satellite phone, listening to the rings that somehow always sounded hollow when dialing internationally.

"Young Buck, how goes everything down yonder?" asked Buddy as soon as he picked up.

"Progress, but I need to know if you've ID'd our boy yet. I'm at a standstill until I get a name. This is a big ass country with a lot of Mexicans in it, so I need a little help."

Buddy chuckled. "Yeah, I reckon Mexico does have a lot of Mexicans in it. Who'd a thought that? I should be hearing back from my contact shortly. Check the board in a couple of hours, okay?"

Roper responded, "Yep. Got something else I need some help with too."

"Whatcha got, young 'un? I hired you to do a job and I'm doing all the damned work. You're probably laid up with some señorita right now anyway," Buddy joked.

"I wish," Roper chuckled before continuing. "I need you to search all incoming flight travel records from the U.S. to Monterrey since the tenth. Also, see if any reservations have been made from the States to Monterrey for the next couple of weeks. Eliminate Hispanic names, that should narrow down the search. Just focus on folks with U.S. passports first."

"Okay, I can do that. Any particular reason I'm hunting for folks flying into an airport that's such a long distance from Mexico City?" Buddy asked.

"It's a hunch, but a good one. My gut tells me your friend from the States has chosen Monterrey as the drop point. If you can get this intel for me today, that'll save us a lot of pain and potential searching later on, if you get my drift," Roper replied.

"I'm on it. Check that board like I told you, but give me a little longer. I'll see if I can group all this information to save you some time and travel to find a computer without a bunch of eyes looking over your ass end."

"Indeed, you are a poet, Buddy. I don't know how you keep all the girls from hanging on you," said Roper.

"It ain't easy," he replied.

New York City, New York, USA
July 17, 2013 7:21 A.M.

Dugan walked to Columbus Circle then down a flight of stairs to the subway station. It was hot down below, the air still and it smelled of dankness and human sweat. Locals and tourists hustled, bustled and bumped into each other, never uttering an "excuse me," "pardon me," or "kiss my ass." Locals wore rudeness like a badge of honor in the Big Apple, and tourists walked around like they were as equally hardened as the people who spent a lifetime defending turf, pride and family.

He pushed his way through the turnstile using his pre-paid metro card and walked to the blue ACE line that would transport him downtown. Dugan could smell everything that was wrong with the city, as it had gotten hotter and mustier the further he walked. In the distance a subway musician, one who made a living playing and singing music in the train stations, was belting out *Stand By Me*. He was playing an acoustic guitar and singing the song like it was something he was born doing. His pitch was perfect and in tune. Dugan sometimes wondered how talent like that had never been discovered. *Probably a drunken bastard*, he thought.

While he stood waiting on the train, a homeless man sauntered up to him and asked for some change.

"Get the hell away from me you nasty son-of-a-bitch," Dugan told the older man.

"Ain't no need to be an asshole," the man responded.

Dugan's hardened eyes met the homeless man's and for an instant, the street bum peered inside Dugan; what he saw frightened him. He saw pure evil, hatred and greed. What he didn't see was a soul, and that's what scared him the most. He held his hands up in the universal sign of surrender.

"Okay man. I don't want no problem. No problem...don't want any," he stammered.

Dugan continued to glower at the old man as he moved quickly away from him. Not lost on Dugan was the fact he now stood alone on the subway platform, others around him could sense the danger and unconsciously had moved away from him.

He heard the train approach and everyone instinctively took a step back from the yellow line, the barrier separating the last twelve inches of the platform and the train. It squealed to a stop on the massive steel rails, and simultaneously the doors opened on the numerous cars. Those whose stop was Columbus Circle or those changing trains to go in another direction, exited. Dugan stepped onto the train and sat down in an empty seat close to the door. The lady seated next to him leaned away unconsciously in an attempt to keep her spirit from being tainted.

The train rolled down the tracks as commuters and tourists got off and others got on at each stop, the train itself continuing its southward pass to what New Yorkers call the "downtown" area of the island. At each stop Dugan remained seated, and at each stop people seemed to shy away from him, not because of his look, but because of his presence.

As the train slowed down at the Canal Street stop, he rose, holding onto a pole for balance. Other passengers looked down at their feet like they had misplaced something atop their shoes, refusing to make eye contact with him. Dugan smirked at his own presumed self-importance.

He exited the train, walked onto the platform, through the turnstile and up the stairs to the sound of sirens and honking horns. Crowds of tourists ambled about in New York's Chinatown, a city and economy all its own. The streets stank of raw seafood stands, open sewers and garbage.

Dugan stepped onto the crowded sidewalk and turned east. He watched as thousands of people crowded into small stores, restaurants and fish markets. Street vendors offered him everything from fake Rolex watches to designer purses to bootleg DVD's of movies released in the last week. Ignoring each of them, he pushed through to the next intersection, stopping long enough to allow an oncoming car to pass.

He made his way to Mott Street, crossed over Canal and walked south. A little over a block later he found what he was seeking and walked into the small Chinatown Community Buddhist Temple. Seating was readily available at this time of morning with only two women and one other man sitting separately in the pews. The strong smell of lavender incense permeated the room while the golden Buddha statue looked out over the parishioners, silently preaching a homily of peace and compassion. Dugan paid little notice to the statue of a now dead man whose very life and existence had been deified. He shook his head at the lunacy of man.

A frail Chinese gentleman dressed in the robes of a Mahayana priest walked into the room and faced the statue of the Buddha. Both hands came together in the traditional pose of supplication and thanks as he bowed deeply, his rosary beads swaying as he did so. He silently asked for blessings on his humble temple before turning and walking to Dugan.

"Mr. Dugan, it is nice to see you again. I pray that your health is good and your life complete," he said respectfully to his guest.

"Thank you, venerable reverend. I appreciate you seeing me on such short notice," Dugan replied uncharacteristically polite.

"What brings you back to our humble temple, Mr. Dugan? The last time you were here you asked many questions of our Chinese culture and history, but nothing of the Buddha and his teachings. Do you wish to explore our cumulative human life, suffering and ultimate death and how we can try to make one another happy in a world filled with so much misery?" the priest asked, seriousness in both tone and posture.

Dugan lowered his voice and tilted his head toward the elderly Chinaman. He had spent a lot of time at the little temple, in this dirty part of the city, befriending the old holy man. After learning that Reverend Loi was the most knowledgeable man in Manhattan on Chinese lore, history, and ancient medicine, he sought him out hoping to glean useful information.

"No, Lao Shi," Dugan replied using the formal title for teacher, "what I'm interested in learning about are incantations and magic used in your culture and country. I realize this request may seem strange coming from a white American, but my interest is purely academic. I would like to pen an article about the mysteries of China, both ancient and current."

He hoped his story sounded real and convincing. The inordinate amount of time he had spent researching spells and magic used in ancient China had led him down winding paths of confusion and chaos. America was a couple hundred years old. China, on the other hand, was steeped in thousands of years of history, and a non-Chinese would find it extremely difficult to wade through centuries of documentation to find what he or she needed.

"I'm happy that you've taken such an interest in my home country, Mr. Dugan. However, this is a most strange request. When you ask about magic and incantations, I think it is important to understand that much of Chinese medicine is based upon sound mathematical calculations, as well as the use of astrology and the meridians and chakras of the human body. The Chinese believe in the power of the mind, the will, nature and the elements. Each of these can be used for healing, but with each of these things can also come destruction or what non-Chinese would refer to as 'evil.' Do you understand?"

He thought about the question for a moment before responding. "I think I have an idea of what you're saying, but perhaps you could elaborate?"

"Some of the ancients believed in healing and destructive powers that moved through the body. This is the concept of chi. All living beings have chi, but only a few know how to harness it and use it. You have heard of the Japanese method of healing called 'Reiki,' yes?"

Dugan answered the old man, "Yes, Lao Shi. I've heard of Reiki and its practitioners that can magically heal another person's sickness by holding their hands over the person's body. Supposedly, the heat generated helps the person receiving the treatment feel better or mysteriously heals them. Personally, I never believed in it."

"That is fair enough, Mr. Dugan. The practice of Reiki is a new concept developed in Japan in only the twentieth century. However, its founder, Mr. Usui, studied for many years in China. He claims to have climbed a mountain in Japan and, while there he fasted, eventually being given the teachings of Reiki. The Japanese love their drama and mountain legends," Loi chuckled, "but the reality is, he learned of the physical healing nature of chakra repair in China."

"Okay," said Dugan, "but what does this have to do with my question?"

Reverend Loi laughed quietly, "Americans and Europeans only see the surface of anything. You never look beyond the here and now, and that is why you are never happy. You see, Usui shifu learned the healing arts of

China. Specifically, he studied the ancient tongue and focus of the masters, which allowed him to use his own spiritual energy to heal. Some would call this 'magic,' but to the learned Chinese it is the natural progression of life. It is the giving of oneself to help others heal. Now, do you understand?"

"On some level, I understand. But what about using that same power to destroy? Was that practiced by the ancients too, Lao Shi?" pressed Dugan.

"Of course. In all cultures there have been those who have yearned to rule over others. Although the old teachers understood how to reverse the positive energy they gave in order to destroy, I'm happy to say that most refused to teach that element of their art. Unfortunately, there were, and still are, those who prefer to profit from the darker side of their art."

Dugan's heart raced, but he fought to contain himself as he continued his line of questioning.

"Can chi be directed to inanimate objects, similarly as it is to living beings?" he asked the old man who was now staring at him intently.

"That's an interesting question, Mr. Dugan. I suppose only the most advanced healer and practitioner would be capable of forcing his will on an object, but I suspect that object would be used as a means to capture the chi or incantation. It is similar to the Caribbean practice of voodoo, if you will, when a doll or object is used to help the spiritual practitioner focus energy onto a person."

"I see," Dugan said, his mind awhirl. "Kind of like a wizard's wand or a witch's broom."

"Yes, similar to that. Or perhaps like a statue of Buddha or a Christian cross. These items contain within them all the prayers sent their way. This is what makes a place holy. You feel the power of a truly spiritual place when you enter it, not because of its physical address, but because of the spiritual energy captured within it.

"Now, Mr. Dugan, I'm afraid that is all the time I have today. I hope what I've told you will be beneficial when you write your article about my home country," Loi said as he began to rise.

"Just a couple more questions, please," Dugan requested.

"Please hurry, Mr. Dugan. I have other matters to attend to. I'm certain you understand."

"Yes sir, I understand. Thank you." Dugan pushed on. "Can the power housed in the focal object be harnessed by another, and if so how is that done?"

Loi studied the man carefully, sensing something not quite right with him, but he answered anyway, if for no other reason than to have him leave as quickly as possible. "Only the person who focused the energy, or a family member, can control it."

"A family member? A blood relative?" Dugan said aloud but mostly to himself.

"Correct, Mr. Dugan. Be well and be safe," Loi said as he rose and walked to the back of the temple.

Mexico City, Mexico
July 17, 2013 1:06 P.M.

Roper was preparing to leave his room when his phone rang. The number was a familiar one, Buddy's. He heard a pop in the line followed by a brief hiss. "Go," was the simple greeting he offered his counterpart.

"Go? What kind of nonsense is go? That's not a very welcoming or nice greeting for the feller who's calling you to give you information, Young Buck," Buddy's thick Appalachian twang bellowed.

"Is the line secure?" Roper asked.

"Does a cat have climbing gear?" Buddy asked.

"Why the hell are you calling me? I was about to go check the board. You're like a bad date who keeps calling after I've told her to leave me alone," quipped Roper.

"It couldn't wait. I needed to get you this information pronto, amigo, besides, if we were dating, you'd have me on speed dial."

"The board would have been fine, but go ahead anyway," Roper said while ignoring Buddy's verbal jabs.

"Alright, first things first. The picture you sent is a known gun runner and two bit thug. His name is Rafael Umberto Chao. Apparently, he's done quite a bit of work for Dugan over the years, from peddling arms to the border, running coke from Guatemala to American border towns, to murder. He's a street savvy feller and a loner. I couldn't find a lot of history on him other than he grew up poor as hell in the Yucatan region of Mexico. He doesn't cross the border because he's smart enough to know he'll do hard prison time or someone will bust a cap right in his Mexican ass."

"That's all good information, Buddy. You said his last name is Ciao, like "see you later" in Italian?"

"I figured you'd pick up on that pretty quickly, amigo. No, it's not ciao like the Italians say it, it's c-h-a-o," he spelled the name out for him. He let Roper soak in what this might mean.

"I don't understand. Was his dad Chinese? That name isn't Latino at all. This fucking case gets stranger by the minute, Buddy," said Roper with an exasperated breath.

Buddy answered him, "Nah. As far as I can tell, both his parents were as Mexican as tamales. Like I said, I don't have a lot of history on him, but it looks like he's been arrested a few times for minor things in Mexico, managed to pay his way out of trouble and still work for Dugan."

"What the hell does this mean, Buddy? You know I'm a global guy, but I'm used to names like Hernandez, Lopez, Garcia and shit like that in the Spanish speaking world. How does a Mexican guy wind up with a Chinese last name if he's one hundred fucking percent Mexican?" Roper continued to ask.

"There's the crux, ole boy. I had the same questions you just prattled off to me, so I did some more research. You sitting down for this?"

Roper sat down on the edge of his bed. "I am now. Shoot."

"Brother, it would seem that there are Mexicans and Guatemalans running around all over the place with names like Chao, Chen, Chan. Seems a lot of these folks somehow managed to comingle with some Chinese folks at some point and time. I ain't playing around, and you're right, this shit is getting weirder, but we need to stay focused on the task at hand."

"You're kidding me? Mexicans running around with names like that? I have no idea how that happened, but does that explain the cartouche being Chinese in origin?" Roper questioned.

"Could very well explain why the damned thing seems to be of Chinese origin yet wound up in Mexico, but here's something more I just learned. Apparently, those people have been there for generations...for possibly two thousand years. You hear me? It looks like a lot of the Mayans had Chinese names and they carried on to modern times. Mayans with Chinese names making cartouches, ain't that something? Now it gets stranger, Buck.

It seems there are only two places in the world that cartouches were made in ancient times – Egypt and the Yucatan Peninsula in Mexico. What amazes me even more are the similarities in pyramid construction and genetics. Both cultures had a serious propensity for building pyramids, staring at stars and doing math. Their slanted eyes and dark complexions may just be a coincidence, or perhaps some of the Chinese culture migrated from China into those areas a long damned time ago. Everyone considers Africa to be the cradle of civilization, but that may not be true.

Now, I'm no scientist and maybe I'm just reaching here, but if that's true, a lot of history is going to have to be rewritten, and a lot of what we know today will be questioned. Things like religion and what happened to the dinosaurs and shit. You hear me, amigo?"

Roper laughed and asked, "What the hell do the dinosaurs have to do with this?"

"Nothing. I just thought I would throw that in there," said Buddy with a chuckle.

"Okay, what else do you have for me?" Roper pressed on.

"Everyone that's flown in and out of Monterrey since the theft has checked out, including all the Americans, so I looked even further for booking dates to see what I could find. There's a reservation on the morning of the twenty-second for a Donald Haden. This Haden doesn't have any background information, employment, arrest record, car registration. He's a ghost...a phantom, which makes it very likely he's our boy flying down to grab the jewel. I can't find any return information on him though, so I don't know what his plans are beyond that."

"That's perfect, Buddy. I have plenty of time to track down the current cartouche holder or intercept Dugan at the airport. I might even see what he would look like in a state of rigor mortis. I'll do that for free, you know what I mean?"

"The focus is getting our hands on the cartouche, Young Buck. Let's try not to start an international incident at a Mexican airport, okay?" Buddy stated this more than he asked.

Xi'an, Shaanxi, China
July 20th, 2013 5:30 A.M.

From the west the sun crept over the mountains and poured its light on the sleepy valley so far removed from the hustle and bustle of the coastal cities of China. The quiet canals flowed through the town as it started to come to life. Gray and brownstone buildings saturated the cityscape, as they did throughout the vast country. Some people dressed in the same colors as the buildings in which they lived and worked. They performed their morning ritual of tai chi, the age-old form of exercise and, some believed, method of fighting and defense.

Even though it was summer time in the northern hemisphere, a cool wind blew from the north, an almost human moan springing from the gust as it whipped through the mountains. A few people practicing their moving meditation actually shivered, some feeling a strange sense of inevitability on the heels of the draft. Others, their heads askew, turned in the direction of the northern mountains trying to hear what the wind was trying to tell them.

In a long-abandoned and overgrown area outside the city at the base of a mountain, a lone stone statue stood, its moss and bird feces covered face one of agony. The same blustery gust of wind swept over the statue as a *ripple* seemed to float across its chest. Had someone been there when that cold wind drifted over the warrior and his steed, they would have sworn, for just a second, that it moved. And had someone been there when that cold wind drifted across the statue's face, they would have thought they heard it moan.

In a manmade pyramid just a few kilometers away, the same ripple appeared to no one in particular. Thousands of stone warrior statues standing at attention inside its base teetered as the gust blew over them.

Monterrey, Mexico
July 21, 2013 11:12 A.M.

Roper spent two days driving unfamiliar roads from Mexico City to Monterrey, a cumulative of 1,057 kilometers. He took it easy while driving, not wanting to arouse suspicion concerning why he was leaving the metropolitan area to go to Monterrey, as his cover story given at the airport would be blown. Tucked into his waistband in the small of his back was the reassuring pressure of the Colt 1911 with a stubbed silencer and laser sites. This had been included in the supply bag Javier had given him, and it gave him some sense of security as he spent more time in the unfamiliar and rogue nation.

After arriving in Monterrey on the nineteenth, he knew he would have time to do some research, so he made his way to the Rain Forest cyber café not far from his hotel. What he found kept him mesmerized for a couple of hours. Roper knew that every culture builds temples to appease their gods. The thought of getting closer to God or the heavens has been documented since the dawn of man; however, few realize that only certain cultures built pyramids to honor their gods. Fewer still understood the complexities of creating a written language made up of hieroglyphs, rather than an alphabet. And even fewer still wrote about their gods arriving to Earth in what appeared to be spaceships. The Mayans and the Egyptians had all of those things in common.

As Roper continued to read he made mental notes of similarities between the two ancient cultures. Incredible math skills and application of math in their respective architecture, an infatuation with mythical dragon creatures, the use of jade in ceremony, language similarities, shamanistic practices and even facial resemblances were all uncanny. But what Buddy had told him earlier chewed at his mind incessantly...Chinese surnames are found throughout old Maya or new southern Mexico.

He further researched the last names of the Mexican Yucatan peninsula and found that numerous Chinese names existed. *I guess this could be a coincidence, but the rest of this stuff adds up to some weird shit,* Roper thought to himself. *This is one of the strangest things I've ever found, and damn it, and I have seen some weird shit.*

He delved further into his research and studied all three cultures and their temples, more specifically their pyramids. What he found floored him. Rumors of primeval pyramids existed in China prior to World War II. At long last, some exploration deep into China occurred and confirmation of their existence became public knowledge; unfortunately photographic evidence was all but nonexistent. Of course, as the world changed and the internet evolved, pictures became available on the World Wide Web, or as Roper called it, the world's brain, and more and more people began seeing them. Still, China denied the pyramids existed, insisting that theirs was a culture of Asian temples and pagodas. What the Chinese couldn't explain, they denied.

What people saw was a photo taken by a U.S. Air Force pilot, James Gaussman, in 1945, of a pyramid that appeared to be missing its top, similar to the pyramid featured on the back of the United States one dollar bill with the *all seeing eye* floating just above the incomplete temple. The Chinese pyramid sat just outside the country's early capital, Xi'an.

"Satellite imaging," he continued reading, "has now allowed those outside China's borders to see aerial shots of pyramids with trees growing on them, intentionally planted by the government to hide them from public view. During his research, he discovered that Thailand also had pyramids." *Damn. Egypt, the Maya, Thailand and China. All of these cultures built pyramids. Why is that? What else do they have in common,* Roper wondered?

"China's Xi'an pyramids were aligned with the constellation of Orion. The pyramids of Giza in Egypt were also built and aligned with the constellation of Orion. Only Chichen Itza in old Maya did not align with a star constellation, but its position allowed for a strange optical illusion of a shadowy dragon descending from its top to the base. This event happens twice per year during the spring and fall equinoxes."

He read more about Chichen Itza and was enthralled with the construction of the star observatory built by the Mayans which resembled modern observatories constructed the world over.

Next, he wanted to compare the ancient writing styles of China and the Maya. The search engine revealed that China, the Maya *and* Egypt all used hieroglyphs in their writing. Of the three cultures, semblances of Chinese hieroglyphs still existed within their written language. These glyphs evolved into their current language and spread to Korea, Okinawa and Japan. Roper read that a trained eye will find pictographs in their respective Asian scripts.

He eased back in his seat and glanced around the room. He twisted his back, stretching it, and took a deep breath, moving his right ear to his right shoulder. A couple of vertebrae popped and the tension in his neck dissipated. He repeated the same movement to the left shoulder and his neck cracked again. The lady sitting on the other side of his partition heard the cracks, stood and looked at him, her jaw slack and a disgusted look on her face. He returned her look with a smirk that said, "Thanks for your concern, now mind your own damned business." She sat back down and minded her own business.

He returned to his research after checking his watch. Not wanting to stay in one place for an excessive amount of time, he planned for another thirty minutes before leaving. His fingers moved to the keyboard, and he went back to the Google search engine.

"China and Mayan similarities" was what he searched next. Pottery and artwork from two countries, two continents half a world apart filled his computer screen. The likenesses between them were inconceivable. Even to

Roper's inexperienced eye, he knew he was looking at something more than mere coincidence. This was real, but none of it explained why he was chasing a Mexican man from Mexico City to Monterrey.

The word "cartouche" appeared in the search bar as his fingers typed the word. He pressed the enter key and watched the monitor populate with links to several sites discussing their use in Egypt of old. As he read about their design, first made of stone and later gold and silver, he grew to learn that a pharaoh or king whose name was emblazoned upon a cartouche was believed to be protected from evil in life and death. Egyptians also believed a wearer of a cartouche would never disappear, even after death. Roper found this belief a difficult one, but assumed their belief was rooted in the acknowledgement of a spiritual soul.

Egyptians were also very careful when their cartouches were cast to avoid an enemy gaining control of it because they believed an enemy could overcome the owner's spirit and physical body if the high priests did not protect the gem with a sacred ward or curse. Roper found that information fascinating. What if this cartouche held a spell that controlled someone's soul? Wouldn't that be just like the United States government to want that power for themselves?

Much less information was found about Mayan cartouches. It would seem a Mayan cartouche was worn in a related manner as that of its Egyptian counterpart. The kings and priests of Mesoamerica wore them to protect themselves from evil, both in the real world and that of the spiritual realm. They, too, believed that any enemy who came into possession of their cartouche could control their physical and spiritual beings.

Roper saw the likenesses of the Egyptian and Mayan cultures, but this did nothing to help him in his search for the Chinese cartouche stolen from the Museum of Anthropology in Mexico City, so he conducted another search for "Chinese cartouche" and found minimal information. *Strange. Buddy is convinced the cartouche stolen from the museum is Chinese or at least, Chinese in origin, yet I can't find a concrete link between their use in China and the Mayan people,* he thought. *But there's something there, even if the connection is minimal.*

Having decided that he'd stayed long enough, and happy that he had gleaned some useful information, but nothing that lead him to the cartouche, he knew the time had come to hash this thing out with Buddy. He cleared the browser history before backing his chair away from the small computer desk, checked around the café, and left.

Stopping long enough to check his reflection in the café's window, he pretended to adjust his clothes and run his fingers through his hair. No one caught his attention or looked like he wanted to kill him, so he began his counter surveillance walk to the Hampton Inn some two and a half kilometers away.

His northerly course turned east as he made a right on Lomas de Vallecillo, allowing only his peripheral vision to see anyone who might possibly be following him. Not detecting anyone, his mind began to drift back to what he had learned at the internet café about the varying cultures and their similarities. The distinctive differences between them provided for serious knowledge gaps that only served to further confuse him about the cartouche and its significance. If he could figure out its value, tracking it would be simpler. Knowing its destination would enable him to head Dugan off at the pass, so to speak.

As he continued walking, he observed more gang graffiti painted on homes and buildings, so typical of third-world Mexico. Bright paint over stucco walls gave the impression of festive neighborhoods. However, the violence many of the people behind those walls lived with was anything but festive. He'd seen this way of life all over the world, and it still sickened him to know a lot of good people would never realize a decent life without fear.

It wasn't his custom to be unfocused, especially while walking strange city streets, but he couldn't stop it this time. *Chinese, Mayan and Egyptian pyramids. Two in alignment with Orion, one built with an observatory. Three separate cultures, each using hieroglyphs as a part of their written language. All three cultures used a cartouche to fend off evil spirits, and each believed the amulets were magical. The Chinese culture is the one believed to have created or influenced the creation of the cartouche that was stolen, but the link to China is ambiguous given the west's inability to access a lot of their history. This is driving me bat shit crazy.*

He turned left onto Sierra Pena Nevada, stopping only long enough to pull up his socks and to check behind him. No one on either side of the street paid him any attention, nor did anyone make any sudden stops or look his way to see what he was doing. The sidewalks on the block were lined with neatly pruned trees, and newer vehicles parked along the street. As he continued to walk, he decided to take out another disposable phone and make a call.

The day grew warmer as he navigated his northeasterly trek down Sierra Pena Nevada. Familiar ringing in his ear began as the connection was made from his phone to Buddy's. On the second ring that reliable southern Appalachian accent answered, "Hey, Young Buck. How're you making it?"

"My brain is going into overload. I've been doing some research, Buddy. This is crazy stuff. Do you understand me? I just haven't been able to piece together the cartouche connection to China, but my research tells me the jewels were used as talisman in both Egypt and Mesoamerica. I realize Egypt wasn't factored into this deal when we first began the op, but there's a distinct connection between the three cultures and countries. Information about Chinese cartouches is sketchy, but it looks like they used them a couple of eons ago."

Buddy hesitated a few seconds before responding, "I've been doing research on my end too, Roper. Trying to keep the fire stoked here by finding out why Dugan is so damned hot and heavy for this fucking thing. We know it has some sort of magical power, but we don't know what it does. I've been honest with you about this damned cartouche. Hopefully, you can intercept it and we can get our hands on Dugan and interrogate him. We need to know what he knows."

"It took you a minute to respond to me. You've given me facts. I want your opinion, Buddy, and I want you to be up front with me," he responded candidly.

"Look kid, I have an idea about this thing...this cartouche...but I don't have any proof, and I don't know how it works. Until I get something more tangible about its use, I prefer to keep speculation out of it," said Buddy.

A red, older model Camaro slowed as it passed. Roper followed the car with his eyes and saw it turn left on a street a few blocks away. He saw nothing unusual about it so he kept walking and talking.

"Not good enough. I want to know what you're thinking, Buddy. I feel like I'm walking into a shit storm without a hazmat suit, and you're not even giving me a can of Lysol," Roper threw back at him.

He could hear Buddy take a deep breath and exhale into the phone. In his mind's eye, he could see the old spook run his fingers through his hair then scratch his scruffy face as he debated internally what to say, not to mention how much to say.

"Off the record, Buck," Buddy began, and then once again hesitated, "and I have no research to back this up, you understand? All that investigation you've done is similar to what I've done here. The missing piece is what is, or was, inside those pyramids. In Egypt they entombed Pharaohs believing the pyramids were the catalyst to the next realm of existence.

In Mesoamerica, the Maya buried their kings and made murals hiding their gods inside their pyramids. In China, their stone warriors were placed underneath a ceiling of pearls made to look like the night sky. These, too, were placed in a pyramid. You are familiar with the Terracotta Warriors my friend?"

Roper listened to Buddy detail some things about what the pyramids housed that he hadn't considered in his research. "Yes, I've read about those old statues. Thousands of them existed from what I've read and seen. It's a pretty impressive collection of art if you ask me."

"Yeah," Buddy continued. "In two of the three cultural areas, cartouches were found still inside the pyramids, guarding and protecting what was inside. It's believed the cartouche found in the biggest of the Giza pyramids had within it a protection spell guarding King Tutankhamen. Anyone who disturbed the tomb would fall victim to its spell. It's common knowledge that archeologist, Howard Carter, and many on his team, died mysteriously after disturbing King Tut's tomb. Each reported a strange vibration and thrum from the cartouche guarding the tomb, and each who reported feeling it later died.

"The same is true of several archeologists who disturbed the Mayan ruins, and let me remind you, cartouches were found there as well, remember. Many died grisly deaths that doctors couldn't explain. It's been reported that two scientists who were on site when the Chichen Itza pyramid was opened died miserable deaths after their bodies began rotting from the inside.

"Only in China has no one befallen a strange death after disturbing the tomb, but the Warriors remain largely intact. Also, no cartouche was found, but it's common knowledge in Xi'an that cartouches were used to protect the living or to curse the dead. Only recently have we found the cartouche we believed to have housed that curse. The weird thing is, the cartouche, as you now know, isn't in China...it's in old Mexico," Buddy said.

"That being said," Buddy continued, "there have been rumors of deaths surrounding a statue not contained within the pyramid. I don't know anything beyond those rumors and have no idea why this one warrior isn't inside with the others, but apparently it stands not far from its brothers."

"So, you believe the cartouche that's here is the one from ancient Xi'an?" Roper asked, already knowing the answer.

"Yes, and I'll tell you why. There are several stories about an exodus from a village in Xi'an two hundred years B.C. Some accounts have them heading due west and ending up in northeast Africa, what we now call Egypt. Other legends tell of them heading north and east through modern Russia and crossing what we know as the Bering Strait, eventually making a home in southern Mexico and Central America. I believe both accounts, Buck.

I think some of the villagers wound up in Egypt and assimilated into their culture bringing with them the knowledge of the stars and pyramids, and I believe some headed east leaving their DNA and knowledge behind all the way from Alaska to Central America. Look at the similarities of the people and look at DNA samples taken across those cultures, and you'll find there is no mistake about this theory.

As with any exodus, a culture's belief and learning follow them. I believe the pyramid builders in Egypt were of Chinese origin, as were those in Mesoamerica. And with those spiritual temples came the magic supplied by the Chinese shaman who passed that knowledge along. The only magic missing was in China. I think this magic left with them and has recently been rediscovered," Buddy said ominously.

"To what end?" asked Roper. "What does this magic do? In the Egyptian and Mayan pyramids, it protected what was in it and cursed those who disturbed them. There's a bunch of statues in the Chinese pyramid...the White Pyramid as it's called...with no statues of deities."

"That's the crux, kiddo. And this is where it gets stranger, but makes sense if you follow human evolution. The Chinese were spiritual people but not particularly religious. They didn't believe in otherworldly gods and such, but their beliefs centered on the earth, the sun and the moon. They believed in the elements: fire, water, wood, earth and metal. In these things they based their magic, not so different from European magicians, wizards, witches and warlocks.

"Legend has it that the Emperor, who was once based in Xi'an, sent his tax collector to the village to collect bushels of rice. On this particular season the rain had not been favorable, and rice production was low. The villagers did not have enough rice to feed themselves for the winter, much less pay the Emperor his ransom. As a result, the tax collector beheaded the local shaman's son and promised to return the next day and continue the onslaught until the taxes were paid.

"It's said the shaman crafted a cartouche made of all five elements and put upon it a curse to turn the tax collector to stone, as well as the Emperor's army. I think Dugan wants the cartouche because he believes he can reverse the spell and control the ancient army. That's my theory, Buck. I know it sounds crazy, but you and I both have seen crazy juju in faraway lands that neither of us like to talk about."

Roper laughed uneasily before replying, "Buddy, this sounds like some farfetched bullshit for our government to be involved in, either officially or unofficially. I can't believe I'm chasing a magic amulet that will release the power of a bunch of short Chinamen with bows and arrows. Do you know how silly that sounds?"

Buddy remained serious. "Buck, I do realize that it sounds rather incredulous. But what if the spell was to be partially reversed and the warriors brought back to life, but in an altered state of physicality? What then? Does that sound crazier or would that worry you?"

"What do you mean, 'altered state of physicality,' Buddy? Spit it out, man," Roper demanded.

"Stone warriors not fazed by bullets or current technology. I mean soulless warriors at the command of whoever holds the amulet. That's what I'm talking about and that's what I think we're facing. Short of a nuclear strike, how would that army be dealt with and who could stop it, Buck?

"That's my theory and that's what I think we're dealing with here. China, if they had the cartouche and held its magic, could invade several countries with an army of hardened stone and destroy weaker nations in days. Many Asian countries don't even have standing armies, and just the fear of the sight of them would be mind-boggling. I think this is what Dugan wants to control, and I believe he'll sell this army to the highest bidder, and that's why you have to find this cartouche before he figures out how to reverse the spell, if he hasn't already.

"And what would happen if a country like Iran or Syria had control of this army? How about Russia or Germany? Control of this army is an unimaginable power, Buck. And think of all the other implications we've discussed before – religion falls apart, nations lose control of the masses, hysteria on a monumental level. And if the magic can be reverse engineered, could it be duplicated in the future? Do you see where this is going?"

"Buddy, this whole damned thing sounds like a bad fairy tale and is based upon a lot of 'what ifs.' What if you're wrong? What if Dugan just digs old jewelry and art? Maybe he's just getting soft," Roper finished.

"Listen, Buck, there's something you need to know," Buddy started.

Roper heard a car slowly creeping up behind him and glanced over his shoulder to see a hint of red. It slowed even more as it approached and the sound of Latin music could be heard bumping through speakers with a cheap sub-woofer.

"I think I've got some company, Buddy. I'll be in touch," he said as he clicked off his phone and put it back in his pocket.

Arlington, Virginia, USA
July 21, 2013 9:34 A.M.

Buddy put his iPod on his docking station and dialed over to his selection of jazz. Deep base and soothing piano began pouring from the speakers as The Mel Brown Quartet allowed their collective heart and soul to flow through their music. He poured a glass of Merlot, relishing in his own social refinement while still embracing his redneck attitude. He smiled at his own diametrically opposed personality as he savored the fruity black cherry and light oak flavors.

"Son of a bitch, I'm sophisticated. I hate that I ran out of beer though," he chuckled to himself as he took another sip of his wine. Mel Brown beat his drum and kept time as his other band mates played their instruments, soothing music streaming through his townhouse. Buddy appreciated their musical genius and silently wished he'd learned how to play the piano instead of learning how to manipulate and kill people. *I wouldn't have made as much money, but my sleep would be a lot less restless.*

He looked at his clock, considered the time of morning, shrugged his shoulders and took another sip of wine as he sorted through his messy refrigerator looking for leftovers. Years earlier he would have reasoned with himself to justify drinking alcohol during the morning hours. Nowadays, Buddy hummed a few bars of Alan Jackson and Jimmy Buffet's duet, "*It's Five O'clock Somewhere*," and drank without thought.

Before lumbering to his computer, Buddy decided he'd be a normal human being and chase his wine with some coffee. The coffee maker stood at the ready, and he filled the reservoir with water and added eight scoops of his favorite blonde roast to make the brew. As it percolated, he made a peanut butter sandwich.

"Yep. Sophisticated is what the hell I am!"

He poured a cup of coffee, took another sip of his Merlot then put the hot coffee to his lips and took a little drink. The burn chased the black cherry flavor all the way to his stomach. A steady finger touched the power button on his laptop and the booting process began. The normal Windows start up commands flashed across the screen as he waited patiently while the little circle signifying the loading process spun relentlessly.

A blue screen with icons appeared on the monitor. He moved the cursor over the Internet Explorer icon and opened the window. He toggled through his favorites and opened his personal bulletin board account. Keeping things as mundane and generic as possible kept Big Brother from being interested, even though he was a part of the U.S. machine. He saw there was a message awaiting him, so he clicked on it.

Change in plans. Asset tracked. Asset will be removed after pick up. Will discuss any additional funding required once the gift has been transferred.

"FUCK ME," Buddy shouted! His fingers ran across his key board as rapidly as he could.

Negative. Asset is not to be removed at this time. He could prove valuable when the gift has been acquired. Confirm receipt ASAP.

Buddy punched the number to the disposable phone and listened to it ring. After five rings and a recording telling him that the number he had reached did not have an active voicemail account, he hung up. He redialed one more time as he became more and more anxious. The sound of distant ringing began...two rings...three rings...four rings...five rings...an automated voice. "Damn it," he muttered and hung up again. The old spook sat and stared at his computer trying to *will* his previous e-mail to be read and a reply sent back to him. Nothing appeared on his monitor before he shut down the computer. He drank the rest of his wine in one gulp.

Monterrey, Mexico
July 21, 2013 12:03 P.M.

The red Camaro rolled past Roper and stopped. He fought the urge to reach for the Colt 1911 in his waistband until it became necessary to do so. Streets and sidewalks were curiously empty, and yards were devoid of kids, parents or pets. Roper stood his ground and moved his right foot back assuming a hidari shizentai position – a left foot forward natural stance.

Four Latinos ranging in age from their mid-twenties to mid-thirties piled out of the car. Each wore jeans and sneakers, two wore tank tops, one a button down, ornately designed short sleeve shirt, and the last a fancy western looking long sleeved shirt. All wore blue bandanas on their heads. Fancy Shirt took the lead and approached Roper.

"You lost, vato? Whachoo doin here, ese?" Fancy Shirt asked, his accent heavy.

Roper eyeballed him and waited several seconds before replying. "I'm just walking.
What can I do for you men? I'm not looking for trouble." he began.

"Orale. You found trouble, gringo. You hear me, cracker? We *are* trouble," Fancy Shirt boasted. He took a step toward Roper, his gang of three circling the man. "You look like a cop from up north. Why're you in our neighborhood, ese? We don't need no fuckin American cops here, comprende?"

Roper felt his heart rate kick up a few notches, and his adrenaline began pumping, making it a little more difficult to speak. Adrenaline has a way of taking a human's body to a more primordial state, which normally doesn't include perfect diction. He reminded himself to control his breathing so he could try to talk his way out of the confrontation, or in the very least buy himself some time.

He turned slowly watching each of the men, keeping an eye on their hands. Should one motion as if he were drawing a weapon, things were going to get messy. Roper couldn't help but wonder at the likelihood of being followed and attacked for a second time while in Mexico. He would work out the "who's and why's" when he finished with the four thugs now confronting him.

"Look my man, I just took a wrong turn while I was walking around the area. My apologies to you men. If you fellas will just let me go, I'll get out of your neighborhood," Roper said as he made a slow turn to check the hands of the each man, his mind focused on relaxing his shoulders and controlling his breathing. He let his thoughts fall to his tanden, that area just two inches below his navel that the Japanese believe houses the human spirit.

Realizing the Latinos were not going to back down, he eyed Fancy Shirt and took a step toward him. Fancy Shirt retreated a half-step and licked his lips, a sure sign of nervousness. The testosterone fest was in full swing.

A couple of blocks away a car passed, its muffler in obvious need of changing. The typical blue sky of southern Mexico beat down on the quintet and no wind offered relief. Roper stepped off the sidewalk and onto the black top road. The footing there would be much better than the sidewalk that had begun crumbling in some spots.

Roper furrowed his brow and slightly tucked his chin, sure to keep right foot forward in a relaxed fighting stance then said, "Well, an old boy back home once told me, 'if you can't get along, you gotta get it on.' Looks like we're going to dance, fellas, so let's waltz."

Tank Top One moved behind him, his pudgy stomach hanging over the top of his jeans. His shuffling steps told Roper he was about five feet behind him, a mile away in fighting distance.

Tank Top Two and Fancy Short Sleeve moved to either side of him. Roper glanced at the three that he could see in his periphery before focusing on Fancy Short Sleeve. He gave him an appreciative nod then offered, "Nice shirt."

Fancy Short Sleeve obviously grew a little unnerved by his opponent's obvious calm demeanor. His eyes darted to his three partners, and he saw all three of them with the same dumbstruck look on their faces.

As Roper bought a little more time to slow his breathing, he thought to himself – *Chances are very high that the guy behind me won't attack first. Most people in the rear are the last ones to attack because they are the most scared. Fancy Shirt has too much of his reputation to protect, so he'll move first. Then one of these guys on the side will decide to take a step; I'm guessing Fancy Short Sleeve won't be the one to move.*

Roper could actually feel his heart rate slow and his breathing normalize. He made a quick half turn so he could glance at Tank Top One to make sure he wasn't reaching for a weapon. When he made the turn, all four of his assailants jumped as though he had made a sudden move toward each of them at the same time. A smirk turned one side of his mouth up.

Fancy Shirt, as he predicted, lurched for him, just as Roper's right foot shot out in an inverted arc, the big toe of his shoe striking the femoral nerve of the attacker's left leg. Fancy Shirt's leg instantly went numb and gave way. The man fell to ground holding his thigh and wincing in pain.

Fancy Short Sleeve surprised him by moving next. From his left side, Fancy charged as Roper turned his body into him, blending as he was taught in his years of judo training. He let his left hand drift to Fancy's right shoulder and drift down his opponent's arm, never breaking continuity with him. Roper's right hand shot to Fancy's left lapel while he snapped hips into him. He pulled with his left while he intertwined his right into the lapel and threw him up and straight back down to the street in morote seio nage, one of his favorite judo throws. Fancy's head bounced twice, and blood oozed beneath it. His eyes rolled up into his skull, and his body involuntarily convulsed, his blue bandana slowly turned red and hung haphazardly from his head.

Meanwhile, Tank Top Two had taken a step toward him but stopped when he saw his buddy's head hit the street. His right hand shot inside his pocket and he pulled out a flip blade serrated knife. He held the blade loosely in his hand, his thumb resting on the case. The blade made small crescent movements as Tank Top Two positioned his open left hand by his chest in a defensive posture.

Shit, this guy has used a knife before. He's got some training, the thought slipped through Roper's mind like water passing over a rock in a stream. *The knife is just an extension of his hand,* he reminded himself. The first slash came, and Roper moved his hips away from the attack, sliding his left foot, then his right.

Tank Top Two slashed perpendicular from Roper's neck to his armpit. Again Roper avoided the slash as sweat formed on his brow, and one droplet trickled down his nose. His attacker reversed the slash, whipping the blade toward his neck. Roper eased his head back an inch to avoid the slash but didn't move his feet.

Across the street a robin chirped in a tree as it watched the battle transpire. A mother walked out of her front door holding her young daughter's hand. The little girl asked her mother what was happening in the street as her mother's jaw dropped while the five men continued their Tango of Death. She whisked her daughter back into the house, slamming the door behind her and locking the deadbolt with a loud and reassuring thunk.

Tank Top Two jabbed the knife at Roper's midsection. He parried the knife wielding hand away from his body. He brought his left hand to the attacker's wrist and simultaneously grasped it with his right, both hands now holding his attacker's knife hand at the wrist. His left foot stepped toward the man's left shoulder then he snapped his hips around straightaway executing a perfect shiho nage, or four corner throw.

Rather than letting go of his assailant, he smashed him to the ground, the impact knocking the air from the man's lungs. As he gasped for air, he dropped the knife as Roper again reversed his feet while holding the man's wrist with his own right hand. After his body turned, the man was lying flat on his back with his arm extended. Roper slammed his arm, just behind the elbow, into his knee snapping it. Tank Top Two let out a blood curdling scream as Roper rose to face his next opponent.

Tank Top One looked at him, his eyes full of terror. "Your turn tough guy," Roper's surprisingly steady voice said. He saw from the corner of his eye that Fancy Shirt was trying to get up while Tank Top Two rolled around on the ground holding his arm. Fancy Short Sleeve had not moved and probably wouldn't be making it to a family reunion again...ever.

In the tree, the robin stopped chirping and the street grew deathly quiet except for the combatant's breathing and agonizing groans. Roper fought to control his heart rate while refocusing his mind on his tanden. Sweat covered his body and dripped down his fingertips to the road below.

The acrid mixture of fear and sweat wafted through the air and slammed into Roper's nostrils like a hammer on a nail. He had smelled this blend of human emotion and porous adrenaline several times in his life and in the jungles of Africa and deserts of the Middle East. True warriorship is measured in how one controls his fear, commands his senses and confronts an enemy in the face of bodily harm, injury or certain death. It was obvious to him that this person was no warrior.

Zanshin is the Japanese term for extreme or remaining awareness. In the seconds, or moments, a person experiences zanshin all sight and sound is magnified beyond anything they've previously known. An individual in this altered state of mind can hear a commuter plane traveling at thirty-eight thousand feet like the aircraft was right next to him. He can hear his opponent's heartbeat and see heat vapor rising from his skin. A dog barking a mile away might as well be sitting in his lap yapping. Anyone walking behind this person would be sensed, his survival skills enhanced to unexplainable levels. Warriors know this sensation, have felt it, but struggle to explain it. A soldier fresh from the battlefield would be perplexed to put this into words, but rest assured, he would know exactly what it was.

The first time he killed a man with his bare hands he had been twenty-five years old, but was already considered a battle hardened veteran among his peers. The Ugandan had snuck up on him while he was relieving himself. A twig had snapped about six feet behind him, and he immediately turned to face his assassin with all his glory hanging out.

The African swung a large gurkha blade at his head. Ducking as the knife whisked over his head, he quickly closed the distance between himself and the man, trapping his arm and knife against his body while wrapping his left arm around him. Roper jammed a thumb into the man's left eye two knuckles deep. A wraith-like scream escaped from the man as his eye ruptured and blood poured from the socket.

His attacker writhed in agony as he attempted to escape the hold, but Roper jerked his thumb from the eyeless socket and allowed his thumb and forefinger to find his assailant's larynx. As fast as his fingers found it, he bore down and pinched just above the Adam's apple, snapping the cartilage and small bone. The African slumped to the ground, a gurgling sound rolling over his lips, a hand loosely wrapped around the gurkha's hilt as though it would save him from a certain death.

Roper grabbed his rifle and ran back to his camp and fellow warriors. Unfortunately for him he forgot to put his man unit back in his pants and zip up. Adrenaline has a way of making a man forget minor inconveniences. His buddies pointed and laughed as he ran to the camp, but slowly stopped giving him hell when they noticed the obvious effects of the adrenaline high – shakes and the inability to speak coherently.

Tank Top One stepped forward and took a wild swing at Roper, connecting with his cheek. His head snapped to one side from the impact of the punch. Sensing a change in momentum, Tank Top pounced on the big American and attempted to put him in a headlock.

Roper, seeing the confidence on his face after his punch connected, let the man wrap his arm around his neck before dropping his hips and bear hugging Tank Top one's waist. He drove his hips into Tank Top's thigh while lifting him off the ground. As he turned his body, Roper drove his adversary to the ground...hard. The air was purged from Tank Top's lungs as his body slammed to the deck. Roper landed directly on top of him, driving an elbow into the man's sternum. He let go of Roper's head as he tried to refill his lungs with air.

The man took a shallow breath and winced. No sooner had the sound left his mouth when Roper drilled a heavy hand into his eye. The soft flesh of Tank Top's eye brow split, and blood splattered in a six inch arc across his face and up Roper's hand. Unconsciousness followed the strike giving Tank Top a brief respite from the pain he would feel after waking.

Roper stood and saw that Tank Top Two was on his feet holding his arm. He started after the injured man who promptly backed up and began begging in broken English.

"No hit! No hit! Por favor, no hit."

Roper thought to himself, *How quickly a man's will bends and breaks when he's injured. Snap an arm and you snap his fighting spirit.* Roper continued to close the distance hoping he could get the man to give up some information about who had sent him and what their orders were. Or were they simply gang-bangers there to rob him? Was he supposed to be captured or killed? He took another step toward the man then...

A sharp pain exploded between his shoulder blades. He felt electricity attack his whole body as every muscle seized and refused to move. His mouth pulled back in an agonizing grimace as his lungs refused to draw a breath. A tunnel of darkness narrowed his peripheral vision as unconsciousness overtook him. An involuntary tear rolled down a cheek as his eyes glazed. His mind registered that he was about to be cataleptic but couldn't reason why. Almost as quickly as it began, it stopped. The muscles in his body released and he crumpled to the ground. Across the street, the robin chirped one last time before flying away.

Monterrey, Mexico
July 21, 2013 12:45 P.M.

A daytime soap opera played on Rafael's television as he lay atop his hotel bed. Despite there being a bathroom only steps from him, he hadn't showered in days. Each time room service knocked on the door he sent them away. The cartouche rested on his night stand because he had stopped putting it back in his pants pocket about the same time he ceased showering.

His brain told him he needed to urinate, but his body didn't want to leave the cartouche's vicinity. The hold it had on him had grown each time he touched it. Now, its call reached to him without touch. The thrumming and vibrations had only gotten stronger and stronger. It was now that he understood, somewhere in the recesses of his mind, that this is how an addict must feel. To part from it was relief and terror, both emotions creating a deeply seeded anxiety.

With a lot of effort he sat up and threw his legs over the bed. His eyes locked on the jewel, but he managed to pry them away after a long moment. The pangs and silent screams from his bladder told him his bed would be soaked in a few more minutes if he didn't make his way to the toilet.

Feet dragging across the cold tile floor, Rafael found his way to the bathroom. His hand reached for the light switch and flipped it up, electricity immediately bringing the fluorescent light bulbs to life. He turned his head away from the sharp light as it pierced and stung his eyes. Since he hadn't left the hotel room in a few days, he had not found a need to turn on a light. His only connection with the outside world had been through his television, which he mostly ignored.

He reached for the toilet seat and lifted it. This small act was seemingly all that was left of his humanity. He unzipped his pants and relieved himself. Dark brown urine splashed in the water below, a sure sign that his body was seriously dehydrated. At long last he finished. An immense relief passed through his body, and he shuddered. Stumbling to the mirror, he saw the reflection of a man he didn't recognize. His gaunt features and emaciated body was reminiscent of pictures he'd seen of Holocaust victims. His tongue flipped across chapped lips then raked against teeth that felt like stubble was growing on them.

"Mierda," he mumbled to no one in particular. The pull of the cartouche was heavy, but his mind forced him to remove his clothes after turning on the shower. His body itched from its own oils, dead skin cells and general filth. Only survival instincts forced him inside the shower, while the cartouche insisted he return to its side. He stepped into the scalding hot shower, the heat making him jump. The water poured over his head and body, somehow revitalizing him. His stomach told him he needed food, or he would be too weak to do anything.

The shampoo he scrubbed into his hair and scalp felt incredible, and the soap he used on his body felt as though it removed all the filth of the world. For a moment he felt guiltless, clean and absolved of all the sins he had committed. Yet, still, the relic called to him.

His shower finished, he toweled himself dry, put on the last clean pair of underwear he had then brushed the grit from his teeth. Toothpaste usually tasted horrible to him, but today it was glorious. The minty paste removed what felt like tile grout in his mouth.

A little life began to course through his thin body, which was how he felt...*thin*. Thin not just in the physical sense, but mentally too. Thoughts began to pour back into his mind; he had been almost lifeless since his arrival in Monterrey.

Ora le, I have to break this hold that thing has on me. I don't understand why it talks to me, but it's like I know it personally. I'm somehow linked to this thing but can't explain how or why. It sings to me, and I see images of Oriental people. I don't understand what is going on. Am I going insane or have I already stepped over that threshold?

He ran his razor over his drawn face that had grown a considerable amount of patchy beard stubble. Since he had run out of shaving cream several days earlier, he was forced to use soap as a lubricant. It wasn't great, but it kept the razor from chaffing his sunken face. The cold water he used also helped reduce the razor burn he normally got from using hot water.

While he dressed and put on his shoes, he fought the call of the old jewel. His stomach told him he had to step out to eat, but he knew he could not leave the cartouche behind, even though he feared touching it again. The jewel, he knew, would consume him.

He opened the closet door and removed the plastic bag the hotel maid service left behind for guests to place dirty clothes in, tore the perforated edge and carefully raked the jewel into the bag with the ink pen lying on the night stand. He didn't want to risk touching it with his bare skin again. His hand jammed the bag into his pocket, and he breathed a sigh of relief. He could feel the cartouche against his leg, but its call was a little more distant, a little more tolerable. Still, his head ached with the mere thought of it.

He tucked his pistol in his waistband and put on his jacket before stepping outside the door. Before the door closed behind him, he made sure the plastic hotel key was in his wallet and his cell phone was safely inside his jacket.

Rafael's finger touched the down button on the stainless panel on the wall that called the elevator to his floor. A quiet ding told him his chariot awaited, and the door slid open. An older couple riding in the elevator stared at him in disbelief before averting their eyes.

Apparently, I look a little worse than I thought. Damn it. His finger touched the lobby button on the Otis elevator's panel and they all watched as the door shut. The couple stood silently, then dashed from the elevator when the door opened.

New York City, New York, USA
July 21, 2013 3:57 P.M.

At New York's LaGuardia Airport, Dugan sat and flipped through his phone's address book. He had sent orders to another Mexican gang of miscreants he sometimes employed to help with various jobs close to the American border. Concern ate at him while he waited to board the plane for Mexico, concern for the cartouche's recovery and concern his gang of four would fail in their mission. Incompetence was something that tripped his bullshit-o-meter and he had had a belly full of it the past couple of weeks.

Deep down he had known the operation was fragile and dependent upon many fools. Rafael had proven a worthy go-to-guy and as angry as he had gotten at him two weeks earlier, he felt it would be a shame to have to kill him, in spite of his smart mouth and growing insubordination. His balls had gotten a little too big for his tidy-whities, especially after he had refused to meet Dugan earlier than planned. In fact, his tone had been downright belligerent, emboldened and hostile.

As he sat at his gate, the smell of restaurant food and coffee cascaded through the terminal. Dugan reflected on the past two years, and how he had come to learn about the cartouche. While in China on an assignment, he had happened across a tour of Xi'an and had seen, at the base of Qin Mountain, a lone statue of a warrior sitting atop a massive horse. The warrior's face was contorted, the emotions raw and telling. It wasn't the face one would think of when one thought about an artist's rendition of a revered and fierce soldier.

Dugan stared at the magnificent statue, the rider's arm raised with sword in hand. His uniform was impeccably detailed. So amazingly detailed was the statue that Dugan's mind wondered how the sculptor could have managed something so marvelous with only crude hand tools.

He walked around the monument, never one to really admire great works of art, but perplexed by this particular one, gazing at its every feature. The back of the warrior was as immaculately chiseled as the front. The muscular definition of its arms was amazing as were the veins, so realistic, protruding from his neck and forehead. A bead of sweat was emblazoned upon one side of his face.

The horse was equally as impressive as its rider. Its mouth, too, was drawn, revealing large teeth. Sweat had formed under his saddle and moisture had been forever sculpted on its sides and neck. Its mane was so meticulously chiseled that Dugan could see every hair. The sculptor made it appear that a mild breeze was blowing through its mane, so exact was his ability and skill. A string of snot ran from the horse's snout and its head was pulled to the right, the reigns tout and the bit notched firmly in its mouth.

One hoof was raised as though the horse was ready to dash into a gallop. The rider's weathered boots rested firmly in their stirrups, poised to spur the horse to run faster should the need arise.

"This has to be the most amazing statue I've ever seen. Almost human," Dugan said aloud.

Next to him stood a local Chinese man. As with many Asians, age could be very deceiving to the untrained eye. At first glance one might think he was in his forties, and in another his sixties. His complexion was clear with few lines appearing around his eyes or mouth. His light yellow skin sat tightly on his face, but his hair had a heavy gray influence and his hands the leathery look of a man that had seen many harsh winters in the mountainous regions of northern China.

"Excuse me sir, I couldn't help but overhear your comment about our statue," the Chinaman said to Dugan in near perfect English.

Dugan eyed the man warily, but soon realized he was no threat and just making casual conversation. Even though he didn't enjoy idle chit-chat, he was so fascinated with the statue, and anxious to learn more about it, that he turned to face the man who spoke to him. He could see in the man's eyes a certain wisdom that comes with age.

The Chinese gentleman continued, "We are very proud of our statue warriors here, sir. Their history is significant and means much to our people. They were discovered by villagers drilling for water a few decades ago. Our Terracotta Army has brought much prosperity to Xi'an."

Dugan's eyes narrowed and a confused look crossed his face. He listened intently to what the man had told him, but something struck him as strange. His green eyes shifted from the man to the statue, then back to the elder again.

"You said 'warriors,' as in more than one, yet I only see one here. Are there others?" Dugan asked.

The man snorted before replying, "You've never heard of the Terracotta Warriors, sir?"

"The what kind of warriors?" Dugan asked, his interest growing.

"Terracotta, sir. It is a form of earthenware. It is said the warriors were crafted by skilled sculptors in honor of our first Chinese emperor, Qin Shi Huangdi. The warriors were made to be placed with Emperor Qin to protect him in the afterlife. They were buried with the Emperor and later discovered by farmers attempting to dig a well. That is what the scientists and archeologists tell us," the man responded.

"Earthenware, huh? Like clay and stuff?" he asked.

"Yes, they have been hardened through a heat treatment process it would seem, not so different than modern artists who place clay pots in firing kilns to harden them and assure the glaze properly adhered to them," responded the stranger.

The American's interest was piqued. "You certainly speak English well and know a lot about these Terracotta Warriors. How do you know so much?"

"Ah, sir, I teach Chinese culture at the Xi'an Jiatong University and studied English while attending University at Boston College. I have been very interested in the Warriors since their discovery in 1974. Strange that over eight thousand warriors are in the pyramid crypt of Emperor Qin, yet this one has remained here all this time isn't it? For over two thousand years the Terracotta Army has gone undiscovered, while this one lone warrior and his horse have stood here in all their agony and pain."

"Yes," Dugan mused, "this one warrior remaining here is very strange. I wonder why he was left here and not taken to the same area as the others? Tell me, have you seen the other Terracotta Warriors?"

The Chinaman smiled as he replied, "Of course, sir. They are maintained by the Chinese government in one of the pyramids of Xi'an, which is not far from where we are now. It is there they stand guard and are protected from the harsh elements, quite unlike their counterpart here. They are truly a remarkable sight to behold. I highly recommend a tour of the uncovered warriors. The soldiers stand or kneel at the ready, and their horses and carriages are works of artistic grandeur. No one knows how the sculptors accomplished such amazing works.

"But to answer your first question, Mr...," he trailed off, his question lingering until Dugan answered.

"Smith," Dugan lied. "My name is Mr. Smith."

"Of course, Mr. Smith. My name is Mr. Wu, and I'm pleased to make your acquaintance. I am also happy to be able to practice my English. It isn't often I get this chance, so thank you very much for the opportunity."

Dugan nodded his head wishing to dispense with the pleasantries and carry on learning about the Terracotta Warriors. There was something about them that fascinated him. Perhaps it was his time spent in the military or participating in shadow warfare, or maybe it was the fact that he operated outside the laws of most countries. No matter the reason, he found himself enthralled and enamored with the statue.

"Anyway, Mr. Smith, our archeologists have not been able to figure out why this particular statue was left here. Oddly enough, this statue's general appearance is significantly different from those inside the pyramid," Mr. Wu said.

"How so, Mr. Wu? Since I haven't seen the other statues, can you explain what the differences are between this statue and the others?"

"Yes, of course," responded Mr. Wu. "The statues housed inside the pyramid do not have the same expressions of pain and surprise as this one. Similarly, the mounts standing with their riders do not look as pained either. The warriors stored inside appear to have been marching or practicing for some military assault. At least that is the look the sculptor, or sculptors, were attempting to depict.

But this statue, as you can see, is considerably different. His face is in agony, and the look of terror is mystifying. Also, the horse is in a peculiar position as compared to the other horses portrayed inside. This one looks as though it was about to begin a mission, while the others were sculpted to look stately and proper. The statue we see here appears...emotional. Should you choose to see the sculpted gallery in the three pits where the statues stand, you will understand what I am trying to say," Wu concluded.

"Hhhmmmm. Has there been any speculation about this particular statue and its pose?" asked Dugan. "Certainly, there has been some study and a scientific reason for it to be here and not with the others."

"Mr...Smith," began Wu again, a hint of cynicism in his voice (it was unclear to Dugan if Wu's tone was because he didn't believe his made up generic last name, or if it was directed more toward the elementary question he asked regarding the study of the statue), "of course there has been much study, but science has been able to prove the similar composition of the statues only. Scientists struggle to explain why a human would leave one statue outside while all the rest were moved indoors and buried. Human nature, Mr. Smith, cannot always be explained rationally. If that were the case, I doubt our countries would be enemies.

"So, with that, Mr. Smith, we must speculate and listen to the stories handed to us from our elders, generation after generation, as to why this warrior stands here, obviously frightened and in tremendous pain. Like every other area of the world, we have our myths and stories about things we have otherwise been unable to explain scientifically. And that is part of why this statue draws so many visitors each year."

Dugan looked at the man with more interest than he intended, but he was truly absorbed in the man's lecture. He let his eyes blanket the statue again. It was almost like it drew him in and talked to him on some unexpected spiritual plane. A mystical, far away voice seemed to tell him to "find the way, find the answer." He had no idea what that meant, but the allure of Wu's story was both mysterious and intense, a mirror of the way he had lived his life.

Dugan pushed for more information from the Chinese man. "What stories does this area tell about this statue and the Terracotta Warriors still standing in the pyramid, Mr. Wu?"

A smile crept across Wu's face as he responded, "I'm happy you've taken this interest in the Emperor's army, Mr. Smith. I am very pleased to tell you our local legend about this statue. It is also directly related to the vast Terracotta Army.

"Local legend maintains that this statue was once a 'real' man. He was a fierce soldier in Emperor Qin's army. When Qin did not have his army sent off to war against the aggressors who would bring harm to our beautiful country, he would insist that this man serve as his personal envoy to collect village taxes in the north. According to records, this warrior's name was Li Wan Zhang.

"Li was a captain, again, according to records, in the Emperor's military. Captain Li was ruthless in collecting taxes, which usually consisted of fifty percent of a village's production in whatever industry its people worked. In most cases, food was collected, in some cases clothing, and in others, animals, furniture and so on."

Dugan, his brows almost touching interrupted, "Fifty percent? You're kidding, right? How the hell could a village survive on only fifty percent of what it grew or created, especially if the harvest wasn't a good one in a particular year? This seems far-fetched to me, Mr. Wu."

"I understand your hesitation in believing our story, Mr. Smith, but please realize that the Emperor ruled with an iron fist, not like our current government that takes care of its people." Wu's eyes shifted around quickly to see if anyone was within ear shot of him as he told his story. Dugan noticed Wu's glance and understood he feared pissing off the wrong people in communist controlled China. He knew all too well that Big Brother maintained an eye in the sky and kept an ear to the ground. Anyone they regarded as a threat, or anyone who spoke out against them could possibly never be seen again.

Dugan nodded his head affirmatively to signal both his understanding of Wu's explanation and to offer the man an acknowledgement that he wouldn't press him any further about the Chinese government. He focused on Wu and the story, deciding to hold his questions until the end.

The Chinaman continued his tale, "One day this man came to collect the village's taxes, as he did each year. As you pointed out a moment ago, the year's rice harvest was not a good one. Water was scarce, and rain did not fall for days or weeks at a time. Fifty percent of the harvest would not be nearly enough for the village's people to survive the harsh winter. Everyone knew this to be true, including the Emperor and his envoy. Still, there was no negotiating the taxes and what was owed to Xi'an, which was the site of China's capitol in that era. The Emperor was known to slaughter entire villages or take the people and force them into labor camps, separating families forever. Either way, lives were destroyed, Mr. Smith.

"On the day Captain Li arrived to collect taxes, a man in his twenties or thirties met him in the road to beg forgiveness. This man's father was the village leader and doctor, the son also a village leader. Both were known for their compassion and love for their kinsman and were looked up to by all the villagers.

"As I was saying, the young man met Li in the road to beg forgiveness. It's said the road was right here where we now stand, Mr. Smith. With no pity, Captain Li struck the man down, beheading him while several villagers looked on. Also watching the slaying transpire was the man's father, Liu Xiu Chan, or Chan as he was known to everyone. Our legend states that Chan did not flinch when his son was murdered, and he openly defied Captain Li. Li told Chan that he would return the next day to collect the taxes, which, as we have already discussed, was fifty percent of the rice produced that year.

As you now know that amount of lost rice would be a death sentence for the village.

"Apparently, Chan told Li if he returned the next day he would never leave again. Naturally, Li returned to collect what was owed his master. And, as you probably guessed, Chan refused to pay. It is said that Li was reaching for his sword to reunite Chan with his son, but Chan cast a spell upon the warrior. That warrior is what you see today, Mr. Smith."

Wu's last words hung in the air as Dugan tried to digest the tale. He held his questions for a moment longer while Wu's eyes darted around again still searching for eavesdroppers and those who might not want China's non-state supported stories leaving its borders. The Chinaman took a seat on a bench just behind the statue and waited for his one man audience to ask any question he might have.

Dugan listened patiently as Wu told him of the statue's history. He asked, "You said this statue was Captain Li? I don't understand. You mean this statue is an artist's rendition of Li, correct?"

Wu chuckled nervously then responded, "No, Mr. Smith. Local legend says this statue id literally Captain Li. It would seem that the spell cast on him by Chan turned him to hardened clay. He looks to be stone, but samples of the statue confirm that he is hardened clay."

"But you said Chan was a doctor and village leader, Mr. Wu. How would he know about stuff like witchcraft and spells?" Dugan asked.

This question made Wu laugh a little louder than he would have liked, and he was forced to look around again. He breathed a sigh of relief when he, once again, didn't detect any unwanted ears in their general vicinity. Wu's hands made an uncomfortable wringing motion before he answered Dugan's question.

"Mr. Smith, your American is showing. Your history is only a couple of hundred years old. Our history is thousands of years old. We believe man's origins are here in China despite what many believe about Africa being the birthplace of mankind. Doctors have, throughout history, engaged in herbal and ritual medicine, not just the modern version of invading the human body. Mr. Chan would have been no different and surely studied those spiritual and herbal arts that would help his kinsmen heal from whatever physical or mental ailments they may have had. It would be safe to presume he was proficient in his medicinal practices or the villagers would not have continued to go to him when they were ill. Records indicate that he was the village doctor for several decades."

"I guess," Dugan asked, "I've missed the most obvious question then, Mr. Wu. How old is this statue?"

"Yes, that is a question many will ask first, Mr. Smith, but you have asked some very good questions before this one, so your oversight is understandable. Archeologists approximate the age of the statue to be twenty-three hundred years old. It is very ancient, but not as ancient as many things are in China, sir."

"Twenty-three hundred years old!" exclaimed Dugan. "How can this be, Mr. Wu? Look at this statue. It doesn't even look remotely that old. Surely, after twenty-three hundred years of standing in the sun, rain, snow and wind, pieces would have eroded and decayed or even fallen off. You can't possibly believe this local legend can you?"

"Of course these tales are nothing more than legend, Mr. Smith. None of them are to be believed. I am an academic and do not believe in folklore and, how do Americans say, old wives tales." As he finished replying, Dugan saw Wu wringing his hands again, his agitation and discomfort more apparent. Something in his response and tone told him that the man wasn't telling the truth about his belief in the supernatural.

"Mr. Wu, it's apparent that you have a very analytical mind, so why are you uncomfortable when telling me about the magic involved in this fantasy tale?" asked Dugan.

Wu allowed his voice to drop considerably, "Mr. Smith, what you call magic, we call reality. Magic is a word applied to those things humans can't explain. It's an easy way out of doing research or attempting to get to the bottom of things. In this case, Chan's medicine was strong and was anchored in a spirit that was as fierce as any warrior. You see, in the days of ancient medicine, one had to demonstrate a very strong resolve as an apprentice before learning the medicinal ways in China. It is said that Chan was a man slight of stature but powerful of spirit. It is also said he was kind and gentle but stood strong in his determination to help his fellow villagers. He was allowed to learn the art of being a doctor. I think it is unfortunate that these ways are only now being rediscovered in my own country, sir."

"How, then, did he use his medicine to turn a man to stone, Mr. Wu?" Dugan continued.

"Not a man, Mr. Smith... 'men.' He turned an entire army to clay after Li murdered his son in cold blood. Our lore tells us he held a small piece of jewelry that he had worked his spiritual magic into before casting it upon Li and the army of Xi'an. It has been told that Emperor Qin was devastated for a considerable time after the loss of the majority of his army who were in the area when the spell was cast. Legend tells us that Chan wished for the entire army in the area to be turned to clay. It would seem he managed to pull this off, Mr. Smith. But, like I said, this is all legend," Wu replied.

"A piece of jewelry," Dugan said before continuing. "What kind of jewelry, and what did it do? I'm afraid I don't understand."

"That is a mystery to us, Mr. Smith. We only know it was a piece of jewelry. What it looks like is unknown to us. It would be most interesting to learn of its make-up and appearance. It appears to have been used as a focal point for Chan, or something used to channel the spell, or magic as you call it, not so dissimilar to the western version of a 'magic wand.' From what I understand, Chinese doctors would cast those spells from the object used to channel their medicine or magic, if you will, and the object held a part of the spirit of the doctor. In other words, the part of him used to cast the spell was *locked inside the object until it could be reversed, should the doctor choose to reverse it. In the English language you have come to know the word 'charm' as a piece of jewelry. My understanding is the word comes from the world of magic; a charm is used to bring about a desired outcome. In this case the outcome would be to change a group of people into something other than flesh and blood. Again, from what I've read and studied, a person's spirit would have to be very strong and the channeling of one's personal chi something that had been practiced for many, many years. Chan must have been just such a person!"*

Dugan's mind dwelled on the possibility that Wu's legend held some truth. He had seen too much in his time to discount all things magical or paranormal. Once, while running a job just outside New Orleans, he'd seen a voodoo priestess cast a spell, or invoke the spirits in what she called gris-gris, over a doll. That doll represented a man being held in the same room. He was bound, gagged and forced to watch the whole thing transpire. When she had finished chanting over the doll, she picked up a pin and stuck it in the heart. The bound man's eyes widened to the size of half-dollars. Within seconds his lifeless head slumped to his chest, the man dead of a heart attack. It had been one of the cleanest hits Dugan had ever seen and it both fascinated and scared the shit out of him.

He couldn't help but allow his mind to float around the prospect that the statue and the eight thousand others of which Wu had spoken, were, at one time, living, sentient beings. He had also mentioned that the spell could be reversed. This last fact is what mesmerized him because of the opportunities it posed.

"Mr. Wu, I have another question," Dugan said. He watched one man who had taken an interest in him some twenty feet away, but Dugan suspected the man was more interested in his non-Asian features than the conversation he was having with Wu. "I realize you told me you don't know why this statue, Captain Li as you called him, was left outside, but has anyone ever attempted to reunite him with the rest of the Terracotta Warriors?"

Wu took a long, deep breath before exhaling loudly then replied, "Of course the Chinese have always been interested in protecting their heritage and art, Mr. Smith. This statue is no different than any other, and the Chinese have attempted to move it several times since the discovery of the other warriors in 1974. Each time it has been tried, however, mysterious circumstances have arisen around the individuals attempting to relocate it. But, please, Mr. Smith" he said almost apologetically, "understand that Asians generally, and Chinese specifically, are very superstitious. As a result of our superstition, we attribute oddities to our lore, most especially when that lore involves spells and the like."

The American nodded his head in understanding. "So, tell me what happened to the people who tried to move the statue, Mr. Wu."

Wu's eyes dropped to the ground for a few seconds as he put together his thoughts and considered his words. "Since 1974, the government has attempted to move the statue a number of times. Each time it was tried something strange would happen. On two occasions movers had heart attacks on the spot. Another time, the statue was strapped to a truck to be moved the next day. The individual who placed the straps on the statue went home that night and took his own life. There have been rumors of others who have died or killed themselves after coming in contact with the rider or his steed. A couple of individuals reported hearing voices in their heads telling them how to take their own lives. Family members tried to calm them down, but each time they successfully committed suicide. It's really quite tragic, but again, it is all circumstantial and steeped in lore and legend."

The wheels spun in Dugan's head to the point that he became moderately dizzy. Another question burned at the back of his mind, but he hesitated to ask since he didn't know Wu personally. But he had learned long ago an itch left unscratched would fester and be scratched in time. He figured he might as well dig in.

"How fascinating this all is, Mr. Wu!" exclaimed Dugan. His enthusiasm was probably a little over-acted, but a large portion of it was real. "Tell me, is it known whether a spell or curse like this has ever happened in China before or since?"

Wu chuckled quietly then replied, "A very intriguing question, Mr. Smith. I wonder why you would ask such a thing?" He allowed the question to hang in the air for almost a full minute before continuing.

"I guess it doesn't matter, as I'm sure your musing is purely academic. Yes, there have been some documented cases of people being turned to stone and clay here in China over the centuries. It's a strange but remarkable piece of our folklore that few outside the country's boundaries have any knowledge of. Most are familiar with our fixation on dragons, but few know about the spiritual scientists that have always lived here.

Their mythos is really not so different than the western version of Merlin the Magician, Mr. Smith. And our stories of turning people to stone fall in line with the western story of Medusa. Isn't that amazing? It would seem the human mind is capable of analogous modes of thought that do not bend to the will of country's leaders or borders. This is one part of the human condition that has always aroused my intellect, sir."

The American tried to measure how much longer he should press Wu. He knew there was much research he could do on his own, but having a professor of Chinese culture at his immediate disposal was something he wanted to take advantage of. The internet provided little uncommon knowledge of China, of that he knew.

"You mentioned that a spell such as this could be reversed. My last question, Mr. Wu is this – in your ancient lore, have any of those spells ever been reversed?" asked Dugan.

Wu loudly swallowed some spittle, clearly nervous with the direction of the conversation, but the side of him that loved teaching about Chinese culture would not allow his tongue to be silenced. A drop of sweat formed on his forehead and rolled gently down the side of his face.

"It is rumored, Mr. Smith, that on one occasion a spell akin to this one was reversed. There is a tale told to mischievous children about a man who was turned to stone then brought back, but when he was brought back he was not a man. He remained stone and was evil personified. The child's story was that he slaughtered unmercifully anyone who got in his way, including small children. Obviously, this is only an old wife's tale told to misbehaving children. Mothers and fathers alike have told the story to children and threaten to call the stone man to their homes if children do not behave properly."

Dugan nodded his head again, then asked, "Mr. Wu, would you mind showing me the Terracotta Warriors in the pyramid, that is, if you have time and are willing? I would be honored if you would accompany me to the terracotta crypt and help me learn more about your country's fantastic collection."

Wu considered Dugan's request then said, "I wish I could, Mr. Smith, but I'm afraid I must be leaving. I have a class to teach very soon. You needn't look far for the exhibit. The pyramid stands just two hundred meters from where we are now. Follow this path down the stairs, and you will see it. At the entrance you may purchase a ticket to see our beautiful Terracotta Army. I wish you the best of luck in furthering your learning about the Terracotta Warriors, sir. It's been an honor discussing them with you." With that, Wu turned and walked away.

As Dugan stood there scratching his chin while watching the Chinese professor walk away, he wondered how much truth could be found in the legend. Legends were, after all, conceived from factual events. What if..., he asked himself? He had seen many strange and bizarre things before and would again if he lived long enough, but the potential compensation for controlling such an army was priceless if the spell was real and could be reversed.

He allowed himself a few short seconds of speculation before he began walking down the path to find the pyramid and Terracotta Warriors. The path led him past tall, green trees and immaculately pruned shrubbery. His hand grabbed the rail as he descended the stairs Wu had described. As he came around a bend, an immense, white pyramid towered above him. Never in all his years, had he seen architecture that could match what faced him at that moment. The sun reflected off the side of the massive structure as he stood, mouth agape, staring at it.

After he took a few moments to gaze at the pyramid, he walked to the front of the entrance to purchase a ticket. A mob of foreigners stood in line in their respective tour groups waiting to get inside. Hosts of hawkers lined the area selling souvenirs of the Warriors and Emperor Qin's burial site.

He hadn't given much thought as to why he had become so entranced by the lone statue in Xi'an, or why he was being drawn to the pyramid to view the rest of the Terracotta Army. Simply stated, he knew there was something there that spoke to him, but what that thing was he couldn't articulate.

The throng of visitors made their way inside to see the three large pits and innumerable clay soldiers. Dugan's mind was awhirl with the absolute enormity of the display. Why would anyone choose to sculpt all of these life sized warriors? Were they forced to create them to protect Emperor Qin in the afterlife as recent science had suggested, or was Mr. Wu's tale of a more sinister motive the truer reason for the inordinate, and almost vain, spectacle of art? What he did know, somewhere deep in his gut, was that this room resonated with life beyond the tourists with whom he walked. Dugan was struck by the intensity of the place and noticed others looking uncomfortably at the warriors' prowess.

He wandered around the location for five hours, having lost track of time and almost forgetting the reason he was in Xi'an to begin with. Arms trading could not wait, and his connection to some rebels in the northern tier of China had funded his bank account beyond measure. He knew they planned some sort of assault against the communist government, but he hadn't asked any details and wanted to be out of the country before the shit hit the fan. His spirit wanted him to remain for a while longer, but his mind told him he had to leave.

On the way out of the museum, he stopped and purchased a small replica of a Terracotta Warrior for his desk back in New York City. He hoped the small replica would help him recapture some of the awe he felt while viewing the warriors. Little did he know that they would invade his heart, mind and soul to the point of obsession. Focusing on his normal tasks would be difficult and require tremendous discipline, but in his free time he would allow his mind to drift back to Xi'an. And he would research the legend of the Terracotta Warriors and the spell that many Chinese believed bound them for eternity. Something deep within him told him that the legend was steeped in truth.

Over two years he researched, and paid others to research for him, the legend of the mystical doctor and the Terracotta Warriors. At first there was little progress, but recently some revelations had come to light about connections to China, Egypt and ancient Maya. He began feeling hopeful when his research team had begun delivering news about the connections, especially given his tour through a pyramid to see the Terracotta Army; a pyramid he entered without question, so absorbed was he to see what was inside. Still, it wasn't until someone stumbled upon the connection of the cartouche to all three that things began to take shape. One of his researchers discovered an ancient Chinese cartouche on display in a museum in Beijing that was believed to have originated in Xi'an.

The question of how a cartouche housing a magical spell wound up in Mexico City was troublesome and problematic, but was soon revealed *through discovery and luck. Research had also dispelled the notion that Norsemen were the first to land on the western shores of America. It was apparent to Dugan that the doctor and his Xi'an tribesmen fled first into Mongolia then Russia, or at least in part. Some of them reportedly crossed the Bering Strait into Alaska before continuing their migration to Central America. Perhaps it took a couple of generations for this migration to happen, but it was obvious to Dugan the influence of the Chinese in American, Mexican and Central American Indian cultures.*

Dugan also surmised that part of the clan had ventured west into India, through the Middle East and into Egypt. Not only were pyramids being discovered at a significant rate around the world, most especially in the United States and into Latin America, but the similarities between the three different region's pyramids in question were uncanny. Additionally, evidence of cartouches had been found along both routes from China to Egypt and China to Latin America.

His team of researchers vetted every plausible prospect regarding the migration of Chan and his people. Needless to say, when they found a significant amount of the Mexican population in the Yucatan Peninsula with Chinese sir names, they were all astounded. Upon discovering certain nuances within languages of Native American tribes and Chinese Mandarin, they knew they were on to something. But when it was revealed that particular DNA strands were the same amongst Chinese people in Xi'an, Alaskan Eskimos, several of the western Native Americans and Mexicans all the way to the Yucatan, Dugan was convinced his hunch had been correct all along.

Even harder than connecting all the intercontinental dots would be locating the item, the cartouche he suspected, that contained Chan's spell. He was convinced the cartouche was the charm used when Chan cast the spell, especially since similar jewels could be found in all three areas of the world his research team were scouring. Once found, figuring out how to reverse the spell and control the most powerful army in the world would be the priority.

Confirming it was the cartouche used in the incantation was a reach, but it was obvious the knowledge of their manufacture was passed along to each region where villagers had migrated. Noticeable to Dugan was that Chan had apprentices in his midst, but the strongest of his knowledge found its way to the Yucatan, which must have meant Chan began migrating to the West. The magic used while wielding the charm had been reported throughout Mayan history.

How far Chan made it was still a mystery, but Dugan was convinced his direct bloodline had continued into the Americas. Everything, in his mind and according to his researchers, pointed him to the region. Had Chan been able to make the trek all the way to southeastern Mexico himself? That was doubtful in Dugan's mind, but there was no uncertainty that the cartouche and its secret would have been passed on to someone else in his line. The legend held that his son was killed by Captain Li, but he knew that small villages were rife with blood relations. Asians were beholden to passing secrets along to family members unlike other cultures who would pass along secrets to non-family members if loyalties were exhibited.

An announcement was made over the intercom that his flight would be boarding in approximately twenty minutes. He was still pissed that he couldn't take a direct flight to Monterrey, but resigned himself to connecting through Dallas. *Hopefully, that fucked up airport won't have a tornado circling the top of it like it usually does. Seems like every time I go through there the airport gets shut down and another mobile home gets destroyed*, he thought to himself.

Dugan had really wanted to take his private jet to Mexico, but he would be flying under an alias to avoid detection. He had chartered a private jet to his destination from Monterrey though, and that made him a little happier about the situation. The cartouche would be in his possession, and a lot of loose ends would be cut off soon enough.

He walked to the restroom to relieve himself then ventured to a Starbuck's to buy a cup of coffee. It would be a long travel day for him, and he needed to work through a few more details in his mind, most especially would be reversing the incantation. Finding a family member wouldn't be an issue, as the DNA strains had already been proven, but how the spell would be undone posed a much bigger problem. Should the legends prove true, knowledge passed down through the family could possibly be found in either practice or in tradition. Either way, he fully intended to unlock the secret and become a multi-millionaire in the process.

Joining him in Monterrey would be that crass son of a bitch, Buddy Smith. If he wasn't the man working to land him the cash with the Christians In Action, he would have put a bullet in his head a long time ago. He knew the U.S. government had been following some of his dealings globally for quite some time, and Smith had been one he suspected of keeping tabs on him. Having the knowledge that he was being watched had been beneficial to the point that it forced him to be even more careful in his dealings in the shadow world, but it didn't mean that at some point in time he wouldn't torture that idiot and make him beg for his life.

Sharing much of the knowledge about the cartouche and Terracotta Warriors with Smith had pained him, but he recognized how ridiculous the story of the curse would seem to the uninitiated. Dugan needed an advocate in order to sell his wares, and while the story was far-fetched, he knew the United States government had invested in the black arts on several occasions. If for one moment they thought they could get the upper hand on the Russians and Chinese, they would pay handsomely. Of special interest to the Brotherhood of Allied Capitalists, otherwise known as the U.S. military, would be taking something from China that was inherently theirs.

Hypocritical bastards that his countrymen were, he accepted the fact that they were opportunists of the highest order.

There was one thing that no one had taken into account, no one, that was, except him. It was that one little thing that would be the game changer and make him the most powerful man in the world, and it was that one thing he would keep to himself a while longer.

The gate attendant announced that his American Airlines flight would begin boarding those passengers flying first class, uniformed military and those requiring special assistance. Also, those flying with small children were invited to board at that time. Dugan shook his head at the feigned politeness of the gesture, knowing the airlines didn't give two shits about anyone they were now asking to board the aircraft; they only cared about their money. He laughed as he thought, *hell, that's what I care about too. Maybe after I make this score I'll start my own airline. Nah, after this score, people will be asking ME if they can start an airline.*

Somewhere Between Reality and Death
July 21, 2013 5:17 P.M.

A half-moon hung in the night sky. In the distance smoke wafted from the center of a building. Warm wind pushed its way around and over the building forcing the smoke to undulate like a spineless exotic dancer. A few other buildings sported similar smoke pillars from their rooftops, but no flame could be seen. The roar of an air assault squadron could be heard in the distance.

No light escaped any of the windows of the buildings and homes. Only the moon offered any illumination. The Watcher could hear no sound accept that of the wind whipping around the buildings and across his face. Scattered about the area he saw the remains from what appeared to be a war time attack.

A young boy lay on his back, his body contorted and awkward, and his backpack hanging loosely from his torso. Blood seeped from his chest, nose and mouth, yet his hand twitched as though clawing for something, possibly clinging to a life now lost, or perhaps a can of food he wanted to take to his family. From the backpack a "tic-tic-tic" could be heard.

To the boy's right a lone black man lay face down. His chest wasn't moving, his breath non-existent. One leg, however, still moved also clinging to life like the child's hand. The leg crept back and forth, its knee trying to lift the flaccid body. Had the Watcher not known the man was dead, the scene would have been comical.

On her side, just a few feet from the twitchy-legged black man lay a woman with a black burka covering her entire body. No breath passed from her nose or mouth, but her eyes fluttered open and shut, the repetition very strange. The Watcher looked at her in silent wonder, the confusion mounting in his brain.

All around lay bodies, some recognizable, some not, but all had two things in common, death and movement of sorts. The amount of death was beyond The Watcher's comprehension. One such body, a middle aged man, sat propped against a shack of a building, a shoe on one foot, the other foot missing altogether. Jagged bone protruded from the stump just above where an ankle used to be. Remarkably, there was just a small pool of blood beneath the destroyed appendage. The man's jaw worked up and down; the white of his eyes was the only color visible in their sockets.

The Watcher looked down at his own feet and saw empty shell casings everywhere. On his back he could feel the weight of a grenade launcher, its feel giving him a gratifying sense of security. There was no heat he could feel from the barrel of the launcher, so he was certain the destruction of the buildings had nothing to do with him specifically. In fact, he was struggling to understand where he was and what he was doing there. It was apparent to him that he had been engaged in mortal combat, but he had no memory of doing so.

Utter silence and a clear sense of being alone struck him, as did a sudden urge to run. He realized he didn't know where to go or how to remove himself from the macabre scene. Confusion began to seep into his mind and desperation forced his heartbeat to quicken.

Somewhere behind him he heard a low, gurgling moan. The Watcher turned to see where the sound had come from, but he couldn't find the source. His feet came alive as his brain screamed at him to leave, but each time he took a step a body blocked his way. For as far as he could see in every direction human remains littered the roads and sidewalks. And no matter what direction he turned, behind him he would hear that low, gurgling moan.

His heart sped up even more and his breathing accelerated. He couldn't scream for help because his vocal chords had tightened. For a moment he thought he would hyperventilate, so sure was he that the sound behind him was getting a little closer. He spun on his heel to check his six but nothing moved. On shaky legs he raised his M16A4 and looked down the scope mounted to the modified receiver. He depressed the infrared sights as he spun his body three hundred sixty degrees, but the red dot couldn't find a target. A tense finger rested on the trigger that would deliver a burst of death so fast nothing would have time to react. At least that was The Watcher's hope.

He closed his eyes for a few seconds in order to calm himself. He dropped to one knee, making himself smaller in the event that he was in the line of a sniper's target. Being on one knee made him uncomfortable; the street had become a crypt and he an unwelcomed visitor. He wasn't a superstitious man, but there was something about the sight and smell of death that always made him anxious, even if he was the one creating it.

A shuffling sound from his left forced him to spin on his knee, his rifle leveled and his eye focused on the lens of his Nikon scope. Its six-time zoom eye box technology enabled him to see a target over a mile away, but this night he saw nothing save dead bodies and the night's shadows. His desert BDU's stuck to his skin as the sweat seeped from every pore. As his mind raced he could hear his heart pounding in his ears.

Given his battle dress uniform and the architecture of the smoldering buildings, The Watcher figured he was in the Middle East, although the more he looked around, the more he questioned his location. He had zero recollection of arriving at the scene and no memory of the attack that had taken the life of so many. Further still, he presumed his locale to be Iraq, but some of the dead didn't fit the area. The black man and topless black woman with a fruit basket replete with spilled jackfruit and papaya didn't compute in his brain.

Directly behind him he heard another shuffle followed by an unnatural raspy breath. He turned as quickly as he heard the sound but something collapsed on his shoulder and intertwined itself in the strap holding his grenade launcher. His eyes locked onto the source of the sound and the 'thing' on his shoulder. A hand! A hand connected to the body of the young Islamic boy wearing the backpack. Something stuck in his throat as the corpse's lips pulled back into a demonic grin, blood slowly dripping from his mouth. In a split second he recognized the face as the young boy he'd shot in Mosul. "This can't be real," he tried to tell himself. "I must be dreaming!"

The corpse exhibited inhuman strength. He slung The Watcher some twenty feet and watched with passing interest as his body fell hard to the road, the wind knocked out of him. His teeth rattled in his head. Black dots sparkled across his field of vision – those dots that form when a person takes a hard shot to the head.

The Watcher shook his head trying to regain his senses. In the silence of the evening he could hear more shuffling and movement all around him. His throat was parched as adrenaline coursed through his veins. He could feel his hand trembling and legs stiffen even as his brain screamed "GET UP!" With considerable effort he stood.

Everywhere around him he heard whispers, "Evers... Evers... Evers." Each time he turned to pinpoint where the sounds were coming from, they would stop. A few seconds would pass before they would start again, "Evers... Evers... Evers."

"Where's my team?" he asked, finally able to speak. "Where the hell are all the people? What the fuck is going on here?" His brain swam in confusion as his heart continued to pound blood through his body. For a few moments he thought he would pass out. Never before in his life had he been so frightened. Never had he been in an area so filled with death. And never in his life had he feared what the dead would do to him. The Watcher had been the bringer of death; now he was death's hunted.

"Evers... Evers... Evers." The whispers called out again. He wanted to slap both hands over his ears but he knew that act of contrition would do little to stop him from hearing the voices. As he looked around at the slain, he noticed something intimately familiar with each of them. Finally, it dawned on him who all these people were. Each had been one of his victims. Each had died by his hands.

From his right came more shuffling. This time the black man with the ruptured larynx he'd killed in Uganda walked toward him. The man's eye sockets were empty, but their blackness was fixed on him. Like the youngster before him, his mouth peeled back to reveal a hideous smile. Something about the smile told The Watcher the corpse was hungry, but for what he couldn't say.

"What the hell is going on?" he asked no one in particular. He fought to control the panting pressuring his lungs as he again leveled his assault rifle. Touching the laser sights on the trigger activated the beam. A red dot rested on the corpse's forehead. As hard as The Watcher was breathing the dot held steady, just between the intended target's eyes.

A grossly disturbing cackle came from the black man's mouth. It was throaty and forced because his larynx had been crushed. Popping sounds followed the laugh, the result of crushed cartilage and bone. The Watcher felt a chill run up his spine as the sound drifted across the hot desert breeze.

One more deep breath and an exhale followed by a squeezing of the trigger and the corpse's head exploded. Pieces of skull and gray brain matter sprayed in a one hundred eighty degree arc. There was little blood after the burst of 5.56mm rounds traveling at twenty-eight hundred feet per second hit him. A disgustingly noticeable "V" formed where the top of his head used to be. So sudden had the rounds hit him that his head didn't snap backward, but held steadfast on his neck. The body made a resounding thud as it hit the pavement.

"Evers... Evers... Evers," he heard again. The sound of his name whispered over and over made him want to scream. He spun in time to see a Sunni Arab man, his turban askew, reach for him. The Watcher recognized him as a man he'd shot several years prior. He was purported to be a rebel leader with direct ties to AQI, Al Qaida in Iraq. A double tap to the man's chest had brought about an abrupt end to his reign of terror. But now The Watcher stared at a dead man's hand reaching for him.

The corpse's raised arm slammed down on The Watcher's head followed by a fist to his ribs. Air was driven from The Watcher's lungs and a new blanket of stars clouded his vision. His head was pulled back as the dead Sunni's fingers wrapped under his chin. The corpse's fiendish smile was similar to those of the others. It opened its mouth and a murky hiss streamed, "Evers."

Somehow he managed to escape the grip the Sunni had on him. He rolled to his back and frantically began looking around. From every direction bodies walked or crawled toward him. Each of the corpses called out, "Evers" in unison. The "ssssss" slithered across their tongues like that of a serpent.

His hand found the Colt .45 he kept strapped to his leg. With machine-like precision he pulled it from the holster and pointed it at the Sunni. Without any thought he double tapped the Arab in the chest, the two holes appearing next to the two he had planted in him the first time he had shot him. The corpse dropped to both knees, looking down at his chest with glassy eyes. No blood trickled from the new wounds as he rose to his feet again.

The Watcher was aghast. He felt a hand grab his neck and clamp down. A flowing black burka stood next to him, bare feet protruding under the hem. The woman's free hand reached for her veil and pulled it down displaying a gray face and sharp teeth. On his right he felt another hand grasp his wrist with an ungodly strength.

Sheer terror ravaged his body and brain. Another cold, steel-like hand grasped the other wrist and he dropped the .45. All around him the corpses closed, their feet shuffling across the pavement. Sharp teeth from the Muslim woman bit into his arm and warm blood flowed from a vein onto her chin.

At long last The Watcher managed a throaty shriek. He began thrashing about attempting to escape the hold the walking dead had on him. More teeth sank into the other arm and a fresh scream filled the air. Blood began pooling on either side of him as other corpses closed the distance, the smell of iron-rich plasma drawing them.

"Evers... Evers... Evers," the dead called. The Watcher kicked his boot clad feet as hard as he could but it did no good. He felt another dead hand grasp his ankle. The frigid fingers dug into his skin through his BDU pants and his body began to convulse from shock and the adrenaline rush.

As the dead feasted on his limbs, he saw a man approaching him. This man looked to be of the living, his color good, his hair white and his face somber. In his hand he held a silver jewel. A shimmer of moonlight reflected off its surface. Strange, foreign words rolled off his tongue. He seemed to be in command of the cadavers. And it was then that The Watcher recognized the man: Dugan.

He screamed again as teeth sank into his neck.

Buddy sat at a Starbuck's table sipping an ice Frappuccino while replaying the events of the last week in his mind. Communication between he and Dugan had been intermittent, but he'd finally received word that Young Buck hadn't been killed. That news lifted a huge weight from his shoulders and gave him at least one good night's rest.

It was more than obvious to him that Dugan wanted to eliminate anyone and everyone associated, directly or loosely, with this mission. What was vague was how, and most importantly when, he planned on the process of elimination. Dugan was an evil bastard, and had no qualms when it came to killing, but he wasn't stupid. He would have a plan he would execute, and he would do so carefully and systematically.

He knew when he arrived in Mexico he would have to be wary in his dealings with the seasoned veteran. Not only was he a dangerous man, he was also connected. His contacts in D.C. alone rivaled those of Buddy's, and that made him terrifying.

Smith's problem with Evers was an even bigger one. If both of them got out of this situation alive his role as double-crosser was going to be hard to explain. Sometimes doing the right thing hurts good people. At least this was how he reasoned his actions in his own head. But he knew Buck wouldn't take this lying down. He didn't want to have to be part and parcel to Evers' murder, but he'd made those hard choices before and lived another day to talk about them.

Still, he had dragged Young Buck into this shit storm and he felt like he owed him some allegiance. Hell, truth be known, he owed him a lot more than just allegiance, and at the end of the day, Evers was probably his one and only real friend in the world.

He put the Frappuccino to his mouth and sipped. "This stuff would be so much better with some smoky Agave dropped over the side. I've got to send my resume to the folks in Seattle. I'd be a heck of a gourmet coffee chef, or whatever the hell they call themselves, if they'd give me a shot. Shit, I'd have every drunk in a ten thousand mile radius lined up to spend six dollars on a pick-me-up at these fucking stores," he laughed and said aloud.

A mature lady in her late fifties, who wore her beauty in a way young women could not, sat at a table across from him. Her white slacks, silk, flower patterned blouse and a hat befitting a woman at Club Med rather than an airport, gave an air of class and societal status. His foul diction had gotten her attention. Buddy winked and blew her a kiss. She rolled her eyes, sighed and pretended to read her paper, but he caught her looking his way two or three times.

"Ma'am, I don't usually apologize for the things I say, but I'd like to afford you that today. I beg your forgiveness for my language. Furthermore, I'd like to ask you your name and for a phone number, if you're not spoken for that is. If you are spoken for then just make up a name; I'm okay with that," he drawled in his north Georgia accent.

"Sir, I find your appearance, your language and your accent offensive. I wouldn't give you the time of day, much less my name or telephone number. It wouldn't bother me in the slightest if you never addressed me again," she replied, her notably thick New England dialect annunciating every syllable.

"Oh, I don't believe that for a minute, lady. As a matter of fact, I think you kind of like this ole country boy's accent and appearance. You know what else? I think you desire a little adventure in your life, and I'm just the excitement you need," Buddy finished with an enormously toothy smile on his face.

"Well, I've never," her New England accent pronouncing the word 'ne-vah,' "been spoken to in such a manner. You, sir, are boorish, crude and rash. Personally, I think you should spend time learning some manners before you speak to another person. Furthermore, your dress is of one that I would expect to find on the streets of a major metropolitan city. I'm really quite surprised that you don't have a cup in your hand begging for change. THAT'S what I think," she sniffed and raised an eyebrow, obviously happy with her impromptu rejoinder.

Buddy guffawed as he reached behind his head and pulled his long hair off his neck. He eased forward over the table, his arms folded in front of him. "You want to know what else I think, ma'am? I believe you'd like me to meet you at some point and time, take you out on the town and show you some fun. Ole Buddy knows a woman looking for amusement when he sees her, and you've got that look in your eyes. You are one hell of a lovely lady and if you go the rest of this day without someone telling you that, well, that would just be a goddam shame."

Blood rushed to the lady's prim face. A reticent glow crossed over her and a perceptible relaxing of her shoulders made her seem at least a little vulnerable. She licked her lips then smiled. "You certainly have a way with words...Buddy...that's indisputable. I'm inclined to believe you have a way with women despite your hard outer shell, vile language and ruddy dress." She pulled a pen from her purse and scrawled down a number and a name on a piece of paper then handed to him. "I live in Woburn, Massachusetts, sir. Should you find yourself in New England please give me a call and perhaps I will show you around my lovely city and provide you with some culture. And just so you are aware, I'm no longer spoken for. I'm a widow."

Buddy looked at the paper then folded it and put it into his shirt pocket. For a few seconds he looked into her eyes then gave her a wry smile. "Why, Pamela, I won't lie and tell you I haven't become acquainted with several women in my day. You and I are both old enough to know that we all have certain needs. I'm just happy you have fallen for my southern charm."

"Come now, Buddy. Do you honestly think I've fallen for that wonderful southern accent and your slick vocabulary? I'm an educated woman and know when I'm being gamed," she primly replied. Her words, as harsh as they came out, weren't convincing. "I would love to continue this discussion, but I fear it's almost time for my flight."

He grabbed her right hand and kissed it. "Good day to you, Pamela. That really is such a regal name. In fact, it's almost as lovely as you. When I get over your way, I'm going to give you a call and show you the time of your life."

She rose from her seat and giggled like a teenage girl at the compliment. Her posture was perfect, her shoulders back and both her hands in front of her waist holding her Louis Vuitton purse. Pamela bent her knees and kissed Buddy on a scruffy cheek before turning and walking toward her gate.

Buddy watched Pamela sachet toward her gate, her heels knocking against the tile floor. He paid especially close attention to her lithe frame and long legs. A last smile touched his eyes and he said to himself, "You sly old fox, you've still got it. Almost had her talked right out of those panties. Yep, I'm definitely going to Massachusetts when I get back." He stopped for a moment then mumbled, "If I get back."

He forced his mind away from his new love interest and refocused himself on the matter at hand. Dugan was heading to Monterrey and he had gotten word back that Evers had been captured. Something told him that Dugan's stake in this game was more than monetary gain, but he couldn't figure out what it was. It was obvious to everyone involved in this strange deal that he would do whatever was necessary to assure acquisition of the jewel.

All he could do now was hope and pray that he got to Mexico in time to avoid a complete disaster. If Dugan escaped with the cartouche, who the hell knew what would happen? Most importantly, what would become of the world if he got away?

Monterrey, Mexico
General Mariano Escobedo
International Airport
July 21, 2013 10:27 P.M.

Dugan smiled as he disembarked the 757 Boeing aircraft that had taken him from Dallas-Fort Worth's international airport to Monterrey. As usual, he had been delayed, but he made the best of it by sipping on gin and tonics and thinking about how his plan was taking shape. Tomorrow would be the cliché day of reckoning. All of his hard work, research and truckloads of money spent would be worth it once he got his hands on the talisman.

He had spoken with Rafael after he arrived in Dallas. The Mexican was making him a little nervous with his conversational distance. In fact, his mumbling and rambling had grown more than just sporadic since he had taken hold of the cartouche. He figured Rafael would make a play for more money or maybe attempt to keep the cartouche for himself. This was a part of the calculation he knew was real and problematic.

There were still so many unknowns and variables in the equation. Risky math wasn't a subject he enjoyed; he preferred to understand the situation, remove anything (or anybody) that created "noise" and solve the problem. A plan and a roadmap to success had always been something he prided himself in having, but the position he found himself in lately felt loose. He wasn't controlling the controllable and that made him exceedingly more agitated.

Like so many public places in the Mexico, General Mariano Escobedo Airport was immaculate. The carpeted areas at the gate were phenomenally clean even though they were trampled daily. The marble floor hallways were highly polished and spotless. Stores were tidy and the people friendly. This was one aspect of the country Dugan liked. He knew a little bit of money would buy a hell of a lot of happiness in Mexico, and the money spent to keep this aging airport looking like new was nominal by comparison.

Dugan carried the one bag that he had managed to stuff into the overhead compartment. As a frequent traveler he'd learned how to pack lightly and avoid the problems of checked luggage altogether. He had debated with himself before leaving New York about taking a cab to the hotel or renting a car. His lifestyle had made the decision fairly easy given the mission and the potential for a speedy getaway.

After leaving the rental center he turned northwest and drove the two-and-a-half kilometers to the Crowne Plaza Hotel. He checked in and dropped his bags in his room on the fourth floor. When he finished taking note of the layout of the room, he drew the curtains on the sliding glass door and stepped on the balcony. The night air was warm and the city buzzed with traffic.

He considered going to bed but decided to hit the hotel bar instead. The hostess seated him at a booth he requested in the back of the shadow filled room. He ordered his favorite single malt scotch from the bartender, a highland Royal Lochnager 12 Year Old. Finding it on the drink menu made him happy. As he sipped, he took special pleasure in tasting the spice and hint of sandalwood. There had been times when a higher end hotel bar would surprise him with their drink menu and this was one of them, even though the Crowne Plaza wouldn't be considered "higher end." He delighted in the fragrance and mellow taste of the liquor so much he decided the find was a good omen.

Dugan eased back in his seat and scanned the room out of habit. No one got his hackles up. He considered calling Rafael back but decided not to; he'd kill the greedy bastard when the time came. For now he was content to sip the Lochnager and lose himself in his plans to be one of, if not the most, powerful and influential men on the planet.

Diagonally, from his table, he could see the entrance to the hotel, in addition to the majority of the lobby. He anticipated the arrival of his acquaintance any moment. A grin took shape on his mouth.

Monterrey, Mexico
General Mariano Escobedo
International Airport
July 21, 2013 10:48 P.M.

Buddy walked down the jet-way toward customs with forty other Americans. Most were dressed in Bermuda shirts and shorts that screamed "Please mug me, I'm a tourist!" It was times like these that made him wonder why he bothered working for a country whose citizens walked around like Lemmings, totally blind and oblivious to the dangers around them. If only a few of them had been exposed to the things he'd seen in his life, they would be much more wary and untrusting. Conversely, it was good for Buddy's personal income that most everyone lived in their comfort zone with little thought about anything outside their personal control.

Before he left Virginia he decided to pack and check a bag. He had thrown a few changes of clothes in it along with his favorite pocket knife. Having his contact in Mexico City see to it that he acquired a firearm would have been perfect, but he had a meeting to keep when he arrived at the hotel. The knife would have to do until he had time to obtain a better weapon.

He tried, with no success, to keep his thoughts out of the past and on the present. His mind gave little consideration to the dangers and trials he had lived through, beyond quantifying and cataloging them in his memory banks for future reference. Perhaps his age was beginning to show by playing on those memories, or maybe it was the sight of so many people oblivious to the world's realities that caused his mind to drift. No matter the reason, decades of jungle and desert warfare memories paraded through his mind like a feature length movie on the silver screen.

"Señor. Señor." Buddy's dark green eyes snapped open when he heard the voice calling to him. The Mexican agent eyed him suspiciously as he awkwardly began fumbling around for his passport.

"Passport, Señor," the customs agent demanded. Buddy felt around for his passport and found it in his back pocket before handing it over. "Your customs declaration, Señor," the uniformed man also requested.

Thus far, Buddy had completely lost himself in thought like some amateur traveler on his first vacation, giddy with excitement. He found the customs declaration he had filled out on the plane in his shirt pocket and handed it to the agent. *Customs declarations were probably the most ridiculous documents to fill out when traveling internationally. If I brought over ten thousand dollars into the country with me, I wouldn't tell you or anyone anyway*, he mused about the question on the form.

The customs agent scanned his passport then shifted his eyes from Buddy to the photo. "What is your business in Mexico, Señor?"

"Just here on vacation. I like Mexico this time of year," Buddy said to the agent.

"How long is your vacation," he asked, his questions on cue and predictable?

"I'll be here a week. Going to unwind and enjoy some tequila and a little bit of nightlife," Buddy offered.

"I see," the agent responded then continued. "Are you feeling okay, Señor? You seem...distracted."

"Ah hell, I'm fine as frog hair, my man. I was just thinking about what I wanted to do tonight once I got checked into my hotel. You know, trying to figure out how a man my age can have a good time in Old Mexico," he finished and gave the agent a wink.

The customs agent gave a little chuckle then glanced over the customs declaration and found nothing noteworthy. He glanced at Buddy one more time before reaching for the Nuevo Leon, Mexico stamp that he would pound onto the passport. His hand stopped as he picked up the stamp.

"Where are you staying, Señor," he asked with a raised brow?

"At the Crowne Plaza, just down the road here. I like to be close to the airport so I don't have to rush around when it's time for me to leave. You know what I mean?"

For a few uncomfortable seconds the agent dropped his eyes and seemed to consider the stamp he held in his hand. Finally, he nodded his head and pressed the stamp onto the passport page he'd opened to. He closed the identification booklet and handed it to Buddy.

"Enjoy your stay in Monterrey, Señor, but try not to enjoy too much of the nightlife," he said with a smirk.

"Yes sir, I'll do my damnedest," Buddy said as he nodded. A hushed sigh of relief whistled through his puckered lips as he tried his best to look at ease. He reached for the passport and replaced it in his pants pocket, picked up his bag and walked to catch a shuttle to the hotel. If everything went according to plan, he would have a ride out of Mexico the next day.

While he waited for the Crowne Plaza shuttle, he reached for one of his Cuban cigars. He fished his cutter from the zipper compartment in his carry-on and nipped the end of the stogie. The aroma of the unlit cigar met his nose and immediately made his mood a little lighter. Customs agents always made him edgy and this last one had made him feel particularly uncomfortable. He couldn't prove it, but he would swear agents all around the world were trained in interrogation techniques.

Smoke filtered from the end of his cigar and encircled his head. Unlike most cigar smokers, he preferred the Ulysses S. Grant method and inhaled deeply. He pushed a brownish-white plume of smoke from his lungs that mixed with the toxic fumes of cars and buses as they stopped to pick up travelers. His shoulders and nerves relaxed as he puffed on what he referred to as "the gift of the Cuban revolution."

Ten minutes passed when Buddy spotted the hotel shuttle in the distance. The distinct crown logo was painted on the front of the white van just above the driver's cab. Buddy tamped the cigar out on the side of the large upright, stone-lined ashtray that stood next to him on the sidewalk, and put the remainder in a Ziploc bag he carried with him when he traveled.

The driver pulled to the loading area where Buddy and five other guests piled onto the mini-bus. He sat next to a large white woman who wouldn't stop talking to a man, presumably her husband, about what they would do after they got to their hotel. Her husband didn't acknowledge anything she said, which seemed to further fuel her need for unrelenting chatter. Twelve long minutes later they arrived at the hotel. Buddy thought his eardrums were going to bleed while the woman gabbed on-and-on. Her husband continued to ignore her. As Buddy rose, he reached over and patted the man on the shoulder. He winked and gave the man a sympathetic smile. The man looked beaten and on the verge of crying.

The shuttle eased into the hotel parking lot before stopping under the burnt orange awning. Buddy stepped onto the sidewalk, grabbed his bag and tipped the driver. For a few seconds he scanned the area paying close attention to the parking lot, points of ingress and egress. Details made the mission, and he was one who appreciated the finer points of his surroundings...just in case. He walked through the entrance, scanned the area, and turned toward the check-in counter.

The hotel lobby décor was typical Mexico, polished stone floor and walls and beautiful paintings hung in strategic locations. A woman wearing a yellow sundress adorned with flowery stitching and heels could be heard walking as the clip-clop of her shoes hitting the stone floor reverberated throughout the room. Three beautiful, young Mexican women greeted guests at the counter as the guests handed over their credit cards to check in.

Buddy smiled at the young lady who asked if she could help him in thickly accented, but perfect, English. "Yes ma'am you can. I have reservations for three nights. Smith is the name."

She pulled up Buddy's hotel reservation on her computer monitor. After confirming his information she requested photo identification and a credit card, both of which he handed her. He hadn't felt the need to travel under a pseudonym since Uncle Sam was already his financial suitor. Most importantly, he didn't anticipate anyone tracking him.

"Yes sir, your room is on the fifth floor," she said as she circled his room number on the key card. "How many keys would you like," she asked?

"Oh, I'm a creature of habit, so give me two, just in case I lose one. My mind just isn't what it used to be, young lady," Buddy replied with a wink.

"Of course, sir," she smiled back a little flirtatiously. "Our free breakfast is served from six until ten each morning in the restaurant directly behind you. The elevators are to your left. Enjoy your stay."

"Damn. If only I were a hundred years younger," he muttered, "I'd whisk you away in a second."

The young lady giggled as Buddy turned toward the elevators. From the corner of his eye he saw someone watching him. Angling his head slightly to his left he saw Dugan seated at a table in the back of the hotel bar. He nodded to Buddy and Buddy gave him a quick nod back. He hit the button on the Otis elevator that would take him to his floor.

His electronic key slid into the card slot. He heard the familiar click of the tumbler unlocking then pushed open the door. After dropping his bags on the bed he turned to the mirror and looked at himself. Few times in his life did he ever doubt his own abilities, but tonight was different.

Slightly shaking fingers fumbled for the bathroom light switch. Incandescent bulbs sprang to life as the old warrior walked to the sink and turned on the cold water. His hands cupped, he pushed them into the stream and splashed some on his face. Long strands of hair stuck to his cheeks as beads of water dripped from his nose and jaw.

Both of his hands landed on the bathroom vanity as he stood there staring at his reflection. Age and a hard life stared back at him. He wondered how much longer he would defy the odds and walk on the Earth. One day...two...maybe a year if he was lucky. Every strand of his fiber told him it was time to pull his hair into a pony tail and find a beach somewhere to sit, sip tequila and watch girls. But his mind and ego wouldn't let that happen and he knew it. It had always been about the mission to him. Forget love of country and pledging allegiance to the flag and all that horseshit, it was the mission, and this one was no different than any of the rest.

What differed about this mission, however, wasn't the danger – it was the man he was dealing with and his ruthless way of doing business. Killing and death came with the job, but Dugan took great pleasure whenever he did it. In fact, Buddy once watched him torture a man to death with a smile on his face and an inner glee of enjoyment.

His hand found the white towel folded neatly in one corner on his vanity. He patted his face dry on rough cotton, flipped his stringy hair back and ran his fingers through it. His chest puffed out from the deep breath he took, and then his cheeks blew outward like a blowfish as he exhaled before walking back to the bedroom and unzipping his suitcase.

Inside the suitcase's zippered panel he reached and found the Case XX knife he'd brought with him and shoved it in his front pocket. He grabbed his room key and slid it in his back pocket then turned toward the door. Outside his room he made his way back to the elevator. Within a few seconds the familiar chime let him know of its arrival. Once inside, his right index finger hit the starred lobby button on the call-button panel.

The door slid open and he stepped out, turned to the hotel bar and restaurant and walked to the entrance. With no one appearing to be out of place or threatening, he turned right to the hotel bar.

Buddy stood just inside the bar's doorway for a few seconds allowing his eyes to adjust to the dim light. There were two patrons sitting at the bar and his old adversary at the same table he had spotted him at earlier. He walked over to Dugan's table and sat down without saying anything. Both men kept their hands on the table out of respect for the other's background and ability.

A few seconds passed before Dugan initiated the conversation. "Why, Mr. Smith, it's been such a long time since we have seen one another. How in the world are you?" he asked. He picked up his glass and took the last sip of the golden brown liquid.

"Unless we plan on having sex later tonight, let's dispense with the walk down memory lane and talk a little business. I'm getting up there in years and don't really give a shit for your mouth today," Buddy curtly replied.

Dugan kept his face neutral having grown accustomed to the crassness of unsophisticated men just like him. The old warrior's callous demeanor didn't faze him, however. In fact, it made the meeting a little easier for him.

"I see," Dugan said. "It's unfortunate two old friends can't have a drink and talk about life's simpler times." Dugan's eyes shot around the bar to assure no one could hear him, "You know, like killing sand niggers, jungle spics and those African tree monkeys. Those were the simple times. Good food in some of those places too, wouldn't you agree?"

Buddy stared at the old man as he fought the urge to reach across the table and rip his throat out. His stomach lurched just sitting down with him, and he was sure his posture revealed his uneasiness. He ran his tongue across his teeth then sucked in, trying to give off an air of indifference. Whether or not Dugan bought his disinterested look was another story altogether.

"Yes, I recall a time or two when you, in a drunken rage, stuck a knife in a young Guatemalan's neck because he told you to 'go fuck a goat.' As his corpse lay by the campfire we had built, you dined on some dried fish we had packed the night before. Do you remember that night, Mr. Smith? That little bastard was our trail guide. We all sat around drinking and joking and he only wanted to join in the game. You are really no different than I, sir, so let's not pretend for a moment that your tenure with various government agencies entitles you to be sanctimonious," Dugan mocked him.

The bartender stepped from behind the bar and approached the table. "Señores, what can I get for you?" he asked. He looked at Dugan and asked, "Another Lochnager for you, Señor?"

"Yes, and get one for my friend. He appreciates a nice Highland single malt, as I recall. He and I go way back you understand. We haven't seen each other for several years. It's like a reunion of sorts," Dugan's sarcasm reeked in reply.

Buddy nodded his approval of the single-malt to the bartender then turned his attention back to Dugan. His eyes locked on the man he hadn't seen in a couple of decades but had tracked for the last seven or eight years. Still, his face remained blank while his guts churned with disdain. It was atypical for Buddy to have a maelstrom of emotions, but this one person seemed to bring out the worst in him.

A few moments passed before the bartender brought the drinks to the table. Dugan instructed him to put them on his tab. With that, the bartender walked back to the bar, grabbed a damp rag and began wiping his work space.

Dugan began speaking again, "So, here we are, two old men together again down in Old Mexico. How fitting. We've eaten together, we've shit together and we've killed together. I think there's enough history between us to allow for a modicum of civility. Besides that, we've entered into a business partnership and both have a vested interest in seeing this job carried out."

Buddy wanted to cringe and deny it, but Dugan was right. They were partners in crime so to speak, which made him just as culpable as the asshole sitting on the other side of the table. As many shady dealings he found himself involved in over the years, he had never felt as greasy and dirty as he did when dealing with the cold-blooded murderer with whom he now shared a table.

"Yes, I suppose you're right," Buddy began, "a measure of civility is called for in this case." His thick southern drawl fell heavily upon 'civility.' Despite his uneasiness, his diction was even and metered. "And, you are correct; we have a common goal here, Mr. Dugan. Perhaps it's time we discuss the business at hand."

"That's much better, Mr. Smith. I always operate at a higher level when all parties are at ease with one another. With that, allow me to brief you on where we are regarding the acquisition of the talisman.

We now have my personal agent here in Monterrey holding the jewel until tomorrow morning. You and I will meet in the hotel lobby at 10:00 a.m. then proceed to the pick-up point. My team is confident that we can reverse the spell and give you your army. As we discussed previously, before the artifact is given over to you and that rogue government you serve, the money we negotiated will magically appear in my account.

I suspect the routing number I gave has been turned over to the appropriate party? And just so you are aware, there's a series of bank re-routes making my true account virtually untraceable. Should your folks attempt to track down the payment, or me for that matter, I will be forced to take matters into my own hands. The money shall be deposited no later than 9:30 tomorrow morning so I can confirm its presence before we leave.

Next, we will depart Monterrey in a chartered jet headed to Xi'an. There will be a couple of stops along the way for refueling purposes. Once there, the spell will be reversed and you will be given the cartouche, or as I fondly call it...the warrior's key."

"You've told me that this warrior's key controls the Terracotta Army, Dugan, but you haven't told me how you know this to be true. How can Uncle Sam be assured that by controlling the cartouche, he will control the army? There's a lot of money at stake here and I've been questioned a few times about the validity of your claim," said Buddy.

Dugan laughed and replied, "Oh ye of little faith, Mr. Smith. I have paid a research team a lot of money to confirm the existence of the magic held in that little jewel. Our own government has confirmed the ability to harness the power of the human mind to predict future events, sir. In the Alaskan tundra a group of soldiers were used in experimental forecasting in what became known as 'remote viewing.' Essentially, each soldier was told to sit quietly with his eyes closed and given a name or place and told to report back what he saw in his mind. If several people reported seeing the same person, object or event, the potential was there that they had just seen a snapshot of the future.

"The United States government, the former Soviet Union, Nazis and the Chinese government, have all dabbled in the arena of magic. Make no mistake, Mr. Smith, the CIA has within its ranks priestesses and magicians who have cast death spells on foreign leaders resulting in their untimely death. Is it so far-fetched then, to believe a spell is contained inside a gem that would give the owner the ability to control an army of eight thousand living, breathing stone soldiers?

"One hitch that kept resurfacing in our research, however, is that only a blood relative can reverse the spell. We have located a couple of candidates in the United States who will meet us in Taiwan. These individuals are Native Americans and fully vested in Earth worship and the belief in spiritual magic. We believe one or both of them will be able to figure out how the spell can be mutated to fit our needs.

"But, I do offer my assurances that this is real and that should it fail I will most certainly pay back any money fronted to me by the United States government. I can't imagine that you and your suitors would find that unsatisfactory," he finished.

Buddy listened intently to Dugan's speech. The plan was simple enough. Too simple as plans go, but this was the information he was sharing at the moment, so Buddy would be forced to go along with it. There was no doubt that Dugan had spent copious amounts of time confirming the cartouche's magic could be used to control the army. Still, he had another pressing concern – Evers.

"What about my asset here? Where is he and what have you done with him?" Buddy demanded.

A wicked smile spread across Dugan's face. "Yes, the ever persistent, Mr. Evers. Rest assured he is in relatively good health for the time being, Mr. Smith. But I'm afraid he has become quite the liability. He was our safety net in the event our jewel thief had second thoughts and decided to make a run with the key. As luck would have it, he didn't run, and unfortunately for William Evers, his time is almost at hand. It didn't take me long to realize the man doesn't see the bigger picture and that he would interfere with our plans."

Buddy's forehead creased, "That doesn't make any sense, Dugan. He was following orders and I'm going to need him to help me lead those warriors out of China. I seriously doubt the Chi-coms are going to just let us waltz out of their country with eight thousand of their most prized cultural treasures without a fight. I think your paranoia is catching up with you."

Dugan laughed then replied, "You and I don't live as long as we have in our professional field without a little dose of paranoia, Mr. Smith. But my mistrust of most things notwithstanding, how do you think he would react when he finds out you and I have been working together the entire time? Have you considered the outcome? Don't you honestly think he would attempt to kill us both?"

"Of course I've thought about it," Buddy responded. "And there's a distinct possibility he would kill me given the chance, but he's a good man and doesn't deserve to die like some kind of rogue cur."

"You really are quite taken with Mr. Evers aren't you?" Dugan glibly remarked. "There's something else you need to know about Mr. Evers. He's tainted. The mark of death haunts him, and that makes him unstable and unpredictable. I've been informed by my team here in Mexico that he screams in his sleep. Emotional connection to those lives he's taken creates a much larger problem with him, you see. No, Mr. Smith, tomorrow William Evers will be forever removed from this world."

Monterrey, Mexico
General Mariano Escobedo
International Airport
July 22, 2013 9:10 A.M.

Pain from the shackles attached to his wrists and ankles was the first thing Roper felt when his eyes fluttered open. His back ached from the hard concrete floor he felt beneath him, as well as where the taser had bitten into his spinal column. His brain vaguely registered the fact that he had no clothing. He could smell fuel and oil, but struggled to determine where he was.

He rolled to his side, the heavy manacles and chains connecting wrists to ankles. A streak of pain coursed from his ribs as he held his breath and grimaced. He looked at his side and saw the gigantic black bruises that covered the majority of his ribcage. His face and head ached and felt as though he had been hit with a sledge hammer a dozen different times. He eased his head back to the floor and took a few shallow breaths, each one subsequently causing as much pain as its predecessor.

His eyes took in his surroundings. Daylight poured through large windows forty feet in the air. Corrugate metal walls and weight bearing beams formed the huge structure. The concrete floor extended from the front to the rear approximately a hundred yards, and half that from side-to-side. There were dark, oily stains in various spots on the smooth concrete. Toward the front of the building sat the red Camaro. Finally, it dawned on him that he was in an airplane hangar, and the nearby roar of a plane taking off confirmed his theory.

Despite his splitting headache, Roper's mind raced to remember the events leading up to his waking in the strange building. He closed his eyes trying to recall everything... anything. Thankfully, his eyelids blocked some of the sunlight, giving his aching head a minor reprieve. Memories flooded into his brain – the drive to Monterrey, the walk from the internet café, his phone call with Buddy, the red Camaro and the four thugs. He remembered most of the damage he'd delved out and the second tank top wearing man begging him not to hit him. Finally, he remembered the pain he'd felt between his shoulder blades. Everything beyond that was a complete and total blank.

Lying on his side proved more painful than being on his back. While the chain connecting his handcuffs and ankle cuffs forced his body into the fetal position, he could at least lie on his back with his knees bent. Mercifully, the pressure on his bruised ribcage eased just a little when he rolled to his back. He wondered if some of his ribs were broken. Even his legs hurt, and he was sure there were bruises on them too. A sticky iron taste had formed on the back of his tongue and he knew it was the sickening taste of his own blood. His tongue circled his mouth and did a quick inventory of his teeth. All of them were in place, but he could feel a large gash on the inside of his cheek. He turned his head and spat blood out of his mouth.

A few feet from him he heard someone laugh. He craned his neck in an attempt to see who else was there. The sound of shuffling feet came closer until he could see who it was. Fancy Shirt towered over him, a nasty, evil grin spreading across his face. His hands held a Russian issued AK-47. He presumed the magazine wasn't empty.

Roper, not recognizing him at first, looked him over from head to toe. "Who the fuck are you?" he winced. "What do you want with me?" He was certain he knew the answer to his second question, but any information he could glean was beneficial, but not as important as buying time from a man with a fully automatic weapon of war. "And where are my fucking clothes?" he finished.

The guy didn't say anything for a moment. He simply stood there looking down at the battered man. At last he said in thick accented English, "Who the fuck I am is not important, gringo. What I want with you is nothing but the money I'm going to make for turning you over to someone who is really interested in you. And fuck your clothes, ese. A man with no clothes is less likely to try anything stupid, you know?"

Roper roared with laughter despite the pain shooting through his innards. "Less likely to do anything stupid you say? I think these shackles would make a man less inclined to try anything stupid than taking his clothes off him, but that's just how my mind works. Of course, you may just like looking at naked men, who knows," he taunted.

The Mexican limped over to Roper, obviously still hurting from the kick he took to the inside of his thigh, and stomped a cowboy boot into his ribs. Roper screamed as pain shot through his entire core. He was on the verge of passing out but somehow managed to remain conscious. Deep breaths were an impossibility for him, but Roper tried to force as much air as he could into his lungs.

"That's who I am, vato. I'm the guy who shot you with a taser and dropped you to the ground. I'm the guy who listened to you cry like a bitch while you were asleep, and I'm the guy who just stomped your white ass," said the angry man.

Recognition appeared on Roper's face. "Oh yeah," he spat as blood trickled down his chin, "now I remember. You're that pussy who got dropped with one kick. I bet that hurt, didn't it?" he mocked.

The Mexican's eyes narrowed to slits and his face burned red with rage. Roper thought about not taunting him, but couldn't resist the urge. "Where are your other buddies?" he asked, his head swiveling in search of them. At the entrance of the hangar he saw one man sitting in a chair, his arm in a sling, another was standing holding a dark red rag to his face. The cloth dripped with blood from the man's face. On the floor he saw one man lying motionless.

"Ha! There they are. You dumb bastards struggled to capture one American. I figured you Mexican fellas would be a little tougher than that," Roper provoked. "Looks like one of your friends will have to learn to wipe his ass with his left hand, and another will be buying some cheap-ass sunglasses to cover that eye, huh? And your last little amigo on the floor there...doesn't look like he'll be knocking back cervezas with you again, now does it?"

His captor's face scrunched into a venomous frown. He lifted his rifle and pointed the business end of it at Roper's head. Roper's eyes grew wide and a terrified look crossed his face. As quickly as the fear touched him it was gone. A toothy grin appeared on his face further infuriating Fancy Shirt.

The Mexican opened his mouth to allow a rage filled scream to fill the hangar. It sounded feral to Roper, like a wildcat cornered and poised to attack. He lunged at Roper and kicked again but this time Roper rolled over and entangled the man's kicking leg in the chain of his shackles. Ropers shackled legs moved hard and fast toward his opponent's leg not wrapped in the chain. The man let out a startled gasp as his supporting leg was swept out from under him and his back slammed to the concrete floor forcing the air from his lungs.

The rifle hit the floor with a thud and discharged a round into the ceiling. He could hear scrambling coming from behind him and knew only remaining friend still capable of walking was coming his way. One of Fancy Shirt's legs was resting on Roper's chest giving him an opportunity to inflict a little more pain. He scooped the leg with his cuffed hands and forced the leg to his mouth. An instant later his teeth were sinking into the Mexican's leg and a blood curdling scream bounced off the metal walls.

The familiar double click of ammunition being chambered into a pistol echoed directly above him. Roper released the leg and tilted his head upward finding himself staring directly into the barrel of a really large pistol.

"Do some shit like that again amigo and I'll kill you before the boss gets here. Comprende?" Tank Top growled.

He relaxed his body and took shallow breaths as the pain rushed back into his torso. Thoughts raced through his mind as he fought to catch his breath from the scuffle and the previous beatings he had taken. To his left he could hear speaking and cursing in Spanish and Roper felt pretty sure that he was the subject of the discussion.

One valuable piece of information he realized after the latest ass kicking he had gotten was that his captors weren't going to kill him. At least they weren't going to kill him right now, which meant whoever the boss was he had a plan for him. Unfortunately, he was more than certain that plan involved his death.

Dugan fired up his personal laptop and waited while it finished loading. He rarely got excited about the prospect of completing a mission; the mission was just his job and he enjoyed doing his job well, but there was no emotional attachment. In his mind a completed contract was the direct result of perfect planning and execution. This one, however, was altogether different.

Everything about this job had begun after a chance meeting while in Xi'an with a professor from a local university. The vividness with which he remembered that day still perplexed him, yet the power and energy he felt as he had stared at the statue of Captain Li was embedded in his memory banks.

His meetings with the Buddhist priest in Chinatown had also capitulated worthwhile information regarding incantations and spells used in China. All the research his covert team had conducted in documenting a Chinese migration through the Americas, coupled with the other information, made him feel more than marginally lucky.

He had made a great living following his gut instincts. Whether those instincts told him to move forward with a mission or not, whether to deal with certain individuals or something as simple as not setting foot in a particular place, they had assured his survivability and prosperity over the course of his lifetime.

"Hell, I may just be the smartest man in the world, and if I pull this thing off, I'll be the most powerful man too," chuckled to himself.

After a couple of moments his computer finished booting up. He double clicked the security firewall he had installed to keep prying cyber-sleuths from seeing what he was doing. The NSA had made spying on people their modus operandi and he would be a fool to presume he wasn't on their watch list. A young NYU graduate student working on a master's degree in IT security had developed the firewall he was using. He had paid the kid handsomely, but Dugan knew he was worth his weight in gold.

Dugan typed the bank's URL into the computer's web browser and watched the page load. He entered his user name and password, clicked "go," then waited while the bank's server verified his log-on credentials. A few seconds later his account window opened and he was staring at the largest amount of money he had ever scored on one mission. An enormous smile spread across his face while he closed the browser and purged his browser history.

Buddy sat on the foot of his hotel bed and stared down at the floor. His hand was wrapped around a Styrofoam cup filled with hotel coffee. Small spirals of steam puffed from the uncovered cup.

The conversation with Dugan the previous night kept replaying in his head. He had dealt with the man off and on for just over thirty years and knew Dugan was no fool. It was beyond reason to assume he only had one plan too. Dugan was much more than a simple gun runner. Planning and organizing multi-layered missions was one of his strengths and was a testament to his cognitive skills. That's what bothered Buddy the most about everything that had transpired over the last week or two.

There was no way Dugan would double cross the United States government and not turn over the cartouche and Terracotta Army and risk having the wrath of it come down on him. So, what then? What was the extra play he had up his sleeve?

And then there was Young Buck. Dugan had taken a tremendous interest in the warrior, giving him significant cause for concern. Now he wanted nothing more than to kill him and was determined to follow through with it.

Killing Evers was never on the table when they entered into the agreement. Evers was a backup plan to assure Dugan's asset didn't bolt with the cartouche. Now Dugan perceived Young Buck as a threat to him. None of this was adding up in Buddy's head.

He thought of every conceivable way to talk Dugan out of killing Evers, but knew that once Dugan was intent on following through with something, there would be no stopping him. Not having a firearm made the situation worse. He had no idea how he would get his friend out of this situation. His pulse quickened as the stress mounted.

The link between the cartouche, the Terracotta Army and Evers was lost on him. *Why is he so adamant that Evers die? Just doesn't make a bit of sense to me,* he thought. He ran the fingers of his free hand through his hair then arched his back to relieve a little tension. A couple of vertebrae popped and a sigh of relief pushed over his teeth.

Dugan's revelation that Evers was having nightmares was also disturbing. He had known many a good soldier who suffered from post-traumatic stress disorder and it didn't typically end well for most of them. Dealing with the realities of war and death always made it hard on a man with a conscious. How a person compartmentalized and separated himself from his job is what kept him from going insane.

Evers, he knew, had never been a heartless soldier, and didn't necessarily kill without remorse, but when called upon to kill he did so efficiently and effectively. That was the primary reason Buddy had employed him after his tours in the Middle East. And as much as he hated to admit that Dugan might be right, if Evers was suffering from PTSD he could be a huge liability. He hoped that Evers would still trust him enough after this mission was completed to allow him to help, that was, if they both made it out alive, which was looking less and less likely.

He lifted the hot coffee to his lips and took a large sip. Scorching heat tore across his upper lip causing him to jump, which resulted in a splash of coffee hitting his hand and lap.

"You gotta be fucking kidding me! If this is any indication of how my day is going to go, I might as well find a gun and eat a bullet now," he drawled a little too loudly.

Rafael finished showering. He put clean clothes on a frame that had shrunk several sizes over a two week period. The blue jeans he wore hung on him like two stove pipes covering a pair of pencils. His light green, button-down shirt fit him like a sail borrowed from one of the boats he would sometimes see in the Caribbean in his hometown of Cancun. Like a zombie, he sat in the chair behind the small desk in his hotel room and put his shoes on, his eyes never leaving the cartouche that sat upon the table, unaware and uncaring about his appearance.

Even his shoes felt looser and his belt was cinched to the last notch. Like his eyes, his cheeks were sunken and sallow. With some difficulty he avoided looking at a mirror because he didn't recognize the fleshly skeleton that stared back at him.

His hand slid across the table and over the top of the talisman. Almost immediately the thrum and reverberation of the jewel began pulsating through his body releasing endorphins. His shallow, dark brown eyes rolled back into his skull and the chanting began again.

"Hua, shi...hua, shi...yong. Hua, shi...hua, shi...yong." He repeated these strange words over and over, the phrases rhythmic and melodic. None of it made sense to him but he didn't question it. In his mind's eye he saw strange men in ancient dress with swords, spears and long bows. Their features were oddly familiar. In fact, their eyes and hair looked much the same as that of his family.

He was sure he was viewing the world through another person's eyes. Strangely enough he could hear this imaginary person breathing heavily as he watched the battle unfold before him. Throngs of similarly dressed warriors plowed forward through a multitude of men on both horseback and foot. Although vastly outnumbered and overmatched, he saw the opposing army charge headlong into their foes' line of defense.

"Hua, shi...hua, shi...yong. Hua, shi...hua, shi...yong." As he chanted, he saw one of the men draw a sword and cut diagonally through another man's neck. The man's face was forever frozen in stark terror as his head rolled off his shoulders.

Rafael was only vaguely aware of the euphoria he was experiencing as he held the charm. Its energy engulfed him, eating at his soul, altering him physically and mentally. Something gnawed at his mind. The vision of the battlefield faded away as new, fresh images began coming to him.

An earthen pyramid and a modern city he didn't recognize appeared to him. And while he knew he had never personally laid eyes on the place and things he was envisioning, a familiarity and longing to see them touched his spirit. Rafael felt a warm tear roll down his gaunt face and find its way into the corner of dry, cracked lips. His tongue flicked it and he could taste its saltiness.

His vision revealed bustling streets with large buses filled to capacity. Sharing the streets with the buses were hundreds of people riding bicycles. The bicycle riders didn't give him the impression of people out for a nice ride hoping to get in a little exercise. On the contrary, they all seemed intent on a final destination, presumably where they worked.

The air was a hazy gray and white, not the way he had seen fog roll into a valley but the way he had seen Mexico City and other metropolitan areas that lacked emission controls. Many of the people wore masks like surgeons do as they enter an operating room.

Lazy green canals flowed silently through the city in stark contrast to the garish sounds of car horns and heavy construction equipment. In his head he could hear and smell everything about this place, a place that no longer felt foreign or strange. His heart longed to see this land and its people – his people.

After what seemed an eternity, Rafael managed to put the cartouche down and finish getting ready for his rendezvous with Haden. How he loathed the man! He had come to grips with the fact that there was no way he would be able to release the jewel to the brash American. Rafael needed the money from this job, and planned to get it, and eliminate Haden at the same time. His hand jammed the relic into his pants pocket then reached for his Ruger and shoved it into his shoulder holster. He pushed his arms through the openings in his dinner jacket and walked out the door.

Buddy walked into the hotel lobby, his hair clean but looking like it had been in a fight with a comb. His Levi's and t-shirt were a wrinkled mess and his dusty sneakers gave the impression that he wasn't overly concerned with others' opinions of him. His demeanor was calm and his face was shadowed in two day beard stubble.

The sun shone vividly through the hotel windows and doors, and should have given Buddy the feeling that the day was going to be a good one. But the hard truth was the day might turn out to be the worst he had had in a long time, and possibly finish with Young Buck's death. If he wasn't careful he could wind up just as dead, but he had lead a good life and had outlived most in the craft, so his demise was, at worst, trivial. Making certain he got his hands on the cartouche and away from Dugan was all that mattered to him right now.

He walked to the entrance of the hotel restaurant and found the free coffee pot. The smell of the rich Arabica blend coalesced with the scent of breakfast foods cooked in the restaurant. The aromas brought him a modicum of cheer. His hand reached for the thermal insulator and placed it over the cup. Afterward, he added some creamer to lighten his dark roasted java. Buddy snapped a lid down on the cup then raised it to his mouth and sipped lightly.

Forever having the resigned face of an old warrior, he couldn't help but allow a look of satisfaction creep over him as he sipped a very good cup of coffee. He glanced around the lobby looking for Dugan who hadn't shown up yet. *That nasty bastard is probably in his room jerking off while he looks at his bank account.*

Small squeaks echoed in the lobby from Buddy's sneakers as he walked across the polished stone floor in search of a free chair on which to sit while he waited. A young Mexican girl around four years old pointed and laughed at the sounds. He gave the youngster a smile and a wink.

Buddy lifted the coffee cup to his lips again as he sat. He crossed his legs and tried to keep a worry free appearance even though his concern was ever present. He thought about his youth when he misbehaved, and knew there would be hell to pay when his dad got home. A whipping with a belt was the usual punishment meted out by his old man, but it was the waiting and apprehension that was the worst part of the ordeal. As the old adage went, "anticipation of death is worse than death itself."

After twenty minutes passed, the familiar ding of the elevator sounded and Dugan stepped out, as usual, his dress was fashionable. His khaki pants were pressed in a tight crease as was his white button down shirt. The black dress shoes looked as though he had just spit shined them. He glanced around the lobby and spotted Smith sitting in a chair drinking his coffee.

"I trust you slept well, Mr. Smith?" Dugan asked cordially.

Buddy shook his head as he sighed audibly. "You are quite the sombitch, Dugan," he said as he stood. He looked Dugan in the face.

"You hold the key to the balance of power for the entire fucking world, you've taken a good man hostage and plan to kill him, and you're talking to me about how well I slept, you sick fuck," he stated.

"Now, now, Mr. Smith, need I remind you of the civil pact we struck last night? I understand that your operator is also a friend, but don't forget two things – A. he's stained, and B. you and the American government entered into a contract with me. Animosity will not win the day, my old friend," Dugan smirked. "Shall we proceed to the meeting location, sir?"

Buddy nodded his head reluctantly. He followed Dugan outside to his rental car where he stopped long enough to look around. The morning air was already hot and the day promised to get much hotter.

"It really is a beautiful country, Mr. Smith. It's a shame they haven't figured out how to exploit their natural resources to help move them toward prosperity," Dugan observed. "As for me, I say fuck 'em. Business is good." He opened his car door and slid into his seat. Buddy's jaws clenched as he did the same.

He watched as buildings and cars passed by while they drove toward the airport. He wanted desperately to ask where they were going, but held his tongue instead. *Patience, old man. You've been entirely too wired up and have been taking things personally on this assignment. If you aren't careful you're going to let your emotions get the best of you and that'll be dangerous for you and Buck. Get your head out of your ass.*

The mental pep talk seemed to calm his nerves only moderately. He took another sip of his hot coffee, continuing to savor its robust flavor and aroma.

Buddy thought that engaging Dugan in a conversation might be of more value than allowing him to think he had a mental edge over him.

"Dan," he started, using Dugan's given name, "what the hell happened to you? You used to be a good soldier."

"Mr. Smith, being a good soldier pays shit. And if you haven't figured it out yet, your government and country doesn't give one damn about you or me. I have learned over the years that one man's evil is another's prosperity. You, of all people, know this to be true. Many may consider me evil, but I like to think that I'm a business man who provides a service to those who seek me out. In some cases I provide weapons to those desiring freedom from oppression, other times they prefer those illicit drugs that take them away from a brutal reality they would rather not have to deal with. And in your case I provide an army to combat other governments who would pose a threat to your way of life. Does that sound so evil, Mr. Smith?" he finished.

"So you justify misery, death and despair by supply and demand? I realize there are those who want what you sell, Dan, but that doesn't mean you have to do it," Buddy tried to reason.

"And what would you have me do, Mr. Smith? Work in some factory for a bunch of rich assholes who don't give a shit about me one way or the other? Perhaps I could start my own small business back home and struggle my entire life to put food on my table. No thank you, sir, I like my chosen profession just fine," he said with some emphasis.

"I will say this one last thing, though, Mr. Smith, there are some things in this world beyond our control, but many that aren't. In my line of work I often seek that which many thought lost or beyond measure and make it mine. I have plans that include much more than just the monetary, you see," he said.

Buddy shook his head but decided reasoning with the man wasn't helping the situation. Something about what he said struck him as odd. He knew men like Dugan always had complex plans and he was certain that his dealings with this dangerous individual were nothing more than one of those complexities. What the rest of his plans were he had no idea, but he hoped to figure it out quickly. It sounded to him like money was secondary and meant much less to him than he previously imagined.

His heart began racing when Dugan hit the turn signal. A speeding car whipped past them before Dugan turned into the airport. Eyes narrowed, he looked at a large airplane hangar whose roll up door was rising as they approached.

Dugan tapped his breaks then eased the rental into the hangar. Although there were windows around the building and the lights were on, it took a moment for his eyes to adjust to their new environment. He maneuvered around the Camaro and saw one of his guys standing over a naked man who lay shackled on the floor. Buddy sat up in his seat at the sight of his friend.

Both men stepped from the car, Buddy a little slower than Dugan. Fancy Shirt nodded at Dugan and handed him a blue United States passport. He opened the document as the man lying on the floor strained to see who stood behind him. A sneer crossed Dugan's face as he looked at the document and walked around in Roper's direct line of sight.

"Well, Mr. Roper is it?" he asked. "Why don't we cut through the shit and be real with each other," he stated more than asked.

"Yeah, I'm not exactly in a position to dance anyway, Dugan," came Roper's reply.

"Right," Dugan agreed. "So, Mr. Evers," he began as he tore the passport up and threw it in a trashcan next to his car, "I would say now is a good time to wish Kevin Roper adieu."

The man who had been Kevin Roper for seven days was now officially Bill Evers again. Trying to see who else was with Dugan proved fruitless, as the shackles and his battered ribs prevented him from moving too far. He had heard two car doors close so he knew there had been someone else in the car.

"Who else is here," Evers demanded. "I know someone else is here. If your plans include killing me at least be man enough to let me see you!"

Dugan smiled and said, "Ah, yes, of course you should see your judge, jury and executioner." He motioned for someone to step next to him. Footsteps materialized into feet and legs. Evers looked up and couldn't believe what his eyes revealed.

"Buddy! You son of a bitch! You double crossing cocksucker. Go ahead and kill me now because if I ever get out of here, YOU'RE A FUCKING DEAD MAN! Do you understand me," Evers screamed! He coughed and panted as his rage grew.

Buddy's eyes dropped to the floor as Dugan laughed. "Sorry, Buck. Sometimes it's just about the mission," he stated.

Evers opened his mouth to let another flurry of expletives fly when a door opened and slammed shut from the opposite end of the building. The door's echoes reverberated throughout the building, bouncing from wall to wall until they finally died off. Everyone turned to see who had walked in, as Fancy Shirt turned and leveled his rifle at the interloper.

Dugan's eyes narrowed as he watched the man enter the room. Vague recognition drifted across his memory banks, but the scrawny body and gaunt face made it difficult to discern who the man was. The man took another step forward before Dugan could make out the unsavory character walking toward him.

"Señor Haden, it is so good to see you again," Rafael croaked.

Dugan's eyes widened in total shock and disbelief at the image of the person standing in front of him. The man's jacket hung from his shoulders like an oversized beach towel and his pants looked to be four sizes too large. He looked as though he had lost fifty pounds and hadn't eaten in months even though he had last seen him just three short weeks prior.

Evers eyes darted from Rafael to Dugan to Buddy while everyone focused on the newest addition to the party. Buddy made eye contact with Evers at that moment and winked at him. For a brief second, Evers appeared startled then relaxed his facial muscles.

"Who the fuck is this zombie, Dugan?" Buddy asked.

"This dapperly dressed young man is Rafael, the keeper of the key and holder of my financial freedom," Dugan replied while eyeing his Mexican operator.

Rafael asked his own question, "Who the fuck is Dugan?" It came out sounding like 'Doooogun.'

Dugan chuckled and replied, "That's me, Rafael. Most of us in this room work under aliases and fake identities. I had always assumed Rafael wasn't your real name but now I'm not so sure."

An evil grin sprouted from Rafael's face, "Whether it's my real name or not no longer matters, Mr. Ha...Dugan." His right hand emerged from his jacket holding the Ruger he had placed in his shoulder holster earlier. With a steady hand he pointed it directly at Dugan's face.

Dugan's hands shot in the air as confusion overtook him. Fancy Shirt brought his rifle to his shoulder and released the safety with a loud click. Tank Top dropped the rag from his eye and ambled over to the scene while drawing his own pistol that was tucked into his waistband. He, too, leveled it at Rafael. The air was thick with tension and a collective deep breath was heard throughout the building.

Buddy shot glances all around and began cackling. "Who the hell would have thought we'd come all the way to Mexico to witness a fucking Mexican standoff? This has to be the funniest thing I've seen in years."

The worried expression on Dugan and his band of criminals' faces was anything but jovial. Buddy walked next to Tank Top and stood. Everyone remained woefully focused on the men holding guns, paying little attention to the old American soldier.

Rafael's free hand reached into his pants pocket and grasped the jewel. In an instant the chant began as he stared at Dugan. "Hua shi...hua shi...hua shi yong." His voice resonated and thrummed in the chests of everyone in the hangar. The smell of fear and sweat dripped from Tank Top and Fancy shirt's bodies. Dugan's head tilted to the right as his eyebrows sloped together. His jaw opened wide enough to catch flies, had one flown close to his mouth. The entire scene would have been both frightening and comical to anyone entering the hangar at that moment.

Buddy seized the opportunity to grab his pocket knife. He had it out and the blade opened in a fraction of a second, the arc of the blade never slowing until it found its mark on the underside of its target's arm. Tank Top's eyes widened and his mouth formed a chasm that only a scream could pass through as he looked down and saw Buddy's sharp blade sever the brachial artery in the arm holding the pistol. Blood pulsed in time with his heartbeat. The gash in his arm was six inches wide, flesh and meat exposed. Red plasma sprayed his torso and face as his hand involuntarily opened and dropped the pistol.

Just as quickly as he had gashed Tank Top's arm, Buddy jammed the blade into the man's neck before the scream was actually vocalized. Wet, gurgling sounds came from his mouth instead as he grabbed the knife's hilt and attempted to pull it from his neck. Blood oozed over Tank Top's hands, the blade buried deep enough to prevent a jettison of plasma. Fancy Shirt turned his head in time to see Buddy fall to the floor and grab Tank Top's pistol, but he wasn't fast enough to prevent two rounds from the gun hitting him in the leg and arm. As he fell to the ground he held tightly to the AK-47.

The room erupted into a discourse of chaos, gunfire and screams. Dugan ducked and tackled Rafael before he could react, losing his own pistol in the process. Rafael clasped the cartouche tightly in his hand even as he dropped his sidearm and fell, both he and Dugan rolling in a wad of flailing arms and legs. A bullet struck Dugan's rental and two more hit the Camaro destroying the passenger side window and shattering the side view mirror into thousands of tiny pieces of plastic and glass.

Fancy Shirt's panic turned into semi-automatic fire in every direction. Nerves and panic ran through his body that didn't permit his untrained brain from being able to focus on the intended target. Instead, a stray bullet ricocheted and struck Tank Top Two in the ribs, the bullet piercing a lung and grazing his heart before it lodged itself somewhere deep in his chest wall. Buddy rolled and squeezed another round from the pistol striking Fancy Shirt in the groin. Blood exploded all over the front of his jeans as he grasped for his mangled penis and testicles. Vomit spewed from his mouth as the intense pain threatened to engulf his sanity. Fortunately, he didn't have to suffer very long as Buddy fired two more rounds into his face and head from five feet away. The acrid-iron scent of blood and brain matter filled the air as Fancy Shirt's life's blood emptied from his head and stained the hangar floor.

Screeching tires caused Buddy and Evers to whip their heads around in time to see Dugan speeding off in his rental car. Another head bobbled around in the passenger's seat. They both presumed it to be Rafael since he was nowhere to be found, but the fact that he had drawn a gun on Dugan would later make both wonder why he would have taken the Mexican with him.

Rising to one knee, Buddy leveled the pistol and squeezed three more rounds at Dugan's car as it sped toward the closed door. The first round bounced off the bumper and careened harmlessly into a corrugate wall leaving sparks in its wake. The second round penetrated the trunk just as the car hit the massive roll-up door. The aluminum door flew into two sections, one large and one small. The smaller of the two fell crashing down on the rental, the other falling haplessly to the floor. Dugan's car whipped right and shot out from under the half-door, speeding off toward the terminal.

Buddy rose and turned toward Evers. "You alright, Buck? I mean other than being shackled and naked on a floor during a gun fight, you're okay," he half-heartedly chuckled.

"Well, my ribs feel like they've been through a sausage grinder, my head is killing me and my wrists and ankles feel like they're about to fall off my body. Oh, and I just saw the guy who hired me to do this job show up with the fucking guy I was hunting! Other than that, I'm dandy," he replied, his sarcasm thick and meaty.

"Yeah, I reckon we need to talk about that, Billy. Let me see if I can find the keys on one of these dead guys so I can get those manacles off you. If I have to look at that small thing you call a dick anymore I'm going to laugh my ass off."

Dugan brought his car to a shrieking halt just a few yards away from a twin engine Learjet 60 he had paid a man handsomely to fly just a few days prior to his arrival in Monterrey. He dropped the keys to the rental on the floorboard then opened his door and ran around to the passenger side. Rafael sat there entranced and mumbling strange words while holding the cartouche.

He forced the Mexican out of the car and to his feet. The back of his hand struck Rafael square across the face causing him to see stars and instantaneously snapping him out of the trance. Dugan looked the man up and down and shook his head.

"Get in the fucking plane right now. If I have to tell you more than once I'll snatch that cartouche out of your hand and rip your throat out. Do you understand me?" he demanded.

Rafael stood there blinking at the American he so woefully had wanted to kill just a few moments earlier. As a matter of fact, by all rights he should have been dead but he couldn't remember what had happened between the second he had pulled the pistol from his jacket until that very moment.

He shoved the jewel into his pocket and dropped his eyes to the ground. With some effort he walked toward the plane and put a foot on the step, pausing long enough to take a long look around. A sickly feeling shot through him telling him he would never see his country again.

Buddy flipped the bloodied messes of bodies over and searched their pockets looking for the keys to the shackles. He tried to be careful not to get any of their blood on his hands while he searched. When he got to Fancy Shirt he heard the familiar jingle of keys in the dead man's pockets. With great care he reached inside and grabbed them. Four keys hung from the key ring. He located the one that looked like it fit the shackles and stuck it into the keyhole.

He turned the key and the manacles opened releasing Evers' wrists. The key slipped into the key hole on the manacles imprisoning his ankles next, releasing them with a similar clank. Bill stood on wobbly legs holding his bruised and battered ribs. He stood like that for a few seconds until he steadied himself. With considerable effort he launched a punch that connected with Buddy's jaw. The punch sent Buddy sprawling to the floor and stars exploded in his head.

Evers limped over to him with great effort. He was about to kick Buddy in the face when Buddy rolled like a cat. He hopped to his feet in a flash.

"Buck, we ain't got time for this shit. I told you we'd talk, but in about sixty seconds cops are going to be pouring through that door and find a naked man trying to fight an old goat with a whole bunch of dead bodies lying around. What say you get some damned clothes on and let's get the hell out of here before we get caught up in an international incident?"

Evers couldn't argue with Buddy's logic so he began searching for his clothes, finding them in a wad where the Tank Top twins had been sitting when he first woke up. He threw his pants and shirt on and snapped his head around when he heard a car door slam and the Camaro's engine roar to life. Buddy gunned the muscle car's engine then came to a sudden stop right next to his protégé.

Bill eyed him warily but reached for his shoes and socks then jumped into the car. Before his door closed, Buddy was already halfway out of the hangar. Exhaust fumes and smoke from the rubber tires drifted over the dead bodies they left behind.

Monterrey, Mexico
Four Points Sheraton Hotel
July 22, 2013 11:48 A.M.

Buddy and Evers drove the twenty-one kilometers from the hangar to the hotel in silence. The old warrior knew he couldn't return to the Crowne Plaza after being seen with Dugan that same morning. Direct involvement in an international incident with a known arms smuggler was frowned upon by his employer, but he certainly didn't want a Mexican investigator to place him and said arms smuggler together in the same hotel just a short time prior to the incident. Going back to the Crowne Plaza could be disastrous if a hotel employee positively identified him. He also needed a place to ditch the borrowed Camaro.

Evers stared out the window trying to make sense of everything that had happened over the past week leading up to be the most bizarre day of his entire life. His breathing had become more labored as the damaged tissue around his ribs began tightening. His bruised legs and back made the pain intensely sharper, but he made every effort not to wince.

The quiet ride to their new hotel had been uncomfortable for both men. Evers wanted to understand everything that had happened and Buddy wanted to explain it. Neither wanted to start the conversation in a car; both were smarter than allowing their tempers to get the best of them while trying to look inconspicuous.

After thirty minutes of driving, they whipped into a Four Points Sheraton Hotel garage and found a parking spot on the second level in a far, unassuming corner. After killing the ignition he allowed himself a sigh of relief before looking at Evers and saying, "Let's get the fuck out of this car." Each man took a few minutes to wipe down the interior and door handles. Buddy wiped the keys before throwing them on the seat. Ditching the car in the parking garage would give them plenty of time to get out of town before the authorities were alerted, or some enterprising soul discovered the keys and drove off in his new ride.

Evers offered no resistance or argument. He longed to lie down in a bed and rest, but he figured that wouldn't be an option. He looked at Buddy and asked, "What's the plan?"

"When we walk into the lobby keep your head down, out of view of the hotel cameras. I'll check us into separate rooms on the same floor. Once we're checked in, I'll give you your key, we'll haul ass to our rooms and chill out for a while. That will give us time to shower and meet for dinner in the hotel restaurant. We can talk about everything there, Young Buck. The only thing I ask you to do is to keep an open mind and not allow your emotions to get you worked up before we meet. Can we agree to that?" Buddy asked.

"Fine," Evers replied, "but don't think that gives you a free pass, Buddy. I watched you pull into a hangar with a fucker you wanted me to deal with today. I understand you helped free me from those bastards, but that doesn't take away from the fact that you showed up with him and he escaped. You understand?" he asked.

Buddy rubbed his sore jaw, then said, "Yeah, you ornery bastard, I understand. And after we talk I think you'll see that we're on the same side. Let's get cleaned up and talk in a bit."

He checked in and paid for two separate rooms just as he had explained. After handing Evers his room key, they both walked to the elevator and jostled inside, Evers trying hard to stand straight and not rub his ribs. People were much more likely to remember an older guy walking around with a slumped over, injured middle aged man than they were two average looking guys simply strolling to their elevator.

The chime sounded prior to the doors opening on the sixth floor. The two of them stepped out and walked to their respective rooms. They slid their electronic keys into the card scanner and entered. Had both men been able to observe the other they would have laughed. Each stopped short of walking past the bathroom, pausing long enough to listen for anyone who could be hiding. Convinced there was no one there, each proceeded to flip on lights and slowly make their way around the main bedding areas, stopping to open the single closet...slowly.

Buddy flipped the curtains back while Evers patted down the set in his room. After both men were certain no one shared their rooms with them they headed for their showers. Evers moved slowly as the pain in his ribs felt like a thousand knives were stabbing him at the same time. On his torso, legs, and arms, skin had been torn from the kicks his kidnappers had given him. It looked as though he had wrecked a motorcycle and had gotten a nice case of road rash in the process. When the hot water hit those areas, he winced and jumped causing an incredible jolt of pain in his side.

Even though the hot water brought him significant pain it also brought a tremendous amount of relief. He thought to himself, *a hot shower removes the day's sins and cleanses a muddled mind.* Once, while in Iraq, he overheard a gunnery sergeant make that remark. It seemed odd and out of place to him then, but now it made perfect sense.

He dressed slowly and decided to go downstairs to have a beer while he waited on Buddy. Evers stepped off the elevator into the hotel lobby and walked to the restaurant's bar. He saw Buddy already sitting at a table waiting on him sipping on a beer of his own. Not particularly fond of the bitter Mexican beers, Evers was pleased to find a Heineken on the drink menu and ordered one.

Buddy sat with his back to the wall facing the windows to the front of the hotel. Evers took a seat to Buddy's right so he could at least keep an eye on the restaurant entrance. The waitress brought Evers his beer and handed menus to both men. It hadn't dawned on him until that precise moment that he had gone two days without eating and he was famished.

Buddy took a long pull on his beer and stared at his old friend, but said nothing. He considered how to broach several subjects with Evers and at last decided the best policy was to get things on the table without sugarcoating anything. And that's exactly what he did.

He kept his voice low so no one but Evers could hear him, "Alright Buck, let's get everything in the open. And when I say 'everything' I mean it. We're not going to sit here and bullshit around. Neither of us have time for that sort of nonsense."

Evers glared at Buddy, staring directly into his eyes. Right then all he wanted to do was grab the fork the waitress had put on the table and slam it right between these old weary eyes. Repeatedly.

"Why don't you start by telling me what the hell you were doing with Dugan. That would be the most appropriate thing to do, don't you think?"

"Fine," Buddy began. "You know as well as I do in our line of work plans always have backup plans, Billy. When Dugan first approached the Christians In Action about that damned cartouche, they wanted nothing to do with it. After some research and speculation they changed their minds. As we've already discussed, that thing has the power to control the deadliest army this world has ever seen and the Agency wants nothing more than to get their hands on it.

"That's how I got involved. They knew I'd had dealings with Dugan in the past and figured if anyone could pull off the deal with him it would be me. He's very skittish of the U.S. government, as he should be, so I contacted him and told him the government wanted to do business. Also, my background...*our* background, yours and mine, Buck, has provided us with the ability to suspend general beliefs and assume magic like this really exists. Dugan knows a few things about some of the shit we've seen, so he was more apt to do business with me as the go-between.

"I wanted you on my team for two reasons, Buck, one, because you're a helluva soldier and a damned good tracker and two, just in case that slick bastard Dugan decided to crawfish on his deal and keep the cartouche for himself, I needed you to try to get it back."

"So I was your backup plan then?" Evers asked.

"Yeah, so to speak. But you were also part of the primary plan. When Dugan started getting suspicious and worried that his man here in Mexico wasn't going to give him the cartouche, I told him we could get you on the case. He was well aware of your abilities but I underestimated his lack of trust in anyone," Buddy explained.

"You underestimated his level of mistrust?" asked Evers sarcastically. "You've got to be fucking kidding me. He's the king of evil, Buddy, and you risked my fucking life on a piece of jewelry that you have no idea whether it works or not!" he hissed.

"You're wrong, kid. We are virtually certain this thing's for real, and we have to get it. Since I was a part of the shit that went down at that hangar, we can rest assured he's going to take the cartouche and sell it to a different country. If he sells it to one of America's enemies, we're dead in the water or forced to use some major firepower to stop that army. Can you imagine dropping a daisy cutter or nuke on a sovereign nation to try to stop them from attacking? How about dropping that kind of ordinance in our own backyard to stop them? The possibility of this happening is beyond comprehension, Buck, but completely plausible."

"There is no 'we,' Buddy. I'm done with this op. You used me, endangered my life needlessly, and double-crossed me. We were friends, Buddy but not anymore. You hear me? I'm out of here."

"Simmer down, Buck. Right now I'm the only friend you have, whether you believe that or not. I didn't double-cross you and didn't use you, per se. I should have let you know that I told Dugan about you, and was going to do so when you told me those four Mexican fellers that took you were pulling up. Do you remember that conversation? When Dugan told me he planned to kill you I had to figure out a way to prevent that from happening. So stop whining like a little girl," Buddy said emphatically as he pointed his finger at him.

Their waitress walked over and took their order. Both wanted nothing more than a greasy hamburger and fries. She walked away and Evers took another long drink from his beer, swishing the smooth lager around in his mouth.

"I don't know how you can drink that skunky smelling shit," Buddy quipped.

"It's the green bottle," Evers said casually, his rage calming only moderately. "It doesn't keep the light out which damages the beer, but the green bottle is iconic so they won't change to brown ones."

"Well, look at the brain on Billy Einstein," Buddy chuckled. "Now, let's get back to our discussion. I'm being one hundred percent up front with you, now it's time for you to do the same with me, Buck."

Evers eyes narrowed and he exhaled slowly, some of the pain subsiding momentarily in his ribcage. "What the hell are you talking about? I've been nothing but honest with you, Buddy."

"Is that right, Buck? You've told me everything I should know? You let me in on everything before you left Alabama to come to Mexico?"

"I don't know what you're talking about, Buddy, but it's time for you to get to the point or I'm getting up and walking out of here right now," Evers curtly replied.

"The dreams, Billy. The nightmares you have. Do you have them every night? Have they affected your judgment at all? You suffer from PTSD Buck, and it almost cost you your life. That's the primary reason Dugan wanted to kill you. He considers you unstable and untrustworthy, a liability. I need to know that you are none of those things," Buddy said matter-of-factly.

Evers slammed the half-full beer bottle on the table causing the few people dining in the area to turn and stare. The bartender walked from behind the bar and asked Buddy and Evers if there was a problem.

Bill turned and faced the bartender and spoke through clamped teeth, "No. There's no problem here. We're good."

The bartender walked back behind the bar and continued mixing and pouring drinks while keeping a cautious eye on the duo. He didn't want a fight or trouble on his watch, as he was certain to lose his job if that happened. The manager always blamed the bartender when fights occurred.

A thousand things swirled through Evers' head at that precise moment. The complete spectrum of emotions ran through him. He sat there, stunned, for a couple of moments not knowing what to say or how to reply to Buddy. If he were to be honest he would talk to Buddy about the nightmares, but he didn't want his old partner working part time as his personal shrink.

Evers also didn't want anyone else to know that he was suffering from the nightmares. He was afraid that it would stymie any future work he might acquire if prospective employers found out about them. Anger and fear flowed through him like water over a waterfall. Logic and confusion moved through his head in waves.

He looked away before he began speaking, "Buddy, that's none of your business. I suppose when I was knocked out those bandidos reported back to Dugan that I was talking in my sleep. But those dreams have nothing to do with how I perform in the field. Do you understand? Have you seen any indication to the contrary?" he asked.

"Buck, you've only been back on the job for a week. I need to know the pressure and stress isn't going to cause you to crack. There's no harm in having a conscience my friend, but if it interferes with the job then you put us all in mortal jeopardy."

A sneer crossed Evers' face, "You mean 'mortal jeopardy' like you put me in, right?"

"Look, I get it – you're pissed. But trying to change the subject and avoid this conversation isn't going to help us get to the bottom of things, or more importantly, help me feel better about hiring you for this operation. Now, for the last time," Buddy drawled, "you were a part of the plan to assure we got the cartouche. I never intended for you to be in any sort of jeopardy, mortal or otherwise. You're simply going to have to trust me on this one, or not...that's your call.

"I need to know how long this has been going on, Billy. Is that why you bought that place in the middle of nowhere, Alabama at the foot of that mountain? Out there you can be alone and wallow in your own self-pity, haunted by the memories of some men you were forced to kill. Am I right?"

Evers looked away again, refusing to make eye contact. He was afraid that Buddy would somehow be able to look into his soul if he did, and that he would be judged for the death and pain he had inflicted "over there" and in Africa.

Silence cloaked the area between the two men while each weighed their next words. At last Evers spoke, "I don't want to talk about it."

Buddy nodded a sad understanding and took his turn staring down at his feet. After a minute he looked up and said, "That settles it then. Go home, Buck. This op is over for you. Do what you planned to do when this conversation began."

The waitress brought them their food and place in front of them. She asked if they would like another beer and both said yes. Without another word they both dove into their burgers and fries. Evers' food was half eaten when the waitress returned with the beers. She stared in disbelief at his plate and the ketchup dripping down his chin. The waitress shook her head and walked away.

Buddy and Evers finished eating and drinking in silence. "You're a real asshole, Buddy. Obviously, you must think that reverse psychology is going to work on me. I said I was leaving and you told me to go home because I wouldn't talk about my dreams." He shook his head while fumbling with his beer bottle.

Buddy's head flipped back and a loud bellow of a laugh shot from him. "Did it work?" he asked.

Evers smiled but it didn't touch his eyes. "Look, let's finish this mission then I'll see what I can do about getting some help. I just don't like the thought of some shrink playing around with my mind, you know? Hell, everyone knows the shrinks and pharmaceutical companies are in bed together. One feeds on the other and makes his partner richer, all at the expense of the soldier who winds up on a pocketful of anti-depressants. It's no wonder so many of my war brothers have succumbed to drugs or drinking, or choosing to eat a bullet to end the pain." His tone was reticent and sad.

"I get it, Buck. People who haven't seen what you and I have seen couldn't understand no matter how hard they tried. Maybe just talking to someone who's been there will help. I don't know what the solution is for you, Billy, but as a friend I want you to get better. As your employer, I can't have that liability in the field."

"That's what you don't understand, Buddy. Being in the field is easy. Taking a person's life is simple," he said as he gripped the edge of the table, his knuckles white. "It's the toll on my conscience that troubles me. Killing someone in cold blood is easy my man. The stain it leaves behind is what gives me nightmares," he finished, his words hanging ominously in the air.

Buddy watched him for a couple of minutes before replying, "I know, Buck, I know." He smiled and continued, "I'm just happy to hear you'll be in control while we're out there," he nodded his head toward a window, the field implied by his motion. From the corner of his eye, he saw someone approaching them.

The bartender walked over with their beers while their waitress took care of another table. "Glad to see you muchachos getting along," he smiled.

Evers cut his eyes at the bartender who felt the heat and ire shoot from his patron. He promptly spun and walked away. Buddy smiled and raised his beer in a silent toast. Evers did the same.

"I'll look into some help when we get home. The bigger question is do you have a plan for getting the cartouche before Dugan unleashes hell on Earth?" Evers asked.

Buddy looked at Evers winked and replied, "Does a bear shit in the woods?"

38,000 Feet Above The Pacific Ocean
July 22, 2013 1:19 P.M.

Rafael stared at Dugan, who sat across from him on the Learjet, holding a pistol he had stashed on the plane. In Dugan's other hand lay the cartouche he had taken from the man he'd hired to steal it. His eyes shifted from the jewel to Rafael and back again.

"What the hell were you saying back there in the hangar? It sounded like some strange chant and it wasn't Spanish. What was that?" Dugan asked, his eyes piercing Rafael's.

"I don't know. It began shortly after I took the cartouche. It *speaks* to me. I do not understand any of this, Mr. Had...Dugan, but it has caused my physical health to begin failing. I hate it, but I cannot keep myself from touching it," Rafael said.

"Yeah, you look like a fucking skeleton with AIDS," Dugan said tersely. He wrapped his fingers around the cartouche and stared at his hand willing it to *talk* to him as it had Rafael, but nothing happened...other than a light thrum he seemed to feel deep within his arm. Growing more and more agitated, he rose, still pointing the pistol at Rafael, and paced for a few minutes.

"Why the fuck did you pull that gun on me? You had to have known you wouldn't get away with killing me? Did you think you could sell this damned jewel to the highest bidder you stupid bastard?"

"No," he responded. "I told you, the cartouche talks to me and it reveals things to me. Places and people I've never seen were shown to me by this thing. It *guides* me to its home," Rafael attempted to explain.

Dugan stared at the thinness of the man who had been quite strapping just a few weeks earlier in the Yucatan of Mexico. He looked around the plane for a moment as though all the answers were stuck to the tubular walls. Everything this guy told him lined up with things his research team had found, except the fact that a Mexican was being shown the cartouche's secrets.

"What do you mean it reveals things to you? Tell me what the hell you're talking about," demanded Dugan.

Rafael looked away and said nothing. He didn't feel that Dugan deserved to know anything that the cartouche had shown him. It also didn't matter if he shot him, which he didn't think he would risk on an airplane in flight.

Sensing Rafael's reluctance to answer his question, Dugan stood and stepped toward him. He raised the pistol to his head, his hand not wavering. "I will bury a bullet in your shrunken head, do you fucking comprende? And after I kill you, I'll dump your skinny body into the ocean and smile as I imagine the sharks tearing it to shreds."

He stared at Dugan as small beads of sweat formed on his face. Still, he didn't say anything. Several agonizing seconds passed and he finally said, "I'm not afraid to die. You need me more than I need you, so if you must shoot me and throw my body in the ocean, go right ahead."

Fury reverberated through Dugan's mind and body, the truth behind Rafael's words causing him to lose control. He looked at the hand holding the pistol and watched as it began shaking. Rage gripped him like never before. With blinding speed, he lashed out with the pistol smacking Rafael across the cheekbone. Dugan heard a satisfying crunch as the steel of the pistol met the naked skin and bone of Rafael's face.

His eyes rolled to the back of his head as he lost consciousness. Dugan wanted to hit him again but feared killing him, given his captive's wasted attenuated body and the uncontrollable rage with which he wanted to lash out. Instead, he stuck the pistol in his waistband and sat back down. After calming his mind he stared at the man's motionless body. He needed him to talk. There was something about the entire situation with the cartouche and Rafael that he hadn't quite pieced together, but if he could find out what else the jewel had revealed to him he would be a step closer to solving the mystery.

Why would the jewel reveal itself to Rafael but not to him? His research team believed only a family member could unlock...

Could it be? Is it possible that Chan's bloodline had found its way to Rafael? His team had already proven the blood of the Chinese shaman was found in various Indian tribes from Alaska, into the western United States and further into Mexico. Never in a million years would I have thought the one person I hired might have the ability to unlock the spell. I thought I would have to find someone in China, but this is a possibility. Chan was forced to leave the country with the rest of the village. It's conceivable that Chan has no existing bloodline left in his mother country. How stupid of me to overlook this and how very fortunate this idiot pulled a gun on me when he did!

His last thought brought a malicious smile to his face. He would have to secure Rafael now and keep him alive long enough to unravel the secret. Perhaps he would be a part of the second half of his plan as well. Only time would tell.

Monterrey, Mexico
General Mariano Escobedo
International Airport
July 23, 2013 6:42 A.M.

Shortly after their dinner and beer at the Four Points, Buddy had called in another favor with Javier in Mexico City. Fortunately, Javier had several connections in Monterrey and was able to help him out, for an exorbitant price. At this juncture in the game Buddy wasn't concerned with money. He would explain everything when he got back home on his expense report.

Using his own passport photo, as well as the one he had had Evers take for the Roper document, Javier's contact was able to create two new United States passports in a matter of hours. His workmanship was incredible, all the way down to the Great Seal watermark and holographic image of "E Pluribus Unum." Buddy had laughed at how naïve the States' Homeland Security could be when it came to counterfeiting documents such as passports. Give an individual with an average I.Q., a computer, the right paper, and a couple of hours, and brand new documents could be created.

His next task was to purchase two tickets to Hong Kong, but he had to avoid re-entry into the States. There was no time for all the questions he would face, and deniability from the CIA about his and Evers' existence would prove very difficult for them should they re-enter the U.S. The plan was to fly to Mexico City then on to the Chinese Island of Hong Kong.

Regrettably, they would have a long layover in Manila, The Philippines and Shanghai, once they got on the mainland, which would cost them precious time. Dugan, however, would be significantly delayed because of the small aircraft on which he traveled. He would be forced to make several stops along the way before getting to Xi'an. Buddy hoped this would be their saving grace and provide them with enough time to find him before he unleashed the cartouche's fury.

They had gone to Evers' room where he checked his agent for broken ribs. Fortunately, everything seemed to be connected. The deep bruising would cause him substantial pain and discomfort for a while, but they would heal relatively quickly. He explained to Evers his plan to get to Hong Kong and about Javier's friend who was making their passports as they spoke.

Their flight to Mexico City was scheduled for 8:02 a.m. on the twenty-third, which gave them both a little time to rest and he some time to figure out how they would get into China largely undetected before heading to Xi'an to stop a madman. How they would stop him was a problem Buddy hadn't sorted out yet. Smuggling guns into China was an area he had not ventured into, but he was certain Dugan had, and that worried him tremendously.

Neither man could really talk about the next phase of the mission in the crowded Monterrey airport, even at that time of morning. In fact, both were simply relieved there had been no problems getting through security with their new passports. Buddy was going to have to destroy his original once they got to Manila. He didn't want to be caught in mainland China with a legitimate United States passport with direct ties to the CIA.

Evers walked over to a nearby coffee shop and bought two cups of steaming hot java. The men sipped their coffee gingerly and made small talk about fishing and hunting. Evers had obviously done more in the wilderness of late than Buddy had, but Buddy told him he would like to spend some time in Alabama at his place once they were finished with the job. Evers nodded his head approvingly.

The gate attendant called out in English and Spanish that their plane would begin boarding momentarily and to please have their boarding passes in hand when they reached the gate. They were seated next to one another on each leg of their flights, which made the possibility of speaking about the mission a little easier, as the sound of the engines and the air flowing through the cabin would help drown out their voices. The men knew their voices would carry around their gate area, and they couldn't afford to have any of the masses overhear them.

They boarded the plane with no luggage. Evers had never made it back to his hotel to retrieve his and Buddy had left his with Dugan in the rental car. "No big deal, Buck. Since we have a twelve hour layover in Manila we can go to the Glorietta Mall in Makati and get some new clothes. Plus, I like walking around there and looking at all those pretty Filipino girls," he said with a perverted grin.

"You're a sick old bastard, Buddy Smith," Evers said with a chuckle. "Where's Makati? Do we really have time to leave Manila?"

"Makati is the financial center of Manila and it's not too far from Aquino Airport. We can take a cab, grab our supplies and be back to the airport in no time. Of course, we'll have to take some time to sip on Lambanog. That's good stuff, son. It'll put hair on your little testicles," Buddy said jokingly. "And that might give me enough time to find me a fine little Filipino woman to pack up in a suitcase and bring back with me. Those women know how to take care of their men. You hear me?"

"Would you stop with the woman talk, Buddy? Let's stay focused. I am curious about Lambanog though. I assume that's some sort of liquor?"

"Hell no, it's not some sort of liquor. This stuff is sometimes called 'gin' or even 'vodka,' but in reality it's wine. It's fermented coconut milk and I'm here to tell you, son, it's the finest thing since sliced bread, and I like sliced bread," Buddy explained in only a way he could.

"Well, I just hate that we have such a long layover in Manila. We need to be getting on with our business on the mainland," Evers said in a lowered voice.

"Nah. It's really a good thing in the grand scheme, Buck. We have to have visas on top of our passports to cross into mainland China. Our Mexican friend didn't have time to work on that for us. Hell, we were lucky to come up with the passports in such short order. But I know a guy in Manila who can help us out. The layover will give him time to make sure the documents are perfect without raising any suspicion," Buddy said.

"Is there a country in this world where you don't know a guy?" asked Evers only half-jokingly.

Buddy thought for a moment then seriously replied, "Nope. Like I said, Buck...a man always has to have a back-up plan. Sometimes that back-up plan means knowing people in certain areas, sometimes it simply means knowing your terrain, and other times it means knowing your opponent's weaknesses. Whatever the case might be, I always try to have a go-to out there just in case things go to shit in a hand basket."

Evers closed his eyes for the duration of the short trip to Mexico City. Mercifully, he didn't dream.

Islas de Socorro
Revillagigedo, Mexico
July 23, 2013 12:12 P.M.

Dugan found some duct tape in a tool box and modified the plastic oxygen tube from one of the plane's oxygen masks in order to fully subdue Rafael. He taped the Mexican's mouth shut and tied his wrist behind his back with the tubing. Duct tape also wound around his ankles securing them to the bottom of his seat. Dugan admired his work as he sat back in his own seat. He stared at Rafael, rather he stared *through* him, as he thought about the connection between the cartouche and its former keeper.

The jet descended onto Socorro Island in order to refuel. Although the plane still had a considerable amount of fuel remaining in its tanks, the pilot had briefed Dugan on the need to stop and get more before the long voyage across the Pacific to Tarawa Island, which lay considerably south of Hawaii and just north of the equator. Dugan had demanded that the plane never touch down on U.S. soil because he didn't know what Smith had told his superiors. As a result of that demand, several stops had to be made along their erratic route to China. From Hawaii all the way to Kingman Reef, the United States had laid claim on the various island chains. He couldn't afford to risk capture in any holdings of the U.S., or anywhere for that matter, so he was forced to fly out of his way to avoid notice.

Islas de Revillagigedo was a Mexican holding with no public airport, but his contracted pilot had made arrangements for them to refuel at a small privately owned airport on the largest island in the archipelago. Leaving Rafael neatly secured, Dugan stepped off the plane while they waited for the fuel truck. The sky was an intense blue and the air fresh with the wonderful salty scent of the ocean.

The island's mountainous terrain was covered in trees and vegetation. Close to the airport was a small sea inlet allowing a few sailboats to cruise across its glassy surface. There didn't appear to be much activity on the small island beyond some tourism and basic island living. *I just don't have it in me to live this way; it's such a waste of time,* Dugan thought.

He milled around for some time, growing increasingly impatient. After forty-five minutes passed, he found his pilot.

"Would you care to tell me what the fuck is taking us so long? I'm paying you to fly, not dick around on some remote Mexican island!" he exclaimed.

"We are on island time, sir. It's much different here than it is on the mainland. People move when they feel like moving. My contact here is at a bar in the village. He said when he was finished he would come over and fuel up the plane," he explained.

"What the fuck are you talking about?" Dugan yelled! "You get that ignorant asshole over here now and tell him to fill up this damned plane, do you understand?"

The pilot looked at his employer with a great deal of patience, almost sympathetically. He nodded his understanding then replied, "Yes, sir. But you must appreciate the sensitivities involved in making demands of the only man on the island with access to jet fuel. No amount of money or screaming will get him here any faster. He lives on his own time and has plenty of money. Should we pursue your course of action he most likely will tell us to get lost and refuse to fuel up the plane. If that happens, you can forget getting to your destination on this aircraft."

"So, what do you recommend?" asked Dugan a little more calmly. He was still perturbed but the pilot's voice of reason caused him to moderate his tone, if only somewhat.

"I recommend stretching your legs, as you are doing now, or going on the plane and resting. Either way, I caution against pushing our host, elsewise we go back to mainland Mexico. Let him drink. If it costs us a couple of hours, what's the harm?" he answered lucidly.

Losing more time didn't make Dugan feel any better about this layover. *At this rate we'll never get to Xi'an,* he thought. He decided to turn his attention back to Rafael. It was his hope he could be reasoned with, even if it meant making promises he never intended on keeping.

"I need you and your co-pilot to exit the plane while we wait, Captain. There is a pressing need for me to have a private conversation with our passenger. I hope that won't inconvenience either of you. And I do appreciate your logical approach and rationale in awaiting your contact here on the island," he said diplomatically.

The pilot nodded his head and stepped into the cabin to retrieve his co-pilot. Both men walked away from the plane pretending to discuss their pending flight path and next stop. They secretly wondered about the ghostly thin man that their passenger had pushed on the plane. Neither the pilot nor co-pilot dared ask Dugan about his guest, as Dugan didn't look like the type of man who felt the need to explain himself.

Dugan stepped back into the fuselage of the plane to find Rafael awake and struggling against his bindings. He sat next to his prisoner, studying him for a few moments before speaking. Rafael stopped resisting against his constraints and met Dugan's gaze. A few uneasy seconds passed and he was forced to drop his eyes in stark resignation. The mental battle was over before it really ever began, and Dugan had won.

His captor reached over and ripped the duct tape from his mouth. He grunted as the pain subsided into burning, his cheeks and chin raw and sticky. His face was a strange paradox of brown and red with two small streaks of adhesive remaining.

Rafael mumbled, "Why are you doing this to me? Why not just kill me and get it over with? I've told you I have nothing else to say to you about the cartouche and what it revealed to me."

Dugan hid his displeasure and impatience, deciding it was better to take a different course with the man. The time he spent in the Agency in the Special Interrogation Unit had afforded him a skill set that had served him well over the years. Despite contrary screaming from the political left, water boarding, and other methods of inflicting mental anguish on a person, revealed significant and essential intelligence. However, those opposed to such methods were correct about one thing: a man will say anything to end his personal torture, so the interrogator was forced to separate truth from fiction. Where his colleagues usually got it wrong, and where he excelled, was understanding how to take a man to his mental break point, but stopping just before pushing him over the edge.

A good interrogator would push forward, stop before breaking the man's spirit completely, then repeat the process for days or even weeks. When the man's will to live was almost depleted he was at his most vulnerable. This was where the rest of his fellow SIU comrades missed the boat, and it was here that Dugan learned to befriend his captive.

The man being tortured understood his captor was capable of becoming the madman who almost pushed him over the mental and physical edge. He also understood the man was now being nice to him and nursing him slowly back to health by allowing him food and drink, and sometimes dessert. Dugan would go so far as finding out his target's favorite cigarette, if he smoked, and bring one to him, light it and put it in the man's mouth.

Over time Dugan gleaned more actionable intelligence than any in the unit. In fact, he was recognized as the go-to guy for high level detainees and domestic enemies of the State. Behind his back his fellow specialists joked and said he was the only man on Earth who could squeeze blood from a turnip.

Dugan leaned forward letting his hot breath hit Rafael in the face. He had been harsh with the man earlier, and now he would switch to feigned kindness. Dugan took a deep breath and exhaled loudly.

"Look, my friend, I don't enjoy having you secured like this. We've always had a good working relationship, and over the years I've taken a liking to you. Your work ethic is what kept me coming back to you each time, but unfortunately, we now find ourselves in a most peculiar situation. I really have no desire to terminate your life. I think we can find a mutually agreeable resolution to this predicament," Dugan said.

"How is that? What do you propose that could possibly bring about an end to this impasse, Mr. Dugan? You have not been honest with me since the beginning. You told me your name was Haden and the cartouche was wanted as a relic in a private collection. I know both of these things are lies," Rafael stated.

Dugan drew a thoughtful breath and replied, "What you said is correct, Rafael. I rarely ever use my real name while dealing in things many consider illicit. That way if the individual working for me, or doing business with me, is caught there is little the arresting body can do to track me down. This is also the reason I deal in cash, and never, ever write anything down. No paper trail and no proper identification. I'm sure you can appreciate my zeal when it comes to self-preservation. Insofar as the cartouche is concerned, there are things about it my client is interested in, but I can't say that I'm fully attuned to his plans. That is the way of business, Rafael. So, to say my client wished to have it in his personal collection may have been a bit of a stretch, but it wasn't entirely untrue.

"As a sign of good faith, sir, I would like to begin with this," he said as he pulled a knife from his pocket and cut the tape from Rafael's ankles, giving him much relief and the freedom to stretch his legs. They ached from being bound.

"As I see it, releasing your feet from bondage is a gesture of my intent, my friend. Your hands can be freed as well. But understand, I still have in my mind the fact that you pulled a gun on me back in the airplane hangar, so forgive me if I remain somewhat skittish and eye you with suspicion," Dugan said with an arched eyebrow.

Rafael continued stretching his legs, flexing them up and down at the knee, attempting to get the blood flowing in his lower extremities. He watched his legs move then looked back over at Dugan and said, "This changes nothing. I have no desire or reason to tell you what the jewel has shown me. In my heart I know it can be of no use to you." He let his last sentence hang in the air for a few seconds without making direct eye contact with Dugan.

"I see," Dugan said. "Well, do you mind if I ask you a question unrelated to the cartouche, Rafael?" He asked this, having now used the man's given name a few times, something he had never done in the course of their relationship. It was with some effort that he forced the niceties to flow. Before Rafael could answer he rose, walked to the rear of the plane and returned with two bottles of water. He twisted the cap off one and pushed it toward Rafael's mouth.

Rafael was happy to slurp down the water. His throat was parched and his mouth sticky with dryness. Dugan poured the water down his throat liberally and watched his Adam's apple bob up and down. A little water missed his mouth and dripped down his chin and chest.

Dugan sat the bottle of water down then asked, "Rafael, do you mind if I ask if that is your real name? I assume it is, but just want to confirm. It's a harmless question, really. Now that you know my name I think it only fair to assure I know yours."

"Yes, Mr. Dugan. My name is Rafael. That is what my father named me, after his father, my grandfather. At least that is what I always understood. Does that satisfy your curiosity?" he asked.

"Of course, Rafael, thank you. You look hungry. Allow me to get some food for you," he said as he rose a second time. Once again he walked to the back of the plane and after a few moments came back with a heated tray of food, obviously warmed in the plane's microwave.

The food's delicious aroma grabbed Rafael's attention. So engrossed had he become with the cartouche over the last few weeks that he had completely neglected his hunger pangs. The smell of processed turkey and green beans filled the cabin making his stomach growl loud enough that Dugan heard it.

As he had with the water, he sat it down then reached across and carefully untied Rafael's hands. He remained within easy reach of his knife if he needed it, but he doubted that would be the case. Rafael had grown increasingly cooperative in the passing moments since their discussion had begun.

Dugan handed him the food and a plastic fork, followed by another bottle of water. Rafael shoveled the food into his mouth. It looked as though his teeth barely touched the meal before he swallowed it. He reached for the water and washed the dry turkey down.

While he ate Dugan began speaking again. "You know, I realize you've only recently known me as 'Dugan,' so I think it's fair that you know my first name – Daniel. Most people I associate with call me Dan. Now you know my first and last name. It's been my experience that knowing someone's first and last name allows a person a certain bond with the individual who hears it."

Rafael chewed a little more slowly as he listened to Dugan, not sure where he was going with the conversation. His mistrust was great but he had removed his bindings and given him food and water.

"I find this a perfect time for us to get to know one another, Rafael. After all, we have little else on our hands now except for...time. So, tell me, what is your last name?"

Rafael looked at his former employer and asked, "You still haven't told me where you are taking me. It's difficult for me to trust someone who can't explain where he's taking me."

"You are quite correct, Rafael. I'll make you a deal – an answer for an answer. How about that? I think that's very fair. You tell me your last name and I'll tell you our destination," he said.

Rafael chomped his food and thought about why Dugan was interested in his last name. He couldn't think of a good reason not to tell the man because, after all, he had freed him and given him food.

"My last name is Chao," said Rafael.

Dugan's heart pounded in his chest as his assumption was confirmed. *A Chinese last name! I knew it. The cartouche has attached itself to a family member just as the story was told.* A grin slowly spread across his face and he had to look away to keep Rafael from seeing his elation.

"Rafael Chao," Dugan repeated, regaining his composure. "Have you ever thought about how strange that sounds, my friend? That sir name doesn't sound very Latino to me. Does it to you?" he asked.

Rafael paused to consider his answer then responded, "I guess I never really stopped to think about how different it sounded, Mr. Dugan. Many of my friends have similar sounding last names. Names such as Chen, Huang and Chao are very common in my area. We tend to look a little more native than many other Mexicans, too. But growing up in our circumstances we never thought about our names. We thought mostly about food and clothes. That's what was important to us then. It's not so different for a lot of the kids now."

Dugan listened to Rafael's social discourse on the plight of Mexico's children with little interest. His desire to unleash the magic of the jewel he had in his possession precluded any sentimentality he would have toward a kid starving in the streets of Mexico, or anywhere else for that matter.

He did, however, have to maintain an open dialogue with Rafael, at least for the time being, so Dugan kept his eyes fixed on him in an effort to simulate interest. He nodded his head in all the right places as Rafael spoke, grunted when he was supposed to, and shook his head on cue. There were few on the planet who could match his skills in the realm of deception and manipulation, and he exhibited this ability during his conversation with Rafael.

After they finished speaking, Dugan stood and gave Rafael a reassuring pat on the shoulder. He didn't worry about tying him up again, as he was certain he had won the heart and mind of the man. Naturally, he would kill Rafael once he no longer needed him, as he originally planned, but at least for now he could rest easy knowing the Mexican wouldn't try to run away or kill him first.

Not wanting to press him any further, Dugan elected to continue the discussion once they were airborne. He walked outside in search of his pilot and co-pilot to see if they had an update from the islander who was supposed to be refueling the plane. They stood along the fence line some twenty-five yards from the plane. Both men had a cigarette in their mouths and stared out at the bay.

The pilot turned to face Dugan after he had taken no more than five or six steps. He shook his head to let him know that he hadn't heard from their fuel delivery man. Perturbed, Dugan walked back to the air conditioned plane. The thought of standing in that heat waiting on some moron to show up drunk and driving an incredibly flammable truckload of jet fuel was enough to send him over the edge.

It's probably best I don't open my mouth again about this guy. He may just make my shit list! Dugan stepped back onto the cool airplane and took a seat a couple rows behind Rafael who had already fallen asleep. His hand drifted to his pocket where it caressed the cartouche. The customary thrum vibrated from his hand to his elbow. Reassured he was about to become an incredibly powerful and important man, he let his head recline on the chair, and, like his prisoner, fell asleep.

Manila, Philippines
Ninoy Aquino International Airport
July 24, 2013 1:33 A.M.

Evers and Buddy arrived in Manila without incident. They had had a relatively short layover in Mexico City and boarded the Airbus A380, the biggest plane that could safely land in Manila. The flight was filled with many Filipinos, Chinese and Japanese heading to various destinations. Evers overheard a few Europeans speaking in their native tongue behind him, presumably German.

After their "heart-to-heart" discussion about his nightmares, Evers was concerned about the long flight over the Pacific and being detained should he have an outburst while dozing. Fortunately, Buddy never left his side. They had discussed little on the full flight, and neither wanted to be overheard talking about their reasons for traveling to the Philippines and beyond.

The pilot taxied the plane to its gate, and after thirty minutes from the time they landed, they finally disembarked. Evers took a few moments to do a couple of back and neck stretches in the concourse. Buddy squatted down and stood back up in an attempt to get the blood flowing in his aging legs.

Evers watched as Buddy pulled his cell phone from his pocket and thumbed through the address book. "We're here. Intercon. Thirty minutes." He clicked off and began heading for customs.

He looked at Evers as he pulled his passport out and stuck five U.S. dollars inside. "The fewer lies we have to tell the better off we are."

Evers stuck a five in his own passport and closed it. "What does this buy us?"

"Our stay here is only going to be a few hours, Buck. Neither of us wants to explain why we're leaving the airport and returning again in a few hours with a final destination to Xi'an. That makes us memorable should someone begin to ask questions. The money makes this process much easier in the Philippines, trust me. Customs jobs here are premium positions because of the money that changes hands."

A customs agent motioned for Buddy to approach as Evers stood in line watching. Buddy handed the agent his passport and gave the man a quick wink. Evers watched as the man opened the passport then grinned at Buddy. His hand shot the money into his pocket then just as quickly stamp his passport. No questions, no comments...just a smile.

"I'll be damned," Evers muttered under his breath.

The same agent motioned him to step forward. He offered the man a tight smile as he handed him his passport. The same scenario played itself out as the man deftly put the bill in his pocket then just as ably stamped his passport.

"Enjoy the Philippines, sir," the agent said in thickly accented English.

Evers smiled at the man again the walked next to Buddy. Both continued onto the baggage claim area, grabbed their luggage and walked to a door leading outside the airport.

The two stepped outside into what could only be described as controlled pandemonium. It felt as though all twelve million residents of Metro Manila had converged at the exact moment they walked outside. Heat, humidity and air pollution hit Evers square in the chest. For a solitary moment he thought he would lose his ability to breath. The air and smog was suffocating, and the toxic fumes of cars, hotel shuttles and Jeepney's, slowly filed through the arrival area.

Buddy pulled out his cell and once again scrolled through his contact list. "I need two rooms, checking out tomorrow. Put them in my name, Joe Presley."

Evers watched him pause after giving them his travel name, apparently being spoken to by whoever was on the other end of the conversation. Buddy smiled and offered a little chuckle.

"Yes, just like Elvis. No, I'm not related. Just hold the rooms for me. I don't want to give my credit card information over the phone. I'll be there in about twenty minutes. Thank you," he said and clicked off again.

"What was that about?" asked Evers.

"I got us a room so we can get a little rest. We're going to need it, so I suggest hitting the hay as soon as we get checked in. We'll stay for a few hours at the Intercontinental Hotel in Makati, the downtown area of Manila and its financial district. It's right next to the mall we talked about earlier. Let's sleep, get up and walk over and get some new clothes then head back here. I've got a meet with my contact here. You know, my guy we talked about back in Old Mexico. He'll handle our visa problems," Buddy said without a hint of doubt.

Buddy looked at home in Aquino Airport, and Evers suspected he'd been there several times before. Part of the warrior's creed included not asking another about past travels unless there was something that could help a person with a new mission. None of that mattered now anyway. All that he wanted to do was lay down in a comfortable bed for a few hours and rest. He knew Buddy was telling him the truth about needing sleep before they ventured into China. What he didn't have to say was how dangerous everything would be once they attempted to get into the country. Hopefully, his 'guy' was as good as he said, and their visas wouldn't raise any questions.

His old friend raised his hand as the Intercontinental Hotel shuttle pulled to the curb. The two hopped aboard and took a seat, each careful to keep his head down and avoid eye contact with anyone else on the shuttle. Old habits died nasty deaths.

"You haven't told me how we're going to get into China, Buddy. There will be questions before we cross the border, and they don't necessarily appreciate Americans, especially Americans who want to bring their

Terracotta Warriors to life then march out of their country with them in tow," he said in a whisper but loud enough for Buddy's ears.

Buddy smiled at him and made the sign of the cross. "Oh ye of little faith, you silly bastard. You and I are going to be Christian missionaries spreading the good Word to those Godless sons a bitches. Happens all the time over here. The Chinese tolerate our Christian folks preaching the Gospel, and we tolerate their cheap shit getting shipped over the pond and placed in our department stores. God Bless em he finished, sarcasm dripping from his mouth."

Evers stared at Buddy, the disbelief in his eyes more than evident. He'd never been a religious man, but realized a border agent, especially a non-Christian Chinese one, would never question his Biblical knowledge. That simple truth didn't make him feel any better about the cover story, though, primarily because he had spent his life avoiding God, and now he would be forced to assume the role of servant. Somehow, he quickly realized his doubt was nothing more than fear of the Big Man Upstairs. *I guess that's just one more thing I'll have to come to terms with when I get home. For now, I'll have to deal with the hypocrisy.*

Buddy watched the wheels turn and ostensibly read what was running through his partner in crime's mind. "Look, Young Buck, I don't think God would want that lunatic Dugan standing charge over any army, much less a virtually indestructible one. Nor do I think he'll stand in judgment of your disguise. Of course if He does, you and I are going to burn together for an eternity. That should put your mind at ease," he guffawed as he slapped Evers on the back.

Evers raised a brow and replied, "That's a visual I can do without, Buddy. The thought of spending an eternity on fire and listening to you talk about all the women you've bedded makes my pickle pucker."

The two men spent a couple minutes laughing before Evers continued.

"So what happens once we get inside China? We've still got to make our way to Xi'an and somehow find Dugan and the cartouche. What's the plan?" asked Evers.

"Hell, that's easy," Buddy said. "We kill the bad guys, take the cartouche and the army, save the world and get the girl. I thought you would have this ending figured out already, Buck."

"What girl?" Evers asked.

Buddy leaned into him and replied, "I haven't met her yet, but when I do I'm going to save her and live happily ever after." He gave Evers a wink and a nod.

Tarawa Island, Kiribati
Bonriki International Airport
July 23rd, 2013 10:52 P.M.

It had taken Dugan several hours to calm down after the owner of the airport in Socorro finally showed up. The man could barely walk and certainly couldn't speak coherently when he showed up. He wanted nothing more than to step off the plane and stick his pistol right between the man's eyes and squeeze the trigger.

Dugan managed to control his temper just enough to let the man live. Begrudgingly, he paid the drunkard and boarded the plane without so much as a nod of appreciation for allowing them to refuel at his airport. The pilot waited for his boss to get on the plane before turning to the man and shaking his hand, thanking him for the fuel and time spent at his airport. Burning bridges or friendships in remote places wasn't wise for the pilot of a small jet.

For several hours, the foursome flew at twenty-six thousand feet through smooth air. As their plane continued on its southwesterly course, Dugan thought the sun would never set. It did give him some time to stare out the window and admire the azure Pacific below. So calm was the ocean that it appeared to be a majestic piece of blue glass.

Rafael had remained silent and calm during their flight, asking only if he could have something to drink and, on a couple of occasions, if he could step inside the restroom to relieve himself. Still, despite his calmness and initial feeling of winning his trust, Dugan sensed a man biding his time and planning to strike like a deadly viper awaiting its prey. He needed to have another discussion with him, but knew it would have to wait until he could be sure that he wasn't going to try something stupid. Not wanting to press too hard or too fast, Dugan did not engage the man until after they landed at Bonriki International Airport.

The small island nation of Kiribati was a former British holding until 1979 and sat close to the equator on the edge of the International Date Line. Its inhabitants had gained their freedom peacefully after petitioning the British parliament. Several cultures lived on the narrow island beaches but Micronesians were in the majority. Dugan hoped for better results than they had gotten during their refueling efforts in Socorro, despite the fact that they were flying to another small island whose inhabitants most likely lacked any sense of urgency.

Lying just to the southeast of the Marshall Islands and due east of New Guinea and Australia, the country boasted a population of some one hundred and thirty thousand residents. Locals suffered from poverty on a scale most couldn't understand, but as with most poor nations the people all seemed to be smiling and happy.

Insofar as international airports were concerned, Bonriki's one modest runway was barely long enough to support a plane much larger than the Learjet. Two old metal hangars sat to the side of the runway and three small single engine props were parked nearby.

Since the small country used to be a British holding, English was the official language even though most people spoke Gilbertese, an ancient and glorious poly-Asian and oceanic language. The runway sat on the ocean's edge surrounded by gorgeous beaches. Heat waves distorted the passengers' vision as the lights from the tail section parted the darkness of the evening.

Dugan squinted out his window willing some human activity to magically appear. Unfortunately, zero movement could be seen in the small airport terminal or on the street right behind it. He hung his head in desperation as the realization they would get no fuel until the following day hit him like a punch to the gut.

The pilot and co-pilot opened their cockpit door and stepped out, anxiety overshadowing the bleak smiles on their faces. "I'm afraid we must stay here for the evening, sir," the co-pilot said to Dugan.

"I could get to China faster if I swam the Pacific!" He punched the seat in front of him.

The Captain flinched at Dugan's outburst. He turned and opened the door to the plane and let the steps fall to the tarmac. "There is a hotel a half mile down the road, sir. We are going to get a room there. I suggest we all do the same and meet back here at 8:00 a.m.

Dugan took a deep breath then released it slowly and loudly. He looked over at Rafael who was staring straight ahead. To Dugan he looked like he was a million miles away, but soon realized he was physically there but mentally two thousand years in the past.

In his pocket the cartouche thrummed, more so than any time it had been in his possession. Slowly, Rafael turned and faced him, his eyes drifting to Dugan's pocket. Had anyone witnessed the bizarre scene, they would have thought someone was filming a scene for a horror movie. Rafael barred his teeth and reached for Dugan.

He rose and shifted away from Rafael who had also gotten to his feet and silently stepped toward his captor. Suddenly, Dugan no longer felt like the predator, but the prey. The thrumming in his pocket grew stronger and Rafael seemed to become more energized. His heart beat loudly in his chest as he stepped back from the skeleton of a man.

A million things ran through his mind at once. Things like creating distance between himself and Rafael, subduing him without killing him, not being killed himself, and understanding the strange connection between the man and the ancient relic.

Rafael placed a hand on the seatbacks just in front of him and on either side of the aisle way. Dugan used the seatbacks to brace himself and as a point of leverage, as Rafael took another slow step toward him. He knew he could pull his pistol out again, but he didn't want to kill the man. As the

Mexican took another step, his weight shifting on his lead leg, Dugan ducked and lunged at it, pulling himself on the seats as he did so. As deftly as a twenty-year old, he took the hypnotized man to the floor and swiftly straddled him in the tight confines of the small aisle.

Rafael attempted to push Dugan off him but the seats prevented either man from rolling over. Dugan drew a balled fist up and immediately slammed it into his opponent's cheek, rendering him unconscious again. His hand began to swell a few seconds after the impact with Rafael's face and he knew it was broken.

"Fuck me," he screamed! "Can this damnable trip get any worse?" he asked no one in particular.

He found the bonds he had used to secure Rafael last time and tied his hands behind his back, although he struggled with his own broken hand. Next, he found the duct tape and taped his ankles, but had to leave him on the floor, the pain in his hand shooting into his forearm.

Few things anger a man like pain. Pain can make a totally rationale person act irrationally. It can make a generally sane person go over the top and do something completely ridiculous by logical standards. Dugan stepped over Rafael's prone body, turned, the pain in his hand and arm intensifying, and kicked him in the face. Blood shot from his nose from the impact of Dugan's foot. Rafael's mouth flew open and a tooth fell on the carpeted floor.

Sweating, Dugan sat down to calm himself and to catch his breath. He surveyed the damage he had inflicted on the man and wondered silently if he had killed him. Rafael's fragile body appeared broken. No sooner had the thought passed through his mind when he saw him take a deep breath.

"At least he's breathing. Pity, we were getting along so well too. Hopefully, I can keep the stupid bastard alive long enough to free the soldiers. He has no choice," he muttered to himself under his breath.

Makati, Philippines
Intercontinental Hotel Restaurant
July 24, 2013 9:07 A.M.

The two met in the Café Jeepney, named for the old World War II buses they had seen earlier at the airport. Although neither man got all the sleep he had wanted, some was better than none, and the hotel beds they slept on were fantastically comfortable. They sat down at their table and ordered breakfast and coffee from a cute little waitress named Maya. Buddy winked at her then blew her a kiss. She giggled as she walked back to the kitchen to get their coffee and freshly squeezed mango juice.

"Now there's a fine little filly, Buck. I bet she would take damned good care of you too," he teased.

Maya brought their coffee to them then took their breakfast order. Buddy asked for a fried egg on fried rice and a side order of mango. Evers decided he would have the same thing and their waitress turned and bounded toward the kitchen to drop off their ticket.

Buddy briefed him on what had transpired earlier that morning. His Filipino contact had showed up around 7:00 a.m. with their forged China visas. He slid Evers his as he spoke. "Now, here's the real shit of the deal, Buck. You and I are like Felix the fucking Cat. You hear me? We've got a new lease on life, so to speak," he said, grinning from ear to ear.

A smirk crossed Evers' face. Buddy always seemed to have a scheme and was always wheeling and dealing in the darkest recesses of different countries' underworlds. There was no doubt he had stumbled upon something that would help them, but Buddy loved to build suspense and wouldn't tell Evers what he had procured until he asked.

"What 'cha got? I hope you're going to tell me you've purchased a tank and a couple of Howitzers that are going to be dropped off at the exact time we arrive in Xi'an," Evers responded.

"Nope, but I have the next best thing," Buddy replied as he reached to the floor and picked up a small navy blue duffel bag. "In this bag I have two pistols, equalizers, if you will. It's better than nothing, Buck, and there is no way in hell we are going to get guns once we're inside the wire with the Chicoms."

"That's perfect, Buddy, but how do you propose two evangelicals, hell-bent on bringing the heathen Chinese to the altar, are going to smuggle those firearms across the border? They'll bury us under a prison then blow it up just to prove a point if we're caught, and you know it," Evers reasoned.

"I thought you would never ask," Buddy smugly replied. "What we have here is the latest in print technology, my friend-plastic guns. Undetectable unless accidentally found. We're going to stuff these bad boys in our bags and walk right across the border, right through their metal detectors and help spread God's Word.

"What the hell are you talking about, Buddy? Print technology? Plastic guns? I have no idea what you're talking about. I guess I'm going to need you to translate for me," said Evers.

"Well, Buck, there are new printers that mold plastic. They're called 3-D printers and the technology is incredible. You can make anything your little heart can imagine in three dimensional form on these printers. The scary part is the parts work! We can build entire pistols and rifles from plastic and they'll fire real bullets. And that's the crux...we'll have to get bullets once we get inside the wire, but those are easier to come by than the actual firearm," he explained.

Evers sat in his seat perplexed and confused. He wondered when this shift in technology had happened. Living in such a secluded area was great, but apparently the world was passing him by. This fact didn't bother him that much, but he was embarrassed that an old-timer like Buddy knew about the technology and he didn't.

Evers turned his head and looked out the window at a car pulling into the hotel driveway. He watched the security guards circle the car with a large round mirror on a telescopic wand and search beneath the vehicle for explosives. The driver opened his trunk so the armed guards could inspect it as well. When he and Buddy had showed up at the hotel a few hours earlier, they had gone through a similar shakedown. Armed guards stood at many public entrances, even at highway tollbooths.

As he stared out at the Glorietta Four Mall Buddy had told him about several hours earlier, he could see the city's smog sit on it like a mother hen protecting its eggs. The realities of a third world country were always difficult for him to fathom, even though he had just left Mexico and had seen similar poverty. Their hotel and the rest of the country were paradoxical shifts between the haves and have not's. In the last 10 minutes, Evers had seen many homeless and destitute, all from the safety of the hotel restaurant's window. He shifted his attention back to Buddy who continued to explain about their plastic weaponry.

"This technology is available to the general public, Buck. My contact recommended it when I told him we were facing a treacherous voyage into China. The damned things fire a forty caliber bullet too. Do you know how much the Filipinos don't like the Chinese? Well, they can't stand them and if we're going to do anything to piss them off, these people will support us. You got it?" he asked.

"Yeah, plastic guns, real bullets, Chinese, death, dismemberment, magic, statues. Understood. I tell you, Buddy, this whole thing is starting to catch up with me. This shit is just getting weird. I mean, I never really questioned any of it at the onset, but I've had plenty of time to think about it on the way over here. I know you think it's real, but I still have my doubts," Evers replied.

"Whatever the truth is, Buck, Dugan feels that he needs to kill for it. Let's go to the mall and get our clothes and we can finish this conversation later," Buddy said.

Buddy put his bag in his room for safekeeping, then met Evers in the hotel lobby a few minutes later. They crossed a very busy East Street to the Glorietta Mall where they were searched by guards before entering. Once inside they found a couple of department stores where they could purchase some new clothes, in addition to new suitcases.

Evers asked Buddy, "Why all the armed guards around here? Bomb searches at the hotel. These folks seem to be pretty diligent about their security."

"Fucking extremist camel jockeys, Young Buck. There are millions of them here. Mostly they hang out on the southern islands, but they have a pretty significant presence in the capital too. They like to blow shit up, kill people...the usual," he finished.

Evers nodded his understanding and carried on with his shopping, buying enough in the way of clothes to last him a week, and toiletries to last a couple of months. He was amazed with the warmth and politeness of the gentle Asian islanders, even in a city as vast as Manila. Everywhere he went people smiled and greeted him with a "hello, sir." It was difficult for him to comprehend why anyone would want to blow up such a loving bunch of people, but he knew evil had no bounds and was indiscriminate.

After they finished making their purchases and Buddy stopped long enough to exchange United States dollars for Chinese Yuan at a currency exchange booth, they walked outside the mall and stared at the palm trees that lined the sidewalks. The temperature was balmy and the air pollution heavy. He watched as people hustled to the Ayala bus terminal. As with most major cities, mass transit was the easiest, most cost effective method of moving around the area.

"It's too much city for me, but I like the people, Buddy. I wouldn't mind having a place here out in the country far removed from the hustle and bustle," Evers mused.

Buddy chuckled and responded, "Yeah, until a typhoon came along and blew you and your house all to hell. Happens all the time over here. Hellacious storms too. Let's go get our shit and get back to the airport. It's almost time to leave, and we've had a little change in plans. Since we have our visas, we're going directly to Shanghai then on to Xi'an. This itinerary will get us there faster than stopping in Hong Kong first."

Taipei, Taiwan
Taipei Shongshan Airport
July 24th, 2013 12:09 P.M.

Dan Dugan grew ever more anxious. His plans, which he had spent countless days and years setting in motion, were unraveling. The frustration of having to stop at several island airports on his way to China was growing exponentially, and was an oversight for which he could not forgive himself. Few times in his life had he flown on a jet that wasn't of a commercial or military variety.

The times that he had found himself on a smaller plane, had seen him delivered and dropped at his location within a couple of hours. He had become so upset with himself at not accounting for the smaller fuel tank on his chartered flight that he wanted to kill someone. His eyes looked to Rafael; he forcibly tore them away from his captive to keep from acting upon the impulse.

They had stopped in Kokor, Palau for fuel. Palau, an island archipelago directly associated with Micronesia, had been settled several thousand years prior by boat faring Filipinos, most likely by accident. As with many islands that had been settled in the western Pacific, fishermen had been blown off course and found themselves occupying a new land.

Typical of Southeast Asia, no one got in a hurry. Dugan didn't care that island life worldwide seemingly encouraged less urgency, or that Filipinos in general took time to enjoy life. None of that mattered to him when his plane landed in Kokor. All he wanted was for someone to put fuel in their plane and get airborne with the least amount of time wasted. Unfortunately for him this wasn't the case.

Kokor had had a rash of international travelers land at their small airport just as his jet landed. Three total planes landing within a timespan of one hour was significant for the small airport, which forced baggage handlers to also be runway attendants, as well as airport security. As strange as it might sound to individuals who travel through metropolitan airports, small budgets forced companies to operate with small workforces. And stranger yet, was the team concept of getting things done. Such was the case in Kokor.

These fucking slopes. They're always so happy for no goddam reason at all and never get in a hurry to do anything.

Dugan was ready to step off the plane and wring someone's neck. Just as he began to rise, the fuel truck pulled up and began filling the tank. A sense of relief overcame him as he watched the workers pump gas into the plane's fuel reservoir.

A short time later the plane was in the air, but then forced to land again in Taipei. The amount of time spent on the aircraft was exhausting, and keeping an eye on Rafael had proven tiresome. Keeping his pistol drawn whenever he released him so he could eat or relieve himself had gotten old quickly. Conversation had been sparse until they had begun their decent into Shongshan airport, the smaller of the two airports in metro-Taipei and least likely to create a stir if a smaller jet landed there.

"You think you can control that army, Señor but you are wrong. The magic that controls them did not originate from a man like you," Rafael said as a sickly laugh slid over his bloody lips. The gap from his missing tooth caused a serpentine hiss when he spoke. He wheezed and coughed, his crooked nasal passages making it difficult to breathe, then looked away.

"What are you talking about you wetback son of a bitch? If you know something you better tell me now, or you'll regret it very soon. Do you hear me?" he screamed!

Rafael continued to ignore Dugan as the plane touched down, its rear tires skidding loudly, the front tires touching down seconds later.

The pilots, knowing their passenger was becoming ever more impatient and prone to violence, taxied to their gate as the refueling truck sped to its side. A host of men wearing gloves ran around the plane and truck connecting the fuel hose to the tank inlet before flipping switches allowing the fuel to flow.

Dugan stood and glowered at Rafael. He reached over and smacked the insolent Mexican on the head demanding his attention. Not even a whimper could be heard from Rafael, which infuriated Dugan further. He punched him in the ribs and pummeled his arms and legs, but no matter the punishment he doled out, Rafael remained motionless and silent.

Finally, out of breath and sweating, Dugan fell into his chair wondering what Rafael had meant about not being able to *control* the Terracotta Army. His mind raced and he ran his fingers through his hair, a nervous habit that he had picked up many years earlier. Everything that had seemed so concrete just a couple of days prior now didn't appear to be so clear-cut anymore.

Being confined to the small aircraft was starting to drive him crazy. There was another stop in Hong Kong before the final leg to Xi'an, which meant at least another eight to ten hours before their arrival into the Forbidden Zone, as it was known in China.

The sky was overcast and the threat of storms loomed in the west. This potentiality made Dugan even more uneasy. He stormed up to the cabin and demanded to know how much longer it would take for the plane to become airborne. His pilot, ever weary, told him at least another thirty minutes.

Dugan was on the verge of explosion. He knew his blood pressure was tipping the scale, and he worried he would have a heart-attack or stroke before they arrived in Xi'an if he didn't bring himself under control. He paced back and forth in the aisle, his neck crooked to one side to avoid hitting his head on the plane's low ceiling. Fatigue and anxiety had begun to take a toll on his aging body. Only his drive to see this mission through kept him awake. Coffee was what he needed so he walked to the back of the plane and pulled out the coffee maker, a packet of coffee, and a filter. As it heated up and dripped into the stainless pot the fresh aroma reinvigorated him.

With intensity etched into his face he stepped over to the window and watched as the men worked to finish fueling up the aircraft. The door at the front of the plane opened. Quickly, his hand felt the pistol hanging in the small of his back as he watched the pilot finish opening it. Eyes narrowed, he stepped forward but was relieved when a small Taiwanese man asked if he could restock their food supply in the galley.

Dugan told him to leave everything at the entrance because he didn't want the man walking to the back and seeing Rafael bound and gagged. The worker looked a little confused then shrugged his shoulders and stacked a couple boxes containing ready-to-eat meals, bottled water, and more coffee behind the cockpit door. The pilot paid the man and tucked the receipt into his wallet, which would find its way to Dugan at the end of the journey.

He relaxed and turned his attention back to his coffee. After dumping a couple packs of sugar and one creamer into his cup, he sipped gingerly. The hot elixir wound its way through his belly into his intestines, and for a moment, he felt some of his sanity return.

The smell of the freshly brewed coffee roused Rafael for the first time since his previous outburst. He stared at the cup in Dugan's hand while Dugan stared back at him. Rafael looked like a man possessed. That thought almost made Dugan laugh, as he had grown to realize that Rafael truly was possessed, held captive by a spell an ancient and distant family member had cast two millennia ago.

Rafael made a muffled sound behind the duct tape across his mouth so Dugan reached over and yanked it off. He winced as the glue from the tape ripped several hairs from his unshaven face and swollen lips. After a few seconds the pain subsided and he spoke.

"I would really like to have a cup of that coffee, sir," croaked Rafael. "I promise not to try anything if you would simply allow me to have some."

"Fuck you. The last time you told me something similar to that you tried to attack me. Why should I believe you now?"

"The coffee smells good, sir. Having some would make me feel human again. That's the only reason I ask. I have no agenda, no strength left to fight, and no energy to try to escape. I only want some coffee. It's really that simple, sir," Rafael finished.

Dugan raised his cup of coffee to his mouth where he took long, slurping sips. He raised his right eyebrow and nodded his head to Rafael in a silent sign of appreciation of the flavor of the java. Rafael imagined he did the same thing to a younger sibling who wanted whatever Dugan had when they were growing up.

Still, Dugan sat in his seat slurping and staring at Rafael. His background in interrogation served him well, when he wasn't allowing his temper and emotions to drive his actions. He relented and retrieved a cup for Rafael, but didn't give it to him. Dugan sat it in the cup holder as he sat back down. Leaning forward he smiled a warm smile at Rafael.

"I'd be happy to give you some coffee my friend, but you have to promise me not to do anything stupid like you did last time. Should you attempt that again, I'll kill you and figure out another way to secure my army. Is that clear?" he asked.

Rafael nodded his head and licked his lips. The smell of the coffee had sparked something in him. In fact, this was the first time he had felt like himself in two weeks. There was something about the aroma that excited his olfactory senses. He remembered times spent sipping tequila, eating good food and asking for a coffee after dinner. Times before the cartouche had entered his life.

Dugan, with significant difficulty, released his bonds giving him an opportunity to stand and stretch. His broken hand made doing things like tying and untying things very challenging. Rafael let out a sigh of relief before uttering a "thank you" then sat back down. A small smile touched Dugan's face when he heard the Mexican thank him. He knew he was getting inside his head and understood that Rafael was beginning to "like" him, much like other captives who learned to love their captors. It was called the Stockholm Syndrome and he had utilized it several times in his illustrious career. Still, he knew the cartouche could take hold of him at any time and turn him into a rabid dog.

Rafael slurped his coffee loudly. Periodic "ahs" were vocalized and a look of pure pleasure would cross his face each time he swallowed his caffeinated beverage. Dugan allowed Rafael to enjoy his coffee in silence before easing back into his line of questioning.

"So, my friend, I think it is time we continue our previous discussion. I would like for you to offer some enlightenment regarding your remarks about me not being able to control the Terracotta Army."

Rafael pulled the coffee from his mouth and eyed Dugan cautiously. Doubt and suspicion passed over his face, like a dark cloud passing in front of the sun, but he relented, realizing his captor had the upper hand. The truth be told, he had always had the upper hand. Rafael just refused to admit it, until now. He put his lips back on the cup and took another sip.

"Mister Dugan, the cartouche's magic was put in place by a man of goodness. He comforted the sick and defended the poor. At no time did he desire personal fortune or fame; he merely wanted good things for his people. When he cast the spell, he did so in defense of his family and his village. Reversing the spell requires someone of his line, and controlling the army would require someone of a good heart. It's really that simple," Rafael stated emphatically.

Dugan stared at Rafael, his mind spinning. *He is telling me I can't control the army because I don't have a good or pure heart. Who the fuck does? I have to figure out how to properly control it before our plane lands in Xi'an.*

"How do you know these things, Rafael? How can you be so certain that what you're telling me is accurate? What would happen if someone who wasn't good tried to control the army? In fact, how do I know you aren't lying to me right now?" he asked.

"I'm not lying, Mr. Dugan. Everything else you ask is unknown. I only know and understand what is revealed to me," Rafael responded.

"You've told me several times that the cartouche has revealed many things to you." He rose and looked at Rafael and his empty coffee cup. "Would you like some more coffee?" Dugan asked with considerable patience.

"Si, Mr. Dugan. That java tastes very good and sits well in my belly," he replied.

Dugan walked to the back of the plane and refilled Rafael's coffee cup. With great care not to spill the near boiling liquid, he made the few strides back to Rafael's seat and handed him the cup. Rafael grabbed it and held it to his nose as if he had never smelled the stuff in his life.

"How do you know all this to be true, Rafael? How does the cartouche reveal things to you?" he asked.

At once Rafael's eyes dropped to Dugan's pocket. His eyes remained there for several seconds, his face as stoic as any Dugan had ever seen. For a moment he seemed to *fade* from existence, like he wasn't of this time or place, but of another many eons prior.

"It speaks to me, Mr. Dugan," he replied at long last. "It shows me things that it will not show anyone else. The cartouche shows me people and mountains and magic from a time long past. It's as though I am standing there, an unseen spectator and the images are portrayed to me. I can't explain how it shows me these things, but I find that hours will pass as it details everything that it has seen in the distant past," Rafael said. "Everything the elder, the creator of the cartouche experienced, I am allowed to see."

Dugan said nothing. He dropped his eyes and nodded his head, understanding, or at least wanting to understand, what Rafael explained to him. What he was trying to articulate, he thought, was that the cartouche was showing him images and emotions connected to the events leading up to the spell being cast over two-thousand years ago. It was like a children's book, complete with pictures, telling a story in such a way that his simple mind would grasp the tale.

In that moment he decided that the Mexican would stay alive and help him gain control of the Terracotta Warriors. Little doubt crossed his mind that Rafael was critical to his plan. In fact, everything he said reinforced what he now believed to be true – Rafael was just as much a part of the Warrior's Key as the cartouche itself.

He also realized the wounds he had inflicted on the man would bring about unwanted attention once they landed in China. He walked to the small galley sink, found a paper towel, and wet it. Dugan also pulled ice from the small freezer and placed several cubes in two separate plastic bags.

He stood towering over Rafael holding the wet paper towel. Dugan dropped the ice packs into the empty seat next to him before turning his attention back to his captive. He handed the wet cloth to the man and directed him to clean the blood from his face.

Gingerly, Rafael moved the wet cloth over his lips, nose, and cheeks. The white towel quickly turned red as it washed over his features. He grunted as he washed as the nasally escape of air through his broken nose made a funny whistling sound.

Dugan took a half-step to Rafael and placed his good hand on one side of the man's broken nose and the edge of his own broken hand to the other side of his nose. With one quick motion he snapped it into place.

Rafael howled. "Pincha cabron!" His own hands flew instinctively to his face seeking to massage the area from which the new-found pain was radiating. Tears began to cascade over his bruised cheek.

Dugan turned and reached for one of the ice bags, shoving it toward the injured man. "Put this on your fucking nose and stop crying. You're a grown man, so shut up. Besides, I couldn't have you walking around with that fucked up beak in the middle of China, now could I?"

As Rafael glared at him, he grabbed his own ice bag and placed it on his damaged hand. He allowed himself a small smile at both the information he'd gathered from Rafael and the additional pain he had inflicted on the insolent bastard. As messed up as the trip to Asia had been, things were looking slightly better after the last few moments.

Manila, Philippines
Ninoy Aquino International Airport
July 24, 2013 1:09 P.M.

Evers and Buddy sat down in their seats and fastened their seatbelts. They had checked one bag each. The 3-D pistols had gotten through security without issue. The China Eastern Boeing 757 was full and the cabin air hot. As much as they hated it, they would have to change planes in Shanghai, which meant more time wasted en route.

"I can't believe this bullshit. Fucking Dugan is going to be long gone before we ever get to Xi'an," Evers whispered to Buddy.

With some conviction Buddy replied, "Hey, hey. Let's remember we're heading to China to spread the good Word. Keep it PG, will ya'?"

Evers looked at his partner in disbelief. "Are you kidding me? We're in a race against time and you're telling me to watch my language and acting like we've got all the time in the world. I cannot fucking believe this," he said between clenched teeth.

Buddy eyes darted around to make sure the two men weren't drawing any undue attention and whispered, "Buck, relax. I happen to know that Dugan is making his way here in a small Learjet. I also know he has to do everything in his power to avoid landing in U.S. airspace. Do you know what that means? That means he'll have his pilot skip all over the place, and travel several thousand nautical miles out of his way to avoid being noticed. It also means he'll have to stop many times to refuel. I suspect our arrival time won't be that far off from one another. That's what God told me. You should pray more often," he quipped as he settled into his seat.

The co-pilot came over the intercom and announced the flight had been cleared for take-off. He instructed the flight attendants to take their seat and fasten their seatbelts. With that announcement the massive plane's thrusters pressed forward and the engines roared to life. In a few seconds the plane was airborne and banking to the northwest.

Evers looked out his window as Metro Manila disappeared under a ten thousand foot cloud deck. Droplets of rain hit his window as the plane climbed to its flying altitude. Clouds were gray and black and the plane made some easy banks to the left then right to avoid large thunderheads. The aircraft's wings bounced and the plane itself jostled as it passed over some moderate turbulence. A few exasperated gasps could be heard from travelers not accustomed to bumps in the air. Buddy put both hands together and feigned silent prayer.

Bill rolled his eyes and shook his head. "I think you're taking this missionary thing a little too seriously."

"A little help from the Big Man upstairs can't hurt, Buck. I've already told you to calm down. Grab a drink when the stewardess comes by with the drink cart. It's better to get all the rest you can while you can get it," Buddy replied.

"Flight attendants, Buddy. They're called flight attendants," Evers corrected. Buddy rolled his eyes at Evers and replied, "Fuck being politically correct. They're stewardesses, and damned good looking ones too."

Evers shook his head, sighed and continued, "There's something else about this mission that's bothering me, Buddy. I don't understand how the hell we're supposed to march out of communist China with a damned army of stone soldiers. Have you considered that yet or is this whole thing just a fly by the seat of your pants assignment," asked Evers.

"Always pragmatic, Buck, always. I love that about you," he said with a smile. "Once we have control of the army, we march to a waiting set of rail cars operated by a few guys who have a vested interest in moving our soldiers north into Mongolia. From there they'll be airlifted and taken to an undisclosed area in the States."

"Undisclosed area, huh? Pre-hired train? Airlift from Mongolia. Sounds like you've thought of everything. I don't reckon you've considered the possibility that the whole damned Chinese army will be four feet up our asses as soon as one of their national treasures starts marching around the streets of Xi'an?" Evers pondered.

"Yeah, that's a distinct possibility, Buck. I can't imagine they won't be alerted, which is why we'll be forced to utilize diversion tactics ahead of the load. We have a team of anti-commie patriots who are willing to create an internal incident by protesting in Beijing. That should keep a large portion of the military occupied for quite some time. All we need is a couple of hours of distraction and we'll disappear like ghosts," Buddy replied.

Evers exhaled loudly before repeating a sentiment he offered previously, "All that is assuming this whole cartouche thing is for real. Sometimes I can't believe I bought into all this nonsense, Buddy. Chinese men and women finding their way to America and Mexico over two thousand years ago, magic jewelry, people turned to stone...somehow someone is able to bring stone men back to life. Doesn't that all sound crazy to you?"

"Listen, Buck, there have been a lot of smart people evaluate this thing. Those same individuals have invested a lot of time, money and resources into figuring out the veracity of Dugan's claims. Do you find it so hard to believe in magic even after you've seen it first hand? There are thousands of things in this world modern science can't explain that we simply accept, things such as the pyramids being built by human slaves, even though those stones weighed two-and-a-half tons apiece, or things like massive amounts of limestone being carried inland in the Yucatan to build their pyramids and massive buildings.

Maybe you accept monolithic stones put in place in the middle of England as ordinary or explainable, or perhaps you have no issue with reports of seven plagues being handed down by an angry god on the people of Egypt? Perhaps you've heard about an Indian feller sitting under a Bodhi Tree and suddenly becoming enlightened? You see, son, there's been magic at play for an eternity. Just because you may not believe in it right now doesn't make it any less real," Buddy finished.

Two flight attendants pushed the food and drink cart through the aisle. Once they reached the two Americans, Evers asked for a beer while Buddy asked for two bourbons and a cup of ice. Both of them sipped their drinks in silence for a few moments, savoring them.

"All I'm saying is that this whole mission seems kind of hodge-podge and thrown together, rather than being planned out. We're risking our lives over something we have no idea even exists. In a short time we'll be in Red China, Buddy, and the last time I checked the Chinese weren't our biggest fans. Don't you think we'll draw a lot of unwanted attention?" Evers asked.

"Nobody twisted your arm to be here, Buck. It's a little late in the ballgame to be worrying about what the Chinese government thinks of us. Personally, after we read a few passages of scripture, I suspect they'll completely ignore us. But, back on the subject of magic and believability, you are a practitioner of the Japanese martial arts, right?" Buddy asked.

Evers nodded his head and wondered where Buddy was taking the conversation. There were a lot of things people could criticize the man for, but a lack of intelligence or reasoning skills weren't on the list. Despite his thick southern drawl, and all the stereotypes that came with it, mentally he was a man to be reckoned with. He had the uncanny ability to draw parallels to things most wouldn't consider, and always had the knack of predicting events before they happened, typically because he deduced his way through them. His ability to rationalize through scenarios was incredible and unmatched in Evers' opinion.

"I'm certain that you've studied meridians, pressure points and chi or ki, as the Japanese call it. Explain to me what 'ki' is, Buck," Buddy requested.

Bill thought about the question and his response before opening his mouth. He thought about his teachers explaining to him how to harness the body's energy and use it to strike or thrown an opponent, or how proper breathing correctly channeled ki. The mystical energy was stored in the body's tanden, or spiritual center, again, according to the Japanese. With considerable practice the Japanese claimed that ki could be gathered and used during battle. Evers believed this to be true, having utilized ki during his own military and paramilitary career.

He did what he could to explain ki to Buddy. "You remember The Incredible Hulk? Bruce Banner was a scientist who couldn't save his family after an auto accident. He read so many accounts of people who had mysteriously summoned great strength to right overturned cars, or pick up huge trees and throw them off of loved ones who had been trapped beneath. So he injected himself with gamma rays in order to capture that amazing strength. You know the rest of the story – get pissed, turn green, stomp the bad guy. Well, ki is like that, minus the gamma rays and turning green. It's that energy Dr. Banner was looking for, Buddy. That's the best way for me to describe ki."

"Ain't that something, Buck? A mysterious energy contained within the human body that can be harnessed and used at a given time. More amazing to me is that you believe in it, say you've used it, and you don't question its existence. Now, to me, that sounds just like magic," he smirked.

Evers started to rebuke him, but shut up fast enough that Buddy could hear his teeth clatter as his mouth slammed closed. He took another breath then opened his mouth, and just as quickly shut it again. Finally he said, "Yeah, well that's different."

His friend cocked his head, raised one eyebrow and looked at him with some humor. "Explain to me what's different between our little jewel we're chasing and your ki, Buck. Everything you described to me matches what most consider magic. It's unexplainable, there's no scientific data to support its existence, and most would call 'bullshit' if you tried to tell them exactly what you told me."

Buddy finished his bourbon then eased his chair back to the fullest extent of its six inches worth of reclining. He closed his eyes, satisfied that he'd properly educated his protégé, and confident he would have more questions when he awoke. Shortly after his eyes shut, he was snoring.

Evers continued to sip his beer, finding the bottom a few minutes later. He thought about Buddy's explanation, dismissed it for a few seconds, but couldn't offer any reason why he was wrong. Everything he said made perfect sense, yet here he sat wondering how in the hell it was possible that some ancient spell could be cast encasing humans in stone, then partially reversed so an army of stone could walk the Earth. The whole concept was ridiculous and preposterous, but he *did* know that ki existed, even if he couldn't articulate exactly what it was.

Is it possible that the magic used in the spell was nothing more than one individual's internal energy captured in that cartouche, and not sourced from what most would call the spiritual realm? If that's the case, then any person, with the proper training, could plausibly cast a similar spell.

This possibility excited Evers. In fact, should he somehow find a way to live through this most bizarre of adventures, he promised himself he would seek out his old sensei and discuss this with him. He considered how his karate and judo would be elevated if he could figure out this aspect of ki and how he could control an opponent.

He had often heard of people who suffered from some terminal illness being healed through the power of prayer. Evers wondered what Buddy's argument would be with a Christian minister who didn't believe in the magic of the cartouche. Was it really a stretch to believe that God heals those who ask for it or through those who pray for healing, but wouldn't permit the power of contemplation and will to be focused in a jewel? The more Evers put himself in a position to think like Buddy, the more he was convinced there could be something to the magical jewel.

He forced the thought from his mind for the time being; he would have time to dwell it once the mission was completed, if it could be completed. For now he was content flagging the flight attendant and asking for another beer, which he nursed for a while. Later, he drifted off to sleep and dreamed of karate and judo and the time he spent with his former teachers of each art. In the recesses of his dreams he envisioned himself holding the cartouche and a foreign but powerful energy surging through his body.

Hong Kong
Hong Kong International Airport
July 24, 2013 6:43 P.M.

While they refueled in Hong Kong, Dugan asked Rafael if he would like to walk inside the terminal to stretch and get some food before their next and final leg of the journey. In reality, Dugan had paid off one of his Chinese airport contacts to inspect the aircraft prior to their departure to Xi'an, which was standard protocol before a private jet could enter Chinese airspace and land at one of their airports. He certainly did not want the agent to see Rafael or his bonds, so it was better that they not be on board while the inspection took place.

Rafael had grown more amicable since Dugan had both released him and given him coffee. Although he was peaceful, Dugan realized he could have another mental meltdown at any time, so taking him inside the terminal was a risk, but a calculated one, especially after he had "repaired" his nose for him. He hoped the new sights and sounds would keep his mind occupied until the plane inspection was complete.

Dugan looked his captive over and saw that his appearance was more than unkempt. His pants were wrinkled and blood from his nose and mouth had poured down the front of his shirt. He rifled through his suitcase for a clean tee-shirt and handed it to Rafael, nodding his head to the man to take the garment and put it on. Dugan then handed him a clean sports coat to put on over the tee-shirt. Finally, he handed Rafael his comb and told him to walk inside the small restroom and comb his hair.

While Rafael was inside the restroom, Dugan changed his own shirt. Blood from Rafael's wounds had splattered on him after their altercation. He raked his fingers through his hair and brushed a few of the wrinkles from his pants. Looking like a travel-weary tourist, he knew no one would pay attention to him as he walked through the airport.

A few moments after entering the restroom, Rafael reappeared in the cabin. His hair was slicked back and the bruising on his face has lessened significantly. His straightened nose didn't look too bad either, and Dugan was happy that the man's eyes had not blackened with the break. Dugan reminded himself to never lose his composure again, something that stupid could land him in an uncomfortable position with law enforcement, or worse.

He motioned Rafael to follow him to the front of the plane. The men walked down the small set of steps attached to the plane's door and made their way to the terminal. Jet fuel permeated the air and the day's hot, sticky air immediately hugged them like a long-lost friend.

As with so much of Hong Kong's infrastructure, the airport was immaculately pristine. The terminals were magnificent works of art, spectacular architecture everywhere they looked. Weight bearing pillars standing at strange angles holding up an amazing glass and metal roof lined the area. Sunshine radiantly reflected off highly polished tile floors, as smartly dressed business men and women hurried to their gates. An endless number of retail stores and liquor shops welcomed customers from all over the world, each store as clean and beautiful as the next.

A massive LED lit sign welcomed travelers to Hong Kong in every imaginable language. In keeping with the sign's theme, numerous languages could be heard over the airport's intercom system announcing arriving and departing flights. Strong smells of cooked food drifted through the terminal as Dugan and Rafael followed their noses to the nearest food court.

Flying in a private jet afforded them certain luxuries not available to the general public flying on commercial airlines. Security measures were not taken as seriously for those capable of paying exorbitant prices for the privilege of traveling privately. And since they would not be leaving the airport, they radioed ahead so they wouldn't have to walk through customs. For a moment Dugan considered how suicidal this global policy was, but quickly pushed it from his thoughts as they made their way through the airport.

They ordered local cuisine and found a table overlooking the harbor and Lantau Island. Hong Kong International Airport sat alone, an island to itself, a considerable drive to Hong Kong proper. Heavy smog clung to the area as the green water of the South China Sea lapped at the sea wall protecting the landing strips.

"What do you think, Rafael? This is Hong Kong and is a part of the land of your ancient family. How do you like it so far?" asked Dugan.

"I'm Mexican, Mr. Dugan, but I must admit this place has called me, especially since I recovered the jewel. I look forward to our arrival in Xi'an so I can see where my blood originated. I have never been outside Mexico until our...uh...trip," replied Rafael.

Dugan put a forkful of rice noodles and chicken in his mouth then chased it with a bottle of water. He chewed slowly, enjoying the flavors, which were unlike any Chinese food served in the States. Even though it was airport food, the Chinese were very careful and cognizant of the many world travelers passing through their cities, and as a result they wanted their food, no matter where it was served, to be the best.

After swallowing it, Dugan said, "Rafael, I suspect when we get to Xi'an you'll get to do more than see the country of your blood. I think you'll be reunited with the blood of your countrymen."

Rafael chewed his food and stared at Dugan unsure of his meaning, and wondering if what he had said was some sort of veiled threat.

Shanghai, China
Shanghai Pudong International Airport
July 24, 2013 6:55 P.M.

Evers and Buddy stepped off their plane and located a kiosk directing them to their next and final gate. Shanghai's Pudong Airport was another Chinese marvel and both men, despite jet lag and travel weary, took in their surroundings. Evers was impressed with the terminal, its level of orderliness and cleanliness, something considerably different than airports back home and in other parts of the world to which he had traveled.

Buddy, on the other hand, was busy watching Chinese women in skirts walking through the terminal. Evers quietly chuckled as he watched Buddy's head snap back and forth each time a young lady walked past them. He shook his head but said nothing, not wanting another lecture on finding a woman to satisfy his XY chromosome and natural male hormonal desires. Naturally, Buddy was right about him needing a good woman in his life but admitting that his mentor was correct put his ego at risk of implosion on a cataclysmic level.

They found a small bar serving Chinese beer and a few imported liquors. Each ordered a drink, neither having much to say. Both of them knew the importance of silence before battle, just as both knew the importance of sharing pertinent information about battle planning. This was one of the times that silence was the necessary mode of communication.

After several minutes of silence Buddy spoke up, "Well, goddam. Here we are about to spread the word of the Good Lord in a godless place while we save the world from certain fucking destruction. I'll drink to that," he said as he raised his glass of bourbon.

Evers smiled and raised his beer. The glass clinked and both men turned their drinks up and gulped liberally. Buddy ran his shirt sleeve across his mouth wiping away the alcohol residue left on his lips. The sleeve-wipe was followed by a mild belch. A Chinese lady sitting next to him turned her head slightly in a disapproving manner. Buddy winked at her then added, "God Bless."

"As soon as we land, Buck, we've got to find where these Terracotta Warriors are and set up a perimeter. It'll be tough since there are just two of us, but the research I've done shows that they're all in one place. That makes things a little easier for us. Once we make contact, we move in. If at all possible we take Dugan out without using the paraphernalia we're carrying; no need to attract attention if it isn't necessary. It's absolutely vital that we recover the cartouche and get it and the army out of the country. Once we're in Mongolia we haul ass out and Uncle Sam will be responsible for moving the soldiers. Like I said, we've got to get close to Dugan and that spic feller traveling with him. Use that 3D pistol wisely. I have no idea how reliable it is.

"At this point it's safe to say this mission is kill and recover. That is, take Dugan and the Mexican out, get the jewel and get out. It's really that simple. We need to do this quickly and quietly," Buddy said.

"It sounds like you're pretty confident that Dugan will show up to lay claim to the soldiers pretty quickly. What makes you think he won't lay low for a while," asked Evers.

"He's a smart man, Buck. Not as smart as me, but he's smart. There's a sense of urgency pushing him to get here and get out, and I think he's planning more than just taking the warriors with him," Buddy whispered.

Instinctively, Evers looked around then focused on Buddy. "What do you mean?"

Buddy sighed then said, "When he and I were heading to that hangar where he was holding you, he said something that's eaten at me the last couple of days. I didn't put it together until a couple of hours ago and, even though he didn't come right out and say it, I'm pretty sure I'm right. He told me there were things in this world beyond a man's control, but there are things that aren't.

I had no idea what he was talking about, but now I think I do. That crazy bastard doesn't care so much about the Terracotta Warriors, Buck. What he cares about is the spell. Specifically, if he can figure out how the spell was cast in the first place, he'll control the fucking world. He wants to learn the secret of the spell so he can cast it. Can you imagine one man having that kind of power?"

Evers face went pale. He knew Dugan took evil to a whole new level, but had no idea he had the kind of ambition Buddy just described. Buddy's reasoning easily explained why Dugan had taken Rafael with him, even though the man had pulled a gun on him. Everyone heard him chanting in a different language, and now Evers realized that language was some Chinese dialect. Obviously, Rafael was somehow linked to the cartouche and the Terracotta Army, and appeared to be the conduit to freeing it from an eternity of stone and damnation.

"Jesus Christ, Buddy," gasped Evers.

"Amen," Buddy replied.

"We are going to need to do some recon of the area when we arrive. Hopefully we'll get there before our friends. The more familiar we are with the terrain the better off we'll be."

"You are exactly right. Let's finish these drinks and go hop a plane. As the younger generation likes to say, 'shit just got real,'" Buddy quipped, seriousness in his tone.

Xi'an, China
Xi'an Xianyang International Airport
July 24, 2013 9:09 P.M.

Evers and Buddy stepped off the plane and were directed to customs. Both were outwardly calm but knew if one, or both, was found with the plastic firearms no amount of diplomatic pleas would ever free them from their Chinese prison. Fake passports and visas in hand, Buddy was called to the agent's glass box.

The customs agent examined Buddy suspiciously without looking at his papers. Buddy tried to look meek, which is the way he knew most Christian missionaries presented themselves. After a few uncomfortable moments the agent examined the passport and visa. His eyes narrowed as he reached for his flashlight to check the holographic watermark. Evers could see Buddy swallow, his composure shaken somewhat.

The agent barked out something in Chinese and another man, similarly dressed, walked over. After a few seconds of conversation the second agent asked Buddy a series of questions. It became obvious that the newer agent was the only one capable of speaking English to the newcomers.

"Why you in Xi'an," he asked in broken English?

"My friend and I, "he started as he motioned toward Evers, "are here to spread the good word of Christianity in your beautiful country."

"The Chinese not care about your Christian god," he stated categorically.

Trying to keep his voice steady, Buddy replied, "I understand that, sir. That's why we're here. We would like the opportunity to share Christ's goodness."

He reached for Buddy's visa and studied it for a few moments before handing it back to the seated agent.

"Where will you be staying while in Xi'an, sir?" he asked.

Fortunately he had made prior arrangements for two rooms in the city before leaving Manila. He pulled his handwritten notes from his pocket and replied, "We are staying at the Jiabao Hotel. I hear it is very nice."

The agent grunted then reached for Buddy's passport. As he had done with the visa, the agent studied his United States government issued passport like it was the first one he had ever seen.

"How long you share the word of your Christ here in Xi'an?" he mocked.

"We will be leaving on August seventh, exactly two weeks from today," said Buddy with considerably more confidence.

For a few more seconds he eyed Buddy before looking at the first agent and giving him a curt nod. The first agent then continued to eye Buddy for a couple of seconds more before grabbing his passport and stamping the official Xi'an seal onto one of the pages.

Buddy thanked them both and grabbed his bag stepping forward to wait on Evers. Evers was called to the same desk that Buddy had just left and was given the same treatment. He fumbled for his forged passport and visa while holding a King James Bible that Buddy had given him before leaving the Philippines.

Several minutes passed as Evers was grilled by the English speaking agent. Feeling a little more at ease after watching Buddy receive the same treatment and still be allowed to enter the country, Evers answered the questions smoothly. His only concern would be the discovery of some flaw on his fake papers.

Satisfied that Evers posed no risk to national security, the second agent again nodded to his counterpart and the familiar pounding of the seal dropped on his passport. He grabbed his carry-on bag and began walking toward Buddy. A small grin touched his mouth.

"Don't go gettin' too happy just yet, amigo. We still have to get through outbound security. I hope you didn't put that little plastic gem I gave you in your bag," said Buddy.

Evers and Buddy walked through the terminal, the walls feeling as though they were collapsing on them. Their non-Asian features screamed "enemy" to the hardcore Communist Chinese, and their American passports, no matter how well they had been made, indicated they were not to be trusted.

The two made their way through outbound inspection. Buddy's bag was chosen and gone through. Nothing unusual was found inside the bag and both were motioned through the line. Evers had put his pistol in his waistband while on the plane and wasn't concerned about the baggage inspection, but he was intensely aware of its weight and what would happen if it was discovered.

As seasoned as each man was in combat, a look of relief crossed each of their faces. Neither had predicted the ease of their entry into Xi'an, but both were appreciative of it. They looked at one another, each recognizing the emotion on the other's face. That recognition caused each to eradicate the look of relief each shared.

They walked into the terminal in search of baggage claim and transportation. Luckily, signs were posted in Chinese and English that pointed them in the right direction. As they walked toward the claim area they took in the layout of the airport.

Comparatively, Xi'an's Xianyang Airport was drab, especially after they had just traveled through Pudong Airport in Shanghai. No one seemed happy to be there, and the merchants were disinterested in any potential customers who happened into their stores. Sleep boxes, large wooden boxes with a window and bed, dotted the terminal. Evers found this very strange having never seen anything like them before. For a small price, weary travelers could get some sleep on a bed in a climate controlled "room." The airport itself was rather grungy and ordinary and the floors lacked any sort of luster.

After a few minutes, they arrived at baggage claim. Luggage was just beginning to funnel onto the carousel. Tired travelers quickly grabbed their bags and rolled them toward the automatic doors. Eventually, Evers and Buddy's bags fell to the carousel.

As the two walked outside they saw people lining up to get a cab. Evers' first sense of Xi'an was the lack of horn blowing and hand waving in an effort to hail a taxi. The entire process was very orderly and cordial. People were polite and quiet.

The next thing Evers noticed was the inordinate number of cameras mounted at every possible angle around the outside premises of the airport. He wondered if the cameras were the reason the majority of the people kept their heads down, avoiding the ever-watchful eye of the Chinese overseers.

A green and white taxi pulled to the curb as Evers and Buddy grabbed their luggage and prepared to throw it in the trunk. "Jiabao Hotel," said Buddy as they closed the rear doors of the cab.

Their cabbie nodded and replied, "Hǎo" Okay.

Both passengers sat in silence as their driver drove the eleven kilometers from Xianyang Airport to the hotel Jiabao. Sullen gray apartment complexes doubled as high rises along the city's skyline. Even in the night the dull, uninteresting appearance was noticeable. Evers knew the Chinese government all but forced the majority of its populace into the crowded cities that dotted most of the country's eastern third of its borders. Grouping its people, he understood, made it easier to control them, much like hording cattle into a fenced pasture.

The drive was uneventful and finished with Buddy paying the chit of seventy Yuan. They grabbed their luggage, checked into their rooms and agreed to meet in the hotel lobby in fifteen minutes. Evers took the time to shower and catch his breath after traveling half a world. Buddy lay on his bed and thought about the night that would follow. He wondered if it would be his last. More often than not he was able to predict events before they unfolded. It was an assumption of his that God had given him that ability as a parting gift for serving in the church. But tonight was different. He faced an unpredictable adversary who held in his hands a power that one person should never wield.

In exactly fifteen minutes the two warriors met in the hotel lobby. Evers saw Buddy standing to the side shaking hands with a Chinese man. Buddy handed him a Bible and bowed his head in apparent appreciation. Neither had said anything to the other since their departure from the airport, and neither felt the need to. Both men understood what was at stake.

Evers had taken the liberty to ask the desk clerk to call another cab for the men just before Buddy had arrived. Within a few minutes the driver awaited his passengers in front of the hotel lobby. Buddy nodded to his protégé as they stepped outside into the hot evening air and climbed inside the cab.

In the back seat Buddy nonchalantly handed Evers a handful of forty caliber bullets for the 3-D pistol. Evers raised a questioning brow but had learned that Buddy's contacts around the world made things happen. *Like magic*, he thought to himself as he remembered the man he saw Buddy speaking with in the lobby. He casually pushed the bullets into his pocket as he looked out the cab's windows.

"Terracotta Warriors," Buddy asked the cab driver?

The driver gave them both a confused look then nodded his head. Evers presumed it was because of the late hour. They would have to be very careful and move quickly to avoid detection by the Chinese authorities. Their cab driver would remember two Americans that he drove to a closed tourist attraction.

Lights from Xi'an's many high rise buildings sped past them as the driver sped toward their destination. Cars and scooters buzzed along as a few people could still be seen on the city's sidewalks. The usual smog that sat atop the city had lightened and become less dense making the cityscape much easier to see.

Twenty minutes later the cab pulled into the pyramid housing one of China's national treasures. Their driver's English was poor and broken as he stammered, "Close. No good."

Buddy paid him the seventy Yuan and stepped out of the car. Evers exited from the other door. Both men quickly scanned the area searching for cameras they knew were there, and for the two men they hunted.

"Close. No good," repeated their driver from his opened window, indicating that the museum was not opened for business. Suddenly, he opened his door and jumped out. Buddy and Evers took a step backward uncertain of the man's intentions. He began motioning them up a sidewalk, his gesture friendly like there was something he wanted them to see. His face was full of excitement as though he had remembered something and wanted to share it with the two of them.

"Okay, okay," Evers responded as he patted the man on the shoulder. They followed him up the sidewalk then up a series of winding concrete stairs until they reached the plateau. At the top, the two men were astounded to see one lone, stone warrior atop a fierce looking horse bathed in white light from a street lamp standing ten feet above the warrior's head. Insects swooped around the street lamp, while an occasional stray would buzz the statue's helmeted head. The warrior's expression made both men pause for a few seconds. Evers glanced at Buddy, but Buddy's face revealed nothing. Instead he reached into his wallet and seized another hundred Yuan and handed it to the cab driver.

Evers thanked the driver before motioning him to leave. The driver bowed and thanked them both for the additional money, money that would go a long way toward feeding his family. He turned and walked back down the stairs to his cab.

"Well, I'm of the opinion, Buck, that this is our boy Dugan's first target. It makes perfect sense. The warrior is outside, he doesn't have to break in to try to reverse the spell, and I believe this statue we're looking at was the focal point of the legendary spell caster. Even though I'm looking at the 'lone warrior statue,' I can't believe the legend is really true," Buddy said considerably shaken at the sight.

"For the first time in a while, Buddy, I think you're right. Amen. Let's move into position so we can keep an eye out for our targets. I'm going to find a good place to lay low and out of sight over here to the left, you take the right," said Evers, the tactical soldier and mercenary coming out of him.

Evers had been careful to purchase darker clothes and sneakers while in Manila, which proved strategic as he looked for camouflage and cover. He found a small row of hedges just beyond the bright street lamp's reach and lay down in front of them, appropriately molding to the ground and vegetation. *Hidden in plain sight*, he thought to himself as he loaded his plastic pistol and stuck it in his waistband. He became deathly still; his only movement was his blinking eyes.

Although his adrenaline had begun pumping he closed his eyes and slowed his breathing and heart rate. Soon the only sound to be heard was the occasional rustling of leaves as a squirrel pilfered the ground in search of food, and the buzzing of the street lamp. On the other side of the statue Evers could detect no movement. He knew Buddy had taken similar cover.

The worst part of being a professional killer is the waiting, that is, aside from the obvious mental defects it sometimes creates after the deed is done. The planning, the meticulous calculations, the travel, the boredom...all of those things are nothing compared to the waiting.

Patience is the one thing I've always struggled with, even in my martial arts training. Yonomo Sensei would tell me, "If you have an annoying fly in your house you can be patient and swat it when it lands, or you can set your house on fire and burn it to the ground. Either way the fly is dead."

That analogy still makes me laugh, but he was certainly right. The end result is the same, but the strategy used to get there is what matters. Patience should always be an integral part of strategy; without it the result can be catastrophic.

"Sensei, I understand the 'whys' of patience, I just don't understand the 'how,'" he had explained to Yonomo. The two of us, student and master, sat in the formal seating position known in Japan as seiza, our knees on the tatami, or mat, and feet tucked neatly behind us, our left big toe crossed behind our right.

Yonomo nodded his understanding at his disciple and silently rose as a curt, "Hai," flew from his mouth.

I was confused, but followed Sensei's lead and rose as well. He motioned for me to stand in front of him then muttered "Dozo, Bill-san. You punch me."

I realized Sensei was about to teach me something, but I was still confused what that teaching would consist of or what this was about, so I asked, "In the face, Sensei, or your chest?"

Yonomo laughed at my question and said, "Doesn't matter. You pick where you want to punch me and when. I will decide whether I block or counter your attack. That is how fights work, Bill-san."

I pulled both hands to my chest like a boxer, as opposed to the usual fighting position traditional karate-ka assumed in the dojo. Sensei always became angered when students would stand in that position when he asked for a uke (partner) when demonstrating a technique. He would tell everyone that no one does that outside the dojo, so why would we practice that way?

Sensei stood, casually, with both hands at his side, his right foot slightly behind him and both eyes locked on mine. I had the keen sense that he could read my mind and knew what I was going to do before I did it, but shook the sensation from my mind.

We stood like that for what seemed an eternity, me on my toes poised to attack my sensei, he relaxed and breathing normally. I had always been a big guy and quick with my hands and feet. As a matter of fact, I took great pride in my ability to move the way I did; most people wouldn't expect someone as large as I am to be able to move that way.

My right hand shot out at Sensei's head, my hips snapping to add power to the punch. Yonomo waited until my hand was a hairbreadth from his face then shifted his feet slightly to the right while his open left hand drilled into my shoulder immediately stopping my punch. My body felt as though a bolt of electricity had traveled from my right shoulder all the way down to my right knee.

In a blur Sensei's open right hand lightly struck the left side of my neck. That was the last thing I remembered before opening my eyes, finding myself lying on the floor, and Sensei again sitting in seiza sipping green tea.

My eyes were watery and a tear rolled down my cheek. I shook my head and it exploded with pain. "What happened?" I asked.

Sensei, a smirk on his face, replied, "Bill-san, I was attempting to teach you a lesson about patience when you decided to go to sleep."

My brain recalled the lesson, my punch and his unfathomably quick reaction right before my hand was due to connect with his face. "How did you do that, Sensei?" I asked as my senses came back to me and the pounding in my head subsided.

He laughed. "Patience, Bill-san; that's how I did that."

The memory that flooded into Evers' head was a not-so-subtle reminder to be in the moment and block external influences that created impatience. He could hear cars in the distance and could almost detect Buddy's breathing as he focused his mind. Being in the moment was another lesson his sensei had taught him, and he embraced it. His military training had heightened and elevated those lessons making them a part of who he was and had become.

Twenty minutes passed, then forty, and soon two hours were gone. Still, Evers remained in the moment, relishing the ground on which he lay and the sights and sounds of this strange, new land. Down the hill by the museum he heard car doors shut – two of them. A couple of moments later he could hear shoes as they labored up the steps leading to the lone Warrior.

Xi'an, China
July 25, 2013 12:03 A.M.

Dugan and Rafael stepped into the bright light of the street lamp. Rafael stopped in his tracks to gaze at the giant stone horse and soldier who sat atop it. He held his breath in stark recognition. After some time he walked over to it and ran his hand across the Warrior's leg and the horse's nose. His eyes took in the whole scene before he looked at Dugan and nodded his head, the silent acknowledgment understood by both.

He walked back to Dugan's side as Dugan's hand slipped into his pocket. When he withdrew his hand he was holding the cartouche, now on a small chain. Rafael's gaze locked on the jewel. This time Dugan handed it to him willingly.

Evers watched as Rafael turned toward the statue, his outstretched hand holding the chain. The cartouche dangled and swayed in the gentle summer breeze. He closed his eyes and the chant began quietly, but quickly grew louder.

"Hua shi yŏng zŭ xiàng...Hua shi yŏng zŭ xiàng...Hua shi yŏng zŭ xiàng," called out Rafael. Evers watched the man holding the jewel he had traveled half a world to retrieve stand in a strange trance and chant words that he had never before heard. From nowhere a cold wind blew through the area directly in the path of the stone warrior, the key bearer, and Dugan.

Just behind the pair, standing in front of the statue, Evers saw Buddy holding the 3-D forty caliber pistol. This was his signal to action. He pulled his own weapon and belly crawled to the edge of the light from the street lamp, circling behind Dugan and Rafael. He rose to one knee and leveled his pistol at Dugan's head.

Buddy stepped into the light and said, "It's over Dan. Time to give me the cartouche like we originally agreed upon. You've received half your money and you'll get the other half as promised when I get home."

Dugan's head snapped to his right to find Buddy standing with the oddest looking gun he'd ever seen. Rafael didn't budge, apparently lost in the jewel's enchantment. His chant continued to grow louder.

"Hua shi yŏng zŭ xiàng! Hua shi yŏng zŭ xiàng! Hua shi yŏng zŭ xiàng!" The sound of his voice reverberated although there were no walls or surfaces to create the echo. A strange thrumming was heard all around them, and another cold blast of wind blew from the mountains towering over the valley.

Evers rose and moved directly in front of Rafael, his pistol now pointing at the Mexican's heart. A third blast of cold air rushed over them and Evers would have sworn that everything became *wavy* for just a few seconds. Rafael's chant grew louder and louder until he was shouting at the top of his lungs. Cold air encircled them all and clouds quickly passed in front of the night's half-moon.

Dugan stared at Evers with his hands in the air and said over the top of Rafael's chant, "Well, you certainly are a resourceful one, Mr. Smith, but I'm afraid you are entirely too late. You are about to witness the most powerful army in all the world come to life! There's nothing you can do to stop that now."

Evers commanded Rafael, "Give me the cartouche right now or I will shoot you!"

Rafael, oblivious to the demands, continued his chant, "Hua shi yǒng zǔ xiàng! Hua shi yǒng zǔ xiàng! Hua shi yǒng zǔ xiàng!" Evers watched the cartouche rock back and forth in Rafael's hand as a soft blue-white glow engulfed the jewel.

There was a strange shifting sound behind Evers. He didn't dare take his eyes off his intended target, but allowed his ears to focus on the sound. Just to his left a strange grinding noise emanated very close to him.

"Buck, look out!" Buddy screamed.

Before he could react something hard and strong hit him squarely in the back, knocking and rolling him fifteen feet from where he stood. His breath rushed from his lungs and his ribs screamed in protest. The plastic pistol he was holding fell very hard to the ground and shattered, its bulleted contents rolling harmlessly in every direction. He struggled to force air back into his chest wall. Slowly, his head turned and he couldn't believe what he was seeing.

As Rafael's chant continued, "Hua shi yǒng zǔ xiàng! Hua shi yǒng zǔ xiàng! Hua shi yǒng zǔ xiàng," the Terracotta Warrior's left arm, the one not holding the stone sword, was moving at the elbow and shoulder. Its fingers wiggled making the strange grinding noises Buck had heard just a moment earlier.

One of the steed's forelegs pawed at the ground beneath it. Evers thought he saw steam blow from the horse's nostrils as Rafael took a step closer to the strangely moving stone statue. The cartouche began to rotate on its chain like a small tornado.

In all the confusion, Dugan seized the moment and kicked Buddy hard in his midsection. He fell to his knees but managed to cradle the pistol to keep it from slamming onto the hard ground. His nemesis moved to stomp his head as he gasped for air.

The cold wind created a bizarre vortex around the men and stone warrior. Leaves that had fallen from the surrounding trees were swirling in the gusts, all keeping time with the rotating cartouche. The Warrior's head turned toward Evers and his mouth moved! Evers had never heard such an ear piercing screech in his life. The sound was wild and primal, its force such that he was momentarily frozen where he stood.

Buddy looked up just as Dugan's foot began its downward motion to smash his face and head. In one smooth arc he raised his pistol, breathing a silent prayer that it wouldn't fail, and squeezed the trigger. A bullet erupted from the gun's barrel hitting Dugan in the back of his leg and exited the top of his thigh. He screamed and fell to the sidewalk holding the wound, which bled profusely. The gunshot's sound echoed loudly all around them.

Evers managed to get to his feet, the air fighting his lungs all the way down and back through his nose. He wheezed as he stepped toward Rafael who was transfixed on the moving statue. His chant continued as loudly as it had over the past five minutes. The cold air whipped all around them, each oblivious to its sound or sensation.

In a blaze of fists and fury Evers unloaded on Rafael's face and ribs. A properly placed hook punch spun the man's head in an almost unrealistic arc on a neck that looked as though it struggled to support everything above it. A disgusting crunch rang out and Rafael's chant stopped. The cold wind, however, continued to swirl and the stone horse's tail twitched in a most odd way.

The Mexican collapsed to the ground, his broken jaw agape and his eyes closed. Evers reached for the cartouche that was still wrapped in Rafael's fingers. He felt the thrum and vibration in the chain from the jewel when he lifted it away from Rafael's hand. The ancient spell coursed through the cartouche, into his body, and was projected to the stone statue. Evers sensed the power of the relic, but watched helplessly as the stone warrior turned his head and attention toward him. All at once Evers realized the soldier recognized the cartouche, as another grizzly howl of anger and pain pushed from its lungs, through its throat, and out of its mouth.

His sword bearing arm began to move as the spell slowly lifted it away from its body. One of the horse's rear legs twitched at the same time its stone neck swayed. Evers, still stunned at the sight, took a full step away from the statue.

Evers felt an arm wrap around his left knee and a punch land in his groin. Yelling from the blow, hot pain rushing from his loins to his guts. He looked down in time to see Rafael begin to stand, his broken jaw swaying on its hinges. Without thought, Evers left fist shot from his side and struck Rafael's trachea. He felt the small bones and cartilage snap in the man's neck. For a second time Rafael collapsed to the ground, this time for good.

An eerie horse's neigh made Evers eyes snap back to the Warrior and his steed. In an instant, the horse and its rider turned, facing the two men head on. The horse's head bobbed up and down as the warrior swung his stone sword arm in preparation to kill. The horse reared up on its back legs just before it charged.

"Buck, throw that fucking charm on the ground!" Buddy screamed.

Without questioning his old mentor, Evers dropped the cartouche on the sidewalk. The horse's forelegs hit the pavement and began charging the two men, the soldier raising his sword to levy a fatal strike on one or both of them. Evers looked up to see the sword on course to slice through his neck.

A loud blast once again boomed all around the men, deafening them for a few seconds. The bullet from Buddy's gun slammed into the cartouche sending pieces flying in multiple directions. Evers watched in horror as the sword closed the distance to his neck.

Sand, grit, and a cold blast of air swept across his neck as the Terracotta Warrior turned to dust. Evers looked around his feet in disbelief as the warm summer breeze that had drifted through the area before Dugan and Rafael had arrived pushed grayish sand across the sidewalk.

"Noooooooooooooo," screamed Dugan! "You stupid bastard, Smith! I've spent the past two years tracking down that jewel and now you've destroyed everything," he snarled as he lay on the sidewalk still holding his bleeding leg.

Buddy smirked at Dugan and said, "Well, ain't that a bitch, Dugan? I'll tell you what, you can explain to the Chi-com police, that are certainly on their way here to investigate, all about how I ruined your dream of stealing their stone army and selling it to the highest bidder. As a matter of fact, you explain to them how you planned on figuring out how to recreate the curse so you could have your own Terracotta Army." He turned his attention to Evers and finished, "Let's get the hell out of here, Buck. We don't need to be here when they arrive."

Dugan suddenly had a look of terror on his face. "You can't leave me here. I'm a fucking American," he croaked.

Buddy looked at Evers and chuckled then threw the plastic pistol to the ground. The gun shattered into hundreds of pieces, and the remaining bullets rolled harmlessly on the sidewalk. Evers smiled at his friend as they turned their back on Dugan, leaving him in a pool of his own blood, and with the knowledge that in a few minutes he would be seized by people not known to be very affectionate.

Langley, Virginia, U.S.A.
January 3, 2014 10:08 A.M.

Evers walked into the Barnes and Noble book store and located the Starbucks sign in the far right corner. He weaved around countless yuppies in search of self-help books and teens and twenty-something's, all dressed in black with bars, studs, and rings hanging from their faces, perusing the gothic and cult sections. The warmth of the store was a welcome relief after walking for a few minutes in the northern Virginia winter.

As he approached the coffee shop he heard what sounded like singing. The singing actually sounded more like a donkey in the throes of blissful passion. Evers was shocked to see Buddy sitting at a table with his computer open, ear buds shoved in his ears, eyes closed, and belting out Delbert McClinton's *No Mississippi*.

> *"I won't go down in a burst of flames*
> *I won't stay locked up in your chains*
> *Yeah, it hurts but it ain't strong enough to whip me*
> *I might stagger and I might fall*
> *But I won't beg and I won't crawl*
> *A tear or two might fall into my shot of whiskey*
> *But I won't cry no Mississippi"*

Buddy's eyes opened and he saw Evers standing there staring at him, his jaw slack. Other patrons were looking at him, some obviously upset at him disrupting their conversations, and others giggling and laughing. He looked at Evers, frowned and looked around at the people staring in dismay.

"What? This is good goddam music. Y'all act like you've never heard a man sing before!" he exclaimed.

For the first time in more months than he could remember, Evers' head tilted back and a loud belly laugh boomed through the store. He put his hands on his knees and continued laughing, while others sitting around Buddy did the same.

"Kiss my ass, Young Buck," mumbled Buddy as he closed his computer and put his ear buds on the table.

Still laughing, Evers took a seat at the table. Buddy scowled at him before finally extending his hand and shaking. Evers looked around the room as people returned to their conversations and latte drinking.

"Interesting meeting place, Buddy. When I got your message on the bulletin board I assumed we'd be sitting in your office at Langley," Evers said.

Buddy's eyes shifted quickly, and a confused look crossed his brow. Finally, he smiled in understanding and replied, "Damn, Buck, you honestly think I'm an employee of the Christians In Action?" It was his turn to offer up a belly laugh, and laugh he did.

Evers watched his friend guffaw at him, while the confused look moved from Buddy to his own face. "Wait. I thought you said you were working for them."

"I *do* work for them, Buck. I'm a private contractor just like you. I have no problem taking hard working tax payers' money, but there's only so much hypocrisy I can put up with. No way would I find myself as an employee of the feds again. Besides, contracting pays much better," he explained.

"What all are you doing for them?" Evers asked.

"You ask a lot of questions, Buck, but I'll tell you that they call me in when they have 'special' projects, not so dissimilar to what you and I worked on a few months ago."

Evers studied him for a moment then said, "Special projects, huh? The kind of projects they don't want their names mixed up in should something go wrong."

"Pretty much sums it up. Had we been caught in Xi'an, we'd been on our own. That would have been bad, my friend," he chuckled.

"Yeah, that would have been bad...," Evers said sarcastically. "Speaking of bad, what have your sources told you about Dugan? I'm certain the Chinese had a time with him before executing him in some dark dungeon."

"You know, we haven't heard anything about or from him. The Chinese have been mum since the whole operation. We received word that they opened the museum the next day and all eight thousand warriors were standing in line like they were going to war. It's been reported that every damned one of their physical positions had changed. Statues that had previously stood at attention are now frozen in mid-stride.

Of course, the Chi-com government denied any weirdness, shut down the museum, and moved the army back into the pits. They haven't let tourists back in there yet. I'm sure they're trying to figure out what to tell people. Comparisons of the army then versus now will be difficult for them to explain," Buddy said.

"We should have killed him when we had the chance," Evers said of Dugan. "I just hope the commies get it done."

"There was no time, Buck. Things happened pretty quickly and I figured him being alive would occupy the Chinese while we made our way to the train. Luckily it worked and we managed to get to Mongolia unimpeded," said Buddy.

Evers rose and walked over to the Starbucks counter to order a cup of coffee. They poured it for him and he walked back to their table and took his seat. "Three and a half dollars for this shit," he muttered. He looked back at Buddy and said, "I don't understand why the rest of the Terracotta Army didn't turn to sand like the statue outside, Buddy. Do you have any idea why that didn't happen to them?"

Buddy took a deep breath before replying, "I can only speculate, Buck. What I think is that the old village man put forth the angst of his own will into that cartouche and focused most of his hatred on the man who had killed his son, as the legend goes. I've been doing some more reading and research on the whole situation, and the locals believe that warrior was the one responsible for killing his offspring. Revenge and magical power can do strange things, I believe.

"The rest of his spell was to exact revenge on the Emperor for sending his son's executioner, but it doesn't appear there was as much hate or ire for the rest of the army as there was for that one lone soldier. Of course, I'm just guessing, Buck, but that at least seems plausible to me," Buddy stated.

Evers sipped his hot coffee and thought about what Buddy was telling him. "So, what does it all mean? The spell has been broken, the cartouche is destroyed, and the Terracotta Army is destined to stand vigil for an eternity in that museum. That's it, right?"

"Is what 'it,' Buck? You mean no more magic and shit?"

"Yeah, that's what I'm asking," Evers responded.

"As long as there are men, there will be unexplainable things that will happen. Some of those things, Buck, will be works of magic, or forces of their will used to influence events or other people. The good thing, however, is that we will have jobs so long as that weird shit keeps happening. Our government will always try to get its hands on stuff like that and that's where you and I come in," Buddy replied.

"Well, I reckon your friends at the Agency are pissed that they didn't get the key to their army, huh," Evers asked?

"At first they were upset, yes. I told them Dugan destroyed it when we tried to seize it. No need in them being mad at us since he made the perfect scapegoat," Buddy laughed.

"I see," Evers responded. "So tell me, why did you have me come all the way up here, Buddy? There are things like telephones and the Internet that will allow us to have conversations without the time and expense of air travel."

"Always cutting to the chase, Buck. Like I told you before, that's why I love ya. What I wanted to say to you, face to face, is that the government, after some prompting and poking from yours truly, has decided to pay us in full. I think they want to keep us happy and to keep us on call. When we met, I told them how unhappy the two of us were to have gone through hell and high water only to find ourselves half rewarded. They finally relented and agreed to pay us. The money should be wired to your personal account within the next two weeks. That's part of what I wanted to talk to you about," Buddy said with considerable cheer in his voice.

A broad smile appeared on Evers' face. He had never dreamed of having that much money. No more working odd security jobs for snobbish business executives or strung out rock musicians. Living comfortably would be something he could at long last look forward to.

Buddy dropped his eyes for a couple of seconds then started speaking again, "Buck, when we were on that mission you promised me to get some help for the nightmares. I expect you to keep your word. Other people, they don't understand what it means to be a soldier and have to kill. They *think* they understand, but until a man looks another man in his eyes before pulling a trigger, well, he could never understand what we deal with inside our own heads. I want to be able to call on you for future missions, but I have to know that you're doing okay. Remember, you promised me."

Evers could feel the anger swelling inside, but fought to keep it in check. He hated being psychoanalyzed, but knew Buddy was only trying to help. Besides, it was true that he had agreed to seek help for the PTSD, if that's what was really haunting his dreams. He measured his response then said, "You're right, Buddy. I promised you that I would get help and I will. I've thought some about it and am pretty sure I know where I can go to get some help, and maybe a little peace of mind too."

Buddy smiled a toothy grin. "That's my boy. Exorcise them demons, son. Get 'em out of your spirit and let 'em rest in peace." He reached for his laptop and slid it into its black cloth case. With nimble fingers he rolled up his earphones and stuck them in a pocket on the case.

"Well, Buck, you go get that help and I'll be in touch. I'm about to head to Boston for a few days," he said.

"Boston? What the hell is in Boston," Evers asked?

Buddy's devilish grin reappeared. "I met a lady who is in need of some country fried Buddy loving. Met her in the airport on the way to Mexico, and she wants me to come up there and give her a little attention," he winked.

"You're a smooth operator, Buddy Smith," Evers replied as he stood and turned toward the door. "I'll be in touch."

Notes

As I wrote Of Blood and Stone: A Bill Evers Novel, it was important for me to convey to the reader the sights and smells of those places Evers, Buddy, and Dugan were visiting. For those who have not enjoyed the luxury of international travel, I felt it important to try to describe how countries other than the United States function.

First, I cannot stress enough how relatively safe we are in the United States. We enjoy a country whose citizenry largely follows the laws set forth by the Federal or state governments, while many in third world, or even some developed countries are not afforded that basic need. This is not meant to be a lecture to you, Faithful Reader; merely, I wanted to explain that my description of each nation was as I found or researched them.

Even with that disclaimer in place, the people I have encountered in numerous trips to Mexico, The Philippines, and China were beautiful, kind, and sincere. People in other nations largely look to the United States for inspiration and hope, despite what you may have heard or read about their disdain for Americans (yes, Americans do need to understand the universe does not revolve around us, but we are not as hated, in my opinion, as many would have you believe).

Next, my inclusion of a protagonist suffering from something as severe as post-traumatic stress disorder (PTSD) has been questioned by some fictional lovers. I admit a certain strangeness for a book's hero to suffer from a psychological disorder, but it was important to me to convey a character who battles something very serious in hopes to bring about more attention to it. Creating a fictional character and making him real is never an easy task, but when he or she suffers from an affliction as we all do, there is a level of connection that is instrumental for a writer to express, and more importantly for the reader to enjoy.

Whenever you travel outside the confines of your own home, maintaining a sense of situational awareness is healthy and necessary. While this does not mean keeping yourself on "high alert" or moving about with an overabundant hyper-paranoia, I do think it important to be aware of an individual's behavior or a group's actions as you walk on familiar or unfamiliar streets.

Bill Evers takes paranoia to a whole new level, but his background and PTSD require his mental state to work in overdrive. Understanding how situations can quickly escalate to the level of violence and required self-defense is important for the traveler, and moving about as a "regular," rather than a tourist is beneficial in keeping you from being the target of an attack.

When and where violence cannot be avoided, Evers's strategy is to bring the greatest amount pain in the quickest, most rapid method available. His military and martial arts background preclude any actionable response he has when danger presents itself. The mindset is simple and effective.

While I do not condone violence, I encourage my martial arts students to be decisive and effective in their response to an attack. I would also stress this to anyone finding themselves in a situation requiring them to respond. Never expect a person intent on bring harm to you to de-escalate the situation. If they have decided that you are going to be a victim, you must prove him incorrect.

It is this mindset that I strive to bring to the reader when describing Evers and how he reacts to violence—no thought or consideration, only reaction and escalating levels of his own violence brought to his attackers to end the situation. More often than not, Evers responses bring about the end of his attacker's life. Understand that I would never encourage this behavior and, in fact, should you find yourself in a similar situation, it is imperative you know that you will be held responsible for any action you take that brings harm beyond the necessary to end an altercation.

Finally, I wanted to describe as accurately as possible the places Evers and Buddy visited. The hangar at Escobar Airport in Mexico and the description of Evers's house at the foot of Mount Cheaha in Alabama are mine alone and live only in my mind, but the streets and surrounding areas in the various cities were as I observed.

Did You Enjoy *Of Blood and Stone?*

If you enjoyed *Of Blood and Stone*, please take a couple of minutes and write a short review on Amazon.com. Your feedback is invaluable to me, and your review of my work helps more than you can imagine.

It is really easy to leave a review! Just follow the steps below:

1) Log in to Amazon.com
2) Type "Of Blood and Stone" into the search bar
3) Scroll down to the end of the reviews
4) Click on "Write a Customer Review"
5) Write your review

It's that easy! So please take a couple of minutes and give me your honest opinion today.

Thank you so much!

A Sneak Preview of Bill Evers' Next Adventure...

Occam's Razor

A Bill Evers Novel

by Howard Upton

We are on the verge of a global transformation. All we need is the right major crisis and the nations will accept the New World Order.
David Rockefeller

We must move as quickly as possible to a one-world government, one-world religion, under a one-world leader.
Robert Mueller
Former Assistant Attorney General of the United Nations

Imagine there's no countries
It isn't hard to do
Nothing to kill or die for
And no religion too
Imagine all the people,
living life in peace
John Lennon

The Grove Luxury Estate
Watford, United Kingdom

The members, all two hundred thirty-two of them, were focused on the man at the lectern. His hair was meticulously combed back and styling gel carefully applied to hold it in place. More gray than brown distinguished itself creating the appearance of age and wisdom. His skin was still smooth, most likely due to expensive face creams and strategic plastic surgery. The dark blue Brioni suit he was wearing was chic, exquisitely groomed, and worth more money than many people would make in a single year. Japanese made, Tenda eyeglasses, framed his chiseled face, the titanium metal used in them light and never short on style.

His sharp English accent cascaded over the assembly. Before he offered his short opening speech, he stood and gazed over the ensemble of the world's elite. His hesitation in speaking was a measured bit of theatrics, but he knew the potential sway it would afford him had a tremendous upside.

"We are all acutely aware of the impact of global climate change, famine, and disease, and their relative influences on mankind as a whole. Gone are the days that one country can influence and reduce causation brought upon us by continued industrialization. We are truly a global village, and with that mantle comes ownership and stewardship of our Earthly environs. At the very least, we must take aim at the purveyors of disinformation and environmental disharmony. No longer can we turn a blind eye to the injustices brought upon our children by those who simply desire additional profit and creature comforts.

"At no time in human history has the prospective for its demise been more at hand. We are a species like no other. Our inherent cannibalistic propensities and inability to curb our reproductive cravings has endangered the planet to the point of total annihilation. People steal our planet's natural assets today without thought nor care for tomorrow. How can we look at one another and not be ashamed?

"Now, my esteemed colleagues, is the time to take a stand. We, with a unified voice, can slowly turn back the hands of time, lowering pollutant particulates in our air, reducing toxic emissions that effect our ability to breath, eliminate dependence on antiquated methods of transportation, and leverage our will against those who rob our planet of its wonderful resources. Collectively, we are the most influential, and if I may be so bold, the most powerful group of human beings ever to sit together in one room. The dynamics at work here, over the next two-and-a-half days, should not be lost on you.

"I beseech you to consider libelous and untrustworthy media sources that have nothing more than their own self-interests at heart. They are the worst kind of enemy. I beg you to pressure those individuals seeking to invade a country whose defenses are no better than a child's play-house, desiring nothing more than the country's natural resources, to change their minds. You can affect change by withholding your generous funds that so many of us gladly hand out in hopes that we might somehow help a starving child or bring water to a parched settlement.

"Alone, few of us have a reach beyond our own limited legislative and judicial elements of government, but together we can shape and mold a world that will have at its very center, prosperity, food, water, and general sustenance for each occupant. We, my friends, have at our disposal unlimited capital that will help pave a future we have only dreamt of and prayed for. The leverage we have in our own country's media and government is incredible and should be expounded upon to the point that our collective desire will be felt.

"We will not rest until we eliminate the old, outdated means of life and bring about a course correction that will forever alter humanity in such a way that there are no more wars, petty squabbling over what isn't really ours anyway, and the ability to kill without forethought. I hope you will each stand with me in this endeavor.

"Now, I would like to introduce our first speaker, the revered Dr. Anthony Little, United States Surgeon General!"

Applause erupted around the room as the attendants rose to their feet. The speaker, Simon Trowton nodded his head and raised a hand in appreciation of the reception he was receiving. Several extended anxious hands in hopes of making contact with the articulate speaker. Others patted him on the back and shouted exultations about his wonderful opening speech.

Trowton pressed through the envious throng of people, shaking hands and smiling along the way. A tall, thin black man walked toward him, others around him understanding his relative level of importance. His infectious smile, tried, practiced and perfected over the previous years, shone brilliantly, compliments of numerous rounds of bleach whitener all on the taxpayer's dime. He offered his hand to Trowton, placing his left on the man's back.

"Well said, well said, Simon. I would love to have some time alone with you to understand your ideas regarding the change you spoke of. Could we arrange a meeting?"

"I will check my schedule, Mr. President. I'm certain that my calendar isn't so full that it would prevent me from sitting with an affluent, influential individual such as yourself," Trowton replied with his own bright smile.

The two men shared a laugh, each knowing full well if the President of the United States desired a meeting, a meeting would be had. Secretly, however, Trowton knew the President, while exceptionally powerful, was nothing more than a puppet. It was the individuals handling and pulling his strings with whom he wanted to confer.

Trowton continued making his way through the mass of glad-handers and applause. A tall, athletic looking man with close cropped blonde hair, also attired in an expensive suit, awaited him by the back door. He placed his hand on the man's back and the two exited The Amber Room.

They stepped into the open atrium, richly designed with soft curtains and perfectly placed seventeenth century murals depicting angelic scenes and gloriously lush landscapes. Plush furniture was strategically positioned, offering sitters little anonymity but plenty of space from other patrons who might also choose to sit or stand. Dark blue carpet muffled footsteps while completing the delicate ambiance the decorator desired.

The pair continued walking toward a darker corner of the large room, away from the large double doors that opened from the banquet hall and away from anyone who might wander into the area in search of a restroom. Trowton turned and faced the man as he reached inside his jacket and produced a letter sized manila envelope.

"Jannick, inside this envelope are twelve separate invitations I need you to hand out to those whose names appear on them. You must do so quietly and discreetly. Understood?"

"Understood, Mr. Trowton. May I be so bold as to ask what they are invited to attend?"

A slight glower appeared on Trowton's face. Just as quickly as it materialized he composed himself. Not a man who enjoyed being questioned by anyone, he lifted his chin and offered a silent response, his answer blatantly obvious, even as his features smoothed.

Jannick nodded, silently acknowledging Trowton's contempt for his question. He turned and walked back to the venue, stopping only long enough to open one of the large doors and quietly slip back inside.

Trowton wandered to one of the posh chairs and took a seat. His mind spun with the possibilities as his heart began to race at the thought of his plan taking shape. Naturally, he knew the most difficult segment was about to begin; convincing twelve of the most powerful men in the world to help him bring about their "Earth solution" would require extreme leverage on his part. He was prepared, however, to use whatever means he had at his disposal to push his blueprint for the future of mankind to fruition.

He pulled a cell phone from his pocket and touched a one-word name on the screen, "Abaddon." The ring on the other end had with it a distinct buzz, as it always did whenever he made this call. Often, he wondered what caused the annoying sound, but eventually chalked it up to a poor connection, although the poor connection only happened when he called this particular number.

Three rings…a fourth…a fifth…and on the sixth ring he heard a click and the distinct voice of his handler, who he preferred to think of as his boss, only because being "handled" seemed to demeaning.

"It is done?" a voice asked in a tone that was more of a demand than a question.

"The invitations will be delivered tonight, after the meeting and presentations have concluded, sir," he replied as his pulse quickened and the familiar queasy feeling returned, the same queasiness he got each time he heard that dark voice on the other end.

"Invitations. How trite, my young apprentice. A more accurate description would be 'life contracts,' I believe. Whatever you call them, Mr. Trowton, you best not fail me, lest you be prepared for pain beyond imagination. That is, tremendous pain before your final breath."

Trowton swallowed hard and his heart rate kicked up several notches, as did his respiration. He felt a trickle of sweat fall from the back of his neck and follow his spine until his undershirt pulled it away from his skin. With a bony finger and thumb, he pinched the bridge of his nose in a feeble attempt to reduce the pressure now hammering away just behind his eyes. For a brief second he considered the peacefulness death would bring him, but just as quickly pushed the thought from his mind.

"I can *hear* your thoughts, Mr. Trowton. Believe me, death would not afford you even a momentary respite from the pain and anguish I would inflict upon you and your family."

Trowton gawked at his phone, amazed that the slithering voice on the other end could possibly "know" what he was thinking, even if the thought was merely passing. He considered the possibility that his boss had someone watching him, but that didn't explain how the man could know what was running through his mind.

He sat there for a few seconds with the phone pressed against his ear, his breathing growing to the point of hyperventilating. Words were lost on him, his mind raced, yet his motor skills were essentially shut down. At few times in his life had he been so scared that he found himself without the ability to speak.

An audible chuckle came from the other end. "Be sure to see this through, my son."

Trowton was relieved when he heard the click on the other end. The silence surrounding him was as warming as a blanket on a cold winter's night. He allowed himself a prolonged sigh of relief; a minor expanse of tension momentarily leaving his body that afforded him a respite from the stress of the call.

His thoughts drifted back in time, six months earlier to be precise. A random call on his cell phone, one that he assumed was a wrong number, but one he felt compelled to take, started the ball rolling. Trowton heard a voice on the other end, one that appeared slippery and dark to him; vaguely his mind processed the emotions the voice perpetuated on him. He felt sickly, marked, and somehow damaged.

"Do not hang up. You and I have never met, but I understand you have a strong desire to save mankind from itself, yes?"

"Who the hell is this," Trowton demanded?

"Who I am is irrelevant at this point and time. What *is* important is our mutual desire to change the human impact man has on an unwitting world. As I've come to understand it, you and I share some ideas about this subject better left off an open line. I suggest a meeting at a time and place of your choosing. However, in my opinion, the sooner we meet the better."

Trowton felt himself quickly confused and equally paranoid. Who could have possibly known his thoughts about containing the virus known as "mankind?" He had not shared his plans with anyone and his mind suddenly dashed to memories of reading Orwell's *1984. Has technology pushed us over the edge so that we're finally forced to succumb to the thought police?*

"Look, I don't know who this is, and I have no idea what you're talking about, but this conversation is finished," he responded, but for some reason could not bring himself to hang up the phone.

"Yes, Mr. Trowton, I do understand your hesitation and concern, but I assure you that I am a man of principle and have a strong belief in an orderly civilization."

"How do you know my name and how did you get my personal cell number," he demanded!

"I will answer everything for you in time, Mr. Trowton, but only if you agree to meet with me first."

And so it was that he had agreed to meet the man who would forever change his life. They met at the very upscale Mari Vanna Restaurant in Knightsbridge, London just before sunset, Trowton having showed up after his newly-made phone acquaintance. The food was the finest Russian cuisine and a décor that screamed love to Mother Russia. Russian made dolls and literature adorned shelves throughout the seating area. Beautifully handmade wooden tables sat at intimate intervals to other diners. Chairs and lushly comfortable couches sat adjacent to the tables, creating a feeling of home and grandeur.

He ordered a gloriously delicious serving of Siberian Pelmini, Russian dumplings filled with onions, lamb, and mushrooms, and a succulently sweet glass of Moscato d'Asti. His dinning partner, who introduced himself as Abaddon, preferred not to eat, but sipped on a glass of Tormaresca, a nice Italian chardonnay instead.

"So, Mr...Abaddon, I fail to understand why you insisted that we meet."

A greasy smile spread over the man's face. His blonde hair was slicked back and his ice-blue eyes pierced Trowton's from behind squared spectacles. Abaddon sported a navy blue herring-bone suit that he wore without a tie and top button left open. The suit did little to hide a slender but obviously muscular frame, the frame of someone who paid special attention to his body, what went into it, as well as the amount of exercise he was to endure. Trowton noticed something odd about the man's facial features, but couldn't quite figure out what the oddity was.

Abaddon spun the stem of his wine glass in his hand, his fingernails carefully manicured. "Mr. Trowton, you will come to know me as a man who is brutally honest, to the point of discomfort with the individual with whom I converse. With that, I want to be completely honest with you—together we are going to change the human landscape, but you must understand, your participation will be worth much to you, both financially and…physically."

"Pardon me for being so forward, Mr. Abaddon, but what *the fuck* are you saying?"

"Everything will be revealed to you soon enough, Mr. Trowton. In the meantime, there are a number of people you associate with that you must persuade to join you. How you devise the plan to ascertain our goal is up to you," Abaddon hissed.

"And what is our goal, Mr. Abaddon? Your cryptic speech is wearing thin on me, and I'm afraid I have other appointments to keep."

Abaddon's forehead creased slightly and his ice-blue eyes seemed to redden. "Let me assure you, Mr. Trowton, I'll not tolerate any insolence in our relationship. You'll be rewarded handsomely for your participation, but should you choose the alternative to our relationship, I fear your time spent among the living shall be sufficiently condensed. Are we clear?" He leaned forward on his elbows and stared directly into Trowton's eyes.

Something in Abbadon's stare told him the man was dangerous, or perhaps evil was the word he was looking for. *No*, he thought, *this individual is beyond evil*. He took a sip of his Moscato d'Asti and swallowed hard. Something electric emanated from the man, something that wouldn't allow him to break the eye-lock on him. He felt as though his soul was being raped and there was nothing he could do to stop it, so succumbing to him was inevitable.

Trowton was first invited to a Bilderberg meeting twelve years earlier. He was enamored at the discussion, all of it kept private and unreleased to an uneducated and unknowing public. But what began as intriguing debate and ideas to help better mankind and take care of a planet in peril soon devolved into empty rhetoric, cocktail parties, and mindless hobnobbing among the world's wealthiest.

He became disillusioned after engaging former French President Lionel Jospin. The man was obviously an idealist, but he laughed when Trowton asked how the organization could make a more powerful statement to the world to curtail the drain on natural resources and curb the growing warming of the planet.

"Ah, Simon, how I long to be young once again, and be filled with fire and passion as you so obviously are. You must understand that the majority of wars waged in our world are orchestrated by our group. We attempt to distract a global populace while we quietly work to further our agenda through the media that many of our members own and support financially. You see? We have a plan and a course of action, but we cannot make evident moves less the people turn on us. Would you prefer to make a flamboyant declaration, only to be drawn and quartered by those you are attempting to protect? This is why we work covertly, my friend. Manipulation of the global markets, wars, and media are just a few of the things we do in an attempt stave off a certain man-made annihilation."

He measured Jospin's words carefully before responding. "So, in essence, you believe we should push our agenda from the quiet halls of luxury hotels and chateaus, all the while keeping ourselves from the line of fire? Don't you find that thought process a little self-aggrandizing and cowardly?"

The French President's expression changed, his face reddened and eyes narrowed. "Do not mock me, young man. I've lived on this Earth long enough to understand the mindset of mankind. I have a firm grasp on the faulty idea of "American exceptionalism," European arrogance, and global Chinese domination. Change cannot be affected in loud explosions only, but by more subtle nuances that bring about universal mindset changes. Do you understand me?" His French accent grew deeper and thicker as the ire in his voice rose.

Trowton dropped his eyes and awkwardly shuffled his feet. How he wanted to engage this powerful man in further debate, but he had quickly realized his mistake in challenging him without concrete evidence supporting his position. This was a mistake he would never make again, and one he marked up to youthful inexperience and his own ideological faith.

"My apologies, Mr. President, I should have chosen my words more carefully. I did not mean to insinuate that you were cowardly or in any way incapable. My zeal for aiding and assisting our fine organization to further our global agenda sometimes clouds my judgment," he responded with as much sincerity as he could muster.

The Frenchman composed himself, while unconsciously straightening his suit. He stuck his chin out and summarily dismissed the insolent young man with whom he had been speaking by turning and walking away.

His eyes darted around the atrium and locked on a man who was eying him curiously from across the grand room. The sight of the man simultaneously confused and angered him. Trowton had been concentrating on his phone call so much that he had forgotten to check his surroundings to insure no one was listening to his conversation. He assessed the situation quickly and knew there was no way the stranger could have overheard his discussion because of the distance between them, and because he had kept his voice low. Still, he glowered at the interloper who immediately recognized his situation, turned, and exited the room.

Trowton took a deep breath and exhaled slowly. The wheels were in motion and the plan in place, the plan that would change the world forever…

Look for the Bill Evers' next adventure, *Occam's Razor*!

Author Biography

Howard Upton spent his professional years in the corporate world, but has always considered himself a writer and storyteller first and foremost. An avid outdoorsman, traditional martial artist, back packer, motorcyclist and global traveler, Howard has been blessed to observe, firsthand, areas of the world about which he writes.

He currently lives in Georgia, but he and his wife travel back and forth to his beloved Alabama with regularity. When he isn't writing, Howard enjoys planning his next adventure with his beautiful wife, Cathy.

Howard's eclectic knowledge in martial arts, military science, international geography, history, and conspiracy theories combine to give him the perfect background for writing Bill Evers' adventures.

Howard Upton can be reached at: www.howardupton.com. Inquiries and feedback are welcome.

www.ingramcontent.com/pod-product-compliance
Lightning Source LLC
Chambersburg PA
CBHW070824180626
46818CB00001B/382